Sealed With A
KISS

Sealed With A
KISS

Essence Bestselling Author
GWYNNE
FORSTER

ARABESQUE®

Recycling programs
for this product may
not exist in your area.

SEALED WITH A KISS

ISBN-13: 978-0-373-53472-2

www.kimanipress.com

Printed in U.S.A.

Dear Reader,

I hope you enjoy this story of Naomi Logan and one of my favorite heroes, Rufus Meade. If you like reading about a sexy, strong, successful, loyal and faithful man who loves his woman and his family, then you'll adore Rufus. Not only is this a romance in which opposites attract—and do they ever—it is also about having a loving relationship and being a single parent.

As in *Sealed With A Kiss*, I try to make every story I write upbeat and humorous, yet I always touch upon serious issues that couples encounter in finding true love. I hope you enjoy this Arabesque reissue, as well as the upcoming reissue of *Against All Odds* and a holiday collection that includes one of my short stories, "Christopher's Gifts."

I receive letters every day about books that I've written over the years, but none of my romances seem to be as popular as the Harrington series. The series includes *Once In A Lifetime, After The Loving, Love Me or Leave Me, Love Me Tonight,* and *A Compromising Affair.*

I enjoy receiving mail, so please email me at GwynneF@aol.com, or write me at P.O. Box 45, New York, NY 10044. If you want a reply, please enclose a self-addressed stamped envelope. Visit my webpage, www.gwynneforster.com, and follow me on Facebook (Gwynne Forster's Page) and Twitter at http://twitter.com/UNOFF. For more information, please contact my agent, Pattie Steel-Perkins, Steel-Perkins Literary Agency at MYAGENTSPLA@aol.com.

Sincerely yours,

Gwynne Forster

ACKNOWLEDGMENTS

My sincere thanks to Monica Harris, the former editor of Arabesque, who read the first three chapters of this story, asked me for the rest and three weeks later offered me a two-book contract that started me on my career as an author. I am grateful to my husband for his gracious acceptance of the time he spends alone while I'm focused on fiction writing; for the wonderful brochures he designs for each of my books; and for the many other ways in which he assists and promotes my work. I also thank my beloved stepson, who takes such pride in my work as a writer, solves my computer problems and encourages me in every way that he can.

Chapter 1

She burrowed deeper into her pillow, hoping to silence the persistent ringing in her ear. Finally, she gave up trying to sleep and reached for the phone.

"It's six-thirty in the morning. Would whoever you are please go back to sleep?"

"Gal, I want you to come over here right away. There's something I ought to tell you." Naomi sighed and sat up in bed. The Reverend Judd Logan's commands did not perturb Naomi. She had dealt with her paternal grandfather's whims and orders since she was seven years old, when he became her guardian and she went to live with him. She tumbled out of bed, her eyes still heavy with sleep, and groped for the bathroom. She hadn't asked him whether it was urgent: of course it was. To him, everything was urgent. And you never knew what to expect when you received his summons, but you could be certain that you were supposed to treat it as if it came from a court of law. She smiled despite herself.

She was twenty-nine years old, but she was still a child as far as he was concerned. However, because she loved him, she didn't have trouble with that. After all, there was nearly a seventy-year difference in their ages. Thoughts of his age gave her a moment of anxiety; his call really could be urgent. She dressed hurriedly, remembering to take a light jacket. Early mornings in October were sometimes chilly.

The drive from her condominium in Bethesda, Maryland, across Washington to Alexandria, Virginia, were her grandfather lived, took half an hour even at that time of morning. She parked her gray Taurus in front of her grandfather's imposing Tudor-style home and rang the doorbell before letting herself in. Judd Logan didn't like surprises. If you handed him one, he lectured you for an hour.

She entered the foyer dragging her feet, wondering at her sudden feeling of apprehension. The spacious vestibule had been her favorite childhood haunt, because her grandfather had put a console piano there for her and always placed little gifts and surprises on it. She would look up from her practice and notice him listening raptly, though he never told her that he enjoyed her playing. The piano remained, but it held no attraction; her childhood had ended abruptly when she was sixteen.

She found him in his study, writing his memoirs, and walked over to hug him, but he dusted her off with a gruff "Not now, gal, wait until I finish this sentence." How typical of him to shun affection, she thought; not once in the nearly twenty-two years since she had gone to live with him had he ever made a gesture toward her that she could confuse with true emotional warmth. She knew that he locked his feelings inside, but she wished he would learn a little something about affection before he left this earth. At times, she'd give anything for a hug from him—or from just about anybody. For some odd reason, this was one of those times.

With a sigh, she sat down, perusing the snow-white curly hair that framed his dark, barely lined face and the piercing hazel-brown eyes that seemed to reflect a knowledge of all the ages gone by.

"What's this about, Grandpa? You seemed a little agitated."

He turned his writing pad upside down, drew a deep breath, and plunged in without preliminaries. "I've had two letters from them and yesterday I finally got a phone call. It's about the baby."

She jerked forward. "The baby? *What* baby? Who called you?"

The old man looked at her, and a sense of dread invaded her as she saw his pity and realized it was for her. "Yours, gal. I tried back then to spare you this. I thought that since the adoption papers were sealed by law, no one would ever know. But they found me, and that means they can find you, too. The adoptive mother says that the child wants to find its birth mother." She saw him wince and knew that the lifelessness that she felt was mirrored in her face.

"Grandpa, I've lived as a single woman with no children, and I've worked to help young girls avoid experiencing what I went through. I'm a role model. How can I explain this?" She pushed back the temptation to scream. "I knew I shouldn't have given in to their pressure, their browbeating. The counselor at the clinic made me feel that if I didn't give the baby up for adoption, it wouldn't have a chance at a normal, happy life. They said a child born to a teenager starts life with two strikes against it. I was made to feel selfish and incompetent when I held out against them. But they finally convinced me, and I gave in. It didn't help that I was depressed, and Chuck didn't answer my letters. Grandpa, I've been sorry every day since I signed that paper. They didn't even let me see the baby, said it was best to avoid any bonding. I wish you hadn't let me do it."

He stood and braced his back with both hands. "No point in going over that now, gal; we've got to deal with this last letter. Take my advice and let well enough alone, Don't turn your life upside down; you'll regret it."

Naomi looked off into space, reliving those days when all that she loved had disintegrated around her. She spoke softly, forcing words from her mouth. "I've spent the last thirteen years trying to pretend that it never happened, but you know, Grandpa, it has still influenced every move and colored every decision that I've made."

"I know, Naomi gal. But where would you be now if you had kept that child and been disgraced?" She looked around them indulgently at the replicas of bygone eras. Judd's 1925 degree from the Yale University School of Divinity, framed in gold leaf, hung on the wall. Doilies that her grandmother had crocheted more than sixty years earlier rested on the backs of overstuffed velvet chairs. And on the floor lay the Persian carpet that the old man's congregation had given him on his fortieth birthday. She smiled in sympathetic understanding.

"Grandpa, out-of-wedlock motherhood is not the burden for a woman that it was in your day. I tried to tell you that."

He shook his snow-white head. "They wanted to reach the child's biological father, too, but, well…"

"Yes." She interrupted him gently. "I remember believing that Chuck had deserted me, and he'd drowned surfing off Honolulu. I didn't know. I'll never understand that, either, you know; he was a champion swimmer. I've wondered if he was as unhappy as I was and if it made him careless."

"I'd feel better about this whole thing, gal, if you'd just find yourself a nice young man and get married. You ought to be married; I won't live forever."

She stared at him, nearly laughing. Wasn't it typical of him to bring that up? He could weave it into a technical discussion of the pyramids of Egypt. She broke off her incredulous glare; he didn't accept reprimands, either spoken or silent. "Get married? I've stayed away from men. Who would accept my having a baby, giving it up for adoption, and never bothering to tell its father? What man do you think is going to accept all that? Anyway, I'm happy just as I am, and I have no intention of offering myself to anybody for approval."

The old man straightened up and ran a hand across his still remarkably handsome face, now nearly black from age. "A man who loves you will understand and accept it, Naomi. One who loves you, gal," he said softly. The sentiment seemed too much for him, and he reverted to type. "You have to watch yourself. You're moving up in that school board and working with that foundation for girls. You're out to change the world, and you don't need this on your neck." She opened her mouth to speak and thought better of it. Judd had managed things for her since she was a child; she was a woman now.

"You let me handle this thing, gal, it's best you not get involved." She didn't care if he mistook her silence for compliance. She had learned long ago not to argue, but she would do whatever she wanted to.

It seemed to her that the drive back to her studio on upper Connecticut Avenue in Washington took hours longer than usual; a jackknifed truck, a two-car accident, rubber necking, and the weather slowed her progress. The day was becoming one big conspiracy against her peace of mind. "Am I getting paranoid?" she asked herself, attempting to inject humor into something that wasn't funny. Having to assume the role of mother nearly fourteen years after the fact was downright hilarious—if you were listening to a stand-up comic. She would not fall apart; she was doggoned if she would, and to prove it, she hummed every aria from *La Traviata* that she could remember.

She didn't get much done that day, because she spent part of it listless and unable to concentrate and the rest optimistically shuffling harebrained schemes to locate her child. She had to adjust to a different world, one that wasn't real, and the effort was taking a toll. She couldn't summon her usual enthusiasm during her tutoring session that evening and could hardly wait to get home. But tomorrow would be different, she vowed. "I'm not going to keel over because of this."

At home that evening, she curled up in her favorite chair, intent on relaxing with a cup of tea and soothing music, determined to get a handle on things. "I'm going to find something to laugh about at least once an hour," she swore. As she searched the dial on her radio, a deep, beautifully sonorous male voice caught her attention, sending shock waves through her and raising goose bumps on her forearms. Well, he might have a bedroom voice, she quickly decided, but his ideas were a different matter. "Educated career women, including our African American women, put jobs before children and family, and that is a primary factor in family breakups and youthful delinquency," he stated with complete confidence.

How could anyone with enough prestige to be a panelist on that program make such a claim? He was crediting women with too much responsibility for some of the world's worst problems.

She rarely allowed herself to become furious about anything; anger crippled a person. But she *had* to tell him off. After trying repeatedly to telephone the radio station and getting a busy signal, she noted the station's call letters and flipped off the radio. Meade, they'd called him. She would write him and urge him into the twentieth century.

Her immense relief at being able to concentrate on something impersonal, to feel her natural inclination to mischief surface, restored her sense of well-being. She embraced the blessed diversion and wholeheartedly went about giving Mr. Meade his comeuppance. But as she walked briskly, almost skipping to her desk, she admitted to herself that the basis for her outrage was more than intellectual. His comments had come bruisingly close to an implied indictment of her, even if she didn't deserve it. She shrugged it off and began the letter.

"Mr. Meade," she wrote, "I don't know by what right you're an authority on the family—and I doubt from your comments tonight in the program *Capitol Life* that you are— but you most certainly are not an authority on women. If a great many American women, and especially African American women, didn't work outside the home, their families would starve. Would that bother you? And if you tried being a tiny bit more masculine, maybe the women with whom you associate might be 'less aggressive,' as you put it, softer and more feminine. Don't you think we women have a big enough load without you dumping all that on us? Be a pal and give us a break, please. And don't forget, Mr. Meade, even *squash* have fathers. Please be a good sport and don't answer this note. Most sincerely, Naomi Logan." She addressed it to him in care of the program and the station.

That should take care of him, she decided, already dismissing the incident. But within a week, she had his blunt reply: "Dear Ms. Logan, if you had listened to everything I said and had understood it, you might not have accused me so unfairly. From the content of your letter, it would appear that you've got some guilt you need to work through. Or are you apologizing for being a career woman? If the shoe fits, wear it. The lack of a reply would be much appreciated. Yours, Rufus Meade."

Naomi hadn't planned to pursue her argument with Rufus

Meade; it was enough that she'd told him what she thought of his ideas and that her letter had annoyed him. A glance at her watch told her that the weekly radio program *Capitol Life* was about to begin. Curious as to whether he was a regular panelist, she tuned in. He wasn't a regular, she learned, but had been invited back because of the clamor that his statement the previous week had caused.

The moderator introduced Rufus, who lost no time in defending his position. "Eighty percent of those who wrote or called protesting my remarks were women; most of the men thought I didn't go far enough. Has any of you asked the children in these street gangs where their mothers are when they get home from school—provided they're in school— what they do after school, when they last had a home-cooked meal, whether their parents know where they are? I have. Their mothers aren't home, so they don't know where their children are or what they're doing. With nobody to control them, the children hang out in the street, and that is how we lose them. Children need parental guidance. When it was the norm in this society for mothers to remain at home, we had fewer social problems—less delinquency and fewer divorces. One protestor wrote me that even squash have fathers. Yes, they do. And they also have mothers who stick with them until they're old enough to fend for themselves. In fact, the mothers die nurturing their little ones' development."

Naomi rubbed her fingers together in frustration. A sensible person would ignore the man and his archaic ideas. She flipped off the radio in the middle of one of his sentences. Wednesday's mail brought another note from him.

"Dear Ms. Logan, I hope you tuned in to *Capitol Life* Sunday night. Some of my remarks were for your benefit. Of course, if you have a closed mind, I was merely throwing chaff to a gusty wind. Can't say I didn't try, though. Yours, RM."

Excitement coursed through her as she read his note. She knew that not answering would be the best way to get the better of him. He wanted her to be annoyed, and if he didn't hear from her, he would assume that she had lost interest. But she couldn't resist the temptation, and she bet he was counting on that.

Her reply read, "Dear Mr. Meade, next time you're on the air, I'd appreciate your explaining what a two-month-old squash does when it no longer needs its mother and fends for itself. (Something tells me it gets eaten.) You didn't really mean to equate the maturity of a squash with achievement of adulthood in humans, did you? I'd try to straighten that out, if I were you. Don't bother to write. I'll keep tuning in to *Capitol Life*. Well, hang in there. Yours, NL."

She only had to wait four days for his answer. "Dear Ms. Logan, you have deliberately misunderstood me. I stand by my position that as long as women guarded the home rather than the office and the Mack truck, juvenile crime and divorce were less frequent occurrences. You are not seriously concerned with these urgent problems, so I will not waste time writing you again. I'm assuming you're a career woman, and my advice is to stick with your career; at least you'll have that. Yours, RM."

Naomi curved her mouth into a long, slow grin. She always enjoyed bedeviling straitlaced, overly serious people, though she acknowledged to herself that her cheekiness was a camouflage. It enabled her to cover her vulnerability and to shrug off problems, and besides, she loved her wicked side. Rufus Meade's words told her that he was easily provoked and had a short fuse, and she planned to light it; never would she forgo such a tantalizing challenge.

Curled up on her downy sofa, she wrote with relish: "Dear Mr. Meade, I've probably been unfair to you. You remind me so much of my grandfather, who was born just before the turn of the century. If you're also a nonagenarian, my sincere apologies. For what it's worth, I am not a 'career woman.' I am a woman who works at a job for which I am well trained. The alternative at present would be to marry a male chauvinist in exchange for my keep, or to take to the streets, since food, clothing, and shelter carry a price tag. But considering your concern for the fate of the family, I don't think you'd approve of the latter. But then, it isn't terribly different from the former, now, is it? Sorry, but I have to go; the Saturday afternoon Metropolitan Opera performance is just beginning, and I'm a sucker for *La Traviata.* Till next time. Naomi Logan." After addressing it to him, she mailed it and hurried back to listen to the opera.

Several days later, engrossed in her work, Naomi laid aside her paintbrush and easel and reluctantly lifted the phone receiver. In a voice meant to discourage the caller, she muttered, "Yes?"

There was a brief silence, and then a deep male voice responded. "Miss Logan, please."

She sat down, crossed her knee, and kicked off her right shoe. That voice could only belong to *him.* She had heard it only twice, but she would never forget it. It was a voice that commanded respect, that proclaimed its owner to be clever, authoritative, and manly, and, if you weren't annoyed by its message, it was sensually beautiful.

"Speaking," she said almost reluctantly, as if sensing the hand of fate. There was more silence. "I'm hanging up in thirty seconds," she snapped. "Why are you calling?"

His reply was tinged with what struck her as a grudging laugh. "Miss Logan, this is Rufus Meade. It seems that your spoken language is as caustic as your letters."

Her world suddenly brightened; she'd made him angry enough to call her. She tucked a little of her wild hair behind her ear and laughed. Many people had told her that her laughter sounded like bells clinking in the breeze. "I thought I had apologized for being disrespectful," she said softly, with an affected sweetness. "If Grandpa knew how I'd behaved toward an older person, he'd raise the devil."

"At the expense of being rude," he replied tightly. "I doubt that there's a ninety-year-old man on the face of this earth who is my equal, and if you're less than eighty, I'm prepared to demonstrate it."

Oh ho, she thought, and howled with laughter, hoping to infuriate him further. "My, my. Our ego's been pricked, and we've got a short temper, too."

"And less patience, madam. You're brimming with self-confidence, aren't you, Ms. Logan?" She assured him that she was. Up to then, his conversation had suggested to her that he didn't hold her in high regard, so his next words surprised her.

"Taking a swipe at me in person should be much more gratifying than having to settle for snide remarks via the mail and over the phone, so why don't you have lunch with me?"

She laughed again, turning the screw and enjoying it. "You couldn't be serious. Why would you think I'd enjoy the company of a man who prefers bimbos to women who can spell? No, thank you."

She sighed, concerned that she might have overdone it and realized that she had indeed when he replied in a deadly soft voice. "I hope you enjoy your own company, Ms. Logan. Sorry to have troubled you."

He hung up before she could reply, and a sense of disappointment washed over her, a peculiar feeling that warmth she hadn't realized she felt was suddenly lacking. It was strange and indefinable. She didn't welcome close male friendship because she couldn't afford them, and she had not been courting Rufus's interest. She had just been having fun, she reasoned, and he wasn't going to have the last word.

She got out her pen and paper and wrote: "Dear Rufus, how could one man have so many quirks? Bimbos, short temper, heavyweight ego, and heaven forbid, spoilsport. You need help, dear. Yours faithfully, Naomi."

Naomi hadn't heard from Rufus in three days, and she was glad; their conversation had left her with a sense of foreboding. She arrived home feeling exhausted from a two-hour argument with her fellow board members of One Last Chance that the foundation, which she had cofounded to aid girls with problems, would overstretch itself if it extended its facilities to boys. In the Washington, D.C., area, she had insisted, boys had the Police Athletic League for support, but for many girls, especially African American girls, there was only One Last Chance. And she knew its importance. How different her life might have been if the foundation had been there for her thirteen years ago, when she had been sixteen and forced to deal with the shattering aftermath of a misplaced trust.

She refreshed herself with a warm shower, dressed quickly in a dusty rose cowl-necked sweater and navy pants, and rushed to her best friend Marva's wedding rehearsal. Dusty rose reminded her of the roses that her mother had so carefully tended and that still flourished around the house on Queens Chapel Terrace, where she had lived with her parents. She couldn't recall those days well, but she thought she remembered her mother working in her garden on clear, sunny mornings during spring and summer. She regularly resisted the temptation to pass the house and look at the roses. She'd never seen any others that color, her favorite. It was why she had chosen a dress of that shade to wear as maid of honor at Marva's wedding.

Marva was her closest friend, though in Naomi's view they

were exact opposites. The women's one priority was the permanent attainment of an eligible man. Marriage wasn't for her, but as maid of honor, she had to stand in for the bride— as close to the real thing as she would ever get. At times, she desperately longed for a man's love and for children—lots of them. But she could not risk the disclosure that an intimate relationship with a man would ultimately require, and to make certain that she was never tempted, she kept men at a distance.

Naomi knew that men found her attractive, and she had learned how to put them off with empty, meaningless patter. It wasn't that she didn't like any of them; she did. She wanted to kick herself when the groom's best man caught her scrutinizing him, a deeply bronzed six footer with a thin black mustache, good looks, and just the right amount of panache. She figured that her furtive glances had plumped his ego, because he immediately asked her out when the rehearsal was over. She deftly discouraged him, and it was becoming easier, she realized, when he backed off after just a tiny sample of her dazzling double-talk.

I'll pay for it, she thought, as she mused over the evening during her drive home. Whenever she misrepresented herself as frivolous or callous to a man whom she could have liked, she became depressed afterward. Already she felt a bit down. But she walked into her apartment determined to dispel it. The day had been a long one that she wouldn't soon forget. "Keep it light girl," she reminded herself, as she changed her clothes. To make certain that she did, she put on a jazz cassette and brightened her mood, dancing until she was soaked with perspiration and too exhausted to move. Then she showered, donned her old clothes, and settled down to work.

She took pride in her work, designing logos, labels, and stationery for large corporations and other businesses, and she was happiest when she produced an elegant, imaginative design. Her considerable skill and novel approaches made her much sought after, and she earned a good living. She was glad that a new ice-cream manufacturer liked a logo that she'd produced, though the company wanted a cow in the middle of it. A cow! She stared at the paper and watched the paint drying on her brush, but not one idea emerged. Why couldn't she dispel that strange something that welled up in her every time she thought of Rufus? It had been a week since her last provocative note to him, and she wondered whether he would answer. It was dangerous, she knew, to let her mind dwell on him, but his voice had a seductive, almost hypnotic effect on her. Where he was concerned, her mind did as it pleased. Tremors danced through her whenever she recalled his deep voice and lilting speech. Voices weren't supposed to have that effect, she told herself. But his was a powerful drug. Was he young? Old? Short? She tried without success to banish him from her thoughts. While she hummed softly and struggled to fit the cow into the ice cream logo, an impatient ringing of her doorbell and then a knock on the door startled her. Why hadn't the doorman announced the visitor, she wondered, as she peeped through the viewer and saw a man there.

"May I help you?" She couldn't see all of him. Tall, she guessed.

"I hope so. I'm looking for Naomi Logan." Her first reaction was a silent, "My God it's *him!*" Her palms suddenly became damp, and tiny shivers of anticipation rushed through her. She would never forget that voice. But she refused him the satisfaction of knowing that she remembered it. She'd written him on her personal stationery, but he'd sent his letter to her through the station; she didn't have a clue as to where he lived. She struggled to calm herself.

"Who is it, please?" Could that steady voice be hers?

"I'm Rufus Meade, and I'd like to see Miss Logan, if I may."

"I ought to leave him standing there," she grumbled to herself, but she knew that neither her sense of decency nor her curiosity would allow her to do it, and she opened the door.

Rufus Meade stood in the doorway staring at the woman who had vexed him beyond reason. She wasn't at all what he had expected. Around twenty-nine, he surmised, and by any measure, beautiful. Tall and slim, but deliciously curved. He let his gaze feast on her smooth dark skin, eyes the color of dark walnut, and long, thick curly black tresses that seemed to fly all over the place. God, he hadn't counted on this. Something just short of a full-blown desire burned in the pit of his belly. He recognized it as more than a simple craving for her; he wanted to know her totally, completely, and in every intimate way possible.

Naomi borrowed from her years of practice at shoving her emotions aside and pulled herself together first. If there was such a thing as an eviscerating, brain-damaging clap of thunder, she had just experienced it. Grasping the doorknob for support, she shifted her glance from his intense gaze, took in the rest of him, and then risked looking back into those strangely unsettling fawnlike eyes. And she had thought his voice a narcotic. Add that to the rest of him and…Lord! He was lethal! If she had any sense, she'd slam the door shut.

"You're Rufus Meade?" she asked. Trying unsuccessfully to appear calm, she knitted her brow and worried her bottom lip. She could see that he was uncomfortable, even slightly awed, as if he, too, was having a new and not particularly agreeable experience. But he shrugged his left shoulder, winked at her, and took control of the situation.

"Yes, I'm Rufus Meade, and don't tell me you're Naomi Logan."

She laughed, forgetting her paint-smeared jeans and T-shirt and her bare feet. "Since you don't look anywhere near ninety, I want to see some identification." He pulled out his driver's license and handed it to her, nodding in approval as he did so.

"I see you're a fast thinker. Can't be too careful these days."

Unable to resist needling him, she gave him her sweetest smile. "Do you think a bimbo would have thought to do that?" It was the kind of repartee that she used as a screen to hide her interest in a man or to dampen his, like crossing water to throw an animal off one's trail.

His silence gave her a very uneasy feeling. What if he was dangerous? She didn't know a thing about him. She tried to view him with the crust caused by his physical attractiveness removed from her eyes. Clearly he was a most unlikely candidate for ridicule; nothing about him suggested it. A strapping, virile male of about thirty-four, he was good-looking, with smooth dark skin and large fawnlike eyes, a lean face, clean shaven and apparently well mannered. She backed up a step. The man took up a lot of psychological space and had an aura of steely strength. He was also at least six feet four, and he wore clothes like a model. So much for that, she concluded silently; all I learned is that I like what I see.

His demeanor was that of a self-possessed man. Why, then, did he behave as if he wanted to eat nails? She was tempted to ask him, but she doubted his mood would tolerate the impertinence. He leaned against her door, hands in his pockets, and swept his gaze over her.

"Miss Logan, your tongue is tart enough to make a saint turn in his halo. Are you going to ask me in, or are you partial to nonagenarians?"

There was something to be said for his ability to toss out a sally, she decided, stepping back and grinning. "Touché. Come on in." She noticed that he walked in slowly, as if it wouldn't have surprised him to find a booby trap of some kind, and quickly summed up his surroundings. After casually scanning the elegant but sparsely furnished foyer and the intensely personal living room, he glanced at her. "Some of your choices surprise me, Naomi." He pointed to a reproduction of a Remington sculpture. "That would represent masculine taste."

"I bought it because that man is free, because he looks as if he just burst out of a place he hadn't wanted to be." He quirked his left eyebrow and didn't comment, but she could see he had more questions.

"The Elizabeth Catlett sculpture," she explained, when his glance rested on it, "was the first sculpture that I had even seen by an African American woman; I bought it with my first paycheck. I don't know how familiar you are with art, but along with music, it's what I like best. These are also the works of African Americans. That painting," she pointed to an oil by the art historian James Porter, "was given to me by me grandpa for my college graduation. And the reproduction of the painting by William H. Johnson is…well, the little girl reminded me of myself at that age."

Rufus observed the work closely, as if trying to determine whether there was anything in that painting of a wide-eyed little black girl alone with a fly swatter and a doll carriage that would tell him exactly who Naomi Logan was.

While he scrutinized the Artis Lane lithograph portrait of Rosa Parks that both painter and subject had signed, Naomi let her gaze roam brazenly over him. What on earth is wrong with me, she asked herself when she realized, after scanning his long, powerful legs, that her imagination was moving into forbidden territory. She had never ogled a man, never been tempted. Not until now. She disciplined her thoughts and tried to focus on his questions. Her heartbeat accelerated as if she'd run for miles when he moved to the opposite end of the room, paused before a group of original oils, turned to her, and smiled. It softened his face and lit up his remarkable eyes. She knew that she gaped. What in heaven's name was happening to her?

"So you're an artist? Somehow, I pictured you as a disciplinarian of some sort." He stared intently at the painting of her mother entitled "From My Memories" and turned to look at her.

"Isn't this a self-portrait? I don't have any technical knowledge of art, but I have a feeling that this is good." She opened her mouth to speak until she saw him casually raising his left hand to the back of his head, exposing the tiny black curls at his wrist. She stared at it; it was just a hand, for God's sake. Embarrassed, she quickly steadied herself and managed to respond to his compliment.

"No. That's the way I remember my mother. Have a seat while I get us some coffee. Or would you prefer juice, or a soft drink?" She had to put some distance between them, and separate rooms was the best she could do.

He didn't sit. "Coffee's fine," he told her, trailing her into the kitchen. She turned and bumped into him, and excitement coursed through her when he quickly settled her with a slight touch on her arm. Her skin felt hot where his finger had been, and she knew that he could see a fine sheen of perspiration on her face. Reluctantly, she looked up, saw the tough man in him searing her with his hot, mesmerizing eyes, and felt her heart skid out of place. He made her feel things that she hadn't known could be felt, and all of a sudden, she wanted him out of there. The entire apartment seemed too small with him in it, making her much too aware of him. The letters had been fun, and she had enjoyed joshing with him over the phone, but he had a powerful personality and an intimidating physique. At her height, she wasn't accustomed to being made to feel small and helpless. And she had never experienced such a powerful sexual pull toward a man. But, she noticed, he seemed to have his emotions under lock and key.

He leaned over her drawing board seemingly to get a better view of the sketches there. "Are you a commercial artist, or do you teach art somewhere?"

"I'm a commercial artist if by that you mean work on contract."

Rufus looked at her quizzically. "Did you want to be some other kind of artist?"

Naomi took the coffee and started toward the living room. She had a few questions of her own, and one of them had to do with why he was here. "I wanted to be an artist. Period." She passed him a cup of coffee, cream, and sugar. He accepted only the coffee.

"Why did you come here, Rufus?" If he was uncomfortable, only he knew it. He rested his left ankle on his right knee, took a few sips of coffee, and placed the cup and saucer on the table beside his chair. His grin disconcerted her; it didn't seem to reach his eyes.

It wasn't a hostile question, but she hadn't meant it as friendly, either. She watched as he assessed her coolly. "You certainly couldn't have put it more bluntly if you tried. Whatever happened to that gnawing wit of yours? I came here on impulse. That last hot little note of yours made me so mad that neither a letter nor a phone call would do. You made me furious, Naomi, and if I think about it much, I'll get angry all over again." She leaned back in the thickly cushioned chair, thinking absently that he had an oversupply of charisma, when his handsome brown face suddenly shifted into a fierce scowl.

She wasn't impressed. "What cooled you off?"

He shrugged first one shoulder, then the other one. "You are so damned irreverent that you made the whole thing seem foolish. One look at you, standing there ready to take me on, demanding to see my ID with your door already wide open— well, my reaction was that I was being a jackass when I let you pull my leg. You've been having fun at my expense."

It didn't seem wise to laugh. "It was your fault."

He stiffened. "How do you figure that any of this is my fault, lady?" This time, she couldn't restrain the laughter.

"Temper, temper. If you didn't have such a short fuse and if you talked about things you know, especially on a radio broadcast, none of this would have happened."

He stood. "I'm leaving. Never in my life have I lost my temper with a woman, or even approached it, and I'm not going to allow you to provoke me into making an exception with you. You're the most exasperating…"

Her full-throated laughter, like tiny tinkling temple bells, halted his attack. He gave her a long, heated stare.

She shivered, disconcerted by his compelling gaze. With that fleeting desire-laden look, he kindled something within her, something that had fought to surface since she'd opened her door. She walked with him to her foyer, where indirect lights cast a pale, ethereal glow over them, and stood with her hand on the doorknob. She knew he realized she was deliberately prolonging his departure, and she was a little ashamed, but she didn't open the door. It was unfathomable. A minute earlier, she had wanted him to leave; now, she was hindering his departure. Less certain of herself than she had been earlier, she fished for words that would give her a feeling of ease. "I meant to ask how you became an expert on the family, but, well, maybe another time."

* * *

Rufus lifted an eyebrow in surprise. He hadn't thought she'd be interested in seeing him again. Despite himself, he couldn't resist a slow and thorough perusal of her. He wanted to…no. He wasn't that crazy. Her unexpected feminine softness, the dancing mischief in her big brown eyes, and the glow on her bare lips were not going to seduce him into putting his mouth on her. He stepped back, remembering her question.

"I'm a journalist, and I've recently had a book published that deals with delinquent behavior and the family's role in it. You may have heard of it: *Keys to Delinquent Behavior in the Nineties.*"

"Of course I know it; that book's been a bestseller for months. I hadn't noticed the author's name and didn't associate it with you. I haven't read it, but I may." She offered her hand. "I'm glad to have met you, Rufus; it's been interesting."

He drew himself up to his full height and pretended not to see her hand. He wasn't used to getting the brush-off and wasn't going to be the victim of one tonight. He jammed his hands in his pockets and assumed a casual stance.

"You make it seem so…so final." He hated his undisciplined reaction to her. Her warm, seductive voice, her sepia beauty, and her light, airy laughter made his spine tingle. He had really summoned her up incorrectly. She was far from the graying, disillusioned spinster that he had pictured. He wanted to see what she looked like; well, he had seen, and he had better move on.

"Couldn't we have dinner some evening?" He smiled inwardly; so much for his advice to himself.

He could see that she was immediately on guard. "I'm sorry, but my evenings are pretty much taken up." She tucked thick, curly hair behind her left ear. "Perhaps we'll run into each other. Goodbye."

* * *

He wasn't easily fooled, but he could be this time, he cautioned himself, and looked at her for a long while, testing her sincerity and attempting to gauge the extent of his attraction to her. Chemistry so strong as what he felt wasn't usually one-sided; he'd thought at first that she reciprocated it, but now, neither her face nor her posture told him anything. She's either a consummate actress or definitely not interested in me, he decided as he turned the doorknob. "Goodbye, Naomi." He strode out the door and down the corridor without a backward glance.

Naomi watched him until he entered the elevator, a man in complete control, and hugged herself, fighting the unreasonable feeling that he had deserted her, chilled her with his leaving; that he had let his warmth steal into her and then, miser-like, withdrawn it, leaving her cold. What on earth have I done to myself, she wondered plaintively.

Rufus drove home slowly, puzzled at what had just transpired. Everything about Naomi jolted him. He didn't mislead himself; he knew that his cool departure from her apartment belied his unsettled emotions. What had he thought she would be like? Older, certainly, but definitely not a barefoot, paint-spattered witch. She'd had a strong impact on him, and he didn't like it. He had his life in order, and he was not going to permit this wild attraction to disturb it. She had everything that made a woman interesting, starting with a mind that would keep a man alert and his brain humming. Honorable, too. And, Lord, she was luscious! Tempting. A real, honest-to-God black beauty.

He entered his house through the garage door that opened into the kitchen and made his way upstairs. All was quiet, so he undressed, sprawled out in the king-sized bed that easily accommodated his six feet four and a half inches, and faced the fact that he wanted Naomi. It occurred to him from her total disregard for his celebrity status that Naomi didn't know who he was. She found him attractive for himself and not for his bank account, as Etta Mae and so many others had, and it was refreshing. If she didn't want to acknowledge the attraction, fine with him; neither did he. If there were only himself to consider, he reasoned, he would probably pursue a relationship with Naomi, though definitely not for the long term. It had been his personal experience that the children of career women didn't get their share of maternal attention. That meant that he could not and would not have one in his life.

Chapter 2

Several afternoons later, Naomi left a meeting of the district school board disheartened and determined that the schools in her community were going to produce better qualified students. She had a few strong allies, and the name Logan commanded attention and respect. She vowed there would be changes. She remembered her school days as pleasant, carefree times when schools weren't a battlefield and learning was fun. A challenge. When she taught high school, she made friends with her pupils, challenged them to accomplish more than they thought they could, and was rewarded with their determination to learn, even to go beyond her. She smiled at the pleasant memory, suddenly wondering if Bryan Lister was still flirting with his female teachers, hoping now to improve his university grades.

Oh, there would be changes, beginning with an overhaul of that haphazard tutoring program, even if, God forbid, she had to run for election as president of the board. She ducked into a Chinese carry-out to buy her dinner. As she left the tiny hovel, she noticed a woman trying to shush a recalcitrant young teenaged boy who obviously preferred to be somewhere else and expressed his wishes rudely.

She got into her car and started to her studio, a small but cheerfully decorated loft, the place where her creative juices usually began flowing as soon as she entered. Sitting at her drawing board, attempting to work, she felt the memory of that scene in which mother and son were so painfully at odds persist. The boy could have been hers. Maybe not; maybe she'd had a girl. What kind of parents did her child have? Would it swear at them, as that boy had? How ironic, that she devoted so much of her life to helping children and had no idea what her own child endured. She sighed deeply, releasing the frustration. She would deal with that, but she wasn't yet ready. It was still a new and bruising thing. It had been bad enough to remember constantly that she had a child somewhere whom she would never see and about whose welfare she didn't know, but this…she couldn't help remembering…

She had stood by the open window; tears cascading silently down her satin-smooth cheeks, looking out at the bright moonlit night, deep in thought. The trees swayed gently, and the prize roses in her grandfather's perfectly kept garden gave a sweet pungency to the early summer night. But she neither saw the night's beauty nor smelled the fragrant blossoms. She saw a motorcycle roaring wildly into the distance, carrying her young heart with it. And it was the fumes from the machine's exhaust, not the scented rose blooms surrounding the house, that she would remember forever. He hadn't so much as glanced toward her bedroom window as he'd sped away.

She heard her bedroom door open but didn't turn around; merely stood quietly, staring into the distance. She knew he was there and that no matter what she said or how much she pleaded, he would have his way; he always had his way.

"Get your things packed, young lady, you're leaving here tonight. And you needn't bother trying to call him, either, because I've already warned him that if he goes near you, if he so much as speaks to you again, I'll have him jailed for possessing carnal knowledge of a minor."

"But, Grandpa…"

"Don't give me any sass, young lady. You're a child, sixteen years old, and I don't plan to let that boy do any more damage than he's already done. Get your things together." She should have been used to his tendency to steamroller her and everybody else, but this time there was no fight in her.

"Did you at least tell him…" He didn't let her finish, and it was just as well. She knew the answer.

"Of course not."

She fought back the tears; the least sign of weakness would only make it worse. "You didn't give me a chance to tell him," she said resignedly, "so he doesn't know."

She looked at the old man then, tall and erect, still agile and crafty for his years. A testimonial to temperance and healthful living. With barely any gray hair, he was an extremely handsome example of his African American heritage and smattering of Native American genes. She thought of how much like him she looked and brought her shoulders forward, begging him with her eyes.

"But, Grandpa. Please! You can't do this. He didn't take advantage of me. We love each other, and we want to…"

"Don't tell me what I can't do. I'm your legal guardian. That boy's nineteen and I can have him put away. You're not going to blacken the name of Logan; it's a name that stands for something in this community. You'll do as I say. And what you haven't packed in the next hour, you won't be taking."

She got into the backseat of the luxurious Cadillac that the First Golgotha Baptist Church had given her grandfather when he'd retired after forty-five years as its pastor. "Where are we going?" she asked him sullenly, not caring if she displeased him.

"You'll find out when you get there," he mumbled.

"I thought you'd stopped driving at night."

"I'm driving tonight, but it's not a problem; the moon's shining. And kindly stop crying, Naomi. I've always told you that crying shows a lack of self-control."

She bristled. Did he even love her? If he did, why couldn't he ever give her concrete evidence of it? She made one last try. "You have no right to do this, Grandpa. I love him, and he loves me, and no matter what you make me do now, when I'm grown, Chuck and I will get together."

She heard the gruffness in his aged voice and the sadness that seemed to darken it. Maybe there was hope…

"I'm doing what's best for you, and someday you'll see that for yourself. You know nothing of love, Naomi. That boy didn't fight very hard for you, gal. Seems to me I gave him a good reason to run off when I warned him to stay away from you. It's a moot point, anyway; his folks are sending him to the University of Hawaii, and you can't get much farther away from Washington, D.C., and still be in the United States. This is the end of it and I know it, so I'm not letting you offer yourself up as a sacrificial lamb on the altar of love. I've lived more than three-quarters of a century, long enough to know how outright stupid that would be." .

Her tears dropped silently until she fell asleep. When they had arrived at their destination, she got out of the car and walked into the building without even glancing back at her grandfather. Two months later, tired of resisting the pressure, she listlessly signed the papers put in front of her without reading them.

* * *

Naomi sat at the drawing board in her studio without attempting to work and tried once more to reconcile herself to her grandfather's incredible news. If they'd found him, they would easily find her. Did she want to be found? Or did she want to find the child and its family? But who would she look for? I've had a few hassles in my life, she thought, but this! She answered the phone automatically.

"Logan Logos and Labels. May I help you?"

"Yes," the deep, sonorous male voice replied. "You certainly may. Have dinner with me tonight." Of course, Rufus meant the invitation as an apology for his abrupt departure from her home, she decided. She searched for a suitable clever remark and drew a blank as thoughts of her child crowded out Rufus's face. Her throat closed and words wouldn't come out. To her disgust, she began to cry.

"Naomi? Naomi? Are you there?"

She hung up and let the tears have their day, tears that had been waiting for release since her grandfather had signed her into the clinic and walked away over thirteen years ago. She got up after a time threw water on her face, and went back to her drawing board, hoping for the relief that she always found in her work. Then she laughed at herself. Solitary tears were stupid; crying made sense only if someone was there to pat you on the back. She looked at her worrisome design and shrugged elaborately. It would be about as easy to get that ridiculous cow into the ice-cream logo without changing the concept as it would be to get her life straightened out, tantamount to getting pie from the sky. She sat up straighter. Mmmm. *Pie in the sky.* Not a bad idea. In twenty minutes, she'd sketched a new ice-cream logo, an oval disc containing a cow snoozing beneath a shade tree and dreaming of a three-flavors dish of ice cream. Why didn't I think of that before, she asked herself, humming happily, while she cleaned her brushes and tidied her drawing board. She held the logo up to a lamp, admiring it. Nothing gave her as much satisfaction as finishing a job that she knew was a sure winner.

Her euphoria was short-lived as she heard the simultaneous staccato ring of the doorbell and rattle of the knob. She opened the door and stared in dismay.

"Is anything the matter? Are you all right?" Rufus asked her, pushing a twin stroller into the room, apparently oblivious to the astonishment that he must have seen mirrored on her face.

She said the first thing that came to mind and regretted it. "You didn't tell me that you are married," she accused waspishly.

She put her hands on her hips and frowned at him. She usually took her time getting annoyed, but she wasn't her normal self when it came to Rufus Meade. She took a calming deep breath and asked, him, "Whose are these?" pointing a long brown finger toward the stroller.

One of the twins answered, "Daddy look." He reached toward the ten-by-fourteen color sketch for the ice-cream logo. "Ice cream, Daddy. Can we have some ice cream?"

Rufus shook his head. "Maybe later, Preston." He turned to her and shrugged nonchalantly, but Naomi didn't care if her exasperation at that ridiculous scene was apparent.

"What was happening with you when I called, Naomi? You sounded as if…look, I came over here because I thought something was wrong and that maybe I could help, but whatever it was evidently didn't last long."

Still not quite back to normal, and fighting her wild emotions, she figured it wasn't a time for niceties and asked him, "Where is their mother?"

This time, it was the other twin who answered. "Our mommy lives in Paris."

"She likes it there," Preston added. "It's pretty."

Rufus glanced from the boy to Naomi. "Since you're al-right, we'll be leaving." He wasn't himself around her. Her impact on him was even greater than when he'd first seen her. Tonight, when he'd faced her standing in her door with that half-shocked, half-scared look on her face, her shirt and jeans splattered with paint, hair a mess and no makeup, he had been moved by her open vulnerability. It tugged at some-thing deep-seated, elicited his protective instinct. He admit-ted to himself that fear for her safety hadn't been his sole reason for rushing over there; he was eager to see her again and had seized the opportunity.

Her softly restraining hand on his arm sent a charge of energy through him, momentarily startling him. "I'm sorry, Rufus. About your wife, I mean. I had no idea that…"

"Don't worry about it," he told her, mentally pushing back the sexual tension in which her nearness threatened to entrap him. Expressions of sympathy for his status as a single father made him uncomfortable. He regretted the divorce for his sons' sake, but Etta Mae had never been much of a wife and hadn't planned to be a mother. She wanted to work in the top fashion houses of Paris and Milan and, when offered the chance, she said a hurried goodbye and took it. Neither her marriage nor her three-week-old twin sons had the drawing power of a couturier's runway. She hadn't contested the di-vorce or his award of full custody; she had wanted only her freedom.

He watched the strange, silent interplay between Naomi and Preston, who appeared fascinated with the logo. His pre-occupation with it seemed to intrigue her, and she smiled at the boy and glanced shyly at Rufus.

"Do you mind if I give them some i-c-e c-r-e-a-m?" She spelled it out. "I have those three flavors in the freezer." He eased back the lapels of his Scottish tweed jacket, exposing a broad chest in a beige silk Armani shirt, shoved a hand in each pants pocket, and tried to understand the softness he saw in her. He couldn't believe that she liked children; if she did, she'd have some. She probably preferred her work.

"Sure, why not?" he replied, carefully sheltering his thoughts. "It'll save me the trouble of taking them to an ice-cream parlor where they'll want everything they see."

"Do they have to stay in that thing?" She nodded toward the stroller.

"You may be brave," he told her, displaying considerable amusement, "but I don't believe you're that brave." His eyes were pools of mirth.

"What are you talking about?" She tried to settle herself, to get her mind off the virile heat that emanated from him. She had never before reacted so strongly to a man, and she disliked being susceptible to him.

His suddenly huskier voice indicated that he read her thoughts and knew her feelings. "Preston can destroy this place in half an hour if he really puts himself to it," he explained, "but with Sheldon to help him, you'd think a hurricane had been through here. We're all better off with them strapped in that stroller."

"If you say so." She knelt unsteadily in front of the stroller and addressed the twin who'd pointed toward the logo. "What's your name?" A miniature Rufus right down to his studied gaze, she decided.

"Preston," he told her with more aplomb that she'd have expected of a child of his age, and pointed to his twin. "He's Sheldon."

"How old are you?" she asked his identical twin brother.

"Three, almost four," they told her in perfect unison, each holding up three fingers.

Naomi looked first at one boy and then the other, then at Rufus. "How do you know the difference?"

"Their personalities are different." He looked down at

them, his face aglow with tenderness, and his voice full of pride.

She introduced herself to the boys and then began serving the ice-cream. On a hunch, she took four of the plastic banana-shaped bowls that she'd bought for use in the logo and filled them with a scoop each of the chocolate, vanilla, and strawberry flavors.

Rufus nodded approvingly. "Well, you've just dealt successfully with Preston; he'd have demanded that it look exactly like that painting. Sheldon wouldn't care as long as it was ice cream."

Naomi watched Rufus unstrap his sons, place one on each knee, and help them feed themselves while trying to eat his own ice-cream. Her eyes misted, and she tried to stifle her desire to hold one of the children. She knew a strange, unfamiliar yearning as she saw how gently he handled them. How he carefully wiped their hands, mouths, and the front of their clothes when they had finished and, over their squirming objections, playfully strapped them into the stroller.

"Do they wiggle because it's a kid thing, or just to test your mettle?"

He laughed aloud, a full-throated release as he reached down to rebutton Sheldon's jacket. She would have bet that he didn't know how; it was the first evidence she'd had that his handsome face could shape itself into such a brilliant smile, one that involved his eyes and mouth, his whole face. He had a single dimple, and she was a pushover for a dimple. The glow of his smile made her feel as if he had wrapped her in a ray of early morning sunlight, warming her.

"Both, I guess," he finally answered.

He turned to her. "That was very nice, Naomi. Thank you. Before I leave, I want you to tell me why you hung up when I called you. Didn't you know that I would have to send the police or come over here myself and find out whether you were in trouble? I brought my boys because I don't leave them alone and I couldn't get a sitter quickly."

"Don't you have a housekeeper, nursemaid, or someone who takes care of them for you?"

Rufus stood abruptly, all friendliness gone from his suddenly stony face. "My children are my responsibility, and it is I, not a parental substitute, who takes care of them. I do not want my children's outlook on life to be that of their nanny or the housekeeper. And I will not have my boys pining for me to get home and disappointed when I get there too tired even to hug them. My boys come before my career and everything else, and I don't leave them unless I have no choice." He turned to leave, and both boys raised their arms to her. Not caring what their father thought, she quickly took the opportunity to hug them and hold their warm little bodies. His expression softened slightly, against his will, she thought, as he opened the door and pushed the stroller through it. "It was a mistake to come here. Goodbye, Naomi." As the door closed, she heard Preston, or maybe it was Sheldon, say, "Goodbye, Noomie."

Naomi began cleaning the kitchen, deep in thought. Did they have low tolerance for each other, or was it something else? She had never known anyone more capable of destroying her calm, not even Judd. And there was no doubt that she automatically pushed his buttons. The less she saw of him, the better, she told herself, fully aware that he was the first man for whom she'd ever had a deep, feminine ache. "I don't know much," she said aloud, "but I know enough to leave him alone."

Naomi parked her car on Fourth Street below Howard University and walked up Florida Avenue to One Last Chance. She chided herself for spending so much time thinking about Rufus, all the while giving herself excuses for doing so. She had just been defending herself with the thought that being the father of those delightful boys probably added to Rufus's manliness. He was so masculine. Even his little boys had strong masculine traits.

Rufus had made her intensely aware of herself as a woman. An incomplete woman. A woman who could not dare to dream of what she wanted most; to have the love and devotion of a man she loved and with whom she could share her secrets and not be harshly judged. A home. And children. Maybe she could have it with…oh, God, there was so much at stake. Forget it, she told herself; he would break her heart.

She increased her pace. It seemed like forever since the foundation's board members had argued heatedly about the wisdom of locating One Last Chance's headquarters in an area that was becoming increasingly more blighted. But placing it near those who needed the services had been the right decision. She walked swiftly, partly because it was her natural gait, but mainly because she loved her work with the young girls, whom she tutored in English and math. She welcomed the crisp, mid-October evenings that were so refreshing after the dreaded heat and humidity of the Washington summers. Invigorating energy coursed through her as the cool air greeted her face, and she accelerated her stride. Not even the gathering dusk and the barely camouflaged grimness of the neighborhood daunted her.

Inside OLC, as the girls called it, her spirits soared as she passed a group playing checkers in the lounge, glimpsed a crowded typing class, and walked by the little rooms where experienced educators patiently tutored their charges. She reached the nurse's station on the way to her own little cubicle, noticed the closed door, and couldn't help worrying about the plight of the girl inside.

Linda was half an hour late, and Naomi was becoming concerned about her. The girl lacked the enthusiasm that she had shown when they'd begun the tutoring sessions, and she was always tired, too worn-out for a fifteen-year-old. When she did arrive, she didn't apologize for her tardiness, but Naomi didn't dwell on that.

"Do you have brothers and sisters?" Naomi asked her, attempting to understand the girl's problems.

"Five of them," Linda responded listlessly.

"Tell me what you do at home, Linda, and why you come to One Last Chance. Speak carefully, because this is our diction lesson for today." Already becoming a fatalist, Naomi thought sadly, when the girl opened her mouth to object, but closed it without speaking and shrugged indifferently.

"At home, I cook, clean, and take care of my mama's children. I study at the drugstore where I work after school and weekends, but I have to be careful not to get caught. I come here for the company, so I can hear people talk good English and see what you're supposed to wear and how you're supposed to act. I can get by without the tutoring."

"Do you enjoy the tutoring, Linda?"

"Yeah. It makes my grades better, but I just like to be around you. You treat me like I'm the same as you."

"But you are the same."

"No, I'm not. You got choices, and I don't have any yet." She smiled then. "But I'm going to have them. I'm going to be able to decide what I want. I'm going to learn to type and use computers. That way, I'll always be able to get a good job, and I'll be able to work my way through college." She paused and looked down at her hands. "I'm not ever going to have any children, and I'm never going on welfare and have people snooping around to check on me. It's humiliating."

Good for you, Naomi thought, but she needed to correct her about one thing.

"I'm sure that motherhood has many wonderful rewards,"

she told her. "When you fall in love and get married, you may change your mind."

Indicating what she thought of that advice, Linda pulled on one of her many braids and rolled her eyes disdainfully. "Not me," she objected, slumping down in the straight-backed chair. "All I have to do is look at my mama and then look at you. There's never going to be a man smart enough to con me into having a baby. After taking care of all my mama's babies, I'd have to be touched in the head to have one."

Naomi didn't like the trend of the conversation. "You'll see things differently when you're older," she responded, thinking that she would have to teach Linda that life was more enjoyable if you laughed at it sometimes.

"Really?" the girl asked skeptically. "I see you don't have any kids." Linda opened her book, effectively ending the discussion. Shocked, and unable to find any other way to get the privacy she needed, Naomi lowered her eyes.

They completed the literature assignment, and as Naomi reflected on Linda's above-average intelligence, the girl suddenly produced a drawing.

"What do you think of this?" she asked, almost defensively.

Naomi scrutinized it and regarded the girl whose face was haunted with expectancy. "You've got good technique, and this piece shows imagination. I like it."

Linda looked up and smiled wistfully. "I love to paint most of all. It's one thing nobody can tell me is good or bad, because I always manage to paint exactly what I feel." As if she had disclosed something that she thought too intimate to tell another person, Linda quickly left the room.

Naomi watched her leave. Crazy about painting and forced to study literature. It was almost like seeing her own youth in someone else, except that she had had all the advantages of upper-middle-class life that Linda lacked. She understood now that her strong attraction to Chuck had partly been escape from loneliness. He had fulfilled her need for the loving affection that she missed at home, and he'd made her feel wanted. Cherished. God forbid that because of a desolate life, Linda should follow in her footsteps, she mused, getting up to replace her teaching aids in the cabinet that held her supplies.

Rufus stole silently away from the open door and, deep in thought, made his way slowly up to the president's office. He was a board member of Urban Alliance and stopped by One Last Chance to discuss with its president participation in the Alliance's annual fund-raising gala. He hadn't known of Naomi's association with OLC and was surprised to find her there. Certainly, he would not have expected to witness her gently nurturing that young girl. She had empathized totally with the girl, whose background was probably the exact opposite of her own, holding him nearly spellbound. He mounted the creaky spiral staircase whose once-regal Royal Bokhara runners were now threadbare, thinking that perhaps he had misjudged Naomi again. He had gotten the impression from her letters that career and independence were what she cherished most and that, like his ex-wife, she thought of little else and wouldn't take the time to nurture another human being.

Maybe she was different from what she represented herself to be. She was tender and solicitous with his boys, who were immediately charmed by her. Captivated was more like it. Not because of the ice cream, either; they ate ice cream just about every day. No. It was more. He couldn't define it any more than he could figure out why she'd had such a powerful impact on him, why she was constantly in his thoughts. She was brash and a little cynical. But she was also soft and giving. He remembered his sudden need to get out of her apartment, away from her; he had never had difficulty controlling his libido until he'd met that woman. He grinned. She affected his temper that way, too.

He sat listening to Maude Frazier outline her plans for One Last Chance's contribution to the gala, aware that her words held no interest for him; his mind was on Naomi Logan. In an abrupt decision, he politely told Maude goodbye and loped down the stairs in hopes of seeing Naomi before she left. He was relieved to find her in the basement laundry room. And what a sight! Without the combs and pins, her hair was a wild, thick frizz, and her slacks and shirt were wet in front. He leaned against the laundry room door and watched her dash around the room folding laundry and coping with an overflowing washing machine.

"Want some help?"

She dropped a clean tablecloth back into the sudsy water, braced her hands on her hips, and stood glaring at him.

"See what you made me do? You frightened me." He observed her closely, but with pretended casualness. Was she trembling?

"Sorry. Anything I can do to make up for it?"

"You can help me fold these things, and you can wipe that cocky grin off of your face." She hated being caught off guard; he didn't blame her. It put you at a disadvantage.

She was obviously wary of him, and he wanted to put her at ease, so he spread his hands palms upward in a gesture of defenselessness. "I'm innocent of whatever it is you're planning to hang me for, Naomi. Now, if you'll show me how you want these things folded, I'll help you." She did, and they worked in companionable silence.

Rufus carefully hid his inner feelings, controlling the heady excitement of being with her, but he wouldn't bet that he'd be able to hold it back for long. He wouldn't put a penny on it. She zonked him.

His impatient nature wouldn't allow him to wait longer before probing. "I'm surprised to see you here."

"And why would that be? Why do you think I don't care about people?" she asked him, a bit sharply.

Didn't she know that her defensiveness was bound to make him suspicious? He was a journalist, after all. He shrugged and decided not to accept the challenge. He wanted to know her, not fence with her. "Did I say that, Naomi? I've seen softness in you." *And I want to know whether it's real.*

"Humph. Me? A career woman?" Her glance must have detected the tenderness, the protectiveness that he felt, because she reacted almost as if he'd kissed her. Her lowered eyes and the sensual sound of her sucking in her breath sent his blood rushing through his veins.

Rufus quickly cooled his rising ardor. He sensed her nervousness but didn't comment on it, as he weighed her consistent refusal to carry on a serious conversation with him. When she finally looked directly at him, he spoke. "You treat everything I say with equal amounts of disdain."

"Be fair. Aren't you exaggerating?" He was sure that his words had stung her, though that was not what he had intended.

"Not by much, I'm not," he answered, running the fingers of his left hand through his hair and furrowing his brow. "Do you volunteer here often?" He switched topics in the hope of avoiding a confrontation and making peace between them. "You seemed to have unusually good rapport with the girl whom you were tutoring. Most kids in these programs don't relate well to their tutors and mentors. How do you manage it?"

He found her inability to disguise her pleasure at his compliment intriguing; it meant that she valued his opinion. If he let her have the psychological distance that she seemed to want, maybe she would open up.

"You saw us?" He nodded. "It isn't difficult; she's hungry for attention and for a role model, and I really like her." They were leaning against the washing machines, and he appraised her with a thoroughness that embarrassed her.

"Is she one of the girls sent here from Juvenile Court? What had she done?"

Naomi's eyes snapped in warning, and her tone was sharp. "Linda found her way here on her own. She had the intelligence to realize that she needed help. I doubt she'll ever become a delinquent."

Her fierce protectiveness of the girl puzzled Rufus; his reporter's instincts told him that something important lay behind it, but he didn't consider it timely to pursue the matter. He looked at the pile of laundry that they'd folded and sorted. "Well, that's finished. Anything else?"

"No. That's it. I've got to get home and deal with my work." When he didn't respond, she looked up, and he had the satisfaction of seeing guilt mirrored in her eyes. Guilt for having been provocative again without cause. He altered his censorious appraisal of her, relaxing his face, letting the warmth within him flow out to her, and her expressive eyes told him that she responded to what he felt. She should have moved, but she didn't, and he reached for her, involuntarily, but quickly withdrew his hand. He looked into the distance, then glanced back at Naomi, who remained inches from him, standing in a way that told him she wouldn't mind if he touched her. He didn't want to leave her, he realized, but he had little choice unless he found a casual way to keep her with him.

"I promised to attend a lecture on the family over at Howard, and I'd invite you to join me if your clothes were dry." He thought for a second. "Well, you can keep you coat on. Think your work can wait an hour or so?" She smiled, and he sensed an inner warmth in her that he hadn't previously detected. He'd always thought her beautiful, but that smile made her beauty ethereal.

He took her hand. "Come on. Say yes." She nodded, and he clasped her hand, soft and delicate, in his. At that moment, he knew he felt more for her than he wanted to or than was sensible and made a mental note to back off.

Chapter 3

They left the lecture in a playful mood. "Okay, I agree that he wasn't a genius," Rufus declared, "but he did make some good points." His changing facial expressions fascinated her. Naomi watched a grin drift over his face slowly, like a pleasant idea dawning, and walked closer to him. She was not inclined to give the lecturer as much credit as he did, though, and they joked about the man's shortcomings.

Arm in arm, they crossed the street to where two boys in their mid-teens stood beneath the streetlight. One cocked his head, gave them a hard look as they approached, and then ran up to Rufus.

"I don't believe it, man. Look who this is! How ya doin', Mr. Meade?" Naomi watched while Rufus autographed the boys' shirts, since they had nothing else on which he could write, answered their questions, and gave them reasons why they shouldn't hang out in the streets. The happy youths thanked him and promised to take his advice.

"Right on, man!" one said, as the two ambled toward what Naomi and Rufus both hoped was home. He's a kind and gentle man, she decided. And not merely with his own children. What other celebrity with his stature, a best-selling author, would stand on a street corner at nine at night and give autographs to two street urchins? She frowned. And when had boys like those begun to read books on delinquency? Maybe they knew his journalistic writings, but she didn't think so. No doubt there was something about him that she didn't know.

At her car, he told Naomi, "I've enjoyed being with you tonight, Naomi. I enjoyed it a lot." He paused, making up his mind, remembering his earlier vow to back off. She was a heady lure, a magnet, and he wasn't going to get mired in her quicksand. He took his time deciding to walk away, all the while searching her face intently. Then he held the door for her. "Good night Naomi, I hope we meet again soon."

Naomi drove away feeling as if he had dangled her from a long pole, gotten tired, and dropped her. She had learned one thing that evening, though: she wasn't merely attracted to him; Rufus Meade was a man whom she could genuinely like, even care for. And therein lay the danger! But she knew he had not forgiven her for suggesting that he hire a woman to care for his boys. If he had, he would have kissed her goodnight, she reasoned, because every move he made said it was what he wanted. And she had wanted him to do it. She had better watch herself.

She entered her apartment and didn't stop until she reached her bedroom. At least I'm consistent, she joked to herself, looking around the dusty rose room, as she pulled off her dusty rose sweater and reached for her gown of the same color. She stretched out on a chaise lounge and thought about the evening with Rufus.

She could hardly believe that he had invited her to the lecture of that she had so readily agreed to go. She hadn't said yes voluntarily; she had been drugged by his charisma. He was smoldering fire, and if she didn't stay away from him, she would be badly burned. Her tinkling laughter broke the silence. All of a sudden, she understood moths.

Rufus took his minivan swiftly up Georgia Avenue, across Military Road, and north on Connecticut Avenue to Chevy Chase and home. His sister, Jewel, greeted him at his front door.

"Who on earth is Noomie? Preston and Sheldon have been telling me stories about her: she's a fairy; she makes ice cream; she has a pink nose; she lives in Thessa; and you are angry with her."

Rufus frowned. "She doesn't have a pink nose, and she lives in Bethesda. Except for that, they're right." He had already learned that when you have small children, you have few secrets.

Jewel put her hands on her hips and wrinkled her nose affectionately. "Anything else?" He knew she always became suspicious when he didn't satisfy her curiosity. Still, he was uncomfortable with the discussion.

"Not that I know of. Thanks for staying with my boys, Jewel; I hate for them to sleep away from home, and if you didn't sit here with them, I wouldn't have a choice." He walked her to her car. "I'll call Jeff and tell him you're on your way so he can watch for you. Don't forget to call me. You know when you babysit for me at night, I'm always uneasy until I know you're safely in your house."

She hugged him affectionately. "Rufus, you are such a worrywart. You know I'll be all right. Look…"

"Go on, say it."

"No. I shouldn't interfere in your life."

He opened her car door. "Of course I worry about you, Jewel. I look after you because you're my sister. Heck. I can't remember a time when I wasn't looking out for you. But I'd be equally concerned for the safety of any other woman leaving me and traveling alone this time of night—though that rarely happens."

Jewel grabbed the chance. "Does that include Noomie? Or do you plan to keep her a secret forever?"

"Her name is Naomi, and there isn't much to tell. She has pros and she has cons and right now, I'm shuffling that deck, so to speak."

"Which side was winning when you left her tonight?"

Jewel understood him better than anyone else ever had, so he wasn't surprised at her blunt question. She always said that pussyfooting around got you nowhere with him. Still, he didn't like being transparent, not even to her. "You're saying I was with her tonight?" He looked down at his sister, a beautiful, happy wife and mother, and grinned when he felt her grasp his arm lightly. Jewel always liked to touch when she talked. Naomi was a toucher, too.

"Yes, you were. There's a softness about you that says you wish you were with her now."

He leaned against her dark blue Mercedes coupe and folded his arms against his broad chest. "I think it best that I don't discuss her just now, Jewel; I don't know where our relationship is going or if it's going anywhere at all." He looked off into the distance. He didn't want to talk about Naomi; he was too full of her.

"Rufus," Jewel began apologetically, as if wary of breaching is privacy. "Are you beginning to care for this woman? If you are, give her a chance, a real chance. There must be a reason why the boys are so taken with her, talking about her almost nonstop."

"I'd rather not go into this, Jewel." He didn't want to legitimize Naomi as the woman in his life by discussing her with his sister. He knew Naomi wasn't like Etta Mae. And he knew that his loveless marriage with his ex-wife wouldn't have worked even if she hadn't wanted a career as a high-fashion model. She had never committed herself to the marriage, and when the twins were born, she didn't commit to them. Only to her career. He hadn't discouraged her; she needed the spotlight, and he had wanted her to be happy. But how could she have left her three-week-old babies and gone on an overseas modeling assignment? And she'd stayed there.

Jewel's grip tightened on his arm. "This is part of your problem, honey. Don't compare her with Etta Mae, whom you still refuse to talk about; it hurts you, so you bury it all inside, where it simmers and festers and gets bigger than it really is. She isn't evil; she just has tunnel vision. Try to stop reopening those wounds; you'll never be happy till you do. Let it go, Rufus."

He moved away, turned, and voiced what he had never before mentioned to her. "What about Mama? She wasn't there for us, either."

Jewel shook him gently. "But she took whatever jobs she could get, and that meant traveling. She once told me that she didn't have a choice."

It was as if he hadn't heard her. "She made a living, but she was never home, and in the end, she didn't come back. When I knew that she wasn't coming back, that she had gone down in that plane, I thought I would die, too. She was going to write a book on cocoa. Cocoa, for God's sake!"

His sister's startled look told him she hadn't realized that after sixteen years he was still in such turmoil about their mother. "Rufus listen to me. You've forgotten something very important. Papa had been an invalid since before I was born, and Mama had to support us. Etta Mae worked because she wanted to. That's a big difference."

The only evidence he gave of his inner conflict was the involuntary twitch of a jaw muscle. "Maybe I shouldn't have voiced my feelings. But I used to cry myself to sleep when I was little, because I missed her. You didn't feel so alone, because you had me. When you were born, I swore I'd take care of you. Mama had a hard life: a breadwinner, a young woman married in name only and forced to be away from her children. Jewel, I don't want a woman I love to be caught up in that kind of conflict, and if I married while my boys are little, well…"

He disliked speaking of his personal feelings, but his love for his sister forced him to continue to try and make her understand the choices he made. "Preston and Sheldon are my life. I left my job at the *Journal* to work at home as a freelancer because they needed me, and I wanted to be there for them. I remember what it was like to be left with a succession of maids, babysitters, and cleaning women to whom I was just a job. And my boys are not going to live like that. Jewel, I can't expect a woman to put my children before her own interests; their own mother didn't do it."

He put an arm around his sister's shoulder. "Naomi has a career and she's devoted to it. She's also very good at what she does, and she deserves every opportunity to reach the top of her field." He paused, then spoke as if to himself. "And I'll be the first to applaud her when she gets there."

He opened the car door. "Enough reminiscing. It's getting late."

Jewel started the motor. "At least you're thinking about her. That's all I want, Rufus, that you'll find someone who truly cares for you and whom you can love in return. When that happens, you'll forget about these other concerns."

Rufus looked in on his boys, got a can of ginger ale from the kitchen, and went to his study. But after an hour, still looking at a blank page, he conceded defeat. He couldn't afford to become involved with Naomi. She was a complicated mixture of sweetness, charm, sexiness, simple decency, and fear. He enjoyed her fun and intelligence and, most of the time, loved being with her. Her cynical wit didn't fool him, and didn't matter much. He knew it was a screen, a defense. And he couldn't dismiss his hunch that there was a connection between Naomi and that girl at OLC, or that Naomi saw one.

He answered the telephone on the first ring, hoping it was the woman in his thoughts.

"Rufus, this is Jewel. I want you to think hard about this. What can be so unacceptable about Naomi if Preston and Sheldon are crazy in love with her? You know they aren't friendly with strangers; in fact, they shy away from people they don't know well. Talk, Rufus. It might help."

He hesitated, understanding that his response to her could become his answer to himself. He knew with certainty only that he wanted Naomi, but he wasn't foolish enough to let his libido decide anything for him. He thought for a moment and answered her as best he could.

"I'm not sure I know the answer, or even that she's as important to me as you seem to think. She has some strangely contradictory traits, and this bothers me. But worry not, Sis; I'm on top of it." He hung up, walked over to his bedroom window, and let the moonlight stream over him.

She's got a hook in me, he admitted. *I'll swear I'm not going to have anything more to do with her, but when I'm with her I don't want to leave her; when I see her, I want to hold her. But I've got my boys, and they come first.*

He stripped and went to bed, but sleep eluded him. One thing was sure: if he didn't have the boys, he'd be on his way to Bethesda, and the devil take the morrow.

* * *

Naomi unlocked her studio, threw her shoulder bag on her desk and opened the window a few inches. The sent of strong coffee wafted up from a nearby cafeteria, but she resisted retracing her steps to get some and settled for a cup of instant. She had barely slept the night before. Rufus had weighted the temptation of kissing her against the harm of doing it, and harm had won out. It wasn't flattering no matter how you sliced it, especially since she had wanted that kiss. When had she last kissed a man, felt strong masculine arms around her? She knew she was being inconsistent, wanting Rufus while swearing never to get involved. Keeping the vow had been easy…until she'd first heard his voice. When she saw him, it was hopeless. She sipped the bland-tasting coffee slowly.

Images of him loving her and then walking away from her when he learned her secret had kept her tossing in bed all night. She'd finished reading his first book, *The Family at Risk,* and had been appalled at some of his conclusions: the family in American society had lost its usefulness as a source of nurturing, health care, education, and economic, social, and psychological support for the young. Spouses, he complained, had separate credit cards, separate bank accounts, and separate goals. Oneness was out of fashion. Homemaking as an occupation invited scorn, and women avoided it if they could. He claimed that the family lost its focal point when women went to work, and without them as its core, the family had no unity. She hadn't realized how strongly he believed that women had a disproportionate responsibility for the country's social ills. He wouldn't accept her past, she knew, so she'd put him behind her.

She laughed at herself. She didn't have such a big problem, just a simple matter of forgetting about Rufus. But what red-blooded woman would want to do *that?* It was useless to remain there staring at the stark white walls. "I'm going home and put on the most chic fall outfit in my closet," she declared, "and then I'm going to lunch at the Willard Hotel."

The maître d' gave her a choice table with a clear view of the entrance. The low drone of voices and the posh room where lights flickered from dozens of crystal chandeliers offered the perfect setting for a trip into the past, but she savored her drink and resisted the temptation; wool gathering slowed down your life, she told herself. Suddenly, she felt the cool vintage wine halt its slow trickle down her throat, almost choking her, and heated tremors stole through her as Rufus walked toward her. But her excitement quickly dissolved into angst when his hand steadied the attractive woman who preceded him. He wasn't alone.

The sight of the handsome couple deeply engrossed in serious conversation stung her, and she lowered her eyes to shield her reaction. She looked at the grilled salmon and green salad when the waiter brought it, and pushed it aside. She just wanted to get out of there. Aware that she had ruined the day for the little maître d', she apologized, paid with her credit card, and stood to leave. A glance told her that Rufus was still there, still absorbed in his companion and their conversation. She took a deep breath, wrapped herself in dignity, and with her head high, marched past his table without looking his way.

The furious pace of her heartbeat alarmed her, and she decided it would be foolish to drive. Dinosaurs. This was a good time to see them. But on her way to the Smithsonian Institute, the crisp air and gentle wind lured her to the Tidal Basin, and she walked along the river, deep in thought. Why was she upset at seeing Rufus with another woman? There wasn't anything between her and him, and there couldn't be anything between them. Not ever. She took a few pieces of tissue from her purse, spread them out, and sat down. She could no longer deny that he was becoming important to her, so she braced her back against a tree and contemplated what to do about it.

"Even if you wanted to be alone, you didn't have to pick such a deserted place. Are you looking for trouble?"

By the time Rufus ended the question, she was on her feet, trembling with feminine awareness at the unexpected sound of his voice. "Don't you know you shouldn't frighten a person like that?" she huffed, not in annoyance, but in pulsing anticipation. "It's downright sadistic, the way you suddenly appear. Where did you leave your date?" She blanched, realizing that she had given herself away, but pretended aloofness. She didn't want him to know that seeing him with an attractive woman had affected her.

He cocked an eyebrow. "I helped Miss Hunt get a taxi, and she went back to her office."

"Why are you telling me that?" she asked, as if he hadn't merely answered her question. "It isn't my concern."

"I didn't suggest otherwise. Are you okay?"

"Of course, I'm okay," she managed to reply, and turned her back so that her quivering lips wouldn't betray her. "How did you get here?" It was barely a whisper.

"I followed you. When you passed my table immediately after your lunch was served, you seemed distressed. I wanted to be sure you were all right."

He walked around her in order to face her. "I was surprised to see you lunching alone in that posh place. I only go there because Angela, my agent, loves to be seen there. She says it's good for her image."

Intense relief washed through her, and she gasped from the joy of it. Her mind told her to move back, to remember who she was and that she had reasons to avoid a deeper involvement with him, but her mind and heart were not in sync, she learned.

Oblivious to the squirrels that were busily hoarding for the winter, the blackbirds chirping around them, and the wind whistling through the trees, she stood with her gaze locked into his, shaken by her unbridled response to him. She was barely aware of the dry leaves swirling around them and the wind's accelerated velocity as they continued to devour each other with the heat in their eyes, neither of them speaking or moving. Feeling chill-like tremors, she rubbed her arms briskly, letting her gaze shift to his lips.

His sharp intake of breath as he opened his arms thrilled her, and she walked into them, her body alive with hot anticipation. He had lost his war with himself, and she gloried in his defeat. She felt him sink slowly to the turf, clasping her tightly. He lay with her above him, protecting her from the hard ground. She knew, when he immediately helped her to her feet without even kissing her, that their environment alone had stopped him. Blatant desire still radiated from him. She didn't remember ever having encountered such awesome self-control.

"Chicken sandwiches and ginger ale taste about the same as grilled salmon and salad," she told him, when they finished.

"Something like that occurred to me, too." He smiled.

They stood at the curb, near her parked car, neither speaking nor touching, just looking at each other. She hadn't noticed that he'd shortened his sideburns or that he had a tiny brown mole beside his left ear. And in the sunlight, she could see for the first time that his fawnlike eyes were rimmed with a curious shade of brownish green. Beautiful. A lurch of excitement pitched wildly in her chest. *Back off, girl, before you can't!* Without a word, she turned blindly toward her car, but he grabbed her hand, detaining her, and forced her to look at him. Then he brushed her cheek tenderly with the back of his closed fist and let her go.

She drove slowly. She could stay away from him, she thought, if he wasn't so charismatic. So handsome. So sexy. So honorable. And oh, God, so tender and loving with his kids. He was a chauvinist, maybe—she was becoming less positive of that—had a trigger-fast temper, and was unreasonable sometimes. But he made her feel protected, and he was the epitome of man. *Man!* That was the only word for him and, if she were honest, she'd admit that she wanted everything he could give a woman—his consuming fire, his drugging power and heady masculine strength—just once in her life. But most of all, she wanted the tenderness of which she knew he was capable. Naomi laughed at herself. Who was she kidding? Well, her grandpa had always preached that thinking didn't cost you anything; it was not thinking that was expensive. She mused over that as she drove, deciding that in her case, both could cost a lot. Once with him would never be enough, she conceded, wondering how he was handling their…encounter.

Rufus steered into his garage and forced himself to get out of his car. He walked around the garden in back of the house, sat on a stone bench, absently turned the hose on, and filled the birdbath. Why couldn't he leave her alone? It had taken every ounce of will he could gather to stop what he'd started down by the Tidal Basin. He couldn't pinpoint what had triggered it, and he wondered how he managed to appear so calm afterward when he actually felt as if he would explode. And why had he felt obligated to ease her mind about Angela? He'd never even kissed her, thought he'd just come pretty close to it. Besides, he and Naomi spent most of their time together fighting. He had been discussing a three-book deal with Angela when Naomi had passed their table; one look at her face, and he knew she'd seen them. He had immediately terminated the discussion and followed her. Get a grip on it, son! He noticed two squirrels frolicking in the barbecue pit, walked over to the patio, and got some of the peanuts that he stored there for his little friends. He went to the pit, got down on his haunches, and waited until they saw him and raced over to take their food from his hand.

Why couldn't he leave her alone? Nothing could come of it. The question plagued him. And another thing. Good Lord! She was jealous of Angela. Jealous! How the devil was he going to stay away from her if she reciprocated what he felt? They didn't even like each other. Scratch that, he amended; only fools lied to themselves. He went up to his room, changed his clothes, and went to get his boys from Jewel's house.

Naomi sat at her drawing board that afternoon and wondered whether she could do a full day's work in two hours. She was way off schedule, and she didn't have one useful idea. "Oh, hang Rufus," she called out in frustration. "Why am I bothered, anyway? Why, for heaven's sake, am I torturing myself?" She dialed Marva, who answered on the first ring. Naomi always found it disconcerting that Marva's telephone rarely rang a second or third time. She would almost believe her friend just sat beside the phone waiting for a call, but Marva was too impatient.

"Are you going to One Last Chance this afternoon?" she asked her. "I think we ought to firm up the plans for our contributions to the Urban Alliance gala. If we don't get a bigger share of the pot this time, OLC will be in financial difficulty."

"I know," Marva breathed, sounding bored, "but it'll all work out. You ought to be concentrating on who's going to take you and what you're going to wear." Suddenly, Marva seemed more serious than usual. "Someday, Naomi, you're going to tell me why a twenty-nine-year-old woman who looks like you would swear off men. Honey, I couldn't understand that even if you were eighty. Don't you ever want somebody to hold you? I mean *really* hold you?"

Caught off guard, Naomi clutched the telephone cord and answered candidly. "To tell the truth, I do. Terribly, sometimes, but I've been that route once, and once is enough for me." Well, it was a half-truth, but she knew she owed her friend a reasonable answer, and she would never breathe the whole truth to anyone.

She changed the subject. "Guess what happened while you were gone, Marva."

"Tell me."

"Well, Le Ciel Perfumes saw the ad I did for Fragrant Soaps and gave me an exclusive five-year contract. I get all their business. Girl, I'm in the big time now. Can you believe it? I talked to them as if I could barely fit them into my tight program. Then I hung up, screamed, and danced a jig."

"You actually screamed? Wish I'd been there."

"But, Marva, that's what every commercial artist dreams of, a sponsor. I treated myself to a new music system. My feet have hardly touched the ground since I signed that contract."

"Go, girl. I knew you had it in you. We'll get together for some Moët and Chandon; just name the hour."

On an impulse and as casually as she could, she asked Marva, "You know so many people in this town, do you happen to know Rufus Meade?"

"Cat Meade? Is there anybody in the District of Columbia who doesn't know him or know about him?"

"I didn't know him until recently, and I didn't realize you read books on crime and delinquency, Marva," she needled gently.

"Of course I don't; I hate unpleasantness, especially when

it's criminal. What does this have to do with Cat Meade? Cat was the leading NFL wide receiver for five straight years. Didn't you ever watch the 'Skins?"

"Oh, come on, girl. You know I can't stand violence, and those guys are always knocking each other down."

Marva laughed. Naomi loved to hear the big, lusty laugh that her friend delighted in giving full rein.

"Now I understand your real problem," Marva told her. "You haven't been looking at all those cute little buns in those skintight stretch pants."

"You're hopeless," Naomi sighed. "What about Meade? Did he quit because he was injured, or does he still play?"

"From what I heard, he stopped because he'd made enough money to be secure financially, and he'd always wanted to be a writer. He's a very prominent print journalist, and he's well respected, or so I hear. Why? Are you interested in him?"

In for a penny; in for a pound. "He's got something, as we used to say in our days at Howard U, but he and I are like oil and water. And it's just as well, because I think we also basically distrust each other. He doesn't care much for career women, and I was raised by a male chauvinist, so a little of that type goes a long way with me. Grandpa's antics stick in my craw so badly that I'm afraid I accuse Rufus unfairly sometimes. Why do you call him 'Cat'? That's an odd name for a guy as big as he is."

Marva's sigh was impatient and much affected. "When are you going to learn that things don't have to be what they seem? They called him Cat, because the only living thing that seemed able to outrun him were a thoroughbred horse and cheetah, and he moved down the field like a lithe young panther. My mouth used to water just watching him." The latter was properly supported by another deep sigh, Naomi noted.

"I hope you've gotten over that," she replied dryly.

"Oh, I have; he's not running anymore," Marva deadpanned. "And besides, it's my honey who makes my mouth water these days." She paused. "Naomi, I've only met Cat a few times at social functions, and I doubt that he'd even remember me. Of course, any woman with warm blood would remember him. Go for it, kid."

"You're joking. The man's a chauvinist." She told her about his statement when he'd appeared on *Capitol Life,* supporting her disdain, but she could see that Marva wasn't impressed.

"Naomi, honey," she crooned in her slow Texas drawl, "why are you so browned off? If isn't like you to let anybody get to you like this. Lots of guys think like that; the point is to change him…or to find one who doesn't."

"Never mind," Naomi told her, "I should have known you wouldn't find it in your great big heart to criticize a live and breathing man."

She assured herself that she wouldn't be calling him Cat. "I don't care how fast he was or is." They'd been having a pleasant few minutes together the night he'd brought the boys to her apartment, and she had asked him a simple, reasonable question. After all, a working journalist couldn't take twin toddlers on assignment, so who kept them while he worked? But he was supersensitive about it. That one question was all it had taken to set him off. Then, down at the Tidal Basin, he'd nearly kissed her. She should never have let him touch her. Why the heck wasn't he consistent? The torment she felt as a result of that almost kiss just wouldn't leave her. She hoped he was at least a little bit miserable. What she wouldn't give to be secure in a man's love! *His* love? She didn't let herself answer.

Naomi's contemplations of the day's events as she dressed hurriedly that evening for an emergency board meeting at OLC was interrupted by the telephone. Linda's voice triggered a case of mild anxiety in her; the girls at OLC were not allowed to call their tutors at home.

"What is it, Linda?"

The unsteadiness in the girl's voice told her that there might be a serious problem.

"I hated to call you at home, but I didn't know what else to do. My mama says I can't go on the retreat. I won a scholarship, and it won't cost anything, but she says I can't go."

Naomi sat down. Maude Frazier and OLC would wait. "Did she say why?"

"Yes. She said I'll do more good here at home helping her and working in the drugstore than I will wasting two weeks with a gang of kids drawing pictures. She said she never wants to see another piece of crayon. What will I do?"

Naomi pushed back her disappointment; how would the girl ever make it with so little support? "I'll speak with your principal. Don't worry too much. We have two months in which to work out a strategy and get your mother's approval, but I'm sure the principal can handle this. Why didn't you tell me that you won a scholarship? How many were there?"

"One. I didn't tell you, because I figured Mama wouldn't want me to go." Naomi beamed, her face wreathed in smiles. She wished that she could have been with Linda to give her a hug. She doubted the girl received much affection; she certainly didn't get the approval and encouragement that her talent deserved.

"Just one scholarship for the entire junior high school, and you won it? I'm proud of you, Linda, and I'm going to do everything possible to help you get those two weeks of training. I'll see you in a couple of days?" The conversation was over, but it had an almost paralyzing effect on Naomi. What was her own child going through? Were its parents loving and understanding? Did they encourage it? *It!* God how awful! She didn't even know whether she'd had a girl or a boy.

She hurriedly put on a slim skirted, above the knee dusty rose silk suit with a silk cowl necked blouse of matching color, found some navy accessories, and left home having barely glanced at herself in a mirror. She knew that color always set off her rich brown skin, and when she wore lipstick of matching color, her only makeup, as she did now, the effect was simple elegance. She arrived precisely on time and was not surprised when, at the minute she seated herself at the long oval table, Maude Frazier, the board's president and arbiter of social class among the African American locals, lowered the gavel. "Now that we're all here, let us begin our work."

Naomi considered Maude's philosophy, that if you weren't early, you were late, autocratic, and unreasonable. One morning, either in this life or the next, Maude was going to wake up and discover that she really wasn't the English queen. Naomi got immense pleasure from the thought.

Maude's announcement that they had a guest brought Naomi's gaze around the table until she found Rufus Meade sitting there looking directly at her. Her reaction at seeing him unexpectedly was the same as always. Tension gathered within her and her heartbeat accelerated when he dipped his head ever so slightly in a greeting and let his lush mouth curve in a half smile. She knew the minute he responded to the fire that she couldn't suppress, that the tension pulsing between them was a sleeping volcano ready to erupt. She felt her heart flutter madly and shifted nervously in her chair as Maude opened the discussion.

She would not have anticipated that the talks would become so heated. The meeting ended, and she realized from Rufus's facial expression that he was furious with her. She believed her argument—that One Last Chance existed to be a buffer between distressed girls and the cruelty of society—was the correct one. And she was amazed when Rufus took the position that what she really wanted was for the foundation to be a shelter for delinquents. She hoped he wasn't a poor looser; several board members sided with him, but the majority supported her.

She was wrong, and he would straighten her out, he vowed, forcing himself to remain calm while, oblivious to onlookers, he ushered her to the elevator and on to the little office where she tutored. "I know there are special circumstances, but we have to be very careful when we're deciding what they are."

"I'm already familiar with your brand of compassion," she told him, with what he recognized as exaggerated sweetness; "it doesn't extend to females. It does cover cute little replicas of yourself, naturally, but it amazes me that you allowed your perfect self close enough to a woman to beget them. I don't suppose it was the result of artificial insemination, was it?" He wanted to singe her mouth with his when she looked at him expectantly, as if deserving a serious, friendly answer, though she knew she'd irked him.

He surprised himself and figured that he probably shocked her as well when he broke up laughing. When he could stop, he looked down at her and, in a playful mode, shook his head from side to side, his single dimple on full display. "Naomi, I refuse to believe that you are so naive as to issue me that kind of challenge. Don't you know better than to tell a man to his face that you doubt his virility? Are you nuts?"

Her intent regard amused Rufus. If she had been aware of the look of fascinated admiration on her smiling face, ten to one she would have banished it immediately. Her answer riled him. He wondered whether her attention had strayed when she asked provocatively, "How far off was I?"

Abruptly, he stopped smiling, forgot caution, and felt his face settle into a harsh mask. He pulled her close to him and absorbed her trembling as he lowered his head and brushed her mouth with his lips. He drew back to look at her, to gauge her reaction, but fire raced through him when she braced her hands against his chest in a weak, symbolic protest and whimpered, and he knew he had to taste her. Her soft, supple body offered no resistance, and as he sensed the giving of her trust, a warm, unfamiliar feeling of connection with someone special gripped him. She burrowed into him, giving herself over to him, pulling at something inside him. Something he didn't want to release.

He fitted her head into one of his big hands and gently stroked her back with the other, trying to temper their rapidly escalating passion. But her gentle movements quickened his need. He nearly bent over in anguish when she wiggled closer, caught up in her own passion. Capitulating at last and in spite of himself, he captured her eager mouth in an explosive giving of himself, his body shuddering and his blood zinging through his throbbing veins.

He sensed a change in her then—a feminine response to his own burgeoning need—and altered the kiss to a sweet, gentle one, easing the pressure before asking for entrance with the tip of his tongue. Her parted lips took him in, and he felt her tremble from the pleasure of his kiss as she wrapped her arms around his neck in sensual enjoyment. He didn't wonder that she returned his kiss so ardently, that she was caressing his arms, shoulders, and neck, that she was loving him right back. His only thought was that she felt so good in his arms, tasted so good, responded to him hotly and passionately, that she fitted him, that she belonged right where she was. He didn't remember ever having had such a passionate response from a woman nor even having had one excite him as she did. He wanted her and he was going to have her even if she was… He jerked his head up and looked down into her passion-filled eyes. Not in a million years. *Never!* He told himself as he put her gently but firmly away from him.

* * *

Naomi grasped her middle to steady herself. He had to know that it was good to her, she surmised. Like nothing she had ever felt. Did he know that her body burned from his kiss? She had waited so long for it. Forever, it seemed. Nearly all her life. Those strong, muscular arms holding her, soothing her; the heady masculine smell of him tantalizing her; and the possessive way that he held her were more than she could have resisted. More than she wanted to resist. And she needed to be held, needed what he had given her, needed *him.* Her eyes closed in frustration. What was it with him?

"Look," she heard him say, as he brushed his fingers across the back of his corded neck, apparently struggling both for words and for composure, "I'm sorry about that. You made me mad as the devil, and I got carried away. My apologies."

She reeled from his blunt rejection, but only momentarily. With more than thirteen years of practice at putting up her guard, she slipped it easily into place. "Looks as if I was right, after all, Mr. Meade," she bluffed, covering her discomfort. "You've got a problem." She whirled around and left him standing there. He would never know what it had cost her.

Chapter 4

An hour later, still puzzled over Rufus's behavior, Naomi forced herself to answer her doorbell. Tomorrow, she was going to speak to the doorman about not buzzing her to ask whether she wanted to receive visitors. What was the point in having such an expensive place if it didn't guarantee her security and privacy? She knew very well that if it was Rufus, the young doorman would be so awed that he wouldn't dare insult him by asking his name and announcing him, as house rules required. With a tepid smile, she cracked the door open and saw him standing there, the epitome of strength and virility. She tried to curb her response to him, a reaction so strong that blood seemed to rush to her head. And that annoyed her. Her next impulse was to close the door with a bang, but she wasn't so irritated that she wanted to hurt him.

"May I come in, Naomi? Not once when I've stood at this door have you willingly invited me in."

Feeling trapped by her attraction to him, and hoping that

a clever retort would put her in command, she gave him what she hoped was a withering look.

"What do you want, Meade? You've already gotten your-self off the hook with an apology, so why are you standing here?" She spoke in a low, measured tone, trying to keep her voice steady.

Rufus was silent for a minute, trying to gauge her real feelings, which he had learned were probably different from what she let him see. Her gentle tone belied her sharp words, and he welcomed it. He watched her bottom lip quiver while she shifted her weight from one foot to the other, trying not to respond to what he knew she saw in his eyes. His gaze traveled slowly over her, caressing her, cataloging her trea-sures—flat belly, rounded hips, wild hair, long legs, a full, generous mouth, and more. He wanted her badly enough to steal her. Badly enough to forget everything else and go for her. But he hadn't come to her apartment for that. Telling himself to get with it, he reined in his passion and assumed a casual stance.

He cleared his throat, impatient with his physical reaction to her. "Naomi, it must be clear to you that we have to reach some kind of understanding. We have to work together for the next month, and if we can't cooperate, that gala will be a disaster. So ease up, will you?"

He was taken aback by her forced, humorless smile. And her words. "Why don't you level with yourself? You didn't come over here tonight to make it easier for us to work to-gether. You're here for two reasons; your testosterone is acting up; and you're feeling guilty about the way you be-haved back there at OLC. Well, you can go home, wherever that is. Your boys will be 'pining' for you."

Rufus could see that she wanted to take back the words as soon as they escaped her lips. Weeks earlier, those revealing remarks had slipped out of his mouth before he could stop them—childhood hurts that remained solidly etched in his memory—and she had thrown them back at him. He knew that she saw pain in his eyes, that his reaction to her barb aroused her compassion. He regretted having exposed himself to her when he alluded to his unhappy childhood, and she could bet he wouldn't make that mistake again. He hated pity. To cover her own insecurity, her own vulnerability, she had used it against him. But she reached out to him then with her heart as well as her hand, and he looked first into her eyes, softer than he had ever seen them, and then at her extended hand, grasped it, and walked in. Into her house and into her arms.

He breathed deeply, savoring the union, as they held each other without the intrusion of the passion and one-upmanship that had marked their brief relationship. When he felt himself begin to stir against her, he moved away.

"Naomi, if you'd put on more clothes, maybe we can talk this thing out."

Her embarrassment at having greeted him in her short silk dressing gown was too obvious to conceal, and he noticed that she didn't try, but expected him to understand that she had forgotten she was skimpily dressed. It was a small measure of trust, but it was something, and he welcomed it.

"All right. I'll be back in a minute. There's a bar; help yourself to a drink." She left him in the living room and returned within minutes dressed, as promised. He liked that.

"Didn't you find anything you'd like to drink?"

"I don't drink anything stronger than an occasional glass of wine at dinner. Thanks anyway." She looked great no matter what she was wearing, he observed, and told her so. "You're really something to look at, you know that? My common sense almost deserted me when I saw you standing there in that red jersey robe, with that thick black curly hair hanging around your shoulders. Dark women look great in pinks and reds."

She sat down and kicked off her shoes, and he could see that his compliments made her nervous. She did not want an involvement with him any more than he wanted one with her. He grinned. In their case, want didn't count for much.

"Thank you," she replied briskly, "but there isn't anything to talk out, as you put it. I am not looking for a romantic involvement with you or anyone else, not now or ever, so we shouldn't have any difficulty working together."

Rufus glanced at her shoeless feet as she tucked them beneath her. A free spirit would do that, he figured. But she had caged that side of her, he guessed, and she had done it years earlier. He leaned back in the sofa and appraised her slowly and thoroughly until she suddenly squirmed. What a maze of contradictions she was! If she thought so little of romantic involvement and marriage for herself, why had she championed it for her young charge at OLC? The thought perturbed him; her adamant disavowal of interest in men didn't ring true. He noted that the shoes were back on her feet.

Rufus leaned forward. "Sorry about that," he apologized, referring to his blatant perusal of her. "But I can't believe you know so little about what happens when a man and a woman get their hooks in each other. So I have to assume that either you're being dishonest with yourself or you just don't care to level with me. That kiss you gave me, Naomi, almost made me erupt; I'm still reeling from it. You were right when you said that's why I'm here."

"You're making too much of this," she told him, obviously uneasy with the drift of the conversation.

Her attempt to minimize it annoyed him. "When you kiss a man like that, giving him everything he's asking for and letting him know that you're loving what he's doing to you,

you're either consenting or making demands of your own or you've gone too far."

He ignored the outrage that he saw in her reproachful eyes and went on. "You and I want each other, Naomi. Don't doubt it for a minute; we want to make love to each other. I confess that making love with you was one of the first thoughts I had when I met you. But I told myself then, and I'm telling you now, that I don't intend to do one thing about it. You and I would be poison together."

Naomi was a worthy adversary, he recalled at once. "Of course you aren't going to do anything about it," she purred, "because *I* won't let you. As for me wanting you, let me tell you how much weight you can put on that. I saw a beautiful pair of green leather slippers in Garfinkel's not long ago, and I wanted them badly. They were the perfect complement to something I had just bought. I took a taxi all the way back up here to Bethesda at a cost of twenty dollars, got my credit card, taxied back, and would you believe those shoes were gone? You know what I did? I shrugged my shoulders and bought a pair of royal blue ones that didn't match a thing I owned. When I left the store, I was perfectly happy. Nothing gets the better of me, Rufus. Believe me, *nothing!*" He disliked her facetious grin. "So you're right; there's no need to make a big deal out of it," she went on, her quivering lips belying her tough words. "You'll find another one—darker or lighter, taller or shorter, but with the same basic equipment—and you'll be just as happy."

He shook his head in amazement. "I don't believe you said that." His blood pounded in his ears when she crossed her knees and let her right shoe slip off as she did so, revealing a flawless size nine foot with its perfectly shaped red toenails. His couldn't take his eyes from her.

He swore softly. "You'd drive me insane if I spent much time around you. Stop acting," he growled in a velvet soft voice. "You're as vulnerable to me as I am to you." He told himself to cool off. "We have to have a meeting Tuesday or Wednesday. Which would you prefer?"

"Neither." His impatient glance provoked a hesitant explanation. "I tutor at One Last Chance in the afternoon of both days this week, and I can't disappoint this girl; she has a lot of problems, and she's known very little caring. The night you saw her with me, she showed me an excellent drawing that she had done with crayons; it was wonderful. She just needs guidance."

"Then you believe she has talent for art?"

"Yes, but I'm not tutoring her in art. I'm helping her with math and English."

"What's the girl's name?" He wondered if now was the time. Her feelings for this girl aroused his curiosity and his suspicions, too, he realized.

"Linda."

Rufus hesitated, aware of a primitive protectiveness toward her, fearful of hurting her. "Naomi. If I'm wrong here, tell me. I get the impression that you have a special connection with this girl, that you have deeper feelings for her than for the others at OLC. And my instincts say that your concern for her has a personal basis." He watched as she readied herself to divert him.

"Really, Rufus, what could have made you think such a thing?"

"I realize that you were tutoring her in English, but I didn't know that you were qualified to teach math as well. What level?"

"She's in her last year of junior high. I taught those subjects in high school for four years."

"Why did you give it up?" Naomi was a complex person, he was beginning to understand, and the more he saw of her, the more he wanted to see. He leaned back against the deeply cushioned brown velvet sofa, watching her intently.

"I never wanted to teach, but Grandpa would pay for my education only if I studied to be a teacher. Teaching is the proper work for girls of my class, he told me a thousand times. I did as he wanted, same as everybody else always does, and I taught until I'd saved enough money to study for a degree in fine art. He hasn't forgiven me for it, but, well, he's done some things that I haven't been able to forgive him for." He nodded, letting her know that he sympathized with her, then lifted his wrists and glanced at his watch.

"I've got to get home; I told Jewel I'd be there by nine." He hesitated to leave. "How did you get involved with One Last Chance?"

He pondered the reasons she might have for taking so much time to answer. "I saw the need for it. I'm one of its founders. Who's Jewel?" On to another topic, was she? The tactic neither fooled nor amused him.

From Naomi's reaction, he realized that his grin had been mocking rather than disarming, as he had intended. "Jewel's my baby sister. Why? Are you jealous?" He couldn't resist the taunt; it was the second bit of concrete evidence she'd given him that her interest was more than casual and his attraction for her more than physical. Yet he doubted that she would ever own up to it.

Her studied smirk as she slanted her head, tipped up her nose, and peered at him had all the arrogance that any crowned European could have mustered. It was admirable. What a gal!

"Well?" he baited.

"Put all your money on it," she bantered, with a brief pause that he knew was for effect, "and then see your lawyer about filing for bankruptcy." He smiled, enjoying the teasing.

"You'd be fun if you'd just forget about sex," she told him, referring to his comment about their heated kiss.

He knew she meant to provoke him, but instead of indulging her, he quipped: "Forget about sex? Sweetheart, that is one thing I'll remember even after I'm buried."

His seductive wink, a mesmerizing slow sweep of his left eye, was aimed to strip her of any pretense about her feelings. And for the moment, it did. He held his breath when she dusted a speck of lint from the lapel of his jacket, pushed the handkerchief further down in his breast pocket, and rubbed a speck of nothing from his chin. The expression in her eyes nearly unglued him, but he kept his countenance and satisfied himself with a brush of his fingers across her cheek. He was unprepared for the warmth that quickly enveloped them and for the sweet, mutual contentment that they had not previously experienced together. Wordlessly, they walked to her door and stood there looking at each other, comfortable with the tension, with their desire in check. Simultaneously they reached out to each other, but didn't touch and withdrew as one, as if it had been choreographed. He sucked in his breath and left without a word.

The rooms appeared to have grown larger after he left her, and her beloved apartment seemed cold and unfriendly. Her footsteps echoed along the short, tiled hallway. Strange, but she had never noticed that before. A restlessness suffused her. She reached for the telephone, then dropped her hand. So this was loneliness. This was what it was like to miss a man. She had to stop it now. Maybe it was already too late. She didn't think she had the strength to face exposure, certainly not his rejection. Rufus already meant too much to her, had too prominent a place in her life, and she couldn't bear his scorn if he ever knew about her past. One Last Chance was important to her, but if she couldn't get Rufus out of her life any other way, she would have no choice but to leave it, to walk away from the most satisfying thing in her world other than her work. He was right; she had wanted him desperately. She still did. But if she walked away from him, away from the sweet and terrible hunger that he stirred in her, away from the promise of love in his arms... She went to bed trying not to think about Rufus and fell asleep imagining the ultimate joy that he could give her.

The next morning Naomi got up at six-thirty, unable to sleep longer, and phoned her grandfather.

"Why are you calling so early, gal? I thought you artist types worked at night and slept most of the day."

She ignored his attempted reprimand for having abandoned teaching for art. "Grandpa, I think we ought to look up those people who want to find me and get it over with; I can't stand this uncertainty. A month ago, I had a quiet life and was contented, all things considered. It's like a death sentence must be; maybe the waiting and not knowing is worse than the actual execution."

"Don't you be foolish, gal," he roared into the phone. "They may give up or I may find a way to discourage them."

"But where does that leave me? Did I have a girl, a boy, twins? And are the adoptive parents loving, abusive, rich, dirt poor? What about my feelings, Grandpa? This is becoming unbearable." She thought about Rufus and how devoted he was to his boys. He put them before everybody and everything, including his career. She recalled his painful allusion to his childhood when, after "pining" all day for someone, no doubt his mother, that someone had gotten home too tired to give him the love he needed. What would he think of her? She heard Judd's insistent voice.

"What was that, Grandpa?"

"Where's your mind, Naomi?" She imagined that he was

rolling his eyes upward, expressing his frustration. "I said that I tried to spare you as best I could. But if you're going to be foolish and go looking for trouble, I'd better hire a lawyer. Never could tell you a thing."

"So the lawyer can tell you that we don't have any options? This is something that has to be done on a personal basis." She hated discussing it with him. Her grandfather would soon be ninety-five; he'd been born the last day of the nineteenth century, and she tried never to argue with him. Not only because he'd taken her in and made a home for her when her father had remarried to a woman who didn't want a stepchild around, and had become her legal guardian when her father had died, but because she cared for him and didn't like to upset him. He's the product of anther era, she reminded herself, a time when a man did what he thought best for his family and expected them to accept it as he knew they would.

"We've got a problem, so we'll get legal advice," she heard him say in his usual authoritarian fashion. The sisters and brothers of the First Golgotha Baptist Church didn't get out of line with their pastor, and forty-five years of such near idolatry had spoiled Judd Logan. "These hotshot lawyers are worthless," he continued, "but you need them sometimes."

"There's no point in asking you not to, Grandpa, because you always do whatever you like. I don't need a lawyer; I need to meet my child's adoptive parents and ask them to let me see my child. If they want to reach me after all this time, there's a good reason." She wouldn't say more about it then; it would take him a while to accept the idea, if he ever did. "I have to go over to One Last Chance, Grandpa. One of the girls is meeting me there at nine." She didn't say goodbye, because she knew he'd have a comment then or later. Twirling the phone cord, she waited.

"I want you to listen to me, gal. Don't rush into anything. And I wish you'd stay away from those places like Florida

Avenue," he complained. "What kind of people do you meet over there? I'm sure Maude Frazier doesn't waste time around there. It's not proper for an unmarried girl of your class to hang around those people." Naomi grinned, stifling a giggle as she did so. The old man was on a roll. He loved to preach, and it didn't matter whether he had an audience of one hundred or one.

"Grandpa, you're talking about seventy years ago." Reminding herself that there was a generation between them and enough years in age for a two-generation gap, she let it pass.

"We're never going to agree on certain things," she told him gently. "You tried to save people's souls. Well, when I'm at One Last Chance, I'm trying to help people mend their lives. There must be a connection there somewhere." She told him goodbye and hung up.

Half an hour after arriving at OLC, Naomi looked at her watch. Linda was late. She knew that the girl wouldn't offer an excuse, and when she arrived, she didn't. Linda had missed several sessions, and Naomi had been tempted to speak with her mother but had refrained for fear of causing trouble.

"I spoke with your principal. Has he told your mother the consequences of your not going to the retreat and completing your art project?"

Linda's eyes widened. "You mean he's going to tell my mama I'll be in trouble if I don't go? Boy, that's super cool! Tell me to tell her I can't go to the retreat unless I have my hair done."

Naomi laughed. "Linda, we tell the truth to the extent possible. The principal won't be lying. That retreat is important to you; your career decisions may hinge on it."

She knew that Linda admired her, but she was stunned

when the girl suddenly told her, "I wish I could be like you, Naomi. I wish I was you."

Naomi tugged at her chin with a thumb and forefinger. "My dear, if you knew everything there is to know, you might not want to be in my shoes at all."

Linda stared directly at her. "With you, I'd take my chances." Shaking her head, Naomi looked at Linda and remembered herself fourteen years before. If you got what you prayed for, she thought with wise hindsight, it could ruin your life.

She went home and began designing invitations for the Urban Alliance gala. There weren't enough sponsors, she decided. Rufus would know what to do about it. She got his number and telephoned him. She was taken aback when his initial response to her call was unfriendly; he was deep into his current manuscript, *Subculture of the American Juvenile,* he explained, and hadn't wanted to be disturbed. But he'd immediately become warm and agreeable.

"Give me an hour, and I can get over there," he stated, as if confident that she would accept his offer. She couldn't help smiling. To begin the day with Judd Logan and end it with Rufus Meade would tax a saint—that is, unless the saint was slightly sweet on Rufus, her conscience whispered.

She pushed the thought aside and asked him, "How far away are you, Rufus?"

"Fifteen minutes. Just over in Chevy Chase. Why? You need something that'll melt? Or maybe something that'll melt you? Hmm?" He laughed, but she refused to join in his merriment. She wished he'd be consistent and stop the sexual teasing, since they had both sworn not to get involved.

"Are you bringing the boys? Should I dash out and get some ice-cream?"

He answered gruffly, yet seemed touched. "Thanks, no.

They're over at Jewel's house, playing with their cousins. I'll see you shortly."

Naomi hung up and leaned against the edge of her kitchen table. Rufus claimed that he would not permit anything to happen between them, and that was fine with her, because she couldn't afford it. But his behavior didn't always suit his words. He teased her, and though he didn't telephone her, when they spoke, he took every opportunity to make her aware of him as a man. A desirable man. She shook her head in wonder, but her bewilderment was fleeting; she spun on her heels and headed for her bedroom.

"Two can play this game," she told herself, as she remembered how elegant he'd been when he'd come to her house, even when he'd had the twins with him. "If he's a phony," she muttered, "we'll both know it soon." She reached into her closet for her silk knit "Sherman tank," a sleeveless cowl-necked magnet for males, dismissed caution, and shimmied into it.

Chapter 5

To her chagrin, Rufus arrived wearing a long-sleeved sport shirt with black jeans under a light overcoat. His dreamy eyes took her in from head to foot, apparently appreciating the svelte curves revealed by her burnt orange knit tube dress. His grin didn't reach his eyes, she noticed. Leaning against the wall with his arms folded across his broad chest, he told her without a trace of a smile and in deadly earnest, "Don't you play with fire, honey. I wouldn't want you to get singed."

She had an awful feeling of defeat, but only temporarily, because she knew that her sharp mind rarely deserted her. She pushed one of the kitchen chairs toward him, hopefully gave him a level stare, and asked in what she had cultivated as her sweetest voice, "You wouldn't be the culprit, would you?" A bystander would have thought that she was seriously seeking valuable information. "You usually back off when things warm up. So I don't have to worry about you, do I?" But she quickly realized that Rufus was not in a joshing mood. She saw his body stiffen and his muscles tense and thought of a big cat about to spring.

He rounded the table. "You like to tease, do you? Well..." She headed him off, sensing something subtly different about him. It wasn't the annoyance; she'd seen him practically furious. It was the steel, a street kind of steel that a man reserves for his true adversary.

She gulped. "I'm not teasing you, I've never..."

"I'm not asking you; I'm telling you. You didn't wear that hot little number all day long, now, did you? And I'll bet you weren't wearing it when you called me."

She backed up a little. Where was that suave, genteel man with the iron control? This Rufus seemed to be itching for friction, to need it. But she was doggoned if she'd let him intimidate her.

"Your reputation doesn't include being a bully, so be yourself and sit back down."

His steely, yet strangely gentle fingers sent fiery ripples spiraling down her arm. "Don't play with me, Naomi. You poured yourself into that thing to get my attention." He grinned, and she realized for the first time that his grin did not necessarily signify amusement. "You've got my attention. I told you that I had no intention of pursuing this...this whatever-you-want-to-call-it between us, and you assumed that I meant I wouldn't take you to bed. That shows how much you know about what goes on between a man and a woman."

He was right. She knew very little about it, but enough that she sensed the danger of her galloping attraction to him. She scoffed at him, pretending amusement.

"You do fancy yourself, don't you? Well, I want you to understand something, Mr. Meade: I don't knuckle under for *any* man."

She watched with frank fascination while Rufus walked away from her, turned, and placed his hands on his hips.

"Naomi, only a fool would wrap himself in a red sheet and go out to meet a thousand-pound bull. I don't fancy myself; but baby, you *do* fancy me." Then he added in a dangerously soft voice, "I'd rescue you from a burning building, Naomi, but if you push me another fraction of an inch, I'll have that dress off of you in a split second. And before you can bat one of your big eyes, you'll be begging for mercy. Believe it!"

Tiny shivers skittered from her head to her toes and a rapidly spiraling heat suffused her as she imagined what he would be like if she dared him. She stared in rapt attention at his hypnotic face, taking in his serious manner, thrilled at the temptation of him standing before her, tense and flagrantly male, excited in a way that she had never been before. She didn't wonder or even care what he thought as she stood there looking at him, trembling. Time had no meaning as her gaze traveled up his long, lean frame, pausing briefly on his powerful chest and strong corded neck and reluctantly coming to rest in the turbulent pools of fire that his eyes had become. Vaguely, she realized she needed to compose herself, but a feeling of helplessness nearly overcame her. She rimmed her lips with the tip of her tongue and, with what sense she had left, turned to leave the room.

Rufus narrowed his eyes at what was one of the most lush examples of honest feminine need he'd ever seen. He reached for her, and she moved to him without caution or care, like a moth to a glowing flame, nail to magnet. He gathered her to him with stunning force, and as if it was what she needed, she moved up on tiptoe, curled her arms around his neck, and let her long artist's fingers weave through the tight black curls at the base of his head. He brushed her lips briefly, molded them softly to his, and held her head while he took his pleasure. Dimly, he realized that she was out of her league when she felt him growing against her and sagged in his arms.

Gently he lifted her and pressed his closed lips to her

breast, hating that offending dress that separated him from
her flesh. "Rufus. Oh, Rufus." Was she begging him for
more, or pleading for mercy? He couldn't tell which, but he
knew he was rapidly reaching the point where he'd need awesome self-control. He lowered her to her feet, held her away
from him, and looked at her. She was as shaken as he, and
his behavior annoyed him, because he didn't want to mislead
her or hurt her. And he didn't trust himself to have an affair
with her, after that kiss, which had been even more powerful, more punishing that the other that they had shared, he
wouldn't count on his ability to keep his head straight. He
moved away from her, certain from the look of her that she
wanted him even closer. And he was pretty sure now that
her experience with men had been minimal. But what was
he supposed to do while she stood there, apparently absent-
minded, rubbing the spot where his lips had been? He swore
softly and pulled her to him again.

"I want you, Naomi." He spoke in low guttural tones, the
quiver in his voice a sure sign—if she had known it—that he
could be putty in her hands. But she didn't know it, he discovered, and she replied with the volley of an ingénue.

"Please let me go. That doesn't flatter me, Rufus. I told
you, it's not going to happen now or ever." If she had been a
hot poker in his bare hand, he could hardly have put her away
from him more quickly. He had almost made a fool of himself over her, and she'd turned him off, just like that. How
could a woman go up in smoke in a man's arms one minute
and arrogantly tell him to get lost the next?

He wiped his mouth symbolically with the back of his
hand and allowed her to witness one of his indecipherable
grins. "Better stop playing it so close to the edge with me; the
next time you behave the way you did tonight, we may both
regret it. And Naomi," he chided gently, almost affectionately, "you deserve better than you asked for just then, and I

should have given you better than you got. But I'm human; try to remember that, will you?" There's something about her that's different, he thought, but couldn't name it. Shrugging it off, he reached both hands toward the ceiling and grabbed fists full of air, stretching his big frame like the great cats for which he'd been nicknamed.

Naomi admitted to herself that her passionate exchange with Rufus was a humbling experience, and she had the guilty feeling that she'd brought some of it on herself. She knew how she looked in that dress, but she didn't intend to worry about it. His last remark convinced her that he really was very likeable, that she could trust him with herself anyplace and at any time. Frankly observing him, she could almost pinpoint the second that he decided to change the tenor of the conversation.

"All right, let's get started," he directed. "I'm sure some of the fraternities would be glad to join this; I can get my frat to go along and you might contact your sorority."

"What's yours?" she asked. "I'm a Delta." She shook with laughter at his stunned disbelief that they belonged to brother-sister Greek letter societies. Her Delta to his Omega. Stranger things had happened, she reminded him, hinting that at last they had found common ground.

He feigned innocence. "You're joking! What do you mean, 'at last'? What kind of ground was that we found when we were setting each other on fire a minute ago? As an English teacher, you should take a page from Shakespeare, 'to thine own self be true.'"

She had backed away from involvements, from attachments that she would have liked to pursue, because she didn't trust a man to love and accept her as she was. And she paid for it in loneliness. Even now, she chose craftily not to reply to his message but to the package in which he wrapped it. "Mr. Meade," she queried, "where is it written that you're not a man unless you mention sex at least once in every sentence?"

"Who mentioned sex? I was talking about whatever it is between us that draws us together, no matter how much we swear we don't want it. I know what I'm backing away from, Naomi, and I know why. But do you?"

She wouldn't have dared to tell him that she was backing away from what she thought she wanted, but hadn't previously *known* she needed; the love of a strong, tender man. A man like him. And she couldn't tell him that it was fear of his rejection, his scorn, that wouldn't let her reveal herself, the self she knew he would like, that he might even love. Nor could she tell him that, if she were true to herself, he might even become hers for a little while—before her world caved in. And never could she utter the words that would tell him what he was coming to mean to her.

A frivolous reply that would hide her feelings was on the tip of her tongue. But his question was too threatening, too intimate for a trivial answer, and she heard herself say, "I've been backing away so long that I do it without thinking." She must have made him speechless; he was quiet for a long time. When he did speak, it was to suggest that they get something to eat. Relieved, she nodded in agreement. "Sounds good to me."

Naomi rarely sat in the front seat of a car when she wasn't driving; when she did, she tended to be uncomfortable. But not with Rufus at the wheel. She turned to him. "Driving a car is an ego trip for a lot of men, but not for you; you're very careful."

She wouldn't have thought that such a simple statement would please him so much. But his face showed genuine pleasure. "Life's a fragile thing, Naomi, and I don't risk mine or anyone else's, if I can help it. Besides, I'm all that the boys have."

There was a silent minute while he seemed to test her interest, and then he added, "Those little rascals are my life; I can't imagine it without them. They're not quite four yet, but I feel as if I've always had them. I have to leave them sometimes, like tonight, and when I get back home the way they greet me…Naomi, they make me feel like I'm king of the world." The dreamy smile on his face told Naomi that he was speaking not only to her, but to himself as well, that he was counting his blessings. She was silent for so long that he apologized.

"You'll have to pardon me for going on about my boys; I forget that they're not as precious to other people as they are to me."

He couldn't be serious. She never tired of seeing or hearing of love between children and their parents. If there was anything more precious, she hadn't heard of it. "Don't apologize. I was thinking how fortunate they are, how fortunate any child would be to have a parent who loved it like that. It's something about which I know little or nothing, but I recognized it when I saw you with them, and I sensed that they know it, too." Her own words jolted her. They told of her youthful needs, but they might also describe the needs of the child she had borne but never seen. She didn't know, but God she hoped not! Her left hand clutched her chest.

"What is it, Naomi? Are you okay?" At her continued silence, he said, "No, I guess you aren't. Did you grow up without parents?"

She had, she told him. "My grandfather gave me a lovely home and anything that I needed, and he took good care of me. But, Rufus, he was forty-one when my father was born, and he's almost Victorian in his thinking. He thinks that any show of emotion is a sign of weakness. Can you imagine a little seven-year-old girl dealing with that? I think he loves me, but not on the basis of anything he's ever said."

"Was he harsh with you?"

She had always found it difficult to talk about the little pricks and hurts that she kept locked deep inside. Although his calm protective mien tempted her to pour out everything, she quickly threw up her guard. She knew she was hedging, and she suspected that he did, too.

"Not really. The problem was that he made mistakes, mistakes that hurt, but he never seemed to question his decisions nor his actions. He's given me some tough rows to hoe, but I love him, Rufus. I love him, because he's always meant well, and as you said, I'm all he has." He turned off Wisconsin onto M Street and parked.

"Where are you going?"

"I'm surprised you didn't ask earlier," he needled. "You independent gals usually want to be in on every decision no matter what it is." He pulled off his overcoat, reached in the back seat, got a suit jacked out of a dry cleaner's bag, and slipped it on. If you wanted service at the Brasserie, you had to wear a jacket.

"More often than you would imagine, our escorts turn out to be men of little minds," she explained patiently, tongue in cheek, "and we've learned to express our opinions in the interest of self-preservation." He put his overcoat on while he walked around the vehicle to the passenger door.

She accepted his hand he offered to help her out of the minivan and jumped when he gave her a delicate little squeeze for the sheer sport of it. She supposed that she looked a little startled, because he explained to her as patiently as she had explained to him: "Excuse me, but that remark of yours closed down my little mind. Temporarily, of course."

Naomi bubbled with laughter and lightheartedness, unable to remember being so happy. She turned around and skipped backward to keep up with his long strides, joy zinging through her, proud and even a little reckless as they ambled along, teasing and bantering. The brisk night air invigorated her, and the low hum of familiar city sounds lulled her into a carefree mood. How could one man change her world so drastically, so completely? They walked into the crowded Italian Brasserie, overlooking the Chesapeake and Ohio Canal, and were seated facing the narrow stream. Soft lights, reflected from the restaurant, danced on the water, and she wished that Rufus would hold her hand. Walking in there with him was an experience she wouldn't forget. She was unprepared for the smiles, stares, and waves that greeted him as they entered, giving her a sense of how famous he really was.

"I don't believe I know any of them," he told her in response to her question. "I played football some years ago, and I guess some people are nice enough to remember. But those days are behind me, Naomi, and I rarely look back on them. I'm grateful for the success I had, though, because it allows me to write, which is what I love to do best, on my own terms. I gather you aren't a football fan."

"No, I guess not. The roughness makes me nervous. I've often wondered how the families of those players can tolerate seeing their loved ones banged around like that. Some of those big guys seem to try to kill the ball carriers. I just can't watch it." He's really modest, she thought. When had she last been in the company of anyone who showed such humility?

Rufus had been studying her intently. "Naomi, that tells me you aren't as hard-boiled as you'd like me to think." He handed her a menu. "Everything's good here," he explained, before she could respond, "but what they do to broiled stuffed mushrooms is sinful." The waiter mixed their orders with those of another table, and Rufus gave him a gentle reprimand, alluding to his greater attention to Naomi than to their orders. Not that he blamed the man, he secretly admitted.

Surprised, Naomi opened her mouth to speak and thought better of it. Rufus was treating the handsome waiter to a lesson in the meaning of male territorial rights: *Don't get on my turf* was the message on his fierce countenance. Of course, Rufus wouldn't allow another man in his yard, she figured; he was too possessive for that. But he wasn't consistent, and that made her edgy; she was beginning to accumulate a lot of questions about him. He had sworn that he wouldn't become involved with her, but he acted as if he had a claim, a right to tell another man to stay away from her. Or maybe he was just demanding that the waiter show him proper respect. Enigma, thy name is man, she thought.

Rufus smiled as if nothing had happened. "I'm sure your thoughts are worth far more than a penny, so I won't offer to buy. Where were you just then?"

"I was feeling bad for the poor waiter. You probably could have shriveled rock with the look you gave him."

"I'm sorry if you were made uncomfortable, Naomi." But not sorry that he'd reprimanded the waiter, she noted. Talk about self-possession; he had it.

"You haven't made me uncomfortable," she corrected. "It's just that every time we meet or talk, you show me another facet of your personality. Riding in a Model-T Ford must have been something like that: bumpy and full of surprises." When he merely shrugged a shoulder and didn't comment, she decided that he didn't bother with self-analysis. Strong, but unpretentious. She liked that. They finished their meal in companionable silence.

"The dinner was lovely," she told him later, digging into her purse. "How much is the bill?"

Rufus reached for his wallet. "This isn't a dutch treat, Naomi. I do not, repeat, *do not* go dutch with females, be they eight or eighty, sweetheart, wife, or sister."

She gave him what she hoped was her most angelic plastic smile. "For your sake, I'm glad your rule isn't etched in stone, because I pay my own way."

Rufus frowned, a muscle twitching in his jaw, and she could see that he was giving his hot temper a stern lecture.

"Naomi, almost every time we've ever been together, our partings have been less than friendly. This time, could we please avoid that?"

She refused to back down. "Of course, we can, dear," she agreed pleasantly, stressing the "dear." "It's very simple; try being less of a chauvinist, and we'll leave here like two peas in a pod."

The deepening of his frown into a fierce scowl delighted her; his temper was going to be his undoing.

"Naomi, you give me a royal pain in the…in the neck." His long, labored sigh bespoke total exasperation with her.

Not caring that she'd gotten his goat, she told him, "Well, at least you can sit down. After I've been haggling with *you,* I usually have to stand up for a while."

He stared, scowling, before his frown dissolved into a hearty laugh, and he reached over and squeezed her hand affectionately. Then he handed her the check. "Here. Pay the whole damned thing."

Rufus fought to come to terms with the lightheartedness that he felt when they stepped out of the restaurant holding hands; neither of them behaved as if it was strange. The early November wind had become stronger and more biting, and after they'd taken a few steps, he tucked their joined hands into his left overcoat pocket. And they didn't seem to find that incongruous with their professed intentions not to become involved with each other, either. Rufus shook his head in wonder. He disliked the fact that she made him happy, and if he had an ounce of sense, he'd put her in a cab and send her home. He glanced down and savored her serene smile. Oh, what the heck!

"Let's stop by Saloon and listen to some jazz," he suggested. "Carter is there, and they have great ribs. Maybe I'll get some of their barbecued ribs to take home. It's just down the street. I remember that you like opera; *La Traviata,* wasn't it? I hope I'm right in assuming that you also like jazz. I like opera, too, but it's never made me want to dance or hug anybody." Not that he needed any added inducements to snuggle up with her. She was as potent a lure as a man could tolerate. And he was rambling, he realized to his disgust, something he never did. Another indication that he should put some distance between them.

Naomi laughed in that joyous way that always made him want to squeeze her to him. So much for his admonition to himself. "You can't resist needling me, can you? I love jazz, and I don't want to shock you, but I also love country music. As for the ribs, well, I'm afraid you can keep those. They're fattening."

He tugged her closer. "Wouldn't shock *me;* I like country music, too. But in my book, no ribs, no soul." Still holding her hand in his pocket, he squeezed it gently. He wasn't overloaded with soul himself, but she didn't have to know it. "And as for needling," he told her, "lady, you've got that down to a very fine art."

They reached the club quickly and found a table in the rear. An attractive waitress walked over with a bottle of ginger ale and a glass of ice for Rufus, spoke to him, and asked Naomi what she would have. Naomi ordered the same.

"I see you come here often. Do you come just to listen to jazz, or for more personal reasons?"

He watched her above hands clasped in pyramid fashion and decided not to growl at her. What was it about the woman that made him want to walk away from her one minute and love her the next?

"Naomi," he began, as patiently as he could, "if I had anything going with a woman who worked in this place, I wouldn't be so insensitive as to entertain you or any other woman here. You said you don't want us to be more than friends. Buddies was the way you put it I think." He threw his head back and rolled his eyes skyward, indicating what he thought of that likelihood.

"Exactly," she said, head high and nose up. That particular affection was becoming familiar to him; she was covering up her real feelings.

Careful here, Rufus told himself, but he wanted to take advantage of the opening that she had unwittingly given him. He said softly, "Sometimes I sense that your razor-sharp tongue hides a lot of pain."

When she stiffened, he quickly added, "Try to ward me off, if you ever anticipate that what I'm about to do or say will add to that pain. Promise me that." For a brief, poignant moment, she relaxed her guard, revealing hurt that he had already begun to suspect was an essential part of her. And he received a thorough shock; for the first time, he couldn't throw off his vulnerability to her. He had to accept his feelings. He wanted to take her and leave, but that, he knew, would be the wrong move.

"Have I offended you?" Her silence weighed heavily on him.

"Of course not," she answered him. "You just surprised me, that's all." When the waitress brought another round of drinks, he noticed the way in which Naomi looked at her and figured that her stare duplicated the one he had thrown at their waiter. Both of them saw the similarity and appreciated the humor of it. They sat in rapt attention while Benny Carter's soulful saxophone gave a memorable rendition of Duke

Ellington's *Solitude.* She drifted into the past, and Rufus took her left hand in both of his, bringing her back to him.

Naomi struggled to hide the jitters that overcame her when Rufus parked and started around to the passenger side of the car. I don't want any of his mind-blowing kisses tonight, she told herself. They make a wreck out of me. She knew he'd be annoyed, but before he could reach the door, she opened it.

"I had a great time. Thanks," she offered, attempting to dismiss him.

"Naomi," he began, in a tone that suggested mild amusement. "You know that I'm going to see you safely to your door, don't you? So you are going to save your breath about how often you get there on your own, now, aren't you?"

She pretended at first to be speechless. "You've been associating with liberated women, haven't you?" She bit her tongue; it was stupid to bait him when he was being so gracious.

He ignored the taunt and held her hand as they entered the elegant lobby; she would have withdrawn it if she could have forced herself to do so, but she knew he wouldn't have permitted it if she'd tried. When they reached her door, he tipped her chin up with a strong but gentle index finger.

"Now you may tell me how much you enjoyed the evening." She had learned that his facial expressions did not always reflect his mood. His lips were laughing, but when she looked into his eyes, she saw that they were serious with sensual longing. She suddenly lost her capacity for either pointed innuendos or meaningless banter.

He prodded her. "Cat stole your tongue?"

She stunned him with her loaded reply. "No. Cat *wants* my tongue." His cool, off-putting response didn't alter the fact of his genuine surprise, she noted, when his eyes darkened with suspicion.

"You know what my nickname is?"

She nodded and worried her bottom lip. "Yes. Marva, my best friend, told me one day last week. Until then, I hadn't even known you'd played football. She said you ran like a lithe young panther." With each word, she moved closer to him. Unconsciously. Tremors streaked through her as she stared at the dark desire in his mesmerizing eyes. Her every nerve tingled with exhilaration, drowning her in a pool of sensuality, when his long fingers caressed the back of her head, wound themselves through her thick, tight curls, and slowly pulled her to him. She parted her lips before he bent his head.

When his mouth finally touched hers, they both moaned aloud from the intensity of what they felt; more than desire; far more. Naomi turned toward the door, whether to invite him in or to escape, she didn't know. But he stopped her, and she shivered as his strong arms pulled her to him. His firm lips brushed hers softly and then kissed her with such tenderness, such gentle sweetness, that she couldn't bear it and sagged against him. The moisture from her eyes touched his mouth, and she trembled when his lips kissed the tears from her face. She rested her head against his strong shoulders and held him. She couldn't disregard her awareness of him; it was too powerful. Sniffling softly, she relaxed in his warm protectiveness while he stroked her arms.

"I can't leave you if I've made you feel bad, Naomi. Why are you crying? Are you afraid of something? Certainly not of me."

"I'm not afraid of you, Rufus. I'm not." She sniffled and snuggled closer.

"Then you're afraid of yourself." She tried to move out of his arms, but he held her there. "You're afraid, because you want me, and for once, you're not in control." She twisted restlessly, and he let her go. "Don't ever let that bother you,

Naomi; I would never take what a woman doesn't want me to have. And I don't mean sex alone. I won't accept anything that she gives grudgingly, nothing unless the feeling is mutual. And *that,* my lovely lady, is definitely written in stone." He tipped an imaginary hat, gave her a brilliant smile, and left her standing there.

She watched him go, telling herself she was relieved. Inside her apartment, she undressed and tried to find oblivion in sleep. Hours later, she got up, showered and went back to bed. She needed Rufus, but she also needed to know her child. A sixteen-year-old isn't capable of making decisions for a lifetime; they pressured me, but I'm the one who has lived with it and agonized over it for over thirteen years. I won't be cheated like this; I deserve to see my child. But once she walked through that door, she knew she could say goodbye to everything that meant anything to her—the board of education, OLC, the twins, Linda…what would Linda say if she knew? And Rufus. After reading his current bestseller, in which he listed the causes of juvenile delinquency and placed mothers' behavior at the top of the list, she knew he'd never accept her past.

Rufus sat up in bed before sunrise and tried to reconcile himself to the emotional charge that had taken possession of them the night before. But no matter how he rationalized it, he faced a no-win situation; either capitulate and take it all the way, or let it go. What a choice! He was exactly where he'd been since the first time he'd laid eyes on her. He thought back to the smooth way in which she had used his nickname. If she knew it, she must also have known who he was. He hadn't thought that her responses to him were calculated, but acting was an honored profession, and he had met many woman who excelled at it. Especially Etta Mae, whose deceit in pretending to have been taking the Pill had ordained their marriage. So, why not Naomi?

He got up and went downstairs to his state-of-the-art kitchen, looked around, and wondered why he needed all those gadgets. He had reluctantly given in to the boys' tearful plea to spend the night with their cousins, so he didn't have to cook breakfast. He squeezed a glass of orange juice, drank it, and glimpsed the fresh fruit bowl on the table as he was leaving. He loved apples and thought they were better snacks than nuts and candy. He selected the largest red apple, polished it, and prepared to relish the tart sweetness. Then he bit into it and frowned. Beautiful and crunchy on the outside. Spoiled on the inside. He threw it into the garbage disposal. Was there a message in that somewhere?

Several mornings later, Naomi skimmed the report of the community school board's monthly meeting, slammed it down on her desk, got up, and paced the floor. Just a lot of loose talk. Unless they got better officers, there wouldn't be any improvement. She walked over to her desk and telephoned Judd.

"Grandpa, I'm going to try for president of my community school board."

"Now, you watch what you're doing, gal. You don't want to get in the public eye with this thing about the baby hanging over you. You could be asking for trouble. It's all right to be on the board, but being its president is too public. 'Course, I know you'll do whatever you want."

His reaction surprised her. She had thought he would be pleased, that he would support anything that enhanced the Logan name. Well, her mind was made up.

"Don't worry, Grandpa, it's just a local board, and it seldom makes news," she told him, vowing not to let it dampen her spirits. "There have to be some changes in those schools, and I'm going to see to it."

A few hours later, as she walked down the steps of the Martin Luther King, Jr., Memorial Library on G Street, where she'd traced the school board's record over the past decade and a half, she thought she heard her name. She heard it again, less faint than before, but it seemed to come from far away. She turned her back to the street to lessen the bite of the wind and saw Rufus and his boys ambling toward her. He restrained the children when they tried to run to her, preventing them from tumbling down the concrete steps. She opened her arms to them when they reached the sidewalk, and the little boys rushed to her, covered her face with kisses, and delighted in the love she returned.

Awed by their reception, she looked up into Rufus's sultry gaze and drank deeply of the warmth and affection she saw there. "Hi."

"Hi. They're obviously glad to see you. I'm surprised they recognized you from that distance. They've been returning library books. I let them do it themselves, and they've made friends with some of the librarians. It's a big adventure and one of their favorite outings. What brings you down here?" She told him about the school board and her decision to seek its presidency.

"Grandpa doesn't think much of the idea, but I'm going ahead with it." Still hunkered down, she continued holding the boys in her arms.

"I think it's a great idea. I can introduce you to a good publicist who'll get you free television interviews, guest shots on panel shows, newspaper coverage, the whole shebang. He's been disgusted with your school board for years, so he might not charge you. I'll do a story on you for the *Journal;* how about it?"

Her eyes widened in alarm, and she released the boys

almost absentmindedly, rubbing her coat sleeves nervously. He reached down and helped her to her feet.

"What is it, Naomi? Don't you want any help? You'll certainly need it." His eyes narrowed quizzically.

"Y-yes, thank you. I...I just hadn't thought that far ahead. I'll let you know when I'm ready." She knew he'd think her wishy-washy, but she couldn't help remembering her grandfather's warning.

He looked closely at her. "If you feel you can make a difference, don't let anybody discourage you."

"Daddy's going to buy us hot chocolate, Noomie. You want some?" She looked at Sheldon, who regarded her expectantly, and hesitated. Finally, she told him she had to get back to her studio. Then she hugged the children, straightened up, and looked into Rufus's cool gaze. Shaken, she told them goodbye and went on her way, aware that her behavior baffled Rufus. She hadn't considered the necessity of a publicity campaign; cold fear clutched her heart at the thought of it. But she'd find a way, she promised herself. After all, she had nearly six months in which to make a move.

Rufus watched her until she was out of sight. The more he saw of her, the more of a puzzle she seemed. Was she reluctant to accept his help, or was it something else? As soon as he'd offered it, her enthusiasm for the idea had seemed to wane. What was behind it? He wanted to give her the benefit of the doubt, but she hadn't made it easy.

With the date of the gala rapidly approaching Rufus began laying out plans for a media blitz publicizing it. He would represent the Alliance, but they'd get more mileage, he decided, if Naomi spoke for OLC, and other organizations also had their own spokespersons. He hadn't seen her in over a week, not since that morning at the library. He had wanted to see her, and not calling her had tested his resolve, but he had desisted. She was far enough inside him as it was. He didn't want to think about her right then; if he did, the morning would be shot, as far as his work was concerned.

He worked on his manuscript until ten o'clock, gave his boys a mid-morning snack, and then telephoned Naomi to ask whether she'd be willing to make a few appearances on local television shows to promote the gala. There was a spot available that evening at seven-thirty.

Naomi agreed to his suggestion, but after hanging up, she began to worry that whoever was looking for her would be able to put a face with her name and would easily find her through her connection with One Last Chance. She wasn't sure she was ready for that yet and fretted about it for hours. She knew that she intended to see her child, to explain why she had given it up for adoption; it would take the United States Marines to prevent it, but she hadn't thought beyond that. The shock of having to face it after trying for so many years to forget it was only now beginning to wear off. Finally, she called Rufus, forced herself to be pleasant, even a little jocular, and gave him a weak excuse. Then she redesigned the gala program to make it impossible for anyone to trace her through it.

Thirteen years. Nearly half her life had been fraught with fear. For over thirteen years, she had let fear of being exposed about something over which she had had almost no control circumscribe her life. And because of that fear, she lived without love, without a family, without real intimacy with anyone. But she hadn't had an idea of what she'd missed. Now she could imagine how it could be with Rufus if there were no barriers between them. Walking away from him might prove to be the most difficult thing she'd ever done, as hard as learning that she could at last see her child, a child who called someone else "Mother" and who would surely judge her harshly. But she could deal with it. She would. She *had* to!

She wasn't so naive that she didn't know how uniquely suited she and Rufus were, but she knew that it couldn't happen. One day soon, she was going to sit down and deal with it, all of it, and fear wouldn't figure in her decisions. Lost in her thoughts, conjuring up her future, Naomi answered the phone, but the sound of his voice sent her heart racing.

"Hi." It was low and suggestive, though she was sure that after their last encounter, he hadn't meant it to be. "Look. I've got a problem, Naomi. Jewel isn't home, and I don't know whether she'll be able to keep my boys for me. Could you tell me where you'll be around three o'clock? If I haven't been able to make an arrangement for them by then, I'm afraid you'll have to go to the station."

"I'll be here," she promised grudgingly. She telephoned Marva. "I can't make rehearsals tonight. Can you reschedule it? Rufus said I may have to appear on WMAL this evening to publicize the gala, and I probably won't get out of there until after nine. I'm sorry, Marva." Marva changed the dates and advised Naomi that after leaving the station she should spend the evening with Rufus.

Rufus called Jewel, and she used the occasion to tell him that it was time he got a live-in nanny for the boys. "You can well afford it, and you won't have to sacrifice your career and your social life while you baby-sit."

Rufus didn't want to be vexed with his sister. She had made the point numerous times over the past three years, but in this instance it really annoyed him. It was one of her more subtle hints that Naomi would be a welcome sister-in-law, and they hadn't even met.

"Jewel, I'm not going over this with you again. If you have to go to a PTA meeting, keeping my boys is out of the question. I'll work it out."

"You could get married, you know," she shot at him. "It's

time you forgave Etta Mae; you've been divorced for more than three years, and she's still ruining your life because you insist on seeing something of her in every woman you meet. Give it up, Rufus; you're hurting yourself."

His long, deep sigh was that of a man whose patience had been exceeded. He knew that his sister was right; forgiving and letting go had always been difficult for him. He chose to reply to only part of her comment.

"I want a companion for myself, Jewel, and if I ever re-marry, it will be to a woman who can be a mother for my sons. Find me that woman, and maybe I'll take your advice. Well-informed, brainy career women make great companions, but in my book, they're not the best wives and mothers because they're never home; nor should anybody expect them to be. And the woman who's likely to stay home all the time, keep house, and live for her family alone might be good for the boys and is probably what today's family needs, but she'd bore the hell out of me. Believe me, single is better."

"I've got a career, and I'm a good wife and mother."

"Yes, you are. You're committed to your children and your husband, and he's committed to you. The two of you are a team, and that's what a marriage should be. But your kind of marriage is not common."

"Thanks for the confidence; you should be eager to get what Jeff and I have. If you don't know a good woman when you see one, talk to my husband and get a few pointers," she admonished him. He hung up thinking about what she'd said and about what he wanted. He wanted Naomi, and no amount of advice from Jewel's husband or anyone else would change that.

She answered after the first ring. "I'm afraid you'll have to go on tonight," he informed her without a trace of regret.

"I've already told the station's program director that one of us would be there. So how about it?"

"I'm sorry, but I just can't. Bring the boys over here, and I'll keep them for you." Why was she stammering, and what had happened to her normal poise? He jerked the telephone cord impatiently, alert to a possibly hidden reason for her refusal.

"I thought you said you'd be busy. If you're busy, how can you take care of my boys?"

"I'm expecting a business call," she told him, digging a deeper hole for herself.

"At night? At home? Are you leveling with me?" He was openly suspicious of her motives now.

"Okay, I'm a poor liar. I just hate speaking in public without notes and without enough time to prepare myself. I'm uncomfortable with it." She was talking rapidly in a high-pitched voice that told him she had lost her composure.

He couldn't buy it. "As fast as you are with the repartee? You want me to believe that? Look, if you don't want to do it, just say so. I'll go if you're still willing to take care of my boys for a couple of hours. I'm due at the station at seven o'clock, so we'll be over at six."

He sat for a long time, pondering her strange behavior. Not for one second would he believe that she'd be nervous speaking about anything so dear to her as One Last Chance. She was a high school teacher, for Pete's sake, trained for impromptu speaking. She was lying. Period. He thought of the way he felt about her, how that feeling was growing with each day, and experienced a tinge of apprehension. His coach had once said that one could excuse a blind man for getting into a hole, but not a man with sight. "I can see," he reminded himself.

Naomi watched Rufus take the greatest of care unstrapping the boys and removing their coats. He hugged them so many times before leaving that she thought she might cry, and to her surprise, the twins waved him off without a tear. She had fortified herself with plastic building blocks, an electrical musical keyboard, and a pair of walkie-talkies that worked. Once they discovered the walkie-talkies, she had no problem with discipline, because Preston sat in the foyer and talked to Sheldon, who remained in the kitchen. Rufus called just before air time and asked to speak with them, but she vetoed the idea.

"I've got a good system going here, and it's working perfectly. The sound of your voice will definitely disturb the peace, so no, you can't speak with them."

"I can't speak with my boys?"

"You got it." She knew that she'd shocked him, but figured that after thinking it over, he'd see the logic. If he didn't, well, she had a full plate dealing with her thoughts of her own child. Afraid of being exposed on the one hand, and on the other, wishing she had it with her. He'd soon be with his boys.

Rufus expected to find Naomi and the boys in total chaos, but when he arrived, he saw the three of them sitting at the kitchen table, laughing and eating. "What on earth did you give them, laughing gas?" He had worried that his boys would wear Naomi out and that she wouldn't be able to control them, and he relaxed visibly. He didn't want to put a damper on their fun, but he was too relieved to be jocular. Leaving the station, he had fought a thrill of anticipation of seeing Naomi with his children. He could barely wait to get back to her. The incredible scene that greeted him gave him hope—something that for years had remained beyond his reach—but he tried to squelch the feeling that rose in him. If he wasn't careful, he'd do something that he would regret for a very long time.

"Laughing gas? Of course not," she objected, affecting what he knew was her favorite pose, that of pretended detachment. "These boys know their roots; I gave them southern fried chicken and buttermilk biscuits."

"This time of night."

She didn't get a chance to tell him that they'd fallen asleep and had awakened hungry. Preston intervened, "And we got a surprise. We saw you on television, Daddy, and Noomie said you were talking to the people."

"Yes," Sheldon intoned, "and we had a nap after it."

He forced himself to look at Naomi, though he didn't want to, didn't want her to see what he was feeling. How had she persuaded his two little hellions to behave civilly? He saw the softness in her and responded to it. And that vexed him. Where was his resolve of just that morning? He didn't want to care for her, didn't even want to like her, but she was likable and he cared; he couldn't deny it. And he would no longer deny that she would probably be lovable if he was ever foolish enough to drop his guard and let himself do the unthinkable.

"Want a biscuit, Daddy?" Preston inquired, reaching toward his father.

"Yes. Don't you want to join us? I've got some string beans, too, but the boys didn't want any, so we struck a bargain, and they're drinking milk instead." She worried her bottom lip and looked at him expectantly. "But maybe you don't like soul food."

Rufus forced a light smile. It was the best he could manage; with every new move, she crawled deeper inside of him. "Sure, I like soul food," he said, pulling up a chair. Sheldon reminded Naomi that she had also promised them ice-cream.

"All we want," he added.

Naomi seemed to know when she was being taken. "Sheldon," she admonished him, "good little boys always tell the truth."

Rufus's eyes rounded in astonishment. "They're dressed identically. How do you know which is which?"

"Same way you do. As you said, their personalities differ."

He tried to reconcile the soft and gentle woman before him—the one who patiently tended his boys, loving and teasing them—with her other strong, clever, and elusive self. If this was the real Naomi, or if her two selves had their proper places in her life, there was a chance that he could have with her what he'd yearned for but hadn't wanted to admit. He needed a woman he loved in his life, his home, and his bed, one who loved him and needed him and loved his children. But she had told him repeatedly that she didn't intend to become involved. Well, he had said the same, but maybe…

Chapter 6

The phone rang once. "Hi." Rufus leaned back against the headboard of his king-sized bed and waited for more of her soothing voice. But she didn't say more, so he plunged in.

"I didn't realize you'd be in bed so early. It's only about eleven o'clock. I didn't thank you properly for taking care of my boys, and I...well, thank you. They seemed to have enjoyed the experience."

"Me, too." She wasn't forthcoming, and it was unlike what he'd come to expect of her. He marveled at the pure feminine spice of her voice; every time he heard it, he felt as if she was toying with him. Deliberately and carelessly seducing him. He searched for something banal to say, something that would guarantee that their conversation didn't become too personal.

"What would you have done if it had been Maude Frazier calling you?"

"If I can greet you with 'hi,' it'll do for Maude." So she

was waiting him out; it was a trait of hers that he admired; patience. She didn't mind silence, and lulls in conversation didn't make her nervous. Since he called, she seemed to imply, he should do the talking.

"What did you think of my interview? Think it was a good advertisement for the gala?"

She apologized and congratulated him on a very professional performance. "I'm ashamed that I didn't mention it when you were here. You did yourself proud, Rufus, but I don't suppose you're asking me for praise." Her voice seemed more distant, as if she had moved further from the phone. "I'm told that your mere entrance into a football stadium brought thunderous roars from your fans. You must be sick of adulation."

He let that pass. She was right; he didn't give a hoot for praise. Never had. "It hadn't occurred to me that you would let my boys watch. It's the first time they've seen me on television. I thank you for that."

She knew that he could have thanked her before leaving her apartment; in fact he had, so she waited for the real reason why he'd called. Probably to interrogate her some more about her refusal to do the television interview, she surmised. Suddenly apprehensive, tendrils of fear began to snake down her back, and she attempted to disconcert him.

"Rufus, what happened to the boys' mother?" She hadn't realized that the question was on her mind, and his long silence told her that he didn't welcome it.

His succinct reply confirmed it. "She didn't care for marriage, motherhood, or domesticity in any form, so she left."

"Did you love her?" She tried to sound as if his answer was unimportant.

"I married Etta Mae because I'd made her pregnant. She wanted glamour, so she got a man whom she thought would give it to her quickly. She got pregnant by pretending that she was taking the pill, though as she later told me, she had never taken a birth control Pill in her life. But she knew I would marry her if she carried my child. I was sick of the spotlight, and I wanted a home. I committed myself to the marriage and to her." His deep sigh was the only evidence he gave of the pain his explanation must have caused him. "We might have made a go of it," he continued, "but her priority was to be more famous and more sought after than Iman or Naomi Campbell. Nothing was going to prevent her being the top African American model in the country, even the top model. Etta Mae is driven. Driven to escape everything that plagued her as a child. Her mother brought her here from Alabama when she was ten. She told me she suffered verbal abuse and ridicule from her schoolmates, because she was poor and different, and that she'd sworn she'd best them all. I suspect she has. Did I love her? No. Etta Mae isn't lovable, Naomi, but she gave me my sons."

His words weren't comforting. The more she learned of his life, the more certain she was that he would never accept her. His attitudes about wives and mothers were deep-seated, a reaction to unmet needs, to what he had been deprived of and what he had seen his sons denied. She doubted whether she would be able to combat that successfully even if she didn't have the load she carried.

"I'm sorry, Rufus. It was none of my business." She wished she hadn't asked. The less she knew about him, the less the likelihood of her becoming more deeply involved.

Surely she doesn't think I called her to talk about myself, he thought peevishly. "Naomi, I need to know something." She wouldn't welcome his questions, but he didn't intend to let that stop him. He craved her and he knew it was foolish. His head told him that she wasn't for him, but the rest of him didn't agree with his mind. He wanted her and that meant he had to understand her, if he could. Getting a grasp of who she really was and what motivated her would either cure him or sink him, and he didn't believe she could pull him under.

"Have you ever appeared on television?" She acknowledged that she had. "Then what frightened you off tonight? You're a competent, self-possessed woman; I can't imagine your being shy about speaking in public. This has me perplexed."

"I already told you. I wouldn't have been comfortable with it. If I hadn't thought you'd be tired, I'd have called to tell you that I redesigned the program for the gala and that as soon as we can get full sponsor approval, I'll…"

So *that* was her game. Did she think she could spin him around like a top? "I didn't call to talk about that, and I don't intend to. If the reason you backed off tonight is none of my business, save us some time and just say so."

"It isn't. Any of your business, I mean."

He knew that his sharp tone had hurt, but she deserved it. As sensitive as she was, she must have realized that he needed more from her than she gave and that what he needed was deep and personal. Well, hell! What should he expect from a woman raised by a grandparent more than three times her age, and a Baptist minister, to boot? If she didn't know when a warm, feminine response to a man was the only acceptable one and the only one that could bring him to heel, it probably wasn't her fault. He asked himself why he was quizzing her and why he was trying to understand her when he was going to force himself not to give another hoot about her.

"Thanks for keeping my boys, Naomi. Good night." He said it as smoothly as he could, without preamble and with exaggerated politeness, and hung up. If she wanted a completely impersonal relationship with him, he wasn't about to care, he told himself.

But he was dissatisfied and dialed back immediately.

She meant something to him, even if he didn't want her to. "Naomi, it's my business to observe and to be sensitive to what is not ordinary in people and in situations. A journalist finds a newsworthy story not in the commonplace, but in the exceptional, in what is unique. I'm good at that, Naomi, and in my book, you just do not add up." He expected a snide remark or a red herring, but he got neither.

"I'm sorry if I've disappointed you, Rufus, but I'm getting along as best I can right now. If you want to be a friend, you'll just have to try to accept me as I am. I can't make myself over for everybody I meet."

"Look, I don't know exactly why, but I need to understand you, and I'm trying. There's something going on here." His treacherous mind suddenly pictured her in her burnt orange dress, and he could smell her, taste her, feel her against him, warm and wildly aroused. She was more woman that he'd ever held, and he was man enough to want what he knew was there. But he wasn't fool enough to walk into a hornet's nest.

"Naomi, how do I fit into your life? Don't answer now; think about it carefully, because I intend to ask you again."

"All right, I'll think about it," she promised. "And if it seems that we're at cross purposes, we'll just have to wave each other goodbye."

She hung up the phone, went to her closet, and took out the dusty rose evening gown that she was to wear as Marva's maid of honor. She hooked the hanger over the door. She wondered if the two of them would remain friends after Marva married. She took a quick shower and crawled into bed. Marva was getting her man; for the first time, not having one of her own gave Naomi a sense of rootlessness.

Hours later, Naomi got out of bed, unable to sleep. She was less certain that she could remain unscathed by what was beginning to develop into a heady, deeply moving entanglement with Rufus. Even their "good night" had been too tender for a man and woman who professed to be casual friends. "I've written my last letter of protest," she declared aloud in frustration. "Not to any public official, entertainer, community leader nor—God forbid—panelist, will I ever again write one single letter of the alphabet." She told herself that she would not allow him to get next to her, then cursed her inability to kill the feeling for him that was steadily growing stronger within her. She thought about how it had hurt her to hold his wonderful, lovable little boys, to take care of them, and to be solely responsible for their well being, remembering all the while that loving and frolicking with her own child had been cruelly denied her. What could she do? What *should* she do? She had made a life for herself, had achieved stature in the community and enjoyed the respect of friends and business associates. But she wanted to know her child. She wrapped her arms around her middle and paced her kitchen floor.

She noticed the daylight and opened the blinds. The breaking day on a clear morning was usually guaranteed to raise her spirits, but on that particular morning, it failed to lift her mood. She had swum in darker waters, faced equally stymieing dilemmas, but none had involved a man who'd affected her as Rufus did. She put the coffee mug to her lips and held it there, images of him flitting through her mind. She had to deal with it. "I'm doomed," she declared when he didn't answer her ten o'clock phone call. She had intended to tell him it was best that they go their separate ways. Now, she'd have to work up the courage. Again.

Morose and having difficulty shedding it, Naomi stepped into the limousine that would carry her to Marva's wedding. The crowd waiting outside All Souls Church created an aura of excitement, but she barely managed to smile as she walked into the sanctuary. The service began, and she started slowly up the aisle. She wasn't jealous of her friend, but she had to acknowledge her longing for marriage and her own family. The bright camera lights annoyed her, but she tried to force a smile as she felt a dampness on her cheek. After the ceremony, she had to smile through the reception and escaped at the first opportunity.

Rufus saw Naomi nearly every day during the next three weeks, but always in connection with their responsibilities for the Urban Alliance gala. He deliberately engineered their meetings. He got the sense that she'd prefer to have him out of her thoughts, her life, maybe even out of her dreams, and he suspected that he'd broken through barriers that she had carefully erected, something her other suitors probably hadn't managed.

As they left OLC together by chance one evening, he decided to corner her. "You promised to let me know what you want from me, but you can't seem to decide. I find that odd for a woman with your talent for self-expression. Care to enlighten me?" When she didn't reply, he spoke in as cold a voice as he could muster. "Then maybe you won't mind explaining this. Did you know that your friend's wedding would draw the television cameras?"

"No, I didn't. I learned that the wedding was being televised when the lights shone in my face as I walked up the aisle." Her voice seemed strained. Why would such an impersonal question make her uneasy? He knew she would think him merciless if he probed further, but she intrigued him. Maybe if he stripped her of her superficial armor, he thought ruthlessly, she would no longer interest him.

"It was reported on the evening news. You outshone the bride, Naomi." He stopped walking. "Tell me. Didn't you know the bride always throws her bouquet to her maid of honor? And are you aware that all of Washington was watching when your friend threw the flowers straight to you, almost hitting you in the face, and you ducked? In fact, if you hadn't ducked, they'd have landed in your eyes. Why did you do that? I've hardly been able to think of anything else since I saw it. What were you thinking about to do such a thing?"

She walked on, speaking to him over her shoulder. "Weddings are emotionally charged occasions; everyone involved is uptight. Be a hero and switch to another topic."

He detained her with a hand on her arm. "Do you think so little of me, Naomi, that you refuse to do me the courtesy of being honest? Something else that I observed from that short clip were your tears when you were walking to the altar ahead of the bride. Why were you crying?"

"Rufus. Please! Why do you think you're entitled to see my bare soul?" She began to walk away from him. "Can't you drop it?"

He stood with legs wide apart and his right hand in his pocket, while his left thumb pressed beneath his jaw and his index finger tapped his left cheek. "No, Naomi. I can't. I can't. I remember telling you that you don't add up." Her steps faltered then, and he grasped her elbow in support, secretly reveling in the feel of her, in being close to her after so many days. He went on.

"You're wicked, fun, and witty, but I'm beginning to realize that you're unhappy. Oh, you cover it nicely, but I notice everything about you. You're a puzzle, and for me, puzzles are meant to be solved." She was far more to him than a puzzle, but he knew her well enough now to pretend otherwise.

"Puzzles entice you until you've solved them," she countered, "and then you probably lose interest. I'm not a puzzle, Rufus, so please don't give me your undivided attention." He was like a bloodhound, on the scent of something and unwilling to back away without his prize. Of late, he'd been delving too deeply and getting just a little too close. How could she tell him that her tears as she walked up that aisle were for what she longed for but could never have—a mutual love, a home, and children? She had to be more careful.

They reached her car and he leaned against the door, skillfully blocking her access. "It's early. How about stopping for coffee?" She would have sworn that he didn't expect her to accept, and her first impulse was to refuse. But that wouldn't be shrewd; he would know at once that he had made her uneasy.

"Okay," she agreed reluctantly. "Someplace not too far, if you don't mind."

He suggested Louella's Kitchen on upper Georgia Avenue. At the door, he stopped her with a firm hand on her arm.

"Naomi, I'm not up to battling with you over your inalienable right to pay fifty cents for your own coffee. So, do we go in, or not?"

She shrugged her shoulders. "Fine with me. I always offer because some guys can't afford it, some don't want to afford it, and a few want something for nothing. So I got in the habit of playing it safe."

"Does that mean you're not going to hassle with me about it?"

She tilted her chin upward and grinned. "I don't hassle, though with you, it's hard to resist. I'm not a feminist, unless that means standing up for my rights any and every time somebody attempts to abrogate them."

He held the door for her and caressed her playfully on the cheek as she passed him. What man could resist her? She was physically beautiful with her flawless, dark tan complexion and enormous dark brown eyes, and man that he was, he was drawn to her feminine attributes. But for him, her spunk and character, the character she tried to hide, were far greater assets. He smiled inwardly; she'd never believe that.

Louella greeted them warmly and gave them a back table nestled in a romantic little nook. "Do you want your cappuccino with a dusting of cinnamon, hon?" she asked Rufus, "or do you want it plain tonight?"

His affectionate regard rested briefly on her time-worn, but unwrinkled, brown cheek before he pressed a kiss to her forehead and sat down. "Cinnamon, please. Lou, have you met Naomi Logan?" His love for Louella was unqualified, he realized; she had been a mother figure during his late teens, guiding him through attempts to achieve manhood.

Louella took Naomi's extended hand. "No, Rufus, but I saw her on television in that wedding the other Saturday." She looked at Naomi. "Honey, that bride had a lot of courage to let you be her maid of honor. She looked great, but you were really something."

"Thanks," she told the woman, "but it was the dress; dusty rose is my best color."

"Pshaw." Louella dismissed Naomi's modest reply. "Go away from here, girl. You'd better enjoy it now while you got it; youth is fleeting, and when it's gone, fifty face lifts won't make you look like you look now. By the time I realized I was good-looking, it was too late to take advantage of it; too late for a lot of things. When I woke up, I was fifty years old, with three restaurants and an award-winning house. But I'm by myself on those trips abroad and expensive cruises, and I haven't got a single heir." She looked steadily at Naomi. "I hope you're smarter than I was. One great thing about Rufus: he *knows* what's important in this life. Don't you, hon?" She gave his shoulder a squeeze and trudged on back to the kitchen.

Naomi inclined her head in Louella's direction. "I could have missed that lecture. Is she always so candid?"

He leaned against the wall and fingered his jaw, deliberately disarming her with apparent nonchalance. "Lou's one of the most respected restaurateurs around, but sometimes I think she'd exchange it for a couple of kids and a husband or even a live-in sweetheart." He was certain that she didn't want him to resurrect the subject of the wedding. But she was relaxed, and now was as good a time as any; you could wait weeks to catch Naomi off guard.

"Why do you dislike the idea of marriage, Naomi? Have you been married?" And why was she squirming? He had yet to see her lose her cool, seemingly unflappable façade; she didn't even let herself get angry enough to lose her temper. But underneath that polished exterior was a warm, passionate woman. A sensitive woman. And he vowed to see more of that woman and less of the one that she seemed to want him to see.

"Why is that so difficult to answer?" he prodded mercilessly. "You either have been or you haven't."

She recovered quickly, he noticed. "It just brought back some bad, best forgotten memories." She was hedging. Not lying, maybe, but he didn't think she was telling the whole truth either.

"Well, have you? Yes or no?"

"I haven't been married," she replied softly, "and I don't plan to be." She paused. "You're probably not interested, but if you are, I don't intend to have an affair, either."

That didn't ring true, coming from a woman who could melt into a man as quickly and as completely as she, with only a couple of kisses for a starter.

He regarded her with seeming casualness. "You're a mass of conflicts. You're liquid fire in your responsiveness to men—at least to me—and don't dispute it, because I *know* it. And I agree that you wouldn't settle for a casual affair; but don't expect me to believe that you don't want marriage. If you're counting on a life of celibacy, honey, you're in for a big surprise."

She watched his sensuous lips part to reveal perfect white teeth as he gave her a slow, mesmerizing grin. "You tempt me to go over the line, Naomi, and I don't think you want that. But I'm just a man, and it isn't clever of you to continue attacking my ego, especially like now, declaring to me that I'm never going to be your lover. This isn't the first time you've done that." The grin disappeared, and his face was as hard as steel. Like an accomplished actor, she thought, fascinated.

"Better let it be the last time, Naomi." The grin was back in place, unsettling her and annoying her almost to the point of anger.

She refused him the satisfaction of seeing how his words affected her. She wouldn't have elected to live without a loving mate, but she hadn't been allowed a choice. She attempted to hide her feelings behind what she hoped was a blank facial expression and to respond in a voice whose steadiness belied her inner turmoil. But her mouth twisted slightly and she shook her head as if denying something unpleasant.

"If you knew me better, you would know that nobody dictates to me. Judd Logan can testify to that, and I'd bet that he's even dictated to the Lord on occasion. We can always discuss things, Rufus, but don't dare me and don't tell me how to behave; neither will get you anywhere." She thrust her head up, convincing herself; she didn't need him to remind her that he had only to take her in his arms and she would willingly dance to whatever tune he played.

Louella brought their cappuccino and slices of her prize-winning caramel cake. "The cake's on the house," she informed them. "And my great-grandmother is supposed to have said that this recipe is the only good thing to come out of nearly two hundred and fifty years of slavery. I figured I had to do something to make the two of you smile, and my cake's guaranteed to do that."

Rufus flashed a grin. "I've been smiling, Lou."

She shook her head. "You've been grinning, and most of the time that means nothing. It's just a mask you put on to hide your real feelings." She looked at Naomi, who was observing them keenly. "Don't let him get away with it. He's not as tough as he seems."

"You seem to know him very well," Naomi prompted. But she failed to get the reply that she wanted and rephrased the question.

"How long have you known each other?"

"Since Rufus was a freshman in college. He worked his way through school in my first restaurant, starting as a busboy, but I promoted him after a week; he must have been the youngest maître d' in the country." She smiled, and Naomi sensed the woman's deep affection for Rufus. "He never gets too important to drop by and see me a couple of times a month. I'm real proud of him."

Rufus reflected on those days when life had been hard for a struggling young orphaned boy who had a younger sister to care for; but it hadn't been complicated. There had been no fame or notoriety to make him question every woman's motives; no heartbreaking, loveless marriage; and no consuming interest in a woman with whom he wasn't sure he wanted a liaison, whom he didn't understand, and who seemed unable to trust him enough to let him know her.

What a difference an hour could make, Rufus thought, as they walked back to his car, each obviously preoccupied with personal thoughts. The psychological distance between them widened during the drive to Naomi's apartment. He could feel her sliding away, closing her protective shield around her. He said nothing when, apparently lost in thought, she waited until he walked around the car to open the door for her. That was out of character for her.

They reached her apartment door and he spoke first. "Most of the time, I enjoy being with you a lot, Naomi." He didn't think it necessary to tell her that tonight hadn't been one of those times. "You're stimulating, compassionate, lovely, intelligent. And you're a real woman; in fact, I'm not even sure you know how much of a female you are. I don't know what I want out of this relationship, but I do know that I can't stand superficial relationships, and I hate conflict. That's what my marriage was—endless conflicts, maneuvers, and challenges. Always a jostling for advantage. Etta Mae thought only of herself, never of *us.* And when I stopped letting her maneuver me and demanded that she treat our marriage as a partnership, our war began in earnest. I'm too old, too weary, and too contented to go that route again. You're holding back something, and it's definitely not a small thing. I readily admit that you're entitled to your privacy, so let's…let's give each other some space; you seem to want it, and I…well, I bow to your wish."

He had the impression that she had carefully digested every word he'd said. Her cynical laugh held just enough of a tinkle, just enough merriment, to rattle him. He stared in a detached awe, as she raised her chin, dropped her head slightly to one side, and smoothly derided everything that had happened between them since the day they'd met.

"Rufus, you sound as if we're ending a love affair, when there hasn't been anything between us to end. Lighten up, honey. As my grandpa likes to say, Franklin D. Roosevelt died and to everybody's surprise, the world kept right on turning. We can both be replaced. Next year, you won't remember that you ever knew me. And I…" She shrugged and let it hang, blew him a kiss, and turned to open her door.

Arms of steel spun her around. "I'm surprised somebody hasn't blunted that sharp tongue of yours. I've told you that I will not permit you to banish me with the wave of your hand as if I'm of no consequence. No other woman has ever tried it, not even Etta Mae, and she was a master of games and feminine shenanigans. I fire you up as no other man ever has, and I can do it at will."

Her tantalizing face-saving smile gave him the impression that she thought she was being indulgent, something that he refused to tolerate. He was already simmering from the effect that her laughter, her flowery, sexy scent, and her beloved feminine presence had been having on him since they'd left OLC. His temper and his libido blazed in response, and he reached behind her, turned the key that she'd just inserted in the lock, pushed the door with his foot, and pulled her inside. The words she would have uttered died inside of his mouth.

She knew he intended it to be a punishing kiss, an expression of his frustration and anger, but to her it was simply his kiss, his passion, and she surrendered to it. He barely touched her and she curled into him, turning his fire into a tender ravishment that electrified her, inflamed her as he'd said he would. She had been so hungry for his touch, so starved for the feeling of protection, of the wonderful masculine strength that she always found in his arms, that she forgot about his anger. Almost simultaneously with his touch; her arms went around his strong corded neck and her lips parted for his kiss. She forgot about caution and her decision to preserve a distance between them. Driven by her need for him, she melted into him, moaning her pleasure, as he deepened the kiss and raised her passion to the level of his own. He brought a hand to her hips, and held her tight against him, but she tried to nestle even closer and stilled his dancing tongue while she feasted on it.

His shudder made her aware of his need for relief, of relief in her, but she was lost in the emotional fog that he had draped around her and was oblivious to the warning.

He slipped his hand inside her coat and caressed her breast through the sweater. She knew only that she wanted, needed more of what he was giving her, and, barely conscious of her actions, she pressed his hand more firmly to her. Naked awareness possessed her and she moaned his name. Was she falling, or had the world spun off axis? Her fingers dug into his shoulders, claiming him for her anchor.

"Rufus. Oh, Rufus!" The words were barely intelligible.

"Naomi, I can't stand any more. Take me to your bed, or send me home," he whispered in a voice husky and thickened with desire, as he put her gently from him. She stood trembling before him, disoriented, wanting him. "Do you want me? We can't go on like this; we're driving each other crazy. Tell me!" His overwhelming need must have pushed him beyond thought of what making love with her might do to them both. She gazed up at him and into eyes that glistened with passion and with a tenderness, a softness that nearly took her breath away.

"Tell me," he repeated patiently.

She shifted her eyes from his consuming gaze, wanting desperately to embrace what she saw there, knowing that she could not. "I want you," she told him softly, swallowing the lump that thickened her throat. "I don't remember ever having had this feeling before—what I feel with you, I mean. But I can't, and I'm sorry I let it get out of hand. At least you proved your point."

From his slow, deep breaths, she sensed that he was attempting to bring his passion under control. "I don't care about points." He shifted his stance and seemed more relaxed. "Neither of us is the winner here, Naomi." He spoke in a voice so low that she strained to understand.

"I'm sorry, Rufus. Good night." *Dear God, make him leave. Please don't let him see me tremble like this.*

She would have expected that after such an experience, a

man would leave abruptly and in anger, so she watched him warily. But he took her hand and walked into the kitchen, opened the refrigerator, poured them each a glass of orange juice, and gently stroked her back while they sipped in silence. Apparently satisfied that she had settled down, he held her tenderly, then kissed her on her forehead and left.

After half an hour, she managed to move from the spot in which he'd left her and lock her front door. How could he be so caring and loving after she had thoughtlessly led him on? And why did he persist with his sweetness and gentleness when he knew she wasn't what he needed? If she let herself believe in him, if she weakened and began to hope, she would be courting disaster, wouldn't she? She wanted to trust him and what he represented, and in spite of her sense of foreboding, she began to hope. She crawled into bed, but instead of sleep, her mind was filled with the memory of his kisses, of the way he had stood with her in her kitchen, calming and stroking her. Protecting her.

"God, don't let me need him," she pleaded.

For Rufus, there was no sleep that night. He didn't bother to go to bed, but sat in a deep lounge chair in the boys' room and thought about his life and about Naomi. He had never been affected by a woman as he was by her; she responded to him eagerly, wholeheartedly, even joyously, and withheld nothing. He was momentarily amused by the thought that it was always he who put out the fire; she never seemed to think beyond what she was feeling. God, but she was sweet, and he wanted that sweetness for himself alone. When she was in his arms, he felt as if he could slay dragons single-handedly. He didn't know when he had begun to need her, but he had.

By daybreak, he had decided that he was going to have her no matter the cost; beyond that, he refused even to guess. He stroked his jaw and sipped from the warm can of ginger ale that he'd gotten out of the refrigerator hours earlier. Naomi was a maze of conflicts, but he was beginning to wonder if the inconsistencies he saw in her were deep-seated. He thought not. After he'd let her provoke him with that burnt orange dress, he'd noticed something different about her, but he hadn't been able to put his finger on it. Now, it came to him; Naomi had discovered feminine power that night. She didn't discover how to use it, but she found out that she had it. He shook his head in wonder. At age twenty-nine? And in spite of her strong attraction to him, she was unusually shy of involvement. But hadn't he told her he didn't want any emotional attachments? And she wasn't as he had first thought, a tunnel-vision person who focused on work and nothing else. Oh, she needed her work, all right, just as he needed his, but she found time to work hard for One Last Chance and to help others. He nodded slowly, having found a piece of the puzzle: Naomi *needed* to help others. That kind of woman usually wanted a nest, but Naomi swore that she didn't. He didn't believe her.

The following morning, Naomi received another early-morning summons from Judd. As usual, his request was urgent, but this time she sensed in his manner a deep concern. Whatever it was, she'd face it. How many more shocks could Judd give her, she wondered, dressing hurriedly. She filled a bag with the chocolate fudge brownies she'd made the previous morning and was soon on her way. Her grandfather loved chocolate and was always pleased when she made brownies for him. She walked into the sedate Tudor house and found him sitting in his study with a man he introduced as his lawyer. The situation had escalated beyond the old man's control, she learned; the child through its mother had retained a private investigator. She knew that the adoption papers were sealed by law, but it appeared that nothing prevented the principals from obtaining information by other legal means.

She discovered that the private investigator had begun his search at the few private clinics in the area that also served as halfway houses and found that only one of those currently operating had ever had an African American client and that had taken place only two years earlier. Records of a defunct clinic showed that there had been one in the year in which Naomi's child was born, and interviews with two former workers had identified Judd, a prominent and highly visible clergyman, as the person who had brought her there. She felt intense pleasure at the fate of the owners of that clinic, who, she learned, had been forced to close when the unusually large number of babies they'd placed in adoption had come to the notice of public officials. The old man seemed to have switched his interest to the right power play. She expressed strong disagreement.

"I didn't create this situation," she informed the two of them acidly, "and I'm not going to let it destroy me. If I have to pay a penalty, I'll pay it. There are such things as decency and duty, Grandpa. At least, that's what you've been preaching to me, and to anybody else who would listen, all these years."

She watched dispassionately as he huffed and shifted in his chair, indicating that he was losing patience with her. He peered at her over his glasses. "I appreciate what you're saying, but if you do something hasty, gal, you'll regret it as long as you live."

Her best bet was to switch tactics, she figured. Judd had his own system of logic. "Now, Grandpa, don't get your dander up," she chided the old man, "there may be a legitimate reason why they're looking for me after all this time. Can't you see that? And it isn't the standing of the name Logan in the community that's important here"—a reference to his argument when he'd bullied her into going to that clinic fourteen years earlier—"there may be a child's well-being at stake, and that child is my flesh and blood." She paused. "Your flesh and blood, too, Grandpa. Didn't you stop to think of that?" She grabbed her bag and left hurriedly, unwilling to let her grandfather see her break down.

Naomi turned the key in the ignition and backed slowly out of the driveway. Nervous and scared, she contemplated her next move. She couldn't remember ever before having had the feeling that she was all alone, on her own, as she was now. Judd Logan had made up his mind, and he had never learned how to reverse himself. It was one thing to defy him when her actions concerned only her, but this was a bigger issue, one that involved a number of people, probably far more than she knew. The bright sunshine reflecting off clean, new snow was blinding, and she lowered the visor. Behind it, she glimpsed the magazine picture of Mary McLeod Bethune that she kept there. Its framed twin hung in her studio. She had clipped the pictures while at the clinic awaiting the birth of her child, and whenever she needed inspiration, she looked at one of them.

She thought of the hurdles over which her idol had climbed. Mary Bethune was an African American, a child of slaves, an educator who had worked throughout the first half of the century to improve education standards among her people in the South. That such a woman had in 1904 founded a college that still flourished after ninety years had inspired her to help create One Last Chance. She had cofounded it to help young girls who were experiencing what she had faced. An unmarried pregnant girl would be advised sympathetically of her options and of the short- and long-term consequences of her decision. And she would receive the nurturing and support that she needed.

She glanced briefly at the picture. "I'm not facing the odds that you did, Mary, old girl," she said aloud. She took a shortcut toward Rock Creek Parkway, oblivious to the scenic beauty created by the unusual late-autumn snow. A bullhorn called out her license plate number got her attention, and she pulled over. She accepted the ticket for speeding and drove into a filling station to try and steady her nerves. What else could happen in one morning?

She noticed a telephone booth, and without even considering what she did, she dug in her purse, found a quarter, and dialed.

"Meade." His voice thrilled her, comforted her; he wasn't in that filling station with her, but he was there, and that was something. She opened her mouth but couldn't make a sound.

"Naomi?" His voice held impatience. "What is it? Why are you calling?"

"Rufus. I...I don't know why I called. I saw this telephone booth and I...I just called you. It's been such an awful morning. I'm sorry I bothered you."

"You aren't bothering me." She hadn't even wondered how he'd known that it was she who'd called. Her one thought was that he was there and she needed his strength. The tremors in her voice had been uncontrollable, and he had heard them, she realized, heard and known that she had reached out to him in distress.

"Where are you?"

She told him.

He was silent for a while. "Why not go home and get into something warm and casual, and the boys and I will pick you up in about an hour. I promised to take them sledding in the park, and it's best when the snow's still fresh. Would you like that?"

"Yes. Yes. I'd love that. It would be wonderful. See you later." He didn't hang up, so she waited.

"Are you all right? Can you drive home?" Naomi assured him that she could. She felt better for having spoken with him, even as her common sense cautioned her that she was courting heartache. Of all the men she'd met, this was the one man who was least forgiving by nature and who would not accept the explanation that she would someday have to give him if she didn't stop now. And what about him? For the first time, she considered how he might be affected if he grew to care for her, learned her secrets, and felt betrayed. I care too much, she admitted.

Rufus watched his children's faces light up when Naomi opened the door. Their joy at seeing her and her pleasure at their excited greetings touched him, and he knew he had done the right thing in inviting her to join them.

"Where's your sled?" Preston asked her, in a mild reprimand.

"You can ride mine, Noomie," Sheldon declared protectively, chiding his brother.

"She can ride mine, too," Preston was quick to add. She hugged them and got hugs in return.

When she finally looked up at Rufus, he fought to remove all but a tolerant expression from his face.

"Hi. Thanks for inviting me to go along. The children are so nice to be with."

His raised eyebrow was his response. He disliked small talk, considering it too strong a challenge to one's honesty. "I'm glad to see you with a bloom on your face. What happened?" He had promised himself to keep things between them impersonal, but when she'd called needing him, he hadn't remembered it. His only thought had been to shelter her.

"I called you just after I got a ticket for speeding at eighty miles an hour on the Shirley Highway and the Washington

Boulevard." She had told him the truth, he conceded, but he wasn't fool enough to believe she had given him the whole story.

"I don't have to ask where you'd been. Does your grandfather upset you like that very often?" Getting a traffic ticket wasn't what had upset her, what he wanted to know was why she'd been so distressed that she hadn't known how fast she was driving.

She grabbed the straw he'd given her. "He's a genius at it." More evasion, he knew, but he hadn't expected anything different. Not yet. Just give me time, he promised himself, and I'll get behind all of it. Didn't she remember that he was a journalist, a good one, and that collecting facts was his business? All he needed were a few sharp clues, and she had already unwittingly given him several. He'd get it; she could be sure of that.

Rock Creek Park was deserted. It was eerily beautiful, Naomi thought, gazing into the distance. The unusually early snow had preceded a blast of cold that left icicles hanging from branches, and snow-crusted evergreens and pines lent color to the white forest. They gamboled in the snow, pulling the sleds as the boys giggled and screamed with pleasure, throwing snowballs and building snow figures. She watched Rufus's handsome face crease in a slow grin when he noticed one of hers.

"Pretty clever," he told her in a voice laced with humor. "I'm not sure I've seen a snow girl before. How'd you get that skirt on her?"

She rubbed her nose and fought the sniffles. "With my nail file. Where there's a will, there's a way. Try it sometime."

He sauntered over to her and rubbed snow on her forehead. "You can't stand peace, can you? It just kills you to be surrounded with so much contentment, doesn't it?" The warm, alluring eyes that could so easily seduce her sparkled with mischief. "I'm glad you're the only female chauvinist I know. Personally, I mean. And sometimes I wonder how the devil I let that happen." He got out of the way quickly as if anticipating the snowball that he knew would be heading his way. She hadn't enjoyed a genuine snow fight in years; the boys loved it, too, she noticed.

Rufus turned to his boys. "Why aren't you defending *me?* You always take sides with me against your aunt Jewel."

"We have to help Noomie," Preston answered, as Sheldon nodded in agreement.

Rufus regarding his offending offspring, puzzled by their deep affection for Naomi, as he began to pack them into his car with the intention of driving Naomi home. But Preston had other ideas.

"Noomie, we have a snowman in our back garden; you wanna see it?"

"Yes," Sheldon urged, "and our daddy says we're having chili for lunch. Aunt Jewel made it. You want some?" Rufus restrained his inclination to squelch the idea. Having Naomi for a houseguest was not in his plans; the entire afternoon had been too cozy, and he didn't want her to misinterpret it. As it was, the course of their mutual attraction, or whatever you'd call it that was happening between them, seemed to be self-propelled.

"Our daddy can't cook chili," Preston added. Rufus had the impression that she didn't want to look at him for approval, but that she couldn't help it. She wanted to go, and she wanted him to invite her; that was obvious. But why? She's more mixed up about this than I am, he thought. I know what I want; I just don't know for how long.

"You're welcome to come," he said, almost reluctantly, silently weighing the consequences. "There's more than enough." Ashamed of the lack of enthusiasm in his voice, he smiled and looped an arm around her shoulder. "We'd love your company, Naomi."

"All right, if you're sure." She looked at him steadily, and he had the feeling she was trying to see beyond his words.

"I'm sure. If I weren't, I wouldn't have said a word." And he was sure. It might not be the right thing, but he wanted it. Her uncertainty showed in the way she worried her bottom lip and in her forced, shaky smile. He hated that he'd made her insecure and squeezed her to him a little. He glanced down at the two identical pairs of eyes that were watching them intently and winked, reassuring his boys.

"Could we drop by my place first? If I drive, you and the boys won't have to bring me home."

He nodded, understanding that she wanted the freedom to leave at will if she found herself uncomfortable. "All right. Then you can follow us home."

He waited until she'd started her engine before heading toward the highway. He didn't feel as though he was merely driving home with a guest, but rather that he had opened a door and entered a place from which there was no exit.

Chapter 7

A strange, almost otherworldly sensation came over her as she parked and looked at Rufus's home—a large, sand-colored modern brick house nestled in wooded surroundings. She had never been there, never seen it, but it was familiar, welcoming. It seemed to beckon her. She had to quell an unsettling desire to run to it, to be enveloped in its shelter. She started toward it, trying without success to focus on the pristine white snow that banked the long, curving walkway like a painter's border for a fairyland scene. Her heart began to beat rapidly, to gallop like a runaway horse. She walked faster, and when she reached the front door, he opened it and smiled. The boys rushed to greet her as if they had been separated from her for days rather than minutes. She fought the urge to weep; this wasn't her family, her home, and it never would be.

Naomi walked through a large foyer to the living room, observing its high ceiling, large windows, and massive stone fireplace. She admired the Persian carpets scattered about the floor and found it oddly comforting that there was nothing chrome to be seen. It was a room for daily living that proclaimed its owner's simplicity and self-confidence. She was tempted to ask him why his sofa wasn't bordered by matching end tables and lamps, until she realized that the room was intentionally unique. Groupings of a small table and two or three chairs were scattered about the large room; a leather recliner beside which stood a small writing table faced a picture window and garden. And there didn't seem to be a bar. A curved staircase led to the second floor, and African sculptures and tapestries decorated its adjoining wall.

Rufus made a fire in the great stone fireplace. "Entertain Naomi for me," he told Preston and Sheldon. He held the kindling in front of him, disbelieving, as he watched them walk on either side of her, each holding her hand as they led her through the house and down to their own little padded world in the basement. He found them there later, head to head. She had her arms around the boys, who were trying with minimum success to explain their video game to her. He watched them unnoticed as an unfamiliar constriction settled in his chest and knew it wasn't caused by a physical ailment, but by what she made him feel. He shrugged off his alarm at the sight of her cuddling his sons and their eager response to it and thought of quicksand.

Back off, buddy, he admonished himself; you're not planning anything permanent here. But she looked up then, vulnerable, with eyes wide and suspiciously shiny, and he stopped himself just before he gathered the three of them into his arms. His grin was meant to be deceptive; she had almost caught him in a raw moment.

"Ready? For lunch?" Both boys jumped out of Naomi's arms and ran to him for the cleaning ritual. To her astonishment, he told them a little tale about each body part that he washed while they bounced and giggled with pleasure. Still sitting on the floor, she wrapped her arms around her drawn-up knees and spoke as though perplexed.

"You're not really a chauvinist, are you? How could you be, when you get so much enjoyment out of giving your boys the kind of care and affection that children usually get from their mothers?" She seemed embarrassed at having voiced her thoughts. He had suspected that some of her brashness was a cover for shyness, and now he was certain of it.

"I'd better be a chauvinist," he joked, "otherwise, you'll lose interest in me. If you discovered I was an egalitarian, you couldn't fight with me; you'd lose the inspiration for your sharpest wit and sarcasm; you wouldn't resent me any longer; and you wouldn't have a need to change me. So don't get any fancy notions about me; I'm the biggest chauvinist you're ever going to meet."

He put a boy in each arm and nodded to her. "Come on, woman, the food is getting cold." After paying proper homage to the chili, Naomi brought out the bag of brownies that she had forgotten to give her grandfather and further cemented the bond between herself and her three hosts.

Warmth suffused Rufus as he furtively watched the interplay between Naomi and his sons. He reclined in his big chair in the living room while they huddled on the floor before the fire. Each time she indicated that she should leave, one of his boys found an excuse to detain her, and she readily acquiesced.

Finally, she told him, "If I don't leave here, you'll be serving me dinner." Without making it obvious, he had been weighing and judging her every act, gesture, and word all afternoon and had found her more puzzling than ever.

"Do you want to go?"

"No," she answered, "but I'm going before I abuse your hospitality."

Preston and Sheldon demanded and got their share of goodbye kisses, using more delaying tactics in the process. Rufus watched with a sense of wonder. What was it about her? His children had always been retiring with everyone except Jewel and her family.

"Since you're being so generous with your kisses, maybe I can have one, too?" He couldn't help it; it was foolish, but he felt excluded from something important, something good.

She told him with what was obviously mock sincerity, "the boys made me a snow girl out back, turned cartwheels for me, and climbed into my lap while I sang them some songs. If you do that or better, you'll get some kisses, too."

A tiny frown creased his brow, and he shoved his itchy fingers deep into the pockets of his slacks. "You want a demonstration of some of my...er, abilities? Is that what you're asking me for? That's hardly fair, Naomi. I could be hauled into court by corrupting the morals of minors. You could, too, for that matter," he deadpanned.

"Your mind's always in the same rut," she informed him, as she reached up to kiss him. He didn't let her off until he'd exacted a small price, grabbing her shoulder and letting her feel the force of his tongue for a split second. She reeled slightly, to his immense satisfaction.

"I owe you one for that, Meade," she said, digging into her shoulder bag for her car keys.

Rufus put his hands back in his pockets, where they'd be safely out of trouble. "I'm looking forward to collecting," he retorted smoothly. "I'd tail you home, but I don't want to take the boys out again." They stood in the foyer, exchanging light banter, the boys clinging to her hands; then she hugged them goodbye again. He wished she wasn't leaving him, then wished he could retrieve the thought. He shrugged. The hell with it; he felt good. He walked her to her car, kissed her quickly, and opened the door for her. It was the first time that their kiss hadn't been the product of fire-hot desire, the first time that they both had felt the need to join in ways that transcended the physical.

"I enjoyed this time with you," he told her, and meant it. He wasn't in the habit of lying to himself; she had touched him. How he'd deal with it was going to be a problem.

Naomi let herself into her condominium, walked slowly down the hallway to the kitchen, and put on a kettle of water. Deep in thought, she stood there until the water boiled, made tea, and sat down to drink it. She didn't pretend that she wasn't emotionally shaken; getting to know the little boys and observing the loving relationship between them and their father had unsettled and disturbed her. She knew she could love those boys with all her heart, and she knew just as certainly that they could love her. What kind of mother would she have been, she wondered. And what kind of mother did her own child have? Her eyes burned with tears that she didn't dare shed for what she had lost. Crying was useless. She had let her grandfather run her life when she'd been helpless to oppose him, but she wasn't helpless now. She understood that her grandfather would have felt humiliated if her pregnancy had been public knowledge. After all, he had preached sexual responsibility to his parishioners. And though he hadn't told her to give the baby up for adoption, he hadn't told her not to do it, and he had certainly facilitated it.

She stood by the telephone and glanced at her watch. Four o'clock. Her mind made up, she would face whatever came with her head up. She picked up the phone, dialed, and set fate into motion. Judd's lawyer answered on the first ring.

"You'd better think this thing through before you make any contact, but it's up to you. What are you planning?"

"I don't know. I only know that I can't bear to go on like this."

"I'm Reverend Logan's lawyer," he reminded her, "and if you're planning to do something against his wishes, I couldn't advise you. It would be unethical."

"I'm not asking for advice. What I want is accurate information. Can you at least give me that? Have you met the family? Is the child a boy or a girl? Are they in some kind of difficulty?" She knew she sounded desperate.

"The child is a boy. He's healthy, intelligent, and not a problem in any sense, as far as I know. I can't tell you more."

When she could get her breath, she tried to thank him. "When will you confer with the family again?"

"I have an appointment at their home Monday morning at ten-thirty. You may call me around noon if you have any questions."

She had a son. But he wasn't really hers, she reminded herself. Monday morning. It was Saturday, so she'd better get busy.

At ten-thirty Monday morning, Naomi parked on a side street off Georgia Avenue in Silver Spring, Maryland, a Washington suburb. She was unrecognizable in a reddish-brown wig of long straight hair and bangs, and contact lenses that changed her irises from dark brown to gray. The car she drove was a rented dark blue Mustang. She had followed the lawyer, as she supposed he'd figured she would, but she'd kept well behind him in case he hadn't counted on her little maneuver. She sat there in the cold until noon, long after the lawyer had left, unable to leave the scene. How many times had she passed that modest red brick ranch-style house on her way to visit Marva, five blocks away? She wrote down the address, turned the key in the ignition, then turned it off. Impulsively, she got out of the car and walked the half block to the house. She didn't see anyone. The boy should have been in school, so she didn't expect to see him.

I just can't ring the bell and introduce myself, she thought, but I can't leave here not knowing anything more. Then she saw the name plate on the lawn: Hopkins. It was something. She hurried back to her rented car and quickly drove away. She couldn't have said why, but she felt more at peace than at any time since she'd learned that her child's family was searching for her and that she could see him; she had a link to him.

Later that afternoon, the telephone rang just as Naomi was about to leave her workshop. "Logan Logos and Labels. May I help you?" It was her automatic phone greeting when she was in the shop.

"You could be more enthusiastic about it," came the bubbly response.

"Marva! Girl, have I ever missed you! How was the honeymoon?"

"What do you mean, how *was* it?" Marva drawled. "It's just started. Honey, you'd better get busy. What this man does to me! Well, I just never even dreamed that anybody could remain just barely conscious all the time and be deliriously happy about it. Love somebody, Naomi; I swear it'll make you a better person. How's Cat?"

"Who? Oh, you mean Rufus. All right, the last time I saw him, which, before you ask, was Saturday. Please don't pressure me about him, Marva. He's nice and I like him, I guess, but we're really oil and water."

"Are you going to the gala with him?" Naomi didn't want to think about the gala and the television cameras that would be all over the place. Whatever happened in regard to her future relationship with her child, she wanted to be the one who maneuvered it. An accidental meeting could be painful.

"I'm going alone, and I'm going to sit at the sponsors' table." She said it almost belligerently.

"Why don't you come along with Elijah and me? Lije has a really nice friend who could join us, and he's tall, too."

"Marva, please. I don't want to have blind dates with any more of Lije's friends. I hate blind dates, and if I wanted a man to take me, finding one wouldn't be difficult. I'm going alone."

"*Jet* magazine will just love that."

"I don't care. I'm not going to run my life according to what people might think." She almost laughed. That was exactly what she'd been doing for Judd's sake.

Marva tried again. "Well, at least wear something really sexy, and be sure it's either dusty rose or burnt orange. Stay out of black. You and I are going to have a talk about your social attitude, honey, and I'm going to make you spill all. I know you think I'm frivolous, but my degree in psychology didn't leave me totally stupid about human behavior. If you're smart, you'll call Cat and ask him to go with you to the gala. Oil and water! Humph! It's probably more like flint and steel. See you at the gala."

A glance at her watch reminded Naomi that Linda was developing a habit of arriving late for her tutoring. She hoped the girl would be more responsive than she'd been at her two previous classes. Naomi had the feeling that Linda wanted her to lose patience, to stop the sessions. The girl arrived breathless and flushed, but not apologetic. She handed Naomi a tablet of her drawings.

"What do you think of these?"

Naomi flipped the pages slowly, astonished at the talent displayed there. "I think you have great potential. Do you mind if I keep these?

Linda's pleasure at the request was obvious in her broad smile and diffident manner. "I did them for you."

Naomi thanked her and decided to have copies made and to circulate them among several universities in the hope of getting a scholarship for her young charge.

The following evening, Naomi checked her appearance in the full-length mirror attached to her closet door. She'd had her hair straightened to make it manageable and styled into an elaborate French twist. Her dress was an off-the-shoulder lavender-pink sheath slit above the left knee, and the diamond studs in her ears were her only jewelry. Her fur-lined black silk evening cape matched the silk evening bag; and her black silk pumps were plain except for their rhinestone buckles. She sprayed some Fendi perfume in strategic places, closed her door, and went down to the lobby to await her taxi.

Maude Frazier had placed her right in front of Rufus at the narrow end of the oval-shaped sponsors' table. It hadn't occurred to Naomi that he'd be sitting near her. When she arrived, he stood, nodded politely, and walked around the table to assist her in sitting. She hadn't seen nor spoken with him since the afternoon she'd spent at his home, but that might have been because she'd deliberately erased the messages on her answering machine before listening to them. Desire knotted her insides when she looked at him. Why did she respond to him the way she did? He was tall, elegant, and drop-dead handsome; the sight of him nearly took away her breath.

"You look lovely, Naomi. Where's your date?"

"He let me out of the house all by my little self tonight, just to see if I could be trusted not to get lost," she taunted, wearing one of her sugary-sweet, plastic smiles. He had an urge to shake her. It was unreasonable, but so was she.

"Try to discipline your tart little tongue for tonight, so that your tablemates can enjoy the evening, *darling*." He spoke to her ears only and drew the word out to make certain that it annoyed her. He'd called her every evening that week, and she hadn't answered her phone or returned the messages he'd left on her answering machine.

"Who's the little femme fatale sitting on your right and throwing darts at me? Poor thing; put her at ease and tell her there's nothing between us." He tried not to react; she might feel reckless, but he didn't.

He inclined his head toward the younger woman seated next to his chair. "She's smart enough to know there's nothing between us. And why do you care, anyway? You took yourself out of the picture." *And left me here in limbo!* He had had a week of emotional upheaval, half eager to see her and half dreading what seeing her would do to him. And she'd walked in looking like a queen, wrapped securely in her protective witch armor. He went back to his seat.

The young woman seated beside Rufus laid claim to his attention most of the evening, but to Naomi's delight, she didn't always get it, and he either sat out the dances or partnered another woman, never asking Naomi. It embarrassed her that Marva's husband was her most frequent dance partner, and she knew that was a result of Marva's prompting. Finally, the orchestra leader announced the last dance. *Jitterbug Waltz,* a slow, sensuous, heat-provoking jazz piece. She wasn't looking when he left his chair, but she knew instinctively that the fingers that brushed her bare shoulders were his.

"Dance with me, Naomi." It wasn't a question. Everyone at the table looked at them. It was the last dance, and he was asking Naomi to share it with him.

Slowly, she rose to her feet, her three-inch heels making her only a few inches shorter than he. "A gentleman dances the last dance with the woman he brought." She didn't try to hide the bitterness she felt. All evening she had ached to be in his arms, to glide across the floor with him, and all evening he had looked elsewhere for his partners.

He brought her a trifle closer. "If I had brought a woman here, I would be dancing with her right now." She missed a step. "I came alone, Naomi."

"But…"

"I met Maude's niece here tonight. You should have guessed that she wasn't with me." He changed the subject. "You look beautiful. You're always beautiful, but tonight you're lovelier than ever." He pulled her to him and rocked her to the pulsating rhythmic beat with a voluptuous tilt of his hips.

"Move with me," he whispered in a low, sultry voice.

"Rufus. I…" She couldn't muster another word. He danced lightly on his feet and moved them with a slow, enthralling glide that sent her heart racing. Thoughtlessly, she moved closer to him, and he welcomed her, clasping her possessively to him as their dance turned into one of riveting desire.

"You're mine right now," he whispered, as his lips gazed her ear, and she shivered against him. He barely moved, merely let their bodies angle this way and that to the beat of the all consuming rhythm.

Rufus knew the minute she remembered where she was and that she had slid her hands up the lapels of his navy tuxedo and rested her head snugly under his chin. As usual, she had let her senses take over.

"Rufus, please! We're in a public place." She tried to move away from him, but he held her and danced a lovers' dance with her.

"Would you make love with me right now if we weren't in a public place? If we were in the privacy of your bedroom? Would you? Tell me." It wasn't a taunt; he whispered it sweetly, lovingly, softly. She didn't answer, but tried to put a little space between them; he wouldn't allow it. His warm fingers stealthily traced the cut of her gown to her lower back and caressed the flesh revealed there, and he felt her capitulate and let him have his way. He had gotten the only reward he figured he'd get; he'd robbed her of her will to resist him, had scrambled her wits.

At last the music ended; the dance was over, and he watched fascinated as she stood facing him, looking at him, drinking him in, seemingly immobile. Then, like the changing seasons, her eyes slowly lost their soft, besotted look and assumed a glare of murderous intent.

"How dare you do that to me on a public dance floor?" She kept her trembling voice low, and he realized that Naomi was angry. For the first time since he'd known her, she was angry. He rethought it: she was mad, and he had best remain silent. He understood, too, that while she was mad at him, she was more furious with herself, and that put him in the mood to placate her.

Back stiff and head high, she walked back to their table, collected her purse, and bade their fellow guests good-night. Then she turned to Rufus and spoke to him between tightly clenched teeth.

"You come with me; I've got a few things to say to you." She began walking, all but ordering him to follow her.

"All right," he told her, when they reached the entrance to the ballroom, "I'll walk you to your car."

He figured she'd like to destroy him with that withering look and pretended he didn't see it.

"I didn't drive tonight. How could I, with this dress on?"

Rufus shrugged elaborately. "Good point. I still haven't figured out how you got into it. May I have your cloakroom ticket?" She gave it to him, along with two one-dollar bills for the tip. He looked first at the money and then at her, started to speak, and clamped his mouth shut. If she was going to explode, she'd do it without any more help from him.

The porter brought his car to the front. Naomi looked first at the silver gray Town Car and then at Rufus. "I should have known that a minivan wouldn't satisfy you." He said nothing, but merely took her arm and walked toward his car. She was upset, and he suspected it was much more than their dance that had ticked her off.

"Why do you think I'm getting into that thing with you?" she asked him, in a tone that was only a little less peevish than it had been earlier.

He sighed patiently. "Be reasonable, Naomi. You said you wanted to speak to me, but you don't have your car, and it's cold out here. I don't discuss private matters in taxis, because I don't want to read about it the next day. What's the alternative?"

"Oh, all right," she huffed. He opened the door and assisted her into the passenger's seat.

"Why are we going in here?" she queried, somewhat ungraciously, when he parked in front of an exclusive late-night supper club.

Rufus turned, put his right arm on the back of her seat, and looked at her. "My patience isn't endless, Naomi, and you've already tested what little forbearance I have. We can go to my place, but one of my boys would awaken and disturb us; I left a sitter with them. We could go to your place, but in my current mood, I couldn't guarantee that I wouldn't be in your bed with you five minutes after we got there. So this is it." He was well aware that she didn't disagree with his reasoning, and it didn't brighten his mood: knowing that she acknowledged an inability to resist him was more temptation than he wanted.

He asked for and got a table in a corner far from the

piano-playing chanteuse, whose songs all sounded the same. It surprised him that Naomi was still so mad, but there was no mistaking it. Slow to anger and slow to yield it, he mused.

"Lighten up, Naomi; nothing that happened could have been as bad as you're making it out to be." She pursed her lips and glared at him.

"All right. All right. Spill it," he urged, conceding himself to the right to a little anger.

Annoyance surged through her, enlivening her. "You had no right to seduce me on that dance floor. No gentleman would have done what you did to me out there. You practically made love to me right out there in front of all those people," she fumed. "You don't respect me, and now everybody knows it." It poured out of her, but not a word described what she actually felt; words couldn't have described it. A wintry desolation had beset her, saturating her consciousness with a deep need for the shelter of his arms, for the solace of his whole self. Apprehensive of her feelings, she took refuge in her annoyance, grasping at straws.

"Shut up, Naomi." It was gently said, without vocal inflection.

"What?" She lowered her voice. "What do you mean, telling me to shut up?"

"Naomi," he drawled, giving her the impression that he was drawing on his last reserve of patience. "'Shut up' is exactly what I mean. I'm the one who got seduced on that dance floor. Me! I was dancing normally, just as I always do, and then you stepped into me." She opened her mouth to protest, but his look suggested that silence would be prudent.

"That's right. You just tucked your little tush under and moved right into me. What do you think I'm made of, huh? And another thing. If you weren't susceptible, you wouldn't have reacted the way you did. That's mostly what this is about, isn't it. You're scared of what you felt. And you're scared of something else, too, Naomi, but that's another story, isn't it?"

She leaned back in the richly upholstered chair and glared at him. "So what happened out there was all my doing, eh? Big, six-foot-four-inch man got snowed by a female who doesn't know that"—she flicked a finger—"about the art of seduction. Get real, Rufus."

Laughter deep and warm rippled from his throat as he glanced at his watch. Their waiter seemed to have taken a break. "Honey, you don't have to know anything about the art of seduction; you just do what comes naturally. Uninhibited, that's you. No *wonder* you try to hold yourself aloof. You're scared of what you might do if you really let yourself go." He drained his glass and stood. "You're enjoying this conversation because it's cooling you off, but it's heating me up, and I've finished with it. If I offended you, I apologize. But, lady, I'm not one bit sorry for anything that happened on that dance floor."

He winked as he reached for her hand, disconcerting her. "I'd do it again if I had the chance, and I'd bet my Rolex that you would, too."

"Not with you, I wouldn't," she threw at him hating his obvious amusement, his cocky grin.

"I don't believe you," he countered, his face as somber as she'd ever seen it.

They walked out of the supper club, and her pride in being with Rufus overrode her anger. He had complemented his navy tuxedo with a ruffled pale gray silk shirt and pale gray on navy accessories, and the combination offset his dark good looks. Tall and elegant, he was the picture of male power. I'm not vain, she thought, but right now I'm glad I'm not bad-looking.

They reached her door. "Rufus, could we please not have

the kind of scene we had when you last brought me home?" She sounded so prim that she annoyed herself. "I want to avoid it."

"I'm not stopping you," he teased. "You have my permission to avoid it." His charismatic smile enveloped her, but she resisted the temptation to forgive and turned toward her door.

"Naomi, how can you stay angry so long? With me, it's over in minutes."

"And a good thing, too, or you'd be angry all the time. Any little thing ticks you off." His censoring frown challenged her statement. "Well, a lot of things do," she amended.

He moved closer, and she'd have stepped back if there'd been anyplace to go. "If you didn't play a part in what happened to us during that dance and if you're not susceptible to me, as you claim, I'd like to be sure of it. Kiss me, Naomi. I won't move, I promise, and there's no music here."

He leaned toward her, and with the closed door for support, braced his hands on either side of her. "Kiss me, baby." Her heart thundered widely at the suggestiveness in his low, husky words. "Put your arms around me and kiss me," he cajoled silkily. His voice had become thick and slurred. She stared into his eyes mesmerized, and then let her glance drift to his sensuous lips. When he parted them ever so slightly, she sucked in her breath and succumbed to his tempting maleness. He closed in on her, his hands still braced against the wall, and his mouth devoured her as she grasped him to her and clung.

Desperate now, she whimpered. "Hold me. Please hold me." But he didn't touch her until her knees buckled. Then he held her with his left arm, took her key, and opened the door.

"Good night, Naomi."

She barely noticed his short, rapid intake of breath and

the look of longing in his eyes, but focused on what she felt. What she needed. "Good...*what?*"

It registered that he was actually leaving her. "I hate you, Rufus. I do. I hate you, and I'm never going anywhere else with you. *Never.*" She hissed it at him, trembling with frustration.

She calmed herself, allowed her good sense to surface, and with reason restored, no longer felt rejected. If he had crossed that threshold, she'd have had some confessing to do, come morning. And she wouldn't have known where to start and certainly not how to end it. She didn't know the end. She did know that Rufus had proved his point incontestably. She not only wanted him; she needed him.

"I know how you feel," he muttered, as he walked away, equally frustrated, but determined to leave her. Gently, and at considerable expense to his shattered emotions, he had pushed her inside her door and left. If the day ever came when she could look him in the eye and say she wanted him and would have no regrets, he'd stay. Not before.

Chapter 8

Rufus received the Reverend Judd Logan's seven-thirty a.m. phone call with astonishment. He had written exactly one paragraph of the thoughts he'd collected and didn't want to be disturbed. But Judd didn't so much invite as command him to his home in Alexandria for breakfast that morning, not even hinting at what had prompted the invitation. Curious, Rufus agreed to go, but mainly because he figured he might learn something about the mystery that he sensed surrounding Naomi. He took his boys to Jewel's house and left them with her husband, a dentist. Jeff's afternoon office hours enabled him to keep the children while Jewel taught, and she relieved him at three o'clock.

Judd's cook, who seemed nearly as old as his employer, led Rufus to the study. Something out of an old movie, he thought, only grudgingly amused, as he looked around at the antique furniture, heavy velvet drapes, and ecru lace curtains. His working day was shot, his deadline was now almost unattainable, and his boys were off their schedule. Judd Logan stood, his stature belying his great age.

"I see you made it. Just have a seat; breakfast will be served in here in a minute." Rufus remembered Naomi having said that Judd seldom bothered to thank anybody for anything, certainly not for obeying one of his unreasonable commands. So he remained standing, raised an eyebrow, and left the expression of incredulity on his face so long that the old man took a hint and said, "I'm glad to meet you."

The breakfast was consumed and the crafty old man still had spoken only of the weather and of similarly mundane things. Rufus tired quickly and demanded, "What may I do for you, sir? I'm sure you know that Chevy Chase isn't just across the street from you. I'm a busy man."

Judd gazed at Rufus intently, obviously appraising him. "So you're Cat Meade."

"I used to be. Yes."

"Well, who are you now?" The old man's sharp eyes bored into Rufus, sizing him up. Rufus was accustomed to power plays; he had learned to be a master at them when he negotiated his football contracts, and bluffing was fifty percent of it. He didn't take up the challenge.

"I gave that up five years ago. I never intended to make football my life's work; I'm a journalist and a published author. What exactly do you want with me?" He wanted to be respectful to Naomi's grandfather, but the man rankled him, and what's more, didn't seem to mind that he did.

"What are your intentions with regard to my granddaughter?" Rufus sucked in his breath and stared wide-eyed at his host. Was this man serious? It was on the tip of his tongue to tell Judd Logan that he'd had a driver's license for nearly twenty years and didn't take kindly to having his behavior questioned. Then he laughed.

"You couldn't be serious! I thought Naomi might be

stretching the truth with some of the things she told me about you. You're way off, Reverend Logan; your granddaughter and I are not on the best of terms. In fact, we're barely speaking now." He didn't add that he'd merely assumed it from Naomi's mood when they'd parted the night before.

Judd appeared irritated. "Are you telling me that you dance like that with a woman you're hardly speaking to? In my days, no decent woman would have permitted you to dance with her that way, and no gentleman would have attempted it."

Rufus sighed. "Maybe that's because cold showers hadn't been invented," he muttered under his breath.

Judd's hearing proved to be fine. "What? I'm serious here. The whole of Washington and every town near it saw that show you two put on," he stormed.

"What do you mean?"

"My God, boy, didn't you know the television stations had their cameras there? African Americans of our status have to set a good example. Everybody expects more from us."

Rufus wasn't impressed with that reasoning; he leaned forward. "Of course, I didn't know that our dance was being televised." Though if he had, it wouldn't have made one iota of difference once he had her in his arms. "There's no point in being upset about this, Reverend; I haven't compromised her, and I won't. As for that dance, Naomi already gave me the devil about it."

The old man peered at him. "You can't make me believe you're not interested in each other. You're the one man I've met who could turn her head. And if she doesn't turn yours after what I saw last night, I want to know what you're made of."

Rufus sat back in the generously overstuffed chair, getting more comfortable, and gave the man one of his intentionally indecipherable grins. "I came here out of respect, but this is really none of your business, sir." He stood.

Judd looked up at Rufus and released a long, tired breath. "I'm living on borrowed time, son. I'll be ninety-five in a few weeks, and I'm all she has. I'd hate to have to leave her all alone. She's so fragile." He'd spoken almost as if to himself. "I hope I haven't caused any hard feelings." He stood tall and straight, for all his ninety-four years.

"None whatever, sir."

"Well, at least I got to meet one of my favorite football players. It was good of you to come."

"It was my pleasure." Rufus stepped toward the foyer and turned, surprised, when the old man's thin fingers grasped his arm.

"I don't care what you said. My Naomi wants you. It's been more than fourteen years since she let herself get as close to a man as she was to you last night. And I know that for a fact."

Rufus opened his mouth to speak and closed it, at a loss for words, not certain that he wanted that information and positive that within its core lay the key to her character.

"I know she acts tough, son. She learned a long time ago to harden herself to life; she had to. But that toughness is just a front; deep down, she's very fragile. My Naomi spends a lot of time hurting. You're strong, just what she needs. Well, goodbye." They parted with a friendly handshake.

Rufus drove toward Washington, pondering Judd Logan's revealing words. He had known almost from their first meeting that Naomi's flippancy was a shield, and he had begun to realize that her insistence that marriage was not for her was nothing more than pretense, her solution to a problem that she had found no other way to handle. He suspected the real Naomi was the woman who cared that a young slum girl needed a role model, who responded to him without ego or inhibition, who gave herself to him totally in every kiss or caress. The real Naomi, he surmised, was the woman in whom his sons had immediately sensed warmth and tenderness; they had been drawn to it. That kind of woman needed a nest and knew it.

He stopped downtown at Garfinkel's to buy long-sleeved T-shirts for Preston and Sheldon. They outgrew their clothes so rapidly that he bought them a size larger than they needed. As he left the store, a thought occurred to him, as he headed back toward the shoe department.

Tired, cold and discouraged, Naomi let herself into her studio, questioning the wisdom of what she'd decided to do. She pulled off the wig and threw it in her desk drawer, stored the contact lenses, and sat down at her drawing table. She had wasted an hour sitting in a cold, rented car, and no one had entered or left that house. But she was doggoned if she would let it get her down. She took out her sketchpad, closed her eyes, and tried to imagine how the design should look. She'd finished the ad campaign for the ice-cream company, but the parent firm had engaged her to design new paper milk cartons. No, she thought, green wouldn't work for milk.

She reached for the phone after its first ring. "Logan Logos and Labels. May I help you?"

"Hi. So you're finally there. Most people are in their office between three and four, Naomi. Do you always take a late lunch?"

She had completely forgotten lunch. "I work when I'm getting results, Rufus." It wasn't a lie, and her whereabouts were not his affair. She told him, "As a writer, I'm sure you've had experience with that. Did you call to apologize?"

If Rufus hadn't remembered his conversation with Judd, he might have interpreted her words as a mild reprimand or even rudeness. He did neither, but inquired, "Should I?" He couldn't believe she was still annoyed because he'd given her that blistering kiss and left her without explanation. Surely she understood why he'd had to get away from her and fast.

"Why did you call?" She hoped her voice didn't reflect her wariness. She wanted to see him, to be with him, but while she'd waited in front of her son's home, she'd decided to put Rufus out of her complicated life once and for all. She was going to focus on finding a way to know her son and his adoptive parents and managing it without her grandfather's interference.

Her brusqueness apparently didn't discourage him. "I called because you're the only woman I'm kissing these days, and my energy is low. Thought I'd get a little sugar."

Naomi laughed. Drat him; he knew how to get next to her. "Well, here goes a kiss right through the wire. Now, hang up, and let me work."

He didn't let her off. "You complain about Judd, but you're certainly his granddaughter."

"*Whatever* do you mean? Of course, I'm his granddaughter. My father was his only son."

"I mean you've either inherited or copied his bluntness and directness, and I have to tell you, it looks better on him than it does on you."

"How do you know so much about him?" She felt the skin crawl on the back of her neck. What had the old man been up to now?

"He wrecked my day with a summons out to Alexandria this morning to explain my intentions toward you."

Naomi let out a mild shriek. "He *what?* Oh, my goodness. He must have seen us on television last night. I saw the cameramen, but then I forgot about them. This is none of his business."

Rufus chuckled softly. "I told him precisely that, but I could have saved my breath."

"You told him it was none of his business?" she asked, in frank admiration. "I wish I'd been there."

"He took it like a man, sweetheart," he told her, and she sensed his sincerity in the endearment. "I liked him. I liked him a lot. I want to see you, Naomi, but I don't want to leave my boys with a sitter again tonight. Could you come over about six and have supper with us? I don't like to feed my boys too late. I'll take them and get some fried chicken and other stuff, maybe some rice and gravy from one of the take-outs just off Connecticut Avenue. Would you like anything special?"

He'd just assumed that she'd accept, and she was tempted to refuse him, to stick to her resolve not to see him again. But she had missed Preston and Sheldon, and the thought of being with them even for a little while raised her spirits from where they'd dropped while she'd sat in that cold car, watching a house in Silver Spring.

"I guess not, but I could bring something, too. See you at six." She hung up, stared at the phone, and thought of the reasons why she should call him back and tell him that she had changed her mind. But she knew she wouldn't do it; an hour and a half was already too long to wait. Her heartbeat accelerated at the thought that she would soon be with him.

"What's in the bag, Noomie?" Preston asked her, pulling at her shopping bag. Rufus watched his sons greet Naomi, dancing happily and plastering wet kisses all over her face, and his anxiety about his relationship with her increased with each passing second.

He and Naomi set the table, put the food, including what she'd brought, in serving dishes, and placed it on the table. Her reaction to his heated look showed her pleasure at his obvious approval.

"You actually cooked greens and baked sweet potatoes?

Do you know how crazy I am about collards and sweet potatoes with fried chicken? Did Jewel tell you?"

Her shy smile told him that his comment pleased her. "I've never spoken with Jewel. I just thought it would be nice to have it."

Four little fawnlike eyes gazed up at them. Rufus looked down at his children and had a ridiculous urge to search them. There were times when they seemed to have special knowledge enabling them to sense any change in his emotions. He dismissed the thought, glanced back at Naomi, and caught her struggling to replace with nonchalance the passion he'd glimpsed in her. He flicked an index finger beneath her chin.

"I want to kiss you, and I'm going to."

"But the children…"

"They already got theirs," he said, heedless of his previous concern. "Now, I want mine." He touched her lips with his own in a brief, sweet kiss, intending to make it chaste. And he would have if he hadn't sensed in her response a need as strong and compelling as his own. What had come over her? He stared at her in amazement. She had moved away when he'd attempted to deepen the kiss, the first time she'd broken his kiss. He looked down at his boys; she'd shown concern for them in a situation where she'd never shown any for herself. Had he been completely wrong about her? He sat down at the table, said grace, and began to eat, but his mind was not on the food.

Naomi watched Preston and Sheldon indulgently as they devoured the greens, sweet potatoes, and fried chicken. Sheldon indicated that he'd like to have it again. "That was good, Noomie. You coming back tomorrow?"

She saw Rufus's back stiffen. "No, Sheldon. But I'll come see you some other time. All right?" She pulled an apple pie out of the other bag and earned the undying gratitude of all three Meade males.

The boys had been put to bed over their strong objections. "They're usually more cooperative than they were tonight," he told her, stretching his long legs out in front of him as the flames flickered in the great stone fireplace. "They know I get more work done when they cooperate, and they take pride in contributing to what I do. I show them how much I've written, but lately, Preston has taken it upon himself to criticize my progress." Rufus smiled. "He doesn't think much of five or six pages for half a day's work. Thank God, Sheldon is kinder and fattens my ego every time Preston takes me down a peg."

Contentment warmed her as she watched him, captivated by the love in his eyes. She stored in her memory the honeyed tone of his voice as he talked about his precious children.

"I'd give anything to have grown up surrounded by that kind of love," she said wistfully. "And I hope I get to experience it just once." She leaned back and sipped her cool coffee. Rufus remained silent, as if comprehending that her words were to herself, that she had not meant to share such private thoughts.

"Grandpa tries; he always has, but he and I are the products of two vastly different eras. I try to remember that."

His penetrating and compassionate look aroused her need to feel his arms like steel bands around her, but she glanced away. Sometimes, she thought, he seems to be looking into my very soul. As if realizing that she was reaching for something deeply personal and beyond his means to provide, he leaned toward her slowly, seeming to fear disturbing her.

"Naomi, will you come over here, sit beside me, and lay your head on my shoulder?" He spoke in a low, gentle voice, as if trying not to break her mood.

"What?" He smiled and held out his hand. But she had snapped out of it.

"Why can't you come over here?"

"I didn't want to seem threatening and you...I was just being a friend."

Naomi looked at Rufus with new eyes. Was there a chance that he had enough room in his heart to love one more person? To love that person just half as much as he loved his boys? She quickly shifted her thoughts from that dangerous path. "I'd better be going; I have a few things to do at home."

He had been looking at her, and she supposed that her need was mirrored in her eyes. "Don't run away, Naomi. You don't need to be alone just now, and I'm here. Lean on me. Just this once, let me take the weight of what it is that burdens you."

She wished she could put out everything, that she could just open up and let it out. Let go of the awesome weight that had been suffocating her for nearly half her life. If he loved her, she might have a chance finally to live a normal life, to love a man and let him love her, because only a man who loved her deeply would understand and accept. Rufus wasn't that man; he was judgmental and unforgiving. She was never going to meet one who would willingly share her awful burden, and she wouldn't risk exposing herself to rejection and maybe even scorn for something over which she'd been too young to control. She glanced up, saw him watching her, and plastered a bright smile on her face.

"Really, Rufus, you're imagining things. I've got to produce a draft design for a milk carton, that's all."

Discouraged by her refusal to trust him, he stood and helped her to her feet. The backs of his fingers scraped through his short, curly hair, and he began to speak slowly, his tone grim.

"Stop fooling yourself, Naomi. Until you admit the importance of whatever it is that you fear, your life won't be what it could be, what it should be. If you face it, you'll move mountains to straighten it out. And you'll find the strength to do it. I know. Come on; I'll walk you to your car."

He'd sworn to himself that he would have her, but he wondered now if the price wouldn't be higher than what he was willing to pay. She carried a lot of emotional baggage, maybe too much. Yet he couldn't help wanting to protect her, to banish the gnawing anxiety that he sometimes sensed in her. But neither could pretend to be undisturbed by her attempt to belittle what they felt for each other.

She gloried in the security of his hand holding hers as they'd walked, but he hadn't kissed her good night, and she went to bed empty and lonely. Her conflicting feelings—her need for Rufus and her longing to know her son—gave her a feeling of hopelessness. Why did it have to be one or the other? And why had she let herself begin to yearn for the love that she knew Rufus was capable of giving? A love that she hadn't known existed until she had seen him with his children. And she wanted the gentleness that she knew he possessed. But somehow, she had to know her son. Maybe, if she could see him, talk with him just once. She didn't want to hurt him or his family in any way. Thinking of that made her question whether she shouldn't stay away. Confused and uncertain, she wondered if she was ready for a clean break from Rufus, giving up One Last Chance, and possibly inviting ruinous public exposure. It was nearly daybreak when she finally fell asleep.

Several evenings later, the One Last Chance board of directors nominated Naomi as its delegate to the National Urban Alliance convention in New Orleans. She had never been there, hadn't been a convention delegate, and had no idea what was expected of her. She fretted about it, then tucked in her pride and called Rufus, who was an NUA officer.

"I'll call you back in a few minutes," he told her. She decided he'd made a power move, but she couldn't blame him. Her behavior with him had been anything but consistent.

He returned the call after half an hour. "Your call surprised me; how may I help you?" She winced at his coolness and forced herself to assume a casual demeanor as she told him of her board's decision, but she wouldn't let him see how his coolness had affected her.

"I've got a lot of material here that might help you. I'll sort through it and bring it over tomorrow night after my own board meeting, if you'd like." His tone was impersonal.

"What about the boys?" She wanted him to bring them, even as she savored the idea of being alone.

"Jewel keeps them overnight when I have a late meeting or another engagement."

You mean when you stay out all night, she thought, feeling a cold tightness in her chest.

"Tomorrow night is fine with me. Thanks, Rufus." She didn't know how to hang up and just held the receiver and said nothing. He, too, seemed unable to break contact. Nervous and ill at ease, Naomi resorted to flippancy, thought it lacked her usual bite.

"Just think, if you'd been as reluctant to hang up on me once before, we probably never would have met."

"I didn't hang up on you." He paused briefly. "Did I?"

"Yes, you did. When your Ivan-the-Terrible temper roared out of control, you said a few cutting words and hung up."

Rufus chuckled, but his deep voice sounded more like a growl. "I've got better manners than that, lady."

"I know. That's one reason why we got acquainted."

"What's another one?" He considered why he enjoyed needling her; a twenty-minute conversation with Naomi when she was at her devilish best could brighten his life for days.

"Your ego's big enough, Meade." She was sorry as soon as she'd said it.

"There ought to be a law against suppressing compliments."

"Well, there isn't," she giggled. "Let's count to ten and hang up."

Rufus laughed. "The last time I did anything like that, I was in junior high. See you tomorrow night. One…"

Rufus left his desk, walked to the window, and looked out at the bare trees. There was something calming about winter scenes; nature was at rest, but you knew that new life would soon emerge. Would it happen to him? When Naomi had telephoned him, rather than talk with her then, he had elected to call her back, giving himself time to get his emotions under control. The sound of her voice had sent his heart racing. Bringing the material to her was a ploy; he could have told her what she needed to know by phone. But he had held his breath while he waited for her answer.

He spent the better part of the next day prowling through his house, eager for the night when he would see Naomi. Around three o'clock, exasperated with himself, he packed the boys in the minivan and drove to Louella's. Lou let them in the tradesman's entrance at the back. He sat on a high stool and helped her clean string beans for the dinner crowd, while the boys watched *Sesame Street*.

"What's wrong, hon? Why aren't you working?" He should have known that she wouldn't let him escape her motherly interrogation, but he felt too raw for a discussion of his feelings.

"I thought I'd bring my boys over to see you."

"Not in the middle of a workday. How's Naomi?"

He laughed. Trust her to cut to the chase. "You old fox.

She's fine, as far as I know, and she's driving me crazy."
Louella sat down beside him and wiped her hands on her checkered apron.

"If it doesn't come easy, hon, just let it go."

He pulled at his chin and looked into the distance. "I can't."

Louella draped an arm loosely around his broad shoulders. "But from what you told me, she's everything you don't want. So what's the problem?"

"The problem, Lou, is that she is also everything I *do* want. *Everything.*"

Louella sucked in her breath, got up and padded over to the sink. "Then you'll just have to decide whether you'll be more miserable with her or without her." He stood and began putting on the boys' coats.

"I don't have to decide. I know."

The camaraderie that Naomi and Rufus had shared by phone the previous evening didn't seem to ease their discomfort when Naomi opened the door. It was like the first time. Excitement coursed through her when she looked at him. They stood there, caught up in unwelcome longing. The clock that had belonged to her mother chimed nine times; by the ninth, his face had formed what she recognized as a forced smile.

"Usually, when someone opens a door to me, I'm told to come in, and that's what I do. But every time I come here, I wonder if you're going to let me in." He walked in without waiting longer for an invitation, raised his free hand as if to caress her cheek, but quickly withdrew it.

"Have a seat." She put her trembling hands behind her. Why had she agreed to this meeting when she knew that being alone with him in her home might be a disastrous move? He remained standing, looking at her intently, the only sound the ticking of the clock.

"Please, sit," she repeated. His response was a half smile. "After you." He gave her the folders, explained the registration procedure and how to get the best rooms, told her of the more interesting committee appointments, and cautioned her about the political maneuvering.

After thirty minutes, he rose to leave, tired of the strain that being with her imposed on him. She had been careful not to dress provocatively, but his desire wouldn't have been less feverish if she'd been wearing sackcloth. He didn't have to see her in sexy clothes to desire her; he just *did*.

"I'd better be going." She didn't respond, but her look of disappointment told him that she didn't want him to leave. He looked at her mass of thick, curly hair hanging around her shoulders, and the way her navy slacks and mauve-pink sweater outlined her tall, slim body and shook his head.

"Why couldn't you be somebody else?" He hadn't meant to say it, but she'd spoken simultaneously and hadn't understood.

"I wish you'd brought the boys; I'd love to see them. They're really special." She was trying to prolong his stay, and both of them knew it.

Rufus wondered how much truth there was in her statement. If only he could... "They ask about you," he heard himself say, though he hadn't planned to tell her. "It's odd, because they hardly ever ask about Jewel, and they know her so much better." He shook his head slowly. "I can't believe they'll be four on Thursday." He leaned against the wall, and his voice became softer, deeper, almost musical. "They want me to keep their birthday until Christmas and let Santa Claus bring it."

Naomi laughed that joyous liquid laugh that always made his spine tingle. "I'll bet that was Preston's idea."

He creased his forehead, wondering how she knew. "Yes,

it was. I'm surprised at how well you understand their personalities and the interplay between them. My brother-in-law has such a problem with their identities that it's their greatest pleasure to play tricks on him. Jewel's the one who tells them about Santa Claus." He straightened up, began to pace, and stopped right in front of her.

"Don't you?" she asked in a shaky voice, betraying to him her struggle not to lose her composure. She clasped her arms where they joined her shoulders and looked at him through half lowered lashes, but he reined in the desire that threatened to erupt. His gaze remained steady, probing, but he answered her as if there was no tension between them. As if he hadn't jammed his hands into his pockets to keep them off her.

"I don't lie to my boys. Not ever. When they ask, I tell them, 'that's what people say.'" He hesitated. "Well, I've got to be going." But he didn't move. He stood still right in front of her, a breath away, looking deeply into her wide, revealing eyes. He knew she was in a turmoil that matched his own. Her eyes adored him, and he stared at her in wonder, mesmerized. Was she as soft and as sweet as she sometimes seemed? Like right now?

"Naomi, I...Naomi!"

"Rufus!" She was in his arms, sobbing his name. And she wilted when his lips found hers in a kiss that was almost feral in its consuming power. Drugging. Humbling. When he finally eased his lips from hers and looked into her dazed eyes, he knew there was a decision to be made, and made soon. Where were they going?

"We can't be platonic friends, Naomi. It isn't possible."

"I know."

"So I guess I'll see you in New Orleans." He still held her to him.

"Who'll keep the children? Jewel?" He detected a hopefulness in her voice and wondered at it. Did she think he'd leave his boys with a casual friend? He smiled inwardly. Or did she think him a philanderer? He grazed her cheek softly with the knuckle of his right hand.

"Yes. I know she'll take good care of them."

Her pensive manner didn't fit with her soft sexiness of moments earlier, and her next words told him why. "Do you mind if I see them for a few minutes Thanksgiving Day, since it's their birthday?"

Rufus released her, shrugging first his left shoulder and then his right, uncertain as to how he should respond. A glance at her face told him that a negative reply would crush her. "Of course. Just call first; we might be over at Jewel's house."

Jewel Meade Lewis answered Rufus's phone. "Happy Thanksgiving. Who's calling?"

A chill went through Naomi. He had told her that she was the only woman he was kissing, but maybe he'd been joking. If not, then maybe he had lied, though that seemed out of character. Well, what did she care? She didn't doubt that Rufus wanted her, and wanted her badly. Let this woman, whoever she was, do the worrying. Nobody intimidated Judd Logan's granddaughter.

"This is Naomi Logan. I want to speak with Mr. Meade, please." She made her voice sweet and seductive, almost a purr.

"Naomi! How nice to speak with you. I've been wanting to meet you. The twins talk about you constantly, but my brother is too tight lipped to satisfy my curiosity. Come on over. We'll wait for you, then we're going over to my place. How long will it take you?"

A steamroller—that's what she was, Naomi thought. But she felt too relieved to resent it and agreed to get over to Rufus's house in twenty minutes.

Rufus opened the door, and the twins were right behind him. He looked at the two huge, gaily wrapped boxes and the single small one before glancing inquiringly at Naomi.

"Don't worry, it won't hurt them." The boys greeted her warmly, and she discovered a kindred soul in Jewel. Her gifts of giant pandas and a video game featuring them enchanted Preston and Sheldon.

"Come and have dinner with us, Naomi. Can you stay?" His eyes beseeched her.

"I'd love to," she replied, attempting to hide the eagerness in her voice, "but it depends on what my grandpa is doing." A call revealed that Judd was being fêted by the sisters of his church and had wanted her to join them. But when he learned that she would be with Rufus, he seemed happy to excuse her. She wondered whether his eagerness to pawn her off on a man hadn't helped to cement her vow to remain unattached. His domineering behavior could also have been a factor. If Judd had been different—less obstinate, more loving and tender—would she be more willing to risk loving a man, to believe that a man's love for her could be so powerful that he would trust her with his happiness? That he would overlook her liabilities?

Naomi wouldn't soon forget her dinner with the Lewises and the Meades. She liked Rufus's sister. Jewel took her in hand immediately and effortlessly made her feel like a family member, as if she belonged. She looked around at the large Duncan Phyfe table laden with food, the country curtains, and the homey touches that gave the room its lived-in character. She noticed that although the table was formally set, neither Jewel, Jeff, nor Jeff's parents had bothered to dress. Rufus, too, wore casual attire. The twins and their two cousins, aged six and four, each said a line of grace. The dinner was a traditional one of corn chowder, roast turkey, baked ham, stewed turnip greens, candied sweet potatoes, boiled tiny white onions, a dish of raw vegetables, buttermilk biscuits, and pumpkin pie.

She entered eagerly into the camaraderie that flowed among them during the meal. Many different levels and kinds of love flowered in the small group, and the knowledge of it thrilled her. The children talked among themselves, the adults to each other, and above it all, a state-of-the-art sound system reproduced the voices of Marian Anderson and Paul Robeson singing spirituals, folk tunes, and operatic songs while at the peak of their vocal powers. Judd had always preached that you weren't supposed to talk while eating; a mistake she concluded.

Exclaiming that the meal was an example of the best in Southern cooking, Naomi asked Jewel, "Were you born in the South?"

"No. We were born here, in the District. Our mother was born in North Carolina and our father was from Virginia. But Mom wasn't much of a cook, Southern or otherwise." Naomi detected a preference for another topic in Rufus's change of expression. Jewel must have noticed it.

"Come on, big bro," she chided, "don't be a stick in the mud."

"What's a stick in the mud?" Preston asked.

"It's a real sweet man who gets his wires crossed," Naomi answered, without giving the matter much thought.

Jeff, Jewel's husband hooted. "Looks to me like things have evened out. There's another sharp-edged tongue at this table today." The bantering continued through desert, and Rufus gradually rejoined the fun, but Naomi knew that her question had cast a temporary pall over the gathering: Rufus had seemed pained by the reference to his mother.

Rufus left his children with Jewel while he drove Naomi back to his house to get her car. She was nervous and a little anxious about being alone with him; each time they were together, her attraction to him became stronger, less manageable. And she was weakening in her ability to focus on his certain reaction to the factors in her past that he would never accept. *But I like being with him.*

At the expense of displeasing him, she risked mentioning his mother. "I'm sorry about your mother, Rufus. And I'm sorry for some of the things I said in those notes I wrote to you before we met. I…Rufus, what happened to your mother?"

That she'd brought it up, knowing how he would react, sent a strong message to him: her action wasn't motivated by curiosity. He looked straight ahead into the clear, starlit night, his mood deeply pensive. For a long while, he said nothing. But Naomi didn't fidget or appear anxious. She simply waited, and her calm soothed him. Comforted him. A woman with enough patience to let a man weigh his words carefully before he uttered them was to be prized, he marveled, and wondered how she had developed it.

He told himself not to resent her question, that she had spoken to him of his mother because she felt something for him and needed to know him. He pushed aside a rising annoyance; Naomi was asking of him what she refused to give.

"Naomi, my mother was in a two-engine jet prop plane between Kumasi and Accra in Ghana, and it crashed." He closed his eyes and his lips tightened. How could the pain be so severe after sixteen years?

"At first, I got angry with her for risking her life to get some ridiculous chocolate recipes for a book on cocoa. And then I cried. I still can't forget how I missed her when I was little, because she had to work to take care of our invalid father, Jewel, and me. And I missed her when I got my degree, when I was named Super Bowl MVP, when my children were born, and when my marriage broke up. I wanted Mama to share my glory, and when Etta Mae left, I needed Mama to help me understand why I didn't hurt, why I couldn't make myself care."

He glanced down at the woman beside him. "Well, you wanted to know. I won't apologize for spilling it; once I started, I couldn't stop."

Naomi moved closer to him and settled for a hand on his right arm. He let her console him that way, though she said nothing, and he was glad; words were not what he needed.

After a while, he continued. "My memories of my father prior to his accident aren't very clear. I do know that he became an invalid shortly before Jewel was born. I was seven then. Mama once said that when Papa was healthy, he was a man among men and that she would love him forever. As an adult, I understand why she was away so much, but as a child, it hurt and I resented it."

Naomi squeezed his hand and spoke softly. "Jewel seems to have come to terms with this."

It amazed him that Naomi could get such a keen understanding of people after having been around them only briefly. His sons. His sister. He wondered if she understood him, too. "You're very perceptive." He looked to his left, as a speed demon drove by. "None of this affected her as it did me, mostly because Jewel had me from birth. And I told myself when she was born that I would take care of her, protect her from loneliness. And I have. Still, Jewel makes certain that she doesn't duplicate Mama's life; she has an old-fashioned profession and old-fashioned attitudes about home. Even her house is old-fashioned. It's Jeff who's modern. He shares the housework and child care with her. They're happy because they're a team. They think of each other and of their children before they consider themselves. Jewel is a devoted wife and mother, and last year she received the PTA's annual award as outstanding teacher. I'm proud of her." Naomi moved closer to him so that their bodies touched and, deeply affected, he accepted the gesture for what it was.

"Jewel is very likeable." While he drove through the night, she searched his facial expression as though trying to gauge his mood.

He shrugged. "Most people think so. She also likes to try to run my life, even though I'm seven years her senior."

"You shouldn't begrudge her the effort; I'm sure she just tries out of habit."

"What does that mean?" He wasn't certain of the implication.

"I'm trying to think of the kind of person who could tell you what to do, and when and how to do it." She explained. "Nobody comes to mind, except perhaps your football coach, and I'll bet you gave him a hard time. Nope. I don't think anybody could run your life; you wouldn't stand for it, and Jewel knows it."

He relaxed his bruising grip on the steering wheel, relieved that she hadn't reacted with one of witticisms. Why had it been so important to him that her comment not be flippant?

"I'm not so difficult, Naomi, and I don't think I'm overly sensitive. But I've had some experiences that I don't intend to have again. And I'm going to do everything within my power to see that my boys are spared what I went through. I used to sit up until all hours and wait for Etta Mae to come home. I would have met her after work, but she never knew what time the crew would finish the shoot. If she got a coveted assignment, she was happy only until she heard that another model had gotten a better one. It was an obsession; nothing else and no one else mattered. In the end, it destroyed our marriage." He eased up on the accelerator and took the car slowly up Hillandale Road on a meander through Little Falls Park and the beautiful surrounding neighborhood.

She wanted to get still closer to him. It was the first time he'd spoken to her that way, and she felt a new kinship with him. Finally, unable to resist, she pressed herself against him, and, as if warmed by her gentle caring, he turned into Wellington Drive and stopped the car.

"Why are you stopping?" She knew that if she commented on his disturbing revelations, he would withdraw and the mood would be destroyed.

Rufus turned to her. "I'm leaving you in your lobby tonight, because if I get past that, I'll be in trouble." He didn't soften it with a smile.

"I'll keep you out of trouble; trust me." She wished she could believe that, but she failed to convince even herself.

"Yeah, I know, Just as you always do." His voice held a hint of amusement, enough to remind her exactly how little immunity to her he had. He braced his right elbow on the backrest and rested his head in his hand.

"I've never had such a puzzling relationship with anyone, female or male. You and I have a great deal in common. We like each other…well, most of the time we do, and we want each other. *All* the time, I'd say. You know, there are times, Naomi, when I feel in my gut that you're right for me, that something really good could develop between us. But there are other times when I doubt that, when I'm positive I don't know you at all, that something important about you is hidden somewhere. And that it's hidden intentionally."

She had been looking at him, listening intently, and getting the uncomfortable feeling that she had already lost her way. She was going to hurt and hurt badly no matter what she did.

"But I don't…" she said aloud, and stopped.

"Don't what? Don't hide what matters most?"

She shook her head and tried to divert him. "You've said a lot in those few words, Rufus; I'll have to consider what you've said. I want to give you honest answers, but you want me to think about things that I've been unwilling to address."

He rested his arm lightly around her shoulders. "Am I ever going to know who you are, Naomi?"

She raised her left hand to his face, acting innocently, motivated purely by her need to touch him, to show him some tenderness, to communicate the deeply compassionate nature that she so rarely allowed him to see. He looked down at her as she caressed his jaw with featherlike touches. "It seems we've both had difficult lives," she said, almost in a whisper, seducing herself with the intimate gesture of stroking his face. "If I get all the answers and if we're still friends when that happens, I'll share those answers with you."

"I want to believe you. Why don't you try trusting me? I won't disappoint you. Believe me, I know how it feels, Naomi, when someone you care for lets you down, when you find that you can't depend on that person." She'd seen him wicked, serious, angry, and in other moods, but he had not previously allowed her to see him in a state of such heart-rending vulnerability. Suddenly, his carefully sheltered need was exposed and she could see the man who'd missed out on the strong parental attentiveness that he'd craved as a child, and who had seen his dreams of his own happy family and graceful home dissolve into bitterness.

She didn't think; her arms stole around his neck. She leaned toward him, and without the least hesitation, he met her with an urgent, hungry kiss, crushing her to him. Everything that had gone on between them throughout the afternoon and into the evening had been leading up to that moment, when his stifled groan told her how much he needed her. Instinctively, she drew him closer to her, kissed his stubbly cheek, his closed eyelids, his chin. She couldn't say the words, knew even in her passion that she had better not say them, but her every gesture said, *I adore you.*

They sat silently, entwined in each other's arms, buried in their separate thoughts. Finally, he reached into the back seat and got a beautifully wrapped rectangular package.

"Open this after you get home," he suggested, almost diffidently she thought. "I hope it'll be okay."

She looked from him to the gift and started to speak, but he shushed her.

"Please accept it, Naomi. If it isn't all right, I'd like you to exchange it for something that is." She took it graciously, her heart pounding; what was the meaning of it?

Naomi hated to think of Marva as her mentor, but she admitted that she turned to her friend whenever she had a serious problem, even though she invariably ignored Marva's advice. She drained her coffee cup and glanced around her friend's new kitchen. Marva had been observing her closely, adding little to what had passed for a conversation between them, and Naomi knew Marva had noticed that she lacked her usual verve.

"How are things between you and Cat?"

"The same. And why to you always call him 'Cat'? I don't like that name; it's not him. Cats are stealthy."

Marva chuckled and, embarrassed, Naomi shifted her glance as she realized she was being protective of Rufus.

"You're getting to be too sensitive," Marva told her, in a voice laden with censorship. "You don't seem willing to match wits and just do girl talk anymore. Why won't you talk?" She propped her chin up. "You like him a lot; you know that, don't you?"

"Yes. I know it. It's time I got back to work; I'm not at leisure, like you are." She quickly collected her handbag and the portfolio that she had brought along in order to test Marva's reaction to her ad campaign layout.

Marva laid a hand on her arm. "You're not yourself,

Naomi, or at least, not the person I think I've known. I've realized for a long time that you have secrets, important ones, but I thought you'd come to terms with whatever those secrets were about. Lately, there seems to be something tearing at you; everything is forced. Your smiles, your laughter, even your humor is forced. Your smiles, your laughter, even your humor is forced, and it's been more and more noticeable since the gala. Get on top of it before you drown in it. You won't talk to me; can't you confide in Cat?"

Marva was only five foot three and had to reach up to put her arm around Naomi's shoulder. "I was certain that after the way the two of you danced that night, you'd have become very close by now. Let him love you, honey," she drawled. "It'll change your whole world; your big problems will get smaller; work will be easier; even the stars will be brighter. Believe me." Her laugh was rich, throaty, and knowing. "And that's just for starters."

"Thanks, Marva. But Rufus is only part of the problem. I'll call you." She wanted to get out of there; nothing was as simple as Marva claimed. She had a husband whom she adored to share her problems and to hold her at night. When a load got too heavy, she could just hand part of it to him. I can't look forward to that, she reminded herself as she started her car, with Rufus or any other man. *And if the stars don't get brighter, that'll just be my tough luck.* She drove to her studio and buried herself in her work; it didn't help.

Naomi got home late that evening, out of sorts and hungry. She went into her bedroom to change and saw the present from Rufus that so far she hadn't had the courage to open. She made coffee, heated the rolls and roasted Cornish hen she had brought in, and sat down to eat with the beautifully wrapped box beside her plate.

I'm being silly, she told herself, and opened the box with

shaky fingers to find a pair of green leather dress shoes that were remarkably similar to the ones she'd told him about. How had he guessed that she wore size 9B? And why had he done it? She thought about it for several minutes and decided that he had wanted to make up for something missing in her life; the shoes were merely a symbol. She slipped them on. They were a good fit and matched the green Chinese silk dress. Her heart lurched as she looked at them. She longed to telephone him, but decided against it, fearful that her raw emotions would betray her. Instead, she wrote him a thank-you note and signed it, "Love, Naomi."

Three evenings later, Rufus walked out of the OLC building and into its back parking lot, a place that he disliked, especially at night. With the simple act of walking through a door, he was transported from a progressive environment to the profusion of crying children and blaring radios and televisions that emanated from the neighboring apartment buildings. He walked swiftly over the buckled pavement and stopped, all his senses alert. With the help of the overhead lightbulbs that shone from the unshaded apartment windows, he could see in the twilight three figures in animated discussion a few feet from his car, and he was certain Naomi was one of them. He moved stealthily closer and leaned against the wooden fence that bordered the lot, ready to defend her if necessary. His eyes became accustomed to the near darkness, and he recognized first Linda and than a young man. Their words drifted to him.

"Naomi, I'm not doing anything wrong. What's wrong about my going to a party?"

"You're going against your mother's orders, Linda, that's what's wrong. You're getting involved with the wrong crowd, and this man is too old for you. And why do you need an overnight bag just to go to a party? When you find yourself in trouble, you'll regret this night as long as you live. I know what I'm talking about. Look around you. Isn't this the environment that you're trying so hard to escape? Well, it's the one you're headed toward, if you go through with this. I know you're hungry for love, Linda, but you won't find it tonight. Wise up, honey, before it's too late."

Would Linda go off with that man and leave Naomi standing there after she'd pleaded with her? And where was the man's common sense? Linda was a minor. He made a quick decision, rounded two cars, and stepped between Linda and her friend.

"You'd better be careful, fellow. This girl is fifteen, and you're at least twenty. Don't you know that if you touch her, you could get a jail sentence? What's your name?"

"My name is Rodney Hall, Mr. Meade," the man told him, surprising Rufus that he was recognizable under the dim lights. "And Linda told me she was eighteen. I don't hang out with underage girls; that stupid I'm not. Linda's real nice, and I like her, but I sure thought she was older. Looks like I'm in your debt, man." He turned to Linda. "Stay out of trouble, kid, it's rough out here in the streets." Rufus watched Rodney walk away, hands in his pockets, his shoulders hunched. Better to be disappointed, he thought, sympathizing with the man, than to face a jail term.

Rufus had some questions to ask Naomi. Her involvement with Linda was personal, he'd swear to it. She identified with the girl as though they were mother and daughter. His conviction about the strength of their tie deepened when Naomi attempted to embrace Linda and the girl responded by turning away, seeming to sulk.

He sensed Naomi's disappointment in Linda and thought, unhappily, that she'd have preferred that he hadn't witnessed that scene, which seemed to have left her shaken. But he had, and he wasn't leaving that lot until she did.

"Hello, Naomi. Linda. It's just six-thirty. Would the two of you join me for a soda or coffee? I can't suggest dinner, because I have to get my boys in about forty minutes." Both declined. He turned to Linda and winced when he saw tears streaming down her face. She must have been deeply hurt or embarrassed, for she dropped her head and turned her back to him.

He walked around to face her. "Rodney may be a nice guy, Linda; I don't know. Whether he is or not, you shouldn't have deceived him. Don't lie to a man about your age. You could ruin his life, and you'll almost certainly ruin yours if you settle for a one-night stand." He regarded her intently.

He didn't like the silent treatment he was receiving from Naomi, who was behaving as if he wasn't there, as if she resented his interference. He walked over to her and reached for her arm, but she backed away, almost stumbling over the uneven pavement.

"I'll see you to your car, Naomi." What had he done to make her behave as if he was poison? He reached for her hand. "I take it you're driving Linda home, so you two come on. I'm not leaving you here in this back lot in the dark, Naomi, and you know it," he growled. After she drove off, he got into his minivan and sat there, letting the motor idle. He'd just been given a clue to who Naomi was, and he didn't know what to do with it. Maybe he should have asked Linda whether she and Naomi were related. Naomi hadn't seemed like herself. She hadn't wanted him to touch her, and she'd barely said a word to him. He was more puzzled than ever.

An hour and a half later, Naomi sat down to a cold supper of fried chicken, baked sweet potato, and milk. She had driven Linda to her home at North Capital and P Street. Not the worst neighborhood, but close, and waited until the girl was inside her door. Had she herself been that naive fourteen years ago, looking for love in the wrong place? She thought back to the scene in the OLC lot. To leave the lot, you either went back into OLC or through the gate and into the dark alley. If Linda had gone through that gate with Rodney, there'd have been no turning back. Naomi marveled that such a gifted, intelligent girl had given no thought to the consequences. Was the need for love so powerful? Did she need Rufus like that, and did it explain her attachment to Chuck?

She answered the phone after its fourth ring. "Hello. I'm busy; may I call you back?"

"In that case, why didn't you just let your answering machine say that for you? If my boys weren't in bed, I'd invite myself over. Could you call a taxi and come over here? That way, I can at least be responsible for your transportation. How about it?" She thrilled at the sound of his deep, masculine voice, but she couldn't talk with him or see him, not when she felt so raw. She'd been through the wringer once tonight, and she wasn't going to subject herself to Rufus's inquisition. She didn't know how much of herself she had exposed to Linda, nor what he had heard. But Rufus was like a master agent; nothing escaped him, and he always got what he went after. She stalled.

"Well, what about it?"

"I'm eating dinner. I'm tired, and I'm going to bed. If you called about Linda, I saw her safely to her door."

"I didn't call about Linda; I called about you."

She leaned her left hip against the table and contemplated the probable effect of telling him that she didn't want to see him anymore. None, she decided. "Rufus, we'll have to discuss me some other time. I'm going to turn in." *Don't lie to a man, Linda.* She hadn't lied to Rufus, but she hadn't told him the truth, either, and she felt as though she was caught in her own trap. He had wanted to protect her when they were in the OLC lot, but she couldn't allow it. If she ever began to depend on him...

"There's no point in trying to run from your problems, sweetheart," he said, getting her attention. "Like the man in Samarra, when you get there, whatever's chasing you will be waiting."

"I don't want to see you tonight, Rufus, and I took Philosophy 101 almost twelve years ago."

"You told Linda to wise up. You wise up! *You* send a man a note and sign it, 'Love,' and the next time you see him, you behave as if he's a leper. And you accused me of being inconsistent. Maybe we'll run into each other in New Orleans. Good night, Naomi."

She replaced the receiver and threw out the rest of her dinner. There were times when he made her truly happy. And then, like now, she could be miserable because of him. She wished she'd never seen him, and she wished she didn't have to go to that convention in New Orleans.

Chapter 9

When she arrived at the registration desk of the conference hotel in New Orleans, Naomi saw that Rufus had just checked in and was deep in conversation with an attractive blond clerk. Of course, the little blonde doesn't care that fifteen or twenty of us are waiting in line to register, Naomi thought crossly. He hadn't noticed *her,* and it was just as well, she figured; her feelings for him just then were anything but friendly. Distasteful was more like it. She recognized the sensation as one of jealousy and soothed herself with the thought that jealousy was as natural and spontaneous as yawning. She laughed softly at herself, but loudly enough for Rufus to hear from a distance of five feet and turn toward her. Sweet, feminine triumph flowed though her when he immediately smiled at her, the pretty registration clerk evidently forgotten.

He greeted her with a captivating smile. "Hi. We should have taken the same flight."

Still slightly miffed at the pleasure he seemed to have been getting from his conversation with the pretty clerk, she replied grumpily, "Why didn't we?"

"Good question. Probably because if you'd wanted us to travel together, you'd have answered the messages I left on your machine yesterday morning." He shoved his luggage aside, and a middle-aged woman immediately sat on it, nodding an apology toward him.

A delicious little quiver darted through her chest. At least he'd called. "It wasn't deliberate," she explained. "That machine has been giving me problems. I didn't get your message." Then, feigning disinterest, she slipped into her old pattern of behaving differently from the way she felt. "Don't let me keep you from your little blond friend over there."

He laughed heartily, and she knew he recognized her annoyance as a cover for jealousy and that it pleased him. "You could have called me and suggested we fly together," he reprimanded. "It isn't etched in stone, as you like to say, that between the two of us, I make all the calls."

She didn't want to give up her annoyance; it was a good defense against the fevered turmoil into which seeing him had plunged her. She couldn't seem to move her eyes from his full bottom lip that always looked inviting—hard and tender at the same time. He raised his hand to rake his fingers over his hair, and her gaze fell upon his strong, tapered fingers, those pleasure giving digits. She could almost feel them stroking her. Her glance rested on his face, and she had an urge to run, because she knew he'd read her thoughts.

He winked, and her recovery was swift. "I'm glad to know that a nineteenth-century guy thinks it's okay for a woman to invite a man to join her on an out-of-town trip," she told him, falling back on flippancy.

"I thought we'd gotten well beyond the stage where you cover your real feelings with sarcasm," he told her, as a grim look settled over his face. "Say what you really mean, what you feel, Naomi, even if it embarrasses you. At least you'll know you were honest."

"I've never been dishonest with you, Rufus." She tried to look past him in an effort to hide from the accuracy of his assessment. "I may not tell you everything you want to know, but I don't lie to you." He stood before her, self-possessed and comfortable with himself, his tall, sinewy bulk blocking out everything and everybody else from her vision, the same way thoughts of him had begun to crowd other people and things from her mind.

He's taking over my life without even trying or wanting to. Why should I be defensive, she asked herself, looked up into his shadowed gaze, and was stunned by what she saw. He regarded her with a look that seemed to say he adored her soft sepia beauty, and she quickly shifted her eyes from his. When she glanced back at him, she was solemn. "Talk's easy done; it takes money to buy land, my grandpa always says. You try facing your personal problems head on and being honest about them even when it might knock you from your pedestal. Try it, I'm going up to my room now; maybe I'll see you later this evening."

Naomi started past the huge marble columns to the elevator and stopped when she heard a man exclaim, "Cat Meade! It's been years, man. What's happening? How's the old clavicle? Still holding together?" And while she waited for the glass elevator to arrive, another and still another old friend greeted him joyously. One of them inquired, "How you doing, man? Who was that fox I saw you talking with just now?" Naomi didn't hear Rufus's reply, but she managed to get a good look at the hopeful smiles of several women and the bright welcome of others who stood in the ornate reception area waiting to register. It was Cat Meade's world, and it seemed as if everyone around wanted to be a part of it. She could have been proud, but he hadn't given her the right to take a personal interest in him. Nor had she decided that she wanted that right.

When she reached her room, the phone was ringing. She let it ring. Her gaze took in the soothing beige and blue decor, and satisfied with the room, she began to unpack. The phone rang and she relented; who but Rufus would be calling her? She knew, too, the reason for his call. With his bulldog tenacity, he must certainly be a great journalist. She tried to remember what she might have said to set his curiosity juices flowing.

"Hello."

"Naomi, could we get together either in your room or mine for a few minutes? I want to talk with you, and we won't have any privacy in the hotel's public areas. Say, twenty minutes?"

"Twenty minutes suits me. We can talk here, and I'll order some coffee and a couple of sandwiches. Is that all right?"

He agreed, and she ordered the food, unpacked, and sat on the edge of her bed waiting for him. Naomi knew she had to solve her dilemma, and soon; the effect was crippling her and maybe others as well. What did she feel for Rufus? She wasn't ready to name it, but she admitted that she couldn't even contemplate not having him in her life. She had avoided involvements successfully for over thirteen years. No longer; Rufus had changed that. And there was her son. Before she'd known that her child's adoptive parents were trying to find her, she'd hidden her experience of motherhood. But she knew now that she could see him, and wouldn't rest until she did. Maybe she could even get to know him and explain that she hadn't wanted to give him up, that she'd been pressured, that she'd been a child herself.

She had to know ether he or his family needed her. That meant breaking all ties with Rufus and his children, because

Rufus would see in her every fault that he'd found with his wife and his mother, and he would coldly scorn her. She was probably going to damage beyond repair the reputation and credibility that she had worked so hard to establish. Leaving One Last Chance would be one of the most onerous and prophetic penalties of all. Well, she rationalized, she would still have her work; commercial artists needn't be identified. *If only she was sure that she was ready to face it all.* From royalty to servitude in a single step; in matters relating to the morals of women, the African American upper and upper-middle classes in Washington, D.C., were unforgiving. Naomi sighed. Well, so be it.

She answered his soft knock. One look at him and she knew the conference wasn't on his mind. He didn't waste a minute. "What are you facing that can knock you off your pedestal, Naomi?" The precision with which she had described her dilemma registered with her then, and her own carelessness and the accuracy with which he had divined the meaning of her words shocked her.

"I was talking about you, not me. You're the one with the public acclaim and adulation," she bluffed.

"But I don't have any personal secrets that could knock me off my pedestal. Your words. So what were you talking about if not something pertaining to yourself?"

He paced the richly carpeted floor. "Sometimes, Naomi, when you're in my arms, you electrify me; you wipe out every pain—real or imagined—that I've ever had. Sometimes, when you're so giving—the way you were Thanksgiving night—I feel as if I'm just beginning to know what life is about. At other times, like now, you make me feel hollow inside, because you're not being straight with me. I know you feel something for me, and it's deep. But you're afraid to trust me with your feelings, your secrets, or your pain."

He grinned unexpectedly. "Have it your way, sweetheart; you're not indebted to me. You can say what you want and do as you damned please. See you around." The grin hadn't covered the dismal expression she'd seen on his face and been powerless to wipe away.

The doorbell rang and she rushed up the three steps leading to the foyer to answer it, thinking that he might have had a change of heart and returned, but it was the bellboy, wheeling in a linen-covered table on which were two elegant place settings, two carafes of coffee, two sandwiches, the standard pickles, and a bill for forty-one dollars, tax included. She paid the bill and sent him away, along with the overpriced fare.

She stood in the middle of the richly decorated room, at a loss, looked around, and saw the package of materials that Rufus had so carefully assembled for her. She could…her shoulders drooped; she could do what? She wished she had been better schooled in the ways, wants, and needs of the modern male. Nonagenarians? She could give a seminar on those. Naomi laughed at herself. She could be miserable, or she could telephone Rufus and talk with him. Anything, just as long as she had contact with him.

While she dialed, a niggling voice demanded: why are you doing this? Either you walk away cleanly or you take a chance, trust him, and tell him everything.

"Meade." Was he really as impatient as he sounded? She drew in her breath and identified herself.

"Why did you call me, Naomi?"

Truth. Tell him the truth, her common sense preached. "I just wanted to talk."

"*What?* I just left you. What changed your mood? That is, if it's changed."

"Rufus, I've…I've avoided entanglements since I was… well, most of my adult life. I've avoided them because I can't commit to a lasting relationship, and I have wanted to avoid hurting anyone or getting hurt. You sneaked up on me." His silence cut her.

"Actually, I was calling to ask if we could go to the dinner dance together, unless you're going with someone else." He still hadn't responded. "Well, if you'd rather not talk…I'm sorry I disturbed you. But you did say that I had a right to invite you out, even across state lines, and this is just a matter of getting on the elevator and going downstairs."

"Cut it out, Naomi," he growled. "For just this once, if you're hurting, for God's sake, let it show. If you need me, damn it, tell me! *Tell me!*"

She uttered a deep, labored sigh and whispered, "I need you."

"I'll be right there."

She hung up and had to fight the tears. *Oh my Lord! I love him. I love him.*

He had been coasting, taking it as it came, because she had become important to him, and he couldn't will himself to walk out of her life and stay out. Not until ten minutes ago. He had meant what he said. But because he cared, he would open his ears and his heart and listen to her.

He stepped into the room with arms open, and she melted into them eagerly and expectantly. But he didn't intend to precipitate a torrent of desire between them. He wanted them to understand each other, to communicate at a meaningful level, so he crushed her to him and quickly stepped away.

Her discomfort was evident, and he understood the emptiness, the yearning for completion that her demeanor communicated to him, because he also felt it. When she tried by gesture and stance to deny it, throwing her head back and smiling a forced, vacant smile, he shook her shoulders gently.

"It's okay to need, Naomi, and it's okay to need *me*." She

leaned toward him, but he stepped away, determined that they should speak with clear heads. He had never attempted to bring about a meaningful understanding between them because he hadn't decided that it was what he wanted. And his indecision stemmed partly from her deliberate efforts to prevent him from knowing her real self by throwing up screen after screen whenever he got close. But he was no longer going to accept any shamming from her—not if he recognized it. And he was going to find out what they meant to each other and why she could burn up in his arms and then downplay the relationship whenever it suited her.

She looked at him openly, letting him see that she hurt. "You say it's all right for me to need you, but you don't mean it deep down, and it's just as well. You and I *both* know that I'm not what you need; I've got a career that I love, and you can't tolerate that."

A note of censure laced his voice, irritation evident, as it usually was when anyone second-guessed him, but he pushed his annoyance aside. "Shouldn't you leave that to me? I'm more than capable of deciding who and what I need and what I can tolerate." He leaned against the door and stuffed his hands in his pants pockets, out of reach of temptation. "And let's get this straight: I never said I couldn't tolerate career women. What I said, in effect, was that women who place their careers *before their children and their family* risk impairing the welfare of their family, and especially their children. If you had listened to the entire program, and if you had read my books all the way through and with an open mind, you'd know that I also emphasize the man's role in family disorganization and adolescent delinquency. So stop misquoting me. And let's get back to the subject." She seemed to relax, and he gained the impression that she was considerably relieved by his explanation.

Her eyes held an expression of longing as she gazed at him. "Rufus, I'm trying to tell you that I don't have anything more to give." He regarded her intently, sensing that insecurity was at the root of her insistence on their incompatibility. If she'd allow their relationship to follow its natural course, she'd discover that they had plenty in common. He didn't have much hope for that, but he had to persevere for his own sake.

"I know you feel that way," he told her, "and you may even be right, but sharing changes things."

"What do you want, Rufus?"

Was he having a hearing problem? She couldn't possibly be serious. "I want you, Naomi. Beyond that, I don't know. And I won't know until you give us a chance, until you let me know who you are. You took a big step when you called me, and also when you told me that you have problems that complicate your life, limit your options."

"I said that?"

"In effect, you definitely did. And you told me that you need me; as long as you do, Naomi, I'll be here for you." Etta Mae hadn't needed him, but for all her posturing and clever tongue, Naomi did, and so did his boys. And they could rely on him as long as he had breath and strength.

He watched Naomi carefully, already sensitive to every change in her. "Don't close yourself off from me, Naomi; I'm not going to hurt you. And promise me you'll stop concealing your emotions behind clever comments. Why do you do that, anyway?"

He stifled the desire that coursed through him when she raised her left hand and brushed aside the unruly hair that nearly hid her left eye. "Is that what I'm doing? Well, you met my grandfather. Can you imagine being indoctrinated by him from the age of seven, when he was already seventy-three? At least twice a day he told me to control myself, that tears were unacceptable, and that you didn't let other people see any weakness in you. He even discouraged my showing him any weakness."

He nodded. "Yeah. I guess he would do that; he was too old for such responsibility." Mention of Judd reminded him of their torrid dance at the gala.

"Do you really want me to accompany you to the dinner dance?" He gazed quizzically at her, purposefully mischievous, his white teeth framing a deliberately roguish grin. "I shouldn't think you'd be willing to risk dancing in public with me again."

"Why not? I may even repay you. I think I'm entitled to that, don't you?"

"Depends. I'll look forward to it." He draped an arm loosely around her shoulders.

She snuggled closer. "Depends on what?"

"As with most risks in this life," he explained solemnly, "whether you should gamble depends on your willingness to live with the consequences." He felt her tremble and held her to him. Then he noticed the quiver of her lower lip and was puzzled as to why she should be nervous. What was it? He had a driving desire to protect her. But from what?

"Sometimes, we have little choice." Her voice seemed small and came to him as if from a considerable distance.

He shushed her. "When you're ready to tell me everything, to trust me, Naomi, we'll work through whatever it is together. Don't dribble it out; I don't think I could handle that."

She leaned closer, as if unconsciously borrowing his strength. "I don't understand, Rufus. Why are you bothering? A smart man wouldn't invest any of himself in me when he's been warned that a serious relationship is out of the question."

"I've already invested a lot of myself in you, and whether

or not you admit it, we've been in a serious relationship almost from the time we met. I finish whatever I start, and I've started something with you. I don't fish often, Naomi; I've never cared much for the sport. But when I do catch a fish, believe me, I don't throw it back into the water." He glanced at his watch. "I'd rather not leave you right now. It's poor strategy to walk out of a negotiation when it's going your way, but I'm chair of a committee that's meeting in twelve minutes."

"Is this going your way?"

"It's going *our* way, Naomi. You're talking to me and you're listening with more than your ears." He squeezed her to him, lifted her chin, and searched her eyes. She glanced shyly away, but what he had seen satisfied him.

"You have something to give me, Naomi, something that's real, and I want it." He kissed her then, quickly, gently, and possessively.

"You can't just ignore what I've been telling you, Rufus: I'm not for you; I can't be. *I just can't!*" But he sensed a wavering of her resolve, as he held her firmly but tenderly by the shoulders and let his gaze roam over her lovely coffee-colored face and her long, curly black tresses before seeking her eyes. It was her eyes that had first captivated him. Dark eyes. Large, wistful eyes that spoke silently of her innocence, her pain, and her longing. Eyes filled with mischief. Eyes that sometimes said, "I hurt." And eyes that could grow dark and sultry with hot desire. He had a sudden impulse to take her and go somewhere, anywhere, where he could have her to himself, but it was a fleeting urge; he was not ready to make a total commitment to her, though he was far from certain that he never would be. She had become more important to him than he would have thought possible even a week earlier.

* * *

Naomi lowered her eyes under his intense appraisal, and he was glad that she seemed to misunderstand his mood. "There's no place for us to go, Rufus; I think we ought to stop seeing each other." He didn't have to be clairvoyant to know that those words had caused her pain. But she laid back her shoulders, raised her chin, and smiled tremulously. God! He admired her!

He quirked his left eyebrow and summoned what he considered his made-to-order noncommittal grin. "You know, it never occurred to me that you might be daft, Naomi." The grin swiftly vanished, and he projected a serious, almost severe mien.

"Can that idea, sweetheart. Don't even dream it. I'll meet you in the coffee shop at eight o'clock." He tipped her chin up with his right index finger and studied her, trying to see beyond what she was showing. Then he tangled his fingers in her thick hair, gave her a quick kiss, and left her standing there, speechless.

After a while, she moved, dreamlike, to the balcony and stood fingering the glossy green leaves of the magnolia tree that thrived there in a large wooden tub. Restless, she stroked the satin-smooth wooden arm of the swing as if it had human properties, as if it were Rufus, then sat down and stared at the floor. She needed to get rid of the load she was carrying, to talk to somebody. But to whom? Rufus had said he'd be there for her. She put her flat palms on her knees and tapped her fingers. She wanted to believe he'd open his heart to her and give her a place that she'd never had, a place where she could leave her anxieties, her heart's wounds, and her inner turmoil, but she didn't think any such man existed. Besides, Rufus couldn't even contemplate what a mess her life was.

She thought of the prizes at stake and wanted to take a

chance. Then she remembered the penalties. She hadn't ever let anything beat her down, and she wouldn't now; she had made her choice, and she'd stay with it. She had to know her son.

Chapter 10

She needed nerves of steel to walk into that huge, crowded banquet hall with Rufus Meade. The commotion he'd caused at the registration desk should have warned her, but she had foolishly asked him to accompany her. Too late, she told herself. All I can do is look my best. And she did. When he greeted her with a sharp catch of his breath and a nod of approval, she was satisfied that her efforts had produced the effect she'd wanted. Rufus insisted on holding hands with her as they entered the hall, but she tried to hold back, claiming, "People will think we're a couple, Rufus."

He acted as if he couldn't care less; he was a man at ease with the choice he'd made. "Fine with me. I don't let what people might think dictate my behavior, Naomi. I believe in pleasing myself whenever I can." She looked first at him, handsome and elegant, and then at the admiring looks that they received, and she couldn't help being proud and squeezed his hand almost involuntarily.

He looked down at her. "When a man has a woman like you, he wants every other man to know it." She bit her tongue. He has said that she should stop covering up her emotions, so she didn't joke about it and she wouldn't ask him what he meant.

Instead, she winked at him and drawled, "We women like to show off when we're with a great looking guy, too." She laughed disdainfully. "We're being just a little too polite for my taste, Rufus. You look terrific, and I'm enjoying the jealous stares these women are giving me." Rufus grinned, and she could see that her comment pleased him.

The fresh fruit cup, chicken à la king poured over flaky pastry shells, green peas, and potato croquettes had been pushed around her plate, and the tricolored three-layer coconut cake had been rejected. Naomi sipped her black coffee and consoled herself with the thought that at least she would lose some weight. The speeches that were somehow the same every year no matter what the occasion or who delivered them were over. People—mostly women showing off their expensive gowns—were table-hopping in order to be seen, and the band members had begun taking their seats on the bandstand.

All through their forgettable standard banquet meal, Rufus had quietly watched Naomi, responding to her rare remark and wondering how she could let long stretches of time pass without saying a word or seeming bored. She didn't feel compelled to talk. He admired that in her and hoped it meant she was comfortable with him. She slanted him a sly smile, and he felt it from his toes to his fingertips. He reached for her hand.

The band swung into its third number, and he squeezed her fingers. "Dance with me?" She moved with him in a slow waltz until he switched to a sensuous one-step, sending her heart into a wild flutter, and she danced a little away from him.

He nudged her closer. "I thought you'd planned on getting revenge. You won't get it dancing a mile away."

Her nose lifted in disdain. "It wouldn't be in good taste to bring you to your knees right here in front of all these people, especially since most of them are your fans."

Rufus angled his head to one side and drawled provocatively, "Say what you mean. You're afraid of falling into the trap you were going to set for me. Go ahead, lady; work your magic." He grinned at her and goaded, "I'm immune." He wasn't and knew it, but what the heck? He got a thrill just from looking at her; if she wanted to do her thing that ought to be something to watch.

The band began a livelier number, and behind Rufus, Naomi saw a couple spinning and gyrating in the earthiest, sexiest dance she had ever seen on a dance floor. It would serve him right, she decided, and took up the challenge.

"Wait until the band plays something earthier," she promised daringly.

He pulled her a little closer, held her there, and taunted, "It'll be my pleasure." As they walked back to their table, a light, carefree mood enveloped her. She hadn't known that their sexual teasing could be so much fun. Happiness. It was wonderful.

The music began, and she leaned toward him. A frisson of fire shot through him at the gentle squeeze of her delicate fingers around his wrist and the provocative glint in her eyes.

"This one."

Surprised, he rose and held out his hand. So she wants to dance a cha-cha, he mused, and swung into the seductive rhythm. He relished moving to the hot, pulsating beat, dancing it off time, taking one step for every two beats of the drummer's stick. Heat suffused him in response to her seductive movements, the slow, tantalizing undulations of her hips, and the provocative invitations of her hands as she tossed her head from side to side in wild abandon.

Caught up in the storm of passion that she ignited, mesmerized by her frankly sexual gestures, he suddenly ceased to tease, and his mood for it deserted him. Blood roared in his head when she gazed at him dreamily, obviously half drunk on him and the music. Her words were almost slurred.

"Had enough?"

His lower lip dropped. The she-devil! "Yeah!" he gripped her to him, wanting her to feel his strength, to revel in his maleness. He took control of the dance, placing her left arm on his shoulder and her right hand around his neck. He held her to him and moved in a sensual step, the cha-cha forgotten.

Rufus came slowly out of his trance when he recognized a tap on his shoulder and glanced around to a man who was asking to dance with Naomi. He scowled ferally; some of those movers and shakers belong to another era. Let the guy find his own woman.

"Man, you must have left your mind back there in your chemistry lab," he threw over his shoulder. Then he looked down at the woman in his arms. "You want to dance with this guy?"

She moved closer. "What guy?" When a second man wanted to dance with Naomi, Rufus glared at him and stopped dancing. Then, without a word, he led her from the dance floor and out of the hall.

Standing with him in the anteroom, she folded her arms and grinned mischievously. "Aren't you supposed to yield when a man taps you on the shoulder?"

"You're putting me on." He couldn't appreciate humor right then. "Some of my fraternity brothers have a weird sense of humor. Yesterday afternoon, Watkins expressed a lot of interest in…what was that he called you. Yeah. 'That little fox,' I believe he said. Then he had the temerity to try busting up my dance. I've seen the day when I'd have made him pay for that stupidity." Rufus laughed inwardly. He saw no need to tell her about the times during his university days when he had cheerfully done the same to Watkins.

"Which one was Watkins?" she teased. His eyes must have reflected his murderous feelings, because she winced.

"You don't need to know. Would you like to go to Corky's and dance? Or to the Maple Leaf? There're a lot of live jazz spots on Oak Street. Or we could go to Preservation Hall and listen to some Dixieland." He let his hand caress her shoulder. "Tell me what you'd like."

"I'm hungry. Let's go around to the cocktail lounge and have some wine or something. Maybe they'll serve hors d'oeuvres with the drinks. That dinner was awful."

Rufus grimaced. "Make that 'something.' I had a glass of wine with dinner. Besides, there's an old Ashanti proverb that says, 'When the cock is drunk, he forgets about the hawk.' And with all these hawks here tonight and half of the wives back at home, I need my wits." She drank white wine and he sipped Perrier while the cocktail pianist plodded along.

He wanted to please her, but he'd had as much as he could tolerate. "Want to go to Preservation Hall?" he asked hopefully. "This brother needs to go back to music school." She got a light stole and they took a taxi to St. Peter Street, but when they stepped out of the car, Rufus glanced around at the revelers, music makers, and crowds of onlookers, and the idea of a hot, noisy, and smoke-filled room held no appeal.

He took her hand. "Let's walk a bit. It's a pleasant night, or it would be, if we could get out of this crowd."

"Okay. The next time I'm here, I want to go down to the levee. Maybe some warm summer night. The Mississippi

should be prettier at night in the moonlight, when you can't
see how muddy the water is."

"It isn't summer, but it's balmy and the moon is shining.
We could get a taxi and go down there now. What do you
say?"

"How'll we get back?"

His arm slinked possessively around her waist as he hailed
a passing taxi. "I'll have the taxi wait."

"Where you want to go ain't exactly across the street," the
driver explained. He turned up his radio, and they heard a
great rendition of *Jelly Roll Blues* as the taxi sped toward the
levee. At the river, Rufus faced the water and Naomi stood
with her back to him, enveloped in his arms. Her conscience
pricked her; she wasn't leading Rufus on, she told herself.
She just wanted to be with him, to push aside even for a little
while the problems that plagued her. She fought the temptation to worry about her future; this was her night, and she
was going to be happy. As if reminding herself to enjoy the
moment, she began to sing softly *As Time Goes By* in a rich
throaty alto.

Rufus didn't speak until she'd finished. "You have a lovely
voice."

"Of course I have," she threw out. "Don't you know that
all black folk are supposed to be able to sing?" They both
laughed, but Rufus cut his laughter short, and she knew immediately that it was because she had done it again.

"Naomi," he asked grimly, "couldn't you simply have said
thanks? Was it necessary to belittle the compliment, to pretend that it was inconsequential? Stop shielding yourself from
me." He tightened his arms around her in a protective gesture, and she rested comfortably against him as they communicated in a way that didn't require speech. The silence
enveloped them, a full moon brightened the sky, and a fresh

breeze swirled around them. Heaven must be something like this, she thought, as the voice of a nightingale pierced the night.

They didn't speak for a long time, and she savored his nearness, relished his strong arms around her, and had to fight the urge to face him and lose herself in him.

"Have you ever been in love, Naomi?" Immediately she wished she hadn't mentioned wanting to see the levee by moonlight. The scent of anything approximating a mystery piqued his interest, and there was no stopping him until he had the answer. She tried to think of a way of distracting him. But the full moon, fresh southern breeze, and mournful saxophone coming from a barely lit vessel that moved eerily and slowly downstream practically guaranteed that his mind would not waver from her.

"Have you?" Emotion colored his low, husky tone. "Look at me. I asked whether you've ever been in love." He took her face in his palms and gazed into her eyes, but with the sweetest, most loving expression she had ever seen on a man's face. She trembled with sensuous anticipation and excitement at his powerful, wordless communication. She should move, but she couldn't. She should remind him that nothing could ever come of their relationship, but she couldn't part her lips. His slow smile lit his eyes, transformed his mouth, and made his handsome face glow.

"You still haven't answered me. Don't you know?" He removed the scarf that had begun to dangle from her shoulder and draped it snugly, but attractively, around her neck, taking the same care with her as he did with his boys. Her heart constricted at his gentle gesture. Why was the forbidden always so desirable?"

It would have been easy to reply with a quip, but she knew he didn't want that and wouldn't accept it. And she didn't want to respond that way, so she took a deep breath and decided to trust him with the truth.

"I don't know the answer, Rufus, and I wouldn't want to... well, I just can't say." She wasn't going to lie, and if she said yes, he would want to know who. She couldn't tell him that she loved him; maybe she never would.

He pulled her to his side. With her nonchalant façade and outward calm, only someone close to her would ever guess she was so vulnerable. He pulled her closer, wanting to shield her from whatever it was that she seemed to do constant battle with. He had the cool Louisiana breeze in his face and a sweet woman in his arms and he was... *Damn!* He was out of his mind! Or was he fooling himself? Maybe. But he had to know her, what she felt, what hurt her, what made her happy, who she had loved, and what he had to do to make her want him, and everything and everybody else be damned.

Why did she resist answering even the simplest question? He had to persist. He'd do it gently, but he'd get it. He was on the verge of falling for her against his good judgment and his repeated advice to himself, and it worried him. But if she had loved once, maybe he could teach her to love again. "Did you care deeply for him?"

Her answer was a startled stare, the look of a deer caught in the rays of high-powered headlights. He didn't need the words.

"Whoever he was, he was a fool not to have kept you with him forever."

She relaxed, and her sigh of relief was so powerful that he felt it. "I did care," she said in a guarded tone. "Or at least, I thought so then."

"What happened to make you question it?" He had the disquieting feeling that she was hedging, and he was certain that she didn't want to talk about it.

She looked into the distance, and after a moment, spoke

as one who carried a tremendous load. "Time and age." *And you.* The light in her eyes dimmed, and she leaned toward him unsteadily.

"Sweetheart, what is it? I told you that I'm here for you, and I meant it." She didn't answer, but raised her parted lips to his. She's what I want, what I need, he thought, when she clasped him to her, asking for more, taking him with her into a torrent of desire. When he was finally able to, he stepped back from her, shaking his head from side to side, running his fingers through the tight curls at its base. At some other time, he might have been amused, but there was nothing humorous about what he felt and the dilemma in which it placed him.

"Naomi, I'd bet there isn't another woman on this earth who starts the kind of fire that you do and never gives a thought about what will happen once it gets going. Honey, I'm in trouble here."

"What does that mean?" She snuggled close to him; talk about fires was clearly of minor interest.

"It means," he explained indulgently, "that I'm human, and one day we're going to exceed my capacity for control."

She chuckled, obviously unconcerned, and teased, "If you lose it, we'll work something out."

His eyebrows arched upward. *"What?"* She continually astonished him; surely she wasn't that innocent.

She seemed to throw away all caution. "Now, now! Don't get your dander up. You told me to trust you, and that's what I'm doing."

"Naomi, I am trying to have a serious discussion with you. Would you please not joke?" Sometimes he thought she might be playing a game. She couldn't be as naive as she seemed, could she? It was near the end of the twentieth century, for heaven's sake; how could such a beautiful woman insulate herself to the point that she knew practically noting about men? *And why would she do it?*

Her voice came to him as if from a distance, disturbing his worrisome thoughts. "You're right, I guess. But I already told you that I haven't had too much practice with this kind of thing. Give me time."

He was about to probe dangerously deep when he remembered Judd Logan's words: *"It's been almost fourteen years since she let herself get as close to a man as she was to you last night. And I know that for a fact."* Naomi forestalled any comment that he might have made by drifting into a soft hum of Duke Ellington's *Solitude.* As she had no doubt hoped, he let the matter of his self-control drop. And there, beneath the Louisiana moon, he opened he jacket of his tuxedo, got as much of her in it as he could, wrapped her close, and began a slow one-step on the bank of the Mississippi.

He disliked ambivalence in himself. After such an evening with a woman, he'd have expected them to spend the rest of the night together. And he was tempted, almost eager for it. But he needed more from her than what he was certain would be mind-shattering sex. He wanted total communication, all of her. The problem was that he didn't know for how long, only that he needed it. When had he come so far, and how? When she was soft and loving, like now, he never wanted to leave her.

She commented on the eeriness of a dingy lit barge that chugged down the river with the help of a ghostly tugboat. A hoarse horn warning an approaching vessel had broken the night silence and their mood. He looked down at her comfortably settled in his arms, but seemingly oblivious to her effect on him, and he wondered how he made her feel. His mood changed, and she eased out of his arms.

"Maybe we should be getting back. That taxi driver probably thinks we've decided to spend the night." She stumbled. "There goes my shoe heel." He checked, saw that it was broken, lifted her, and began walking toward the taxi.

He held her closer when she shifted in his arms and demanded that he put her down. "I may need help, as you impressed upon me on more than one occasion," he reminded her, "but at least I know how to accept it when I get it. You've got to learn how to accept help—and compliments, too—graciously. I'm not putting you down. You can't walk if one shoe has a three-inch heel and the other is flat." He opened the door and put her in the taxi.

"You're attentive, and I like that, but I don't want to be suffocated," she mumbled grumpily. He sensed that she was distancing herself, putting her emotional barrier back in place, and he was getting tired of it.

It was best to tell her good night in the hotel lobby. He wanted to spend the night with her, but he didn't want to have to pick his way through her minefield of personal conflicts. And he had a choice of that or settling for physical release, something he rejected. Both of them deserved better. Rather than deal with the heat he knew would consume them if he walked her to her door, he'd just look up some old buddies. At the elevator, his kissed her quickly and left her.

He changed his ticket so that they could fly back to Washington together. Even after the two-hour flight, she was still withdrawn. He instructed the taxi driver to take her home first. At her door, he told her that he would be away for a week or ten days.

"I have to go to Lagos, Nigeria, to get material for a magazine piece that I agreed to write. I could have refused, but not without some backlash. I won't see you again before I leave, but I'll call you."

Her surprise was evident. He knew that her mental wheels were busily turning and that she would reach the wrong conclusion: he hadn't hinted about it during three days in New Orleans, when they had been together almost constantly, nor during their flight back to Washington.

Her response wasn't what he'd expected. "What about Sheldon and Preston? Will they stay with Jewel?" He shook his head in dismay. Why in the name of God did she cling so tenaciously to her rigid self-control?

"Yes. Of course." He leaned casually against the door. "She takes good care of them, but…I don't know. I hate to leave them again so soon, especially to go out of the country. I like to be here for them if they need me." His voice trailed off.

"When will you leave?"

He studied her carefully. Did it matter to her? She was behaving as if their relationship was entirely impersonal.

"Day after tomorrow. I have to get back before Christmas." He continued to look at her for a good while and would have walked away, but she stepped closer, grazed his lips slightly and quickly with her own, and whispered, "Come back safe—and soon." He kissed her then, turned, and left. But a keen sense of dissatisfaction enveloped him. His own feelings were more ambivalent than they had been the night before, while they'd held each other on the bank of the Mississippi. He knew that was partly due to Naomi's coolness. She was baffling. Their relationship was baffling. He was convinced that it was in his best interest to stay away from her, but he didn't seem able to; he was drawn to her, and the pull was unlike anything he had experienced with any other woman. But she would swear that there could be nothing between them, and in less than five minutes, she could be in his arms, heating him up until he wanted to explode. And you're no better, his conscience nagged at him. Maybe by the time he got back from Nigeria, it would be out of his system. He laughed derisively; there wasn't much hope for that.

* * *

Naomi unpacked, put her soiled things in the laundry, and went to the refrigerator to see what she could find for dinner. Was there another like him? A man, a quintessential male who enjoyed nurturing his small boys, who fretted about leaving them in good care only for a week? Didn't he see in his own dilemma what his mother must have faced countless times?

"I'm not going to think about Rufus," she told herself adamantly. She wasn't sorry that she had gone to New Orleans, nor that they had gotten close to each other while there. But she wished she hadn't let him know that she cared for him. She hadn't been able to help herself. When he had indicated that he was fed up and left her, she'd thought she'd never be with him again and had weakened. And she *had* needed him. Then he'd walked back into her hotel room with his arms open and gathered her to him, and she had felt for the first time since her mother's death that someone cared for her and wanted to protect her.

He claimed that his shoulders were big enough for whatever burden she was carrying and that together they could work through any problem she had. All she had to do was open up her soul to him, tell him about her mistakes, what hurt her, the dilemma she faced. He didn't want much—just for her to lay her heart on the line and give him proof positive that she wasn't what he thought, so he could turn his back and crush her heart. I'd rather have a broken heart and his respect than to have his scorn *as well as* a broken heart, she told herself. I was right all along; there's no place for him in my life.

Chapter 11

Sleep didn't come easily for Naomi that night. The decision she'd reached was a troublesome one, but it was time to put order into her life. She got out of bed before sunrise and waited impatiently until she could telephone Judd's lawyer. He didn't welcome her call nor the information that she had followed him and had been policing the Hopkins house. But she got what she wanted from him: the boy did not attend school out of town, but worked after school and on weekends. Sitting in front of the house, waiting for him to come home from school, had been a waste of time.

She switched tactics and began morning surveillance. On the second day, she saw him just as she drove up. Her heart pounded painfully as she watched him jump off the porch onto the walkway and breeze away on his in-line skates with his book satchel on his back. He was tall for his age, as she'd expected he'd be, and had his hair cut in the style of a Mohawk warrior. She couldn't see his facial features, except for the café-au-lait complexion that he'd inherited from his father, along with towering height; but she didn't doubt he was hers. She couldn't doubt it; every molecule in her body had reacted to him. She tried without success to steady her hands on the steering wheel, and for an hour, she sat there trying to summon enough calm to drive home.

Her spirits lifted when she found in her mailbox letters from chairs of fine arts departments at three universities, each asking for more information about Linda. The girl's sketches had impressed them, and their carefully worded letters allowed Naomi to hope that Linda would get the training her talent warranted.

Naomi's attempts to work proved a waste of time. Disconcerted, she intermittently pondered what to do about her son or sat catatonic-like, stunned by the proof that she had a child almost as tall as she was. She noticed the flashing red button on her answering machine and played her messages back without really listening to them—until Rufus's voice pierced her dim consciousness. "I'm sorry you weren't able to return my call last evening and that you had to leave home so early this morning. I'm on my way to Washington National Airport. Take care." She replayed it three times. No goodbye. No "See you when I get back." Nothing. A bottomless, piercing ache dulled her insides, and she knew that its only cures—her son and the man she loved—were out of her reach. She swallowed the bitterness, stood up, and looked around her. Her bedroom appeared to be the same; so did her hands when she glanced at them. But nothing was the same, and it never would be again. The whole world had changed. She had a boy who was at least five feet eight inches, and she had never touched him. She took a deep breath and steadied herself. "I'll be damned if I'll cry."

* * *

Two mornings after that, Naomi stood by a window in her studio, painting a winter scene from a photograph that she had taken in Rock Creek Park the previous winter. Realizing that she had absentmindedly juxtaposed on the scene of pristine white snow and evergreen shrubs the shadowed silhouettes of a man and two small boys, she put her brush aside and threw the canvas into the wastebasket. "Just like I'm messing up my life." She answered the telephone reluctantly to hear Jewel ask the unthinkable and the impossible.

"I can't do that, Jewel," she pleaded. "I can't keep Rufus's boys. He'd never forgive you. Things aren't good between us, and they aren't going to get any better." But she finally acceded to Jewel's request. With her husband hospitalized for a ruptured appendix, Rufus's sister couldn't care for her own children, and since the boys wanted to stay with her, she reasoned, she couldn't refuse. Jewel couldn't leave them with a stranger. She lost the battle with her conscience and her heart.

"I don't have room enough here, Jewel, so you'll have to let me stay at Rufus's house with them. He won't like it," she warned again.

She had her telephone calls transferred, got some crayons and a small sketchpad for the children to use, packed a few personal things, and left. At the elevator, she stopped and considered taking her work with her, thought better of the idea, and continued on her way. She was unprepared for the boys' joyous reception; they danced, laughed, and smothered her with hugs and kisses. She knelt and held them in her arms, her heart lighter with the feeling that she was no longer so alone and that the horrible ache that had plagued her all morning had dulled and become almost bearable. She closed her eyes and hugged them to her.

Naomi looked up, embarrassed, to find Jewel watching them and knew the conclusion that Rufus's sister had reached.

But she couldn't hide her feelings for the children. Jewel gave her the keys to Rufus's cars and the money he'd left with her and went home.

Naomi packed the happy boys into the back seat of her car, strapped them in, and went grocery shopping. Rufus had obviously taught them to be helpful, because they advised her on brand names, the color of grapes—they always bought green ones—and the size, shape, and color of the milk container, among other things. She didn't believe Sheldon's claim that Rufus always bought them a big bag of candy and ignored it.

She couldn't remember a happier time in her life. She devoted her days to the children, discovering that they loved to draw and to sing, helped them make welcome-home drawings for their father, and plastered them all along the wall for him to see as he climbed the stairs. Rufus's grill was too heavy for her to move out of the garage, so she put together a makeshift one and they roasted hot dogs on the back terrace.

The days passed swiftly, and she realized she didn't want her time with the little boys to end, didn't want to return to her own life, with its web of secrets, uncertainty, and heartbreak. But Rufus was to return the next day, so in the evening she cooked what she knew he liked, got the house in order, gave the boys their bath, and helped them into their pajamas. She read them a story that she had written and illustrated for them. It was about two little boys, their daddy, and a fawn that had wandered lost into their garden. The boys loved the story and had demanded it each night after that.

She had slept every night in Rufus's big bed, rationalizing that she should be near the boys, who had the adjoining room, rather than at the end of the hall, in the guestroom. She loved to read in bed and was enjoying a historical romance when a powerful clap of thunder seemed to shake the house. A brilliant bolt of lightning followed. Thunderstorms made her nervous, but there was no time to indulge in fear. At the second and even louder burst of thunder, both boys came running into the room and tumbled into the bed on each side of her. She got out of bed and turned on all the upstairs lights so that the lightning flashes wouldn't seem so ominous, then crawled back into bed between the twins and decided it was as good a time as any to teach them *Jingle Bells.*

Rufus said a prayer of thanks as the big jet rolled to a stop at Washington National Airport. The trip had been twice as long as scheduled and fraught with peril and near disaster; at one point, he'd wondered if he'd ever get home. An attempted hijacking at an airport in Africa had been tragically foiled; at Heathrow Airport in London, the plane had landed in a heavy rainstorm; and the flight from there to Washington had been diverted to Philadelphia due to the storms hovering over the lower half of the eastern seaboard. It had taken hours to get a plane out of Philadelphia. More than once during the ordeal he had thought of his mother, whose life had been ended while she was on a business trip only a few hundred miles from Lagos. He got through customs quickly, hailed a taxi, and decided to go directly home to get the minivan. Glancing at his watch, he saw that it was eight-thirty, but he wanted to see his boys and he wanted them home with him. Anxiety gnawed at him when he saw that every room on the second floor of his house was brightly lit. No one was supposed to be there.

He unlocked his front door and opened it carefully. Nothing seemed amiss. The storm might have caused a short circuit or something similar; at least, he hoped that explained it. He set his luggage in the foyer and moved carefully into the hallway, where he could see the staircase and the light in the upstairs hall.

Halfway up the stairs, he simultaneously noticed the

childish drawings and clay figures and heard the singing. He bounded up the remaining steps three at a time. They didn't hear him, and he stood unnoticed at his bedroom door and took in the incredible scene. Preston and Sheldon sang lustily at the tops of their little voices, laughing and jumping around Naomi, hugging and teasing her, and she was adoring them, showing them in numerous tender ways that she loved them. He heard her patiently explain to Sheldon that the word was jingle and dingle, then watched her take his little face into the palms of her hands and tell him that he was smart and wonderful and that she "loved him to pieces." Preston sat in her lap, and she cuddled him playfully, and then the boys knocked her backward and the three of them laughed hysterically.

His heart swelled in his chest until he almost burst with joy. Could he be dreaming? It was his house, his bed, his boys, and Naomi. He clutched at his chest as if to stop his heart's wild pound, as if to control the dizzying delirium that sped through him. He loved her. Right there, he knew that he loved her totally, profoundly, and irrevocably. He thought of his reservations about her, his convictions about independent women, his sworn resolve to put her out of his life. None of it mattered. Even his suspicions were unimportant. He loved! For the first time in his life, he loved! He pushed away from the door, his only thought being to get to them and to her and to get them into his arms. Naomi and his sons saw him and welcomed him with shrieks of joy. He gathered them to him and held them, and the boys began talking excitedly, but Naomi only gasped her amazement at his unexpected presence, clearly overwhelmed.

She struggled to detach herself from the aura of unbridled joy that permeated the room. He had so much love to give, and he showered it on his boys. She longed to be a part of it, to belong to them, but she had made her decision and she would abide by it. She watched enviously as he hugged and teased his boys, giving himself to them without reservation. Nearly an hour elapsed before he calmed them and got them to sleep.

"No reading tonight," he told them. "It's already two hours past your bedtime." They didn't want to cooperate, but sleep soon claimed them, and he finally turned his attention to her. She remained in the middle of his bed wearing her cotton ski pajamas, too shocked to be embarrassed. He hadn't been angry, but happy…and almost lighthearted. She got up slowly and reached for her robe, which she'd thrown across the foot of his bed.

"Where are you going?" His voice was low and husky, almost a growl. And there was a tinge of belligerence, too. She looked up at him, wonder if his earlier pleasantness had been a sham.

"I'm going home. Now that you're here, there's no need for me to stay." She backed away a step, almost bumping into a bookcase, when he walked over and stopped right before her. He brushed her cheek with the thumb of his left hand and searched her eyes, and her heart began a furious pounding in her chest. She stifled a sob and turned quickly away. Her heart wanted her to stay with him always, but her head admonished her to remember her son and her vow that he would be a part of her life.

His hand rested lightly on her shoulder. "What happened? I left the boys at Jewel's house." She told him.

"Jeff's recovering from an operation for a ruptured appendix, and Jewel is taking care of him. He's been very sick, but he's coming along nicely. Their kids are with Jeff's parents, and I agreed to keep your boys." He nodded. She hated that he'd found her in his bed wearing dreary, unfeminine pajamas, and that because she hadn't been expecting him, she'd been uninhibited in her welcome. She wasn't certain whether he was pleased to find her there with his boys, and he seemed to sense that.

He took her hand, walked over to the bed, and sat down. "I hope you realize," he said in a warm, reassuring voice, "that if my boys couldn't have remained with Jewel, you're the *only* person I'd have wanted them to be with. They love you, and you love them. I can't tell you how much I appreciate what you've done." She wanted to go home. She didn't want his appreciation; she couldn't let him thank her for the happiness she'd had with his children. She spoke dispassionately, in a detached voice.

"It was my pleasure, Rufus. Please don't take that away by thanking me. I'm glad you're home safe. Now I have to go."

He looked at her and thought of the way she'd been in the middle of his big bed, gamboling with his sons. Thought of the nights when he had tossed in that same bed, wanting her so badly that it pained him. Thought about how much he loved and needed her, needed to love her, to give himself to her. Desire flared in him, but he had promised himself that he wouldn't touch her unless and until she assured him that she wanted him and would never regret holding him in her body. He tried to cool the heat that invaded his loins, but the fire intensified.

"Don't go, Naomi. Stay here...with me. Please stay." He didn't attempt to hide the low shimmer of his voice or the pleading tone that sprang from the pit of his gut. She reached out to caress his face, and the feel of her silky fingers gently soothing him was more than he could bear; he grasped wrist and pulled her to him. "I need you. *Naomi, I need you!*"

She gazed at him as though disbelieving her ears, as if she was afraid to hear his words, afraid that he might be serious.

She glanced up, intending to tell him that she was definitely leaving, and gasped at the naked, vulnerable look of longing on his face. The temptation was so great; she could go home and have all her worries greet her when she got there, or she could stay with him and…and then what? She stood, determined to be sensible.

Then she thought back fourteen years, when she hadn't said no; back more than thirteen, when she'd writhed in pain as a consequence; and back ten days earlier, when she'd thought he was gone from her life forever.

She shook her head to blot out the confusion she felt, but then he said, "Oh, sweetheart, I can't make it like this," and pulled her to him. He swallowed her protest into his mouth, and she trembled against him as his tongue brushed her lips, begging for entrance into the sweet haven of her mouth. She opened to him, and when he thrust into her deeply and possessively, she whimpered and capitulated, pulling his tongue into her mouth and sucking it voraciously until his whole body quivered. She felt him hard against her and held him closer, and when he spread his legs, she moved quickly into the cradle he'd made for her.

Remembering that she never gave a thought to the consequences once her libido got possession of her, he warned her huskily, "Sweetheart, if you're going to stop me, please do it now." If she heard him, she didn't make it evident, but reached up and pulled his head down, captured his mouth, and took what she seemed to need.

"Naomi, for God's sake. Think about what you're doing. I want you. I want the sweet warmth of your body, and I want it badly. I need it. I need *you!*" She brought both hands to his buttocks and pressed him tightly to her. Close to exploding, he pulled up her pajama top and tossed it across the room, picked her up, and fastened his mouth on her nipple. Her uninhibited cry of passion excited and thrilled him, and he lay her on the bed and stood looking down at her, getting himself under control for what was to come. For the pleasure that they would give to each other.

She gazed up at him, silently, searchingly. How could he make her feel as if she were half a person, needing him and him alone for completion? He turned away, and she sat up quickly, suddenly self-conscious and wary.

"Oh, no you don't," she exploded. "You don't do this to me again. You started it, and you're going to finish it…if you can, that is."

Rufus turned toward her, plainly shocked. "You really thought I was going to walk out of here, away from you? And even if I had intended it, don't you know how to make sure that I don't leave this room if you don't want me to?"

She shook her head, embarrassed. Now he knew that she'd had practically no experience. "Where were you going?"

"To hang my jacket on the back of that chair." He pitched the jacket toward the leather-covered wing chair, walked back, and stood in front of her. Gazing deeply into her eyes, he kicked off his shoes, methodically removed his shirt, belt, and pants, letting them fall, and reached for his shorts. Her lips parted, seemingly of their own accord, and her eyes widened. With trembling fingers, she stilled his hand. She had never seen a nude man, and she hadn't dreamed that the male body could be so beautiful and enticing. In a dreamlike state, she licked her lips, reached for his shorts, and began slowly to peel them off him. He jumped to full readiness, and as if charmed by a beautiful snake, she leaned forward and quickly kissed him. His groan sent a hot ache to the seat of her passion, but she slid away when he reached for her and stood to gaze at his male beauty.

"Naomi, love, for God's sake." Her frank, open adoration of his maleness seemed to make him proud and to excite him almost beyond control. Looking at him, tendrils of heat snaked through her, and she reached for the headboard to steady herself as arousal weakened her.

"Baby, come here to me." She didn't move. And it wasn't

fear that held her rooted in the spot, but riveting, searing passion. She tried to raise her lead-heavy arms, but they remained dangling at her side. "Come here," he growled unsteadily. "If you want me, sweetheart, come to me." She took one shaky step, and he reached out and pulled her into his arms, into the first skin-to-skin embrace that she'd ever experienced. Her erect nipples caressed his hard chest, his full arousal pressed against her belly, and she responded like a leaf in a violent wind, trembling uncontrollably. She felt him hold her closer to steady her and then, enthralled by his nearness and his tenderness, she only sensed his fingers grip the elastic top of her pajama bottoms and ease them below her hips, dropping them to the floor. At first, she gasped at the sudden intimacy of their total nakedness, but when he shifted his hips and undulated against her, she eagerly returned the suggestion, lifted her arms to his powerful shoulders and her gaze to the shimmering love in his fawnlike eyes, and gave herself to him.

Her responsiveness had always excited him, and it was balm to his ego that she seemed to think of nothing but him and her feelings whenever he touched her. But her action now told him that she had always held something back, or perhaps what she felt now was different, more powerful; he only knew that she was different. It was as if she was no longer *in* a hurricane, but had *become* the hurricane. He lifted her, removed the pajamas from her ankles, and lay her in his bed. Then he leaned over her and brushed her lips in a kiss that was merely a promise.

"I'm going to lock the door," he told her, remembering how she had reacted earlier when he had turned away. "The boys walk in here whenever they like. You're the only woman who's ever been in this bed, and I don't want them to grow up too fast."

In seconds he was back. "Are you sure?" She nodded. "Tell me that you will never be sorry. Say the words, Naomi."

She raised her arms to him in a gesture instinctive to every woman, welcoming him to her. "I'll never be sorry. It's what I've wanted and needed since the first minute I saw you."

"You're sure?" he asked one final time. "Tell me now."

She gazed at the tender, loving smile that glowed on his face, leaned forward, and pulled him down to her. She might be sorry for a lot of things, she thought, but never this; it would probably have to last her for life. "I've never been more certain of anything. Come to me, now." He climbed into bed and clasped her to him, molding their bodies from shoulder to knee. She felt him strong and hard at the portal of her passion and tried to urge his entrance, but he refused to relinquish control.

"You're not ready for me, love. Just relax; we've got plenty of time." Her breath quickened and her eyelids fluttered closed with the weight of passion at the light brush of his lips and the gentle stroke of his fingers on the inside of her bare arms. Heat surged through her and she felt herself sinking deeper into a spiraling rush of desire as his big hand feathered down her hip and teased the inside of her thigh. She thrashed about as passion overcame her, and fissions of fire burned her wherever the dancing, stroking electric rods that his fingers had become singed her. Unashamedly frantic for his possession, her undulating thighs trapped his hand between them, signaling her readiness for more. He put his left hand beneath her head, covered her mouth with his in a hard, passionate kiss, and found the core of her with his talented fingers.

The intrusion caused her to jerk upward, but her deep sigh of pleasure immediately followed, and she gave herself up to his double assault on her senses. With his bold tongue, he let her know what he planned for her, all the while stroking her to full passion, driving her to frenzied madness, out of her senses. Oh, Lord, where was her anchor? She was a rudderless boat tossing in a raging storm far from shore. She grabbed his hips.

"Rufus, please."

"Please what? Tell me what you want, love. I want to please you."

"I want to please you, too, and make you feel like I feel. Help me." She damned her innocence, her lack of experience, because deep in her heart she wanted to bind him to her and she didn't know how. He stroked her faster, and she lifted her hips, frantic for completion.

He took her hand and closed her fingers around him. "You are pleasing me, and you will. Just relax, love, we'll get there; I promise." A wave of exquisite pleasure washed over her, and her nerves tingled as if wired to electric current when he bent his head to her breast and suckled her slowly and rhythmically while his fingers worked their magic. She cried out and pulled him over her.

"Rufus," she moaned. "Oh, darling, please. I need you."

And she did, he realized, as the warm love liquid flowed over his fingers and she spread her legs in eager anticipation. He thrust into her, but she winced visibly, muffling a cry, and he paused and looked down at her searchingly, trying to curb his passion.

"What happened?" he asked urgently. "Did I hurt you? Talk to me, Naomi. Is this your first time?"

She shook her head. "No, there was one other time, but that was a long, long time ago. I'm all right." Fourteen years ago? he almost asked, and caught himself. He didn't doubt that any such question would have ended it immediately, so he banished the thought and kissed her, holding himself back with difficulty; his control tested to the limit by the loving clutch of her velvet warmth.

He knew that she feared he might end it because he'd hurt her and watched her carefully. She smiled and held him tightly to her while her body adjusted to him.

"Love me, Rufus," she pleaded. "I think I'll die if you don't." Then she reached down and stroked his buttocks lovingly. He trembled in her slim arms, gathered her to him, and began to move. Strong. Possessive. With every powerful stroke, he branded her. You're mine, he told her wordlessly, and I'm claiming what's mine. Instinctively, she wrapped her long, silken legs around his waist and let him lead her.

He wanted to give her everything, to wipe out whatever had been hurting her for fourteen years. He put his hand between them, stroking her, adding the pressure until she begged him for relief. His heart raced joyously and his body shook when he felt her sweet quivers as she tightened around him. With all the control he could muster, he quickened his pace and drove masterfully within her. Stunned by the intensity of her passion, he raised his head and looked down into her emotion-charged face as she cried out his name over and over and fell apart in his arms. Never before had a woman given herself to him so completely, relinquishing all sense of self. It shattered him, and helplessly he gave her the essence of himself in a thunderous release.

Still lying above her, locked within her, he gazed down into her face, looking for some sign that she felt for him what his heart held for her. But he wasn't going to press it; he didn't need to make another mistake. And he hoped to hell that love didn't turn a man into a fool, because if it did, he was ripe for it. He nudged her nose gently with his, wanting to see into her tightly closed eyes.

"Look at me, baby." He tried unsuccessfully to control his gruff, unsteady voice.

Slowly, she opened her eyes and risked looking into his beloved face, risked exposing her heart and soul to him. She wanted to tell him that she loved him, that he was air and breath to her, but if he then asked for a commitment, no matter how small, she wouldn't be able to follow through. She'd done it up this time; not having him was going to be living hell, but she wasn't sorry. She had known the consequences, so she locked her feelings in her bursting heart and merely smiled at him.

"Any regrets?" he asked her hoarsely, with the urgency of one awaiting sentencing. Naomi looked at him and frowned.

"How could I regret it? I feel as if I've just come alive." Then she realized that he was also asking something more.

"It was wonderful," she added quickly. "I never dreamed that a person could feel like that, I…I hope it wasn't one-sided." She eyed him anxiously.

Rufus laughed. "Sweetheart, I have never felt that way before in my life, either. Ah, baby, that was pure soul mating, and it will only get better." He separated from her and reached out to gather her to his side. She was leaving the bed.

"Where are you going?" His voice was calm, she noted, but he was not. She wouldn't let that deter her; she couldn't yield to her feelings.

"Home," she answered casually. As soon as he'd alluded to a future relationship between them, she'd questioned the wisdom of what she'd done. After the cherished way he'd made her feel, she couldn't expose herself, and she couldn't risk a deeper involvement with him without telling him everything; it would be unfair. She had to go, and she had to go right then, before she weakened and crawled back into his arms, back to his warm, strong body that she already craved again—feverishly. "I have to be getting home," she emphasized, wondering how her voice could be so strong.

Rufus couldn't believe what he was seeing and hearing. He lay there with both hands locked behind his head, fear coiling in the pit of his belly. "Let me get this straight," he said slowly in a low, controlled voice. "You make love to me the way you did just now, rocking me out of my senses, then coolly tell me that it was wonderful and you've got to get home. Just like that. As if I was…as if what we did here was just a quick…" He bit his tongue and said it: "Just a quick lay."

Naomi didn't answer him. He jumped off the bed and grabbed her shoulders, feeling them stiffen at his touch when only minutes earlier everything about her, all of her, had been soft and supple, in complete submission.

"Talk to me, Naomi. Is what you had here with me a one-night stand? Something that means so little to you that you can shut me out and just walk off?" He started to squeeze her shoulders in a quest for warmth, for any kind of reaction, but he dropped his hands instead. She still hadn't spoken, and from the set of her chin, and her closed expression, he could see that she was determined to leave. He went into the bathroom to control his temper and to deal with his anguish. Who was she? What was she, and why had he thought that because he'd fallen in love with her she'd be different?

When he came out, she was walking slowly down the spiraling stairs with her small bag. He slipped quickly into a pair of jeans and his shoes, grabbed his short shearling coat, and caught her at his front door. "What will I tell my sons, Naomi? That you've finished with them? That you've taught them to love you, but you're sorry if they mistook what you felt for them as love? What about that? And what about me? Why in God's name did you get into that bed with me?"

She reached for the doorknob, and he could see her lips quivering in spite of her obvious effort to control her emotions. He stopped her.

"Look at me, woman. I am not just so much refuse that you can accumulate and discard at will. You felt something for me, felt it deep down, and you'll never convince me otherwise. What is this all about? Look at me!"

He forced her chin up and looked into her eyes. "*My God! What is it?*" He shuddered. What in heaven's name could be responsible for her ashen face and the gut-searing anguish that he saw mirrored in her eyes before she snatched the door open and slipped away?

He stood silent, arms akimbo, while the noise from her car engine faded until he could no longer hear it. Twenty minutes. Just twenty short minutes earlier, he'd had it all. The woman he loved, who loved his children, and who had thrashed wildly and helplessly in passion beneath him, his name spilling over and over from her trembling lips. She had no control, had been totally at his mercy, and he knew it. Gone!

"Daddy, I had a bad dream." Rufus turned to see Sheldon at the top of the stairs, rubbing the sleep out of his eyes. He mounted the steps slowly, taking in the drawings and clay sculptures that were his children's presents to him. And he could see Naomi's loving hand in it as she'd taught his sons to write, "I love you, Daddy"; "Welcome home, Daddy"; and "Kisses, Daddy." Wearily, he took Sheldon back to his bed and soothed him until he fell asleep.

He sat for a long time near his children's beds, thinking about Naomi and the strange way in which she had behaved. Try as he might, he couldn't be angry with her, because he couldn't forget the tortured look in her eyes when she'd left him. He was certain that some demon was riding hard on her; she hurt, and hurt badly. He wondered…what was it Judd had said? *My Naomi spends a lot of time hurting.* He couldn't let her go. He loved her. Oh, God, how he loved her! To have known at last what it meant to share his body with a woman whom he loved…he swore softly. Naomi cared deeply for him, or she wouldn't have made love with him after fourteen years of abstinence. And for her, abstinence had definitely been by her choice.

He walked slowly down the winding stairs to his office. Reminders of her were everywhere. He dialed her number and got a busy signal, not even her answering machine, he thought in frustration. After repeated attempts, he decided that she'd disconnected her phone. And disconnected him from her.

Naomi hardly remembered how she got home. She threw her bag into the hall closet and made it to her bed by will-power alone. Disconsolate. Shattered. She hadn't known that she could hurt so badly, and she had hurt him, too. She had wanted to make it right, to tell him that it was killing her to leave him, but she knew that if she offered a single word in her defense, all that pained her, every wish and every secret, would flow out of her in an unbridled torrent. She wanted him to call her, to tell her that he could forgive anything, but the phone didn't ring and she wondered why she had even hoped it would. Hours later, she showered and got ready for bed. Looking in the mirror, she laughed mockingly at her ashen face and haggard eyes.

"Rufus, you're not only the lover that women dream of, you're a magician," she said aloud. "I haven't fallen apart like this since Grandpa left me at that private clinic all those years ago." She went to the kitchen, got some ice, and held it to her forehead. She climbed into bed, reminding herself that she'd never let anybody or anything demoralize her. I might lose it all, she told herself, but not without a good fight. As she dozed off, she remembered that she had transferred her calls to Rufus's number and that if he did call her, he would only get a busy signal from his own number. Seven-thirty the next morning found her knocking on Judd Logan's front door.

Chapter 12

Judd was obviously taken aback by Naomi's sudden appearance; she hadn't rung the bell as was required, she wasn't smiling, and she'd barely murmured a greeting. As though sensing that something was wrong, he clung anxiously to his usual manners and routine.

"You've forgotten what I taught you, Naomi gal; you should've rung the bell and announced your presence. Sit down over there and I'll have Calvin bring us some breakfast."

Naomi looked at her grandfather, who seemed visibly older each time she saw him. I've got to do this, she reminded herself.

"Tell me everything you know about that clinic and my child, Grandpa."

He shifted in his chair, uncomfortable, she realized; a man unused to being held accountable, too proud and too virtuous to lie.

"I've told you the situation, Naomi." She reminded him

that the records were sealed and demanded to know more about how the family had located her. Judd admitted that he wasn't infallible; the clinic guard had recognized him when he'd brought Naomi, and everyone at the clinic knew her first name. It hadn't been difficult for the family's detective to locate her.

"I'm sorry, Naomi gal."

She smothered the pity that she felt for the old man. "I don't want sorry, Grandpa. What I need is a solution. I'm in love with someone, and I have to get my life straightened out. I don't know what, if anything will come of it because from now on, my son comes first with me. But I have to give myself a chance with this man."

The distant gleam that lit his old eyes told her that it was what he had waited years to hear. She didn't let his apparent indifference lull her into unwariness; Judd was an expert at controlling and hiding his feelings.

"You marrying him?" he asked casually, as if it were of minor importance.

"He hasn't asked," she cautioned, "but if he does and if I decide I want that, I can't go to him living a lie and worrying about being found out. I want the woman's telephone number."

"But suppose they're after extortion money?"

"Grandpa, they can do that now," she pointed out, "but if we cooperate, make an offer, maybe she'll let me see my boy."

"Don't think of him that way, gal; it'll only cause you pain."

Naomi reached for the black coffee that the cook had placed on a small antique table beside her chair. "I saw him. Don't look so shocked. I just followed your lawyer and identified the house. One morning when I was parked there, I saw him, and I'll never forget the feeling that I had, watching him skate down the street with his books strapped to his back. I've got to meet him, Grandpa, I've got to."

She imagined that as usual, Judd would weigh the gains and losses before making a move, a trait that had made him a champion chess player; he would want to know what was at stake.

"Who've you fallen in love with, Naomi? Is he good enough for you, gal?"

"After that trick you pulled, summoning him out here as if he were a teenager and demanding to know his intentions, I shouldn't tell you a thing."

The sedate Reverend Judd Logan whooped for joy. "Cat Meade? You're in love with Cat Meade. I knew it. I just knew it," he exclaimed gleefully. "I told him you wouldn't dance like that with him if he wasn't special to you."

She gave him what she hoped was a withering look. "You were out of line, Grandpa."

She sat forward, amazed at the transformation in him. Humility. "Anything I've ever done, gal, was because I love you and want the best for you." She stared open-mouthed as he went on. "Cat Meade, huh? Now, *there's* a real man; not a bit like most of these young fellows today. He's strong, Naomi, and if he gives himself to you, he'll be there for you always. He'll never leave you."

She lowered her head to prevent his seeing her loss of composure. "Grandpa, that's the first time you ever said you love me; all these years, it's what I've wanted most to hear you say. I didn't know you did." She had to struggle to control her trembling voice. Maybe if he had showed her that he loved her, she wouldn't have needed so badly to find love with Chuck. Maybe…

"How could you not know, Naomi gal?" His voice was weak, suddenly old. "You were all I had. But after Hazel left me, my heart just sort of constricted. I loved her so; I still do. One reason why the thought of dying doesn't bother me is because I know she's waiting for me. I kept you away from me because I didn't want you to hurt so badly when I have to leave you, not the way I suffered when your grandma went." She saw a tear roll down his age-roughened face. "I loved her in a way that I've never had the words to express."

She walked over to him and hugged him tightly to her. "I wish I could know a love like that, but I don't hope for it, Grandpa. I'm carrying too much baggage."

He wiped his eyes. "Now, gal, I've taught you not to be negative; think on the good side. You'll find it, and you'll find it with Cat Meade. I've been watching people for almost a hundred years, and I watched him; he's a good man. And he cares for you, or he wouldn't have come out here when I asked him to. I'd die real happy, gal, if I could leave you with him."

Naomi felt a warmth that she hadn't known before and wondered if her son was seeking what she had just been given—the gift of parental love. "Grandpa, I hope you're with me in this, but if you aren't, I'll have to go it alone. And I'm not doing this for Rufus; I'm doing it for myself."

He nodded slowly. "All right, I'll call my lawyer and get the information you need."

Naomi drove into the garage beneath her condominium building, turned off the motor, and sat there. On the way home, she had tried to take her mind off the changes in her life during the preceding twenty-four hours. Now, her mind and heart were flooded. She thought of Rufus, the all-consuming power and passion with which he'd made love to her, and the unbelievable joy she'd known in his arms. She shivered when her mind focused on their parting and the chasm that she'd had no choice but to put between them. She thought of her grandfather's loneliness, of the forty years during which he'd silently and stoically mourned the loss of such a powerful love, and she rejoiced in the healing knowledge that he deeply loved her, his only grandchild. It gave her a measure of peace that she couldn't deny, in spite of her emotional turmoil about her son. About Rufus.

She opened her apartment door to hear Jewel's voice on her answering machine. Preston had fallen down the basement steps and injured himself and Rufus was with him at Children's Hospital. Sheldon was with Jewel.

Naomi didn't question the rightness of it; she went immediately to the hospital and found Rufus in the waiting room, his long legs spread out in front of him and his forearms resting on his thighs. His surprise was obvious, and she could see that he tempered his pleasure at her having come to him.

"I'm rather surprised to see you. I suppose Jewel called you." He didn't want her to think that he had asked his sister to notify her, and she understood his message.

"Do you have any news?" He moved over so that she could sit beside him on the leather sofa.

"Nothing yet, but I suspect he might have dislocated his shoulder; he was in terrible pain. It's the first time he's deliberately done what I told him not to do. Both of them seemed to resent my working this morning. I know it's because I've been away so much recently, only three days between my New Orleans and West African trips. I shouldn't have taken that assignment." He dropped his head into his hands.

She put a hand lightly on his arm. "You couldn't have guessed what he would do, so don't blame yourself." She soothed him before quickly changing the subject. "You didn't tell me whether you were satisfied with your trip."

No, he thought. I fell head over heels in love with you and couldn't think of anything but you and how much I wanted you. Aloud he said, "I didn't bring back the story that I went for. The real story isn't the children in the street, though there certainly are some. I got a different story, one that my eyes wouldn't let me leave without, and I checked it with short trips to three adjacent countries. Poverty, armed conflict, disease, and drought are at the bottom of just about everything that happens over there, including the problem of street children. And that's my story. I got it in personal interviews with real people about the problems in their daily lives. I feel real good about it."

"I know it may not mean anything to you," she told him, "but I'm so proud of you."

Rufus looked down at her, his mouth twisted in disbelief, almost angry. "Why shouldn't it mean something to me?" he asked scornfully. "Do you think I made love to you without caring what you think of me?" He noticed the look of horror on her face and told himself to calm down. "Thanks." It was grudgingly offered. "My publisher is making it the lead article, but he wants it next week, and I'm not going to abandon Preston for the sake of it."

"Are you going back to investigative journalism?" she asked, giving herself time to think.

Rufus sighed deeply, indicating his impatience with the question. "Naomi, Preston almost broke his neck with me right there in the house. I'm not leaving them again until they're old enough to play college basketball."

"Go ahead and write your story. I'll stay with them while you work."

He couldn't keep the bitterness out of his voice. "Are you sure you can handle being around me for any amount of time? I work all hours, night and day." Rufus regarded her intently, pushing back the rising desire. He had made soul-shattering love with her, the most electrifying experience of his life, but he didn't know her. He watched her squirm uncomfortably under his blatant scrutiny.

"Do you want me to leave?"

He didn't spare her. "When I wanted you to stay, you wouldn't. And I wanted it badly. Now, you may suit yourself. If you stay, stay for Preston, because if you stay for me, be prepared to explain yourself. By that, I mean, lay all your cards on the table."

She rose to leave, and he would have let her if he hadn't glimpsed again that grim, desolate look in her eyes, the same look she'd had the night before, when she'd left his house. He couldn't bear to see her in pain; she was his first love, his only love, and his only thought then was to comfort and protect her. He stood quickly and pulled her gently into his arms. When he looked around, seeking privacy for them, he saw none, so he just held her to him, stroking her back slowly, trying to soothe her.

"What is so awful and so powerful," he began softly, "that it rules your life? When we met, you were laughing at life. What's happened to make you so unhappy? I know that you care for me; why can't you open up to me?"

She shook her head slowly—in denial, he thought.

"Oh, yes. You care, and I know it. You were in my arms, and I was inside your body. Remember?" He didn't need her answer; the quickening of her body and her accelerated breathing were enough. He gazed down at her, cursing his powerful, uncontrollable response to her nearness.

"That's the whole point, isn't it?" he asked bitterly. "You either want to forget it or you've dismissed it. *Why are you here, Naomi?*"

She raised troubled eyes to his, but she laid her shoulders back in graceful dignity and told him, "I thought you might need me. That's all. If you do, just let me know and I'll be there."

The doctor came in at that moment and settled the matter. Preston had a dislocated shoulder, a mild concussion, and bruises on an arm and leg. He would have to remain still and absolutely quiet.

Naomi's eyes pleaded with Rufus. "Let me help. Let me

be with him while you work; I need to be with him, Rufus."
He was torn between his need to protect her, comfort her, and
bind her to him and his fear that his children would become
more deeply attached to her. She was asking him to let her
care for his son; he could not have denied her anything.

Naomi tried to make herself invisible to Rufus, spending
her time with Preston and Sheldon. She had taken the guest
bedroom, explaining to Rufus that unless and until she was
able to sort out some personal problems they should avoid
intimacies. He had accepted it, because it was what he felt,
but both of them suffered and were unable to hide it.

Rufus finished the article at about ten-thirty one night and
couldn't resist sharing his excitement with Naomi. He brought
it to her in the living room, where she sat illustrating a story
for the boys.

"It's finished, all printed out and ready to go."

Still holding her brushes, she glanced up at him, taking
in the lines of exhaustion in his haggard face. "What's finished?" Her heart was in her throat. Did this mean she had
to leave? That she had to put the four glorious, idyllic days
behind her and tackle the most difficult situation she would
probably ever face?

"My story—I'd like you to read it." She put aside the illus-
trations, took the story from him, and began to read. By the
time she finished, her face was bathed in warm tears; tears
for the subjects of his interviews, for the magnitude of the
problems that the people faced, and tears of joy for Rufus.

"It is a masterpiece," she whispered in awe. "I never imagined that your writing was so forceful, so powerful. I feel as
if I know those people, as if I've been a part of their lives. It's
wonderful." She walked over to him.

"Congratulations!" Her hand delicately grazed his cheek,
and she reached up and kissed him fleetingly. But he must

have been hungry, for the moment she touched him, he became full aroused and brought her to him. His man's scent, the feel of him, sent tremors through her, and her eyes glazed over as desire gripped her. The devil with her good intentions; he was hers to take, and she meant to have him. Right there. Right then. And as if to make certain that she didn't change her mind, she made the most brazen gesture of her life, found him, and with exquisite, dazzling efficiency let him know that she remembered well what he had taught her only a week earlier. He uttered a tortured groan, the cry of a wounded animal, clamped his open mouth upon her parted lips, and surrendered to his passion.

Rufus gripped her tightly as she moved against him, but he wouldn't be rushed; gently and tenderly, he cherished her, worshipping her with sweet, fleeting kisses. She squeezed him to her, silently asking for more, but he refused to let the demands of his throbbing desire override his love for her.

"Noomie! Noomie, Preston is crying," Sheldon called from upstairs. She froze, and within seconds, was racing up the stairs.

He stood where she'd left him, immobilized in the helpless clutch of passion. His first thought was that if she'd wanted him as badly as she'd pretended, she couldn't have forgotten him in a second. Then he grimaced in self-disgust. Get a grip on yourself, man, he told himself, she responded the way you should have. She wanted him, all right, he acknowledged, and there was no better evidence of her feelings for his boys than the fact that she placed their needs above her own, above his.

He got down on his haunches, took a few deep breaths to get his passion under control, and raced up the stairs.

"What happened?"

"Preston rolled over on his shoulder," she told Rufus, still holding the boy, soothing him. Sheldon stood by with his little hand on her thigh, anxiously watching Preston.

"Is he going to be okay, Noomie?" She hugged the child and gave him the answer that he needed.

Rufus had remained in the doorway, watching Naomi love his sons. It occurred to him that Sheldon hadn't called him, but Naomi, and suddenly he knew what he wanted, and he also knew that he stood a very real chance of never getting it. He swore softly. Why can't she let me love her, protect her? he wondered. Even if she's committed murder, even if she's a fugitive, there would have to be good reasons. Can't she see that I'm here for her? She sang both boys to sleep and then went into the guestroom and began to pack.

She had been in his home for four days and nights and had scrupulously avoided any intimacy with him until he'd gone to her with his finished article. He knew he could write, but her reverential tone when she appraised his work had heightened his sense of self, had been balm for his ego. She'd sat there reading his article, swinging her foot and alternately frowning, shaking her head and finally crying. Knowing that he'd moved her so deeply made him feel invincible, all-powerful.

"Leaving? Tonight?"

She looked at him and smiled weakly. "You don't need me anymore, so I'd better catch up on things at home."

Rufus paced the room, fingering the evening stubble on his cheeks. He stopped and watched her. "I won't argue with the last part of that sentence, but the first part is open to question." He considered what good reasons she might have for rushing off. "How did your client like the logo you designed for their new perfume line?"

"I didn't finish it," she said, barely loudly enough to be heard.

"But you had a deadline, didn't you?" Then he realized

what she'd done. "You gave up that lucrative contract to…?" She turned away from him and continued packing.

With the swiftness that had made him king of NFL wide receivers for five straight years, he was beside her. "Naomi, look at me. *Look at me!*" She shivered as he carefully forced her chin up, wanting to make her see in his eyes the over-whelming need he felt to hold her, to love her.

Naomi didn't expect love from Rufus and didn't see it brimming in his eyes. She grabbed her coat and bag.

"Let's be in touch." She avoided his eyes and walked toward the stairs. He caught her and loped down with her.

"The boys will want to see you Christmas; I hope you'll be able to make time for them." What about you? her heart screamed.

"I want to see them, too. If it's all right, I'll come over for a while." She had to get out of there. Away from the stilted conversation that had no place between lovers; away from the man who possessed her heart and from whom she never wanted to be separated. She turned toward the door.

"Naomi, don't leave like this. Half an hour ago, you were making love to me; in seconds, we'd have been on that carpet."

No. She couldn't leave him again without an explanation—something. "I know. Rufus, please. Someday you'll under-stand. It isn't you; it's me, and I'm trying not to do any more damage than I already have. When I know where I'm going, I'll tell you whatever you want to know. Everything."

He looked off, stuck his hands in his pockets, and gave his expensive Persian carpet a good kick. "Just tell me this. Is there a man involved?"

She hesitated for a second; technically, there was a male involved. "No. There's no man. I couldn't have made love with you if there had been."

He relaxed visibly. "That's what I thought. All right. I'll

try to be patient, but I can't stay in limbo indefinitely, so do whatever it is you have to do. And thanks, Naomi. Your being here these days has meant everything to me."

She got home and looked at her watch. Too late to call her grandfather, so she'd have to wait until morning. She took a shower and prepared for bed, feeling even lonelier than when she'd been passing time in that clinic. She slept fitfully, awakened early, and phoned Judd. Resigned, he gave her what she wanted, and at eight o'clock precisely, she telephoned Rosalie Hopkins.

Chapter 13

Naomi's hand hung heavily over the phone. If she took that step, she could never undo it. She couldn't banish her anxiety, the certainty that she was shadow-boxing with fate, and she withdrew her hand. Her mind wandered back to those moments out of time when Rufus lay above her, completely vulnerable to her, the light in his eyes telling her that she was precious to him. No, she shouldn't focus on that; she'd heard that you couldn't rely on what men said and did in the heat of passion. But she couldn't forget how Preston and Sheldon had tugged at her hands and clothes, kissing and hugging her at will, behaving as though they owned her. And she remembered the tears in her grandfather's old eyes when he spoke so touchingly of his beloved Hazel and his abiding love for her after forty years.

Could she have that with Rufus? Not unless she took this first step—and maybe never. With or without him, she had to know her son. For half her life, she had let fear control

her, cause her to pass up the pleasures that belonged only to
the young, make her brittle when it was against her nature.
Not anymore. Somewhere she had read, "It is better to light
a candle than to curse the darkness." She squared her shoulders, punched the numbers, and waited.

"Hopkins residence, Rosalie Hopkins speaking." Naomi
shuddered, feeling as though the bottom had dropped out of
her stomach.

"This is Naomi Logan. I understand you've been trying
to reach me. Mind if I ask why?" The woman's gratitude for
having received the call was unmistakable.

"Miss Logan," Rosalie Hopkins began, "my son has
become adamant about meeting his birth parents. He's a good
boy, but he's become so obsessed with it that it's affected
his behavior at home, his school grades, even his interest in
school. So I decided to take a chance before it's too late and
I lose him to the streets."

The woman's perfectly natural reference to the boy as
her son cut Naomi to the quick, but she fought off the pain.
"Where is your husband, Mrs. Hopkins?" The woman told
her that she was a widow, but that her son's identity crisis
hadn't begun until one of his classmates, who was also adopted, had met his biological father and seen himself in the
man. Father and son had since become very close.

"So my Aaron got the idea that he was missing something,
and he can't seem to think of anything else."

Naomi didn't know what she'd expected, but it wasn't this.
She sucked in her breath; it was no longer a matter of "the
boy" or "the child"; her son had a name—Aaron. She wanted
to repeat it until it became a part of her. She brought her mind
back to the conversation.

"Mrs. Hopkins, I'm sure your private investigator told you
about Aaron's father."

"Please call me Rosalie. Yes, he did. I'm sorry, Naomi; that must have been terrible for you. After we found out, Aaron was more anxious than ever to see you. I want you to know that if for any reason you don't want to meet us, I'll just drop it, because I don't want to interfere with your life. But our PI said you weren't married, so I thought I'd try."

At noon the next day, Naomi sat at a corner table in a restaurant near her studio, waiting for Rosalie Hopkins. Her sudden desire to get on with the meeting was in sharp contrast to the feelings of dread and fear that had dogged her earlier. She'd gained courage and strength from her determination to swallow whatever medicine she got without complaining. She was going to see her son, and that was worth whatever price she had to pay, even the price of losing Rufus. Her heart pounded furiously when she thought of him. She had promised to tell him the truth, and she would, no matter the cost; he deserved to hear it.

She liked the woman on sight. About forty, she surmised, intelligent and friendly. She learned that her son's adoptive mother worked as a head operating-room nurse and that before she'd been widowed, she'd had a happy marriage. To Naomi's surprise and barely suppressed terror, Rosalie suggested she bring Aaron to meet Naomi Sunday afternoon. Two days. Just two short days.

Naomi viewed her apparent calm as a new kind of hysteria. It started Sunday morning, when she began a minute-by-minute countdown while she waited for them. Fourteen years of consternation: concern about exposure and social censure; apprehension at getting close to a man who liked her or who she might have liked; and once she learned of the possibility of meeting her son, worry about her future relationship with him. Now she would see him, but she was afraid he would hate her.

Tentacles of painful uneasiness flashed throughout her body as the sharp, staccato peals of the doorbell startled and unnerved her. Calm down, girl, she warned herself, as she walked unsteadily to the door, rested her hand on the knob, uttered a prayer, and made herself open it. A powerful surge of happiness rocked her and her heart raced in her chest when she looked into her son's face for the first time. He was tall and handsome, and except for his light complexion, his features proclaimed his Logan genes. She saw in him her large, wide-set brown eyes, thick, curly hair, beautifully shaped mouth, and strong chin. Nearly breathless with emotion, she grasped the door for support and summoned her natural calm as an indescribable joy threatened to overwhelm her.

Rosalie spoke first. "Naomi, this is Aaron." Naomi didn't move her gaze from her son's face; when she opened her mouth to speak, no words came. Rosalie stepped forward, ushering them into the apartment, draped her arm around Aaron's waist, and gave him a light nudge. But he made no outward response, merely gazed at the woman who'd given him birth.

"I think it would be best if I left the two of you alone," Rosalie said, and stepped around to Aaron's side. "Remember what I told you. This is what you wanted, but if you find you've made a mistake, you'll still have learned something. I'll be at home, so call me if you need me." He nodded without taking his gaze from Naomi. Rosalie inclined her head to Naomi, her expression one of sympathy. "I don't know how to thank you, Naomi. We'll be in touch." Naomi looked toward Rosalie as she walked out and closed the door. She struggled to control the wild skittering of her nerves now that she was alone with her son.

Aaron began to fidget, and she realized that her reaction to seeing him had made him uneasy. Her struggle to smile was rewarded when he seemed to relax and tossed off a nod of his head.

"I'm glad you're here, Aaron." Somehow, a simple hello was too banal greeting, too far removed from her fierce urge to wrap him in her arms, to hold him to her heart. To lay claim to her right as his mother. But she had no right. She fell back on the control that she had drilled into herself for fourteen years. He walked in and looked around with pretended casualness. He was neither hostile nor friendly, she decided, just a nervous adolescent who was facing a major crisis and feigning nonchalance. What an actor, she thought, mildly amused.

He glanced slowly around, seeming to take in everything. Then he stopped and looked at her as if seeing her for the first time. They silently appraised each other.

"So how's everything?" It was a stunt she might have pulled at about his age. But she was going to start their relationship right. She was the adult, and she knew that no matter how tempting it might be to court his goodwill, she had to set the tone of their relationship. She felt older than her years, but she strove to reply in a motherly manner.

"Not so good, Aaron. Not with me and not with you. So I'll get us a couple of sodas, and we'll sit down and talk. I'm going to answer any question that you have about me, no matter how badly it hurts, and I hope you're prepared to do the same."

"Why should it hurt?" She was surprised that his voice had already changed. Somehow, it made talking with him more difficult; almost as if she was dealing with a man rather than a child.

She stared at him in amazement; he had a lot of chutzpa, but so did she. "Is that a serious question, or are you being fresh?"

Aaron cocked his head to one side, looked hard at the

woman who'd given him birth, and must have decided to back down. She was slightly unnerved by his laconic reply.

"Fresh. Where do you want to sit?" She decided that it was best to be informal and told him to walk with her to the kitchen. Walking ahead of him, she wondered why she wasn't nervous. He pulled out two kitchen chairs, plopped down in one, and put his feet, legs crossed, in the other.

Naomi recognized the challenge. Her work at OLC had prepared her for any stunt a teenager could conceive of. She walked over and placed a hand lightly on his shoulder, tempering discipline with tenderness.

"Your feet belong on the floor, Aaron. Which one of us is going to put them there?" he put them on the floor and looked up at her to see what effect he'd gotten. Satisfied that she was unimpressed, he apologized. She gave him a Coke and got a ginger ale for herself.

"Got any ice-cream?"

She smiled, remembering her first meeting with Preston and Sheldon. "Vanilla. Would you like some?"

"Could you put it in a big glass? I'd like to make a shake with it." Spiraling warmth seeped through her, commencing a process of healing that had long been denied her. Even that little piece of information about him was precious. He finished it quickly, and she made another one in the blender and, to his delight, topped it with a slice of candied ginger.

When were they going to get down to business? She was afraid to ask why he wanted to meet her; after all, it was natural that he would. She was considering her next move when the telephone rang.

"He's right here," she told her grandfather, for once, thankful for his interference. "Maybe he'd like to speak with you. I'll ask him."

Aaron was beside her before she could ask him. "Who is it? Who do I want to speak with?"

She took a deep breath, looked steadily into eyes that were identical to hers, and told him, "Your great-grandfather."

His mouth hung open and his eyes became enormous in an astonishingly close resemblance to her father when he had been surprised. "My *what?*" She repeated it.

"That's your grandfather?" She nodded.

"How old is he?" She told him that Judd would be ninety-five within a few weeks.

"Well, I'll be…" He caught himself and reached for the phone, still wearing a stunned expression on his youthful, handsome face. She didn't know whether to laugh or cry.

"Hi ya, Gramps. Where? Alexandria? Come on! That's across the world, man." A long pause ensued.

"Uh…" He frowned, as though displeased. "Uh…no, sir. Sorry, sir. I'll ask her, sir. Me, too. Goodbye, sir." She didn't need to have heard the other side of the conversation; Judd was Judd, and Aaron had needed exactly what his great-grandfather had given him—a good verbal spanking.

Aaron hung up and looked anxiously at Naomi. "Guess I blew that, didn't I? He's strict, huh?" She risked laying a hand on his shoulder and her heart fluttered with joy as she realized he didn't mind if she touched him.

"He was strict with me, too," she explained, "but he loves me. He raised me from the time I was seven so for most of my life, there's only been Grandpa and me."

Aaron digested her words—thoroughly, it seemed—and Naomi began to realize that he wasn't as frivolous as he had at first appeared, though he certainly had her talent for flippancy.

"You didn't have any brothers or sisters?" She shook her head. "You got any other children?" She closed her eyes briefly in a prayer of thanks: he had acknowledged that he was her child. Again, she shook her head.

"So how come you're not married? You're real pretty."

Naomi took her son by the hand and walked toward the living room, where she could face him while she spoke. She needed to know his reaction to her every word. But Aaron must have sensed that he was about to hear what he came for, because he began to drag his feet, walking almost as if she was pulling him. And in a sense, she was. She was pulling them both, because they were both scared. He backed up.

"Where are you going?"

"I forgot my shake."

Naomi took his hand, hurting for him and for herself; she had to pay the piper, and this young boy had to deal with the secrets he had unsealed and the painful wounds he'd opened.

"You've already finished your soda. Come on. I know this won't be easy for either of us. Sit down, Aaron." He sat across from her, dropped his head for a moment, and when he raised it, his eyes blazed with defiance. The intensity of his emotion stunned her and she stared, riveted by his hostility, and the honesty with which he expressed it. She admired him for it.

"Okay, why aren't you married?"

What on earth was he thinking? "I loved your father, Aaron," she told him, earning his smile and relieving the tension. She related truthfully what had happened, careful not to turn him against Judd.

"I haven't married," she want on, "because I didn't believe that a man would understand and accept what I've just told you, so I discouraged men who liked me and avoided a man if I began to like him until…"

"Until what?" He leaned forward, eyes narrowed, as if waiting to pounce.

"We'll get to that later. Right now, I have to finish this." She told him what her life had been like from the time she knew she'd conceived him. "A little over two months ago," she explained, "I learned that you wanted to find your birth parents. Until then, I hadn't known whether I'd had a girl or a boy. I hadn't been allowed to see my baby, because the counselors at the clinic believed that if I bonded with you, I wouldn't give you up. I wasn't even awake during the birth. I didn't want the adoption, but I couldn't hold out against their logic that it was best for the baby.

"About the time I learned that Rosalie was looking for me, I met a man who slipped through the wall I'd built around me, even as this news about you tore me into shreds." She told him of wanting to see him; to get to know him; to learn whether he was loved, well cared for, and happy; and of her certainty that the man with whom she was falling in love— the first to touch her in fourteen years—would not accept her having given a child up for adoption.

She flinched at the scorn in his voice when he interrupted her. "But you just said you didn't want to give me up for adoption."

"And I didn't. But how could I prove it to him? Besides, my friend suffered personally from parental inattentiveness, and so have his little twin sons. He's bitter about parents who don't take care of their children."

Aaron leaned back against the sofa, obviously drinking in her every word and gesture. "Is he in love with you?"

"I don't know," she confessed painfully. "I know he cares, but he hasn't said he loves me." The low quiver in her voice betrayed her growing distress, and she struggled to control it.

The boy's ability to wait patiently for her words, to sit quietly and think, to mull over what she'd said before responding, unnerved her. How was it possible that he had her personality when he had lived for over thirteen years without ever having seen her? The eerie quality of it made her shudder.

He rested his left elbow on the back of the sofa, propped the back of his head up with his hand, and told her sympathetically, "Looks to me like you should just tell him. If he can't handle it, find yourself a guy who can." He could have been speaking to a child. "Do you like his kids?" She nodded.

The diffidence was gone, along with his nervousness. She knew with certainty then that he was old beyond his years, and as he sat there coolly sizing her up, she felt pride in him, pride tinged with a little gnawing fear. Was he capable of harsh revenge?

Aaron crossed his right knee and began swinging his foot. "You planning to tell him about me, or you just going to chicken out and pretend that me and him don't exist?" This child had a man's mind, Naomi realized, and tried to imagine the kind of life he'd had. It didn't seem as though he'd spent much of it being a child.

"I promised him that he and I would have a frank talk, and I keep my promises." Had she gotten through to him, made him understand the circumstances of his birth well enough to forgive her and at least like her?

He didn't keep her in suspense. "I listened to what you said, but I can't buy it. You didn't say anybody forced you to have me adopted, so you agreed to it—right?"

"You have to believe me. I've told you things that no one else, not even Grandpa, know, because it's important to me for you to understand that I wouldn't have given you up if even one person at that clinic had supported my wanting to keep you. Everyone was against it, and my grandpa refused to interfere. Can you imagine how I feel when I think that I missed your first steps, first words, first day in school? I don't know whether you had all your shots, if your teeth are strong and healthy, if you're left-handed or right-handed…" Her tears began to flow in torrents, cascading down her face and onto her dress.

He jerked up and dashed over to her. "I'm left-handed. Please, don't cry. For God's sake, stop it! Look, I didn't mean to upset you." She tried to calm herself but couldn't; instead, her sobbing intensified. Aaron responded as if he'd never seen anyone hurt so badly. Clearly shaken to the core, he flopped down on the arm of her chair, pulled her into his young arms, and held her until she became quiet.

After a time, he stood. "I'd better call my mom."

She reached behind her, got a portable phone, and handed it to him. They had been together for little more than an hour, but in that time, her world had changed. Her son had put his arms around her, commiserated with her, tried to soothe her. It was sweet. And it had the bitterness of gall. She would love Rufus forever but she would never regret having made her choice—putting him out of her life and reaching out to her son. The seeds of love for her child had germinated within her heart and taken root. She would no sooner disown his existence or trade him for another love than she would sever her hands from her arms. She closed her eyes and leaned back.

"She's having a hard time of it," Naomi heard Aaron tell Rosalie Hopkins. "I think I'll stick around till she gets her act together. Yah, she *is* nice." Slowly placing the phone in its cradle, seemingly deep in thought, he looked warily at Naomi.

"You got anything here to eat? My mom says I eat her out of house and home. Say…" He paused for a long while, contemplating his next words, she thought, sensing his mood change. "What do you want me to call you?"

There was one name he would never call her, so it didn't matter. "Whatever you like." But she realized from that question that he wasn't planning to make it a one-time visit and breathed more easily.

He joined her in the kitchen, and she fought to cope with the intense emotion that swirled within her, first catapulting her into euphoria and then jerking her back to humbling reality. He could decide that having seen her was all he wanted, or…please, God, she didn't want to be just a curiosity to him. She quickly banished the idea and concentrated on the joy of cooking for her child.

She fried a chicken, baked some sweet potatoes in the microwave, warmed up leftover collard greens and buttermilk biscuits, and had a mid-afternoon meal with her son. He no longer seemed nervous or anxious, and she was grateful that he didn't appear to be censorious. She knew that the acute pain he'd witnessed in her had softened him, forcing him to empathize with her. But she needed his acceptance, not his pity and not the barrier that he had erected between them. It was like a thin veil, but it was there.

"Hey, uh…this is good stuff. My mom can't cook worth a…she can't cook." He put his fork down and looked at her, his eyes piercing in their intensity. "You don't cook like this just for you. Does that guy live here with you?" Before she could reply, he answered his question. "I guess he doesn't if he's got two little kids. How old are they?" She told him.

"What do they call you?"

"Noomie. It's easier for them to pronounce."

He bit into a chicken leg, savored it, finished chewing his mouthful, and said, "Noomie, huh? I like that. Think that's what I'll call you. So where'd you go to school, Noomie?" She wondered if her heart would burst.

"Howard University and Columbia University," she told him, pleased that he was interested. She couldn't imagine why he was astonished to learn that she had studied fine art and was an artist.

"I can't believe this; that's what I'm planning to study. I guess I got that from you, huh? Did you do all this stuff here and in the living room?" She showed him the paintings that were hers and learned that he played the guitar and sang in the boys' choir at school, and that painting and drawing were his special hobbies.

He thanked her for the meal and stood to leave, but she needed something else; she had to know what he thought of her, how he felt about her. Maybe it was unfair to ask him after one short visit, but the ache that permeated her body, the dread in her heart, overrode logical thought. She walked on unsteady legs to the door with him, paused before opening it, and saw at once that she'd made him edgy. I won't back down now, she told herself, squarely facing his searching look.

"Aaron, do you think you can tell me where I stand with you?" She learned then that he was blunt and honest.

"I think we can get on, but the rest...well, I don't know. I'm still not sure about that part where you were pressured into giving me up."

She reached deep into herself for the composure that she needed. Had any woman ever had such a conversation with a child to whom she had given birth?

"I don't have any proof, Aaron, so whether you believe me will depend on your faith in me." After an awkward moment, she succumbed to her deep yearning, pulled him into her arms, hugged him, and released him. She smiled at the cocky thumbs-up sign he gave her as he left her standing in the doorway watching him walk to the elevator. He hadn't believed what she needed most to have him accept, and it hadn't even occurred to her that he would find that terrible truth implausible. Pain stabbed her chest; he had barely tolerated her hug.

"Oh, Rufus," she moaned softly, "I need you. If you only knew how I need you." She closed the door, changed into an old jogging suit, and began to clean her apartment. It didn't help; if Aaron didn't believe her, neither would Rufus. What could she tell him? Maybe she shouldn't tell him anything. But he had said that no matter what troubled her, they would work through it together. Maybe he believed; she was less sure.

Chapter 14

How could she have held her son in her arms the night before and yet look no different this morning? She moved away from the mirror and dressed hurriedly, anxious to get into the Christmas spirit. She hadn't worn a cap in the shower, and her hair was frizzly and unmanageable. I don't care, she told herself, as she tied it back with a small silk scarf, I'm going to be happy, and I'm not going to worry about my hair or Aaron or Rufus.

But as soon as she got caught up in the crowd of shoppers, she had an overwhelming desire to talk with someone with whom she could open up and tell all—the things that hurt her and the joy that flowed inside of her. Rufus. She needed him desperately. If screaming would have brought him to her right then, she'd have stood there in the middle of F Street and done exactly that.

In the fourteen years since that fateful day when she'd grown up summarily, her studies, her work, and the music that she loved had been her companions. Not even Marva had been her confidant. Today, she was unaccountably, woefully lonely. The city wasn't a place for a person alone. But was any place? She finally brought presents for Judd and Marva, as usual, found a child's guitar for each of the twins, and got an old-fashioned gold-plated fountain pen for Rufus. She ruminated about buying a gift for Aaron, uncertain as to how such a gesture from her would be accepted, and realized that that was the source of her forlorn mood. She didn't even know what her child would enjoy. Refusing to indulge further in self-pity, she called Rosalie for advice.

"Do you mind if I give Aaron a small Christmas present?" Rosalie didn't.

"I think that's a wonderful idea, and I suspect Aaron would be disappointed if he didn't get something from you." There was a pause. "Thank you for asking me about it, Naomi," she said, and offered a few ideas. Naomi completed her shopping and rushed home to wrap the gifts. As she absently caressed her gift to Aaron, she considered the probable effect of changing her position on several amendments that the OLC board proposed to attach to the foundation's constitution. She couldn't continue to oppose boys' use of the foundation's services; she had a boy of her own.

She took her seat at the OLC monthly board meeting that evening with five minutes to spare and earned a reproving frown from Maude, who called it to order immediately as a reprimand.

Maude announced that she had invited Rufus Meade to join the board and asked for a vote. As Naomi expected, it was unanimous in his favor.

"Would someone go to my office and ask Mr. Meade to join us?" She looked directly at Naomi, who ignored her and left the task to another board member. Rufus walked into the room, took the seat that Maude had left vacant beside her, and looked around. The sensation that her heart had stopped beating flustered her. She was never prepared for the powerful aura of masculinity that enveloped him everywhere and all the time. Her face burned, and she wondered if everyone present could tell that she had been in his bed and that he had made love to her until she had practically flown out of her body in ecstasy. She caught her breath and pinned her gaze to the table, certain that she was giving herself away, but finally, unable to resist, she *had* to look at him.

She gasped audibly. Rufus's gaze was locked on her, soft, tender, scintillating, and she realized with a shock that he didn't care who knew what he was thinking and feeling. She glanced quickly at Maude, who fixed her eyes alternately on Naomi and Rufus. The rogue, Naomi thought, when she could collect her wits. He's doing this deliberately.

But Rufus wasn't playing a game; he didn't play about serious matters, and he had become serious about Naomi. Gone was his uncertainty. He no longer equivocated about what he wanted from her. He had fallen in love with her, and he knew it was forever. She could use whatever ruse she chose, but he was going to get her and he wouldn't be satisfied until she loved him as hopelessly as he loved her. It was the main reason why he'd suggested to Maude that he would be interested in joining OLC's board; it allowed him to see Naomi while he waited for her to keep her promise. He had known that Maude would be delighted and he meant to work hard for the foundation, but his purpose in being there was Naomi Logan and he didn't plan to let either her or himself forget that. He tuned out the boring drone of Maude's monotonous voice and toyed with the notion that maybe he could reach Naomi by mental telepathy.

"A leading national magazine wants to run a cover story on OLC," Maude said. "I realize that you have refused newspaper and television interviews, but this one is very important to us, Naomi. Would you consider it?" Naomi would, she advised the board. Rufus stopped wool gathering and put his mind on the meeting. So Naomi had made a practice of avoiding publicity; it hadn't just been the occasion when he'd substituted for her on local television.

"…And we have to admit boys into our programs," Judge Kitrell, the eldest board member, declared. "If we don't, we'll lose financial support of some of our most dependable donors. I think we ought to take a vote."

Rufus watched in stupefaction while Naomi let it pass without saying a word. He remembered the finesse with which she had successfully fought the move six weeks earlier. Something of immense importance had happened with Naomi, he decided, and reckoned that she didn't plan to tell him about it.

Oh, but I'll find out, he silently vowed.

He blocked her way as she was leaving the boardroom. "Tell me that you weren't planning to leave without speaking to me," he chided gently. Rufus knew it wasn't a fair statement; Naomi had spoken to him, but they had been in a circle with three other board members. He wanted a more personal greeting, and he didn't doubt that she understood as much.

"How are Preston and Sheldon? Has Preston's shoulder healed?" She knows I don't want an impersonal conversation any more than she does, he told himself, but she isn't ready for a serious discussion; maybe she never will be ready.

"Children's bodies heal rapidly, Naomi, but it takes their hearts and minds a bit longer." He stopped to make certain that his blow struck its mark. "Sheldon wants me to teach him how to use the telephone, and he wants your number. I'm going to give him the number and teach him how to use it.

Then he can telephone you whenever he likes. If you object, take it up with Sheldon."

"The last time I saw Sheldon, he was four years old, not quite old enough to run his life. I presume that hasn't changed."

"Not to my knowledge. One thing has changed, though; instead of asking for you two or three times a day, your name is almost every other word, and they talk constantly. What are you planning to do about your little friends, Naomi?"

She stared at the faded green in the frayed Persian carpet that covered the hall floor and was reminded of the shoes that Rufus had bought her. Probably an impulsive, impersonal act, she thought irritably. Be fair, she admonished herself. He wouldn't do that or much else on impulse, and damming him wouldn't make her life more bearable. She looked up at him and her breath caught in her throat when she saw the bitterness etched in his face. Oh, God. She shouldn't have joked about Sheldon's age; now he would think that after allowing the boys to care for her, she was callously deserting them.

She paused beside her car, not wanting the evening to end without her having so much as held his hand, but she couldn't think of a way to bridge the chasm that separated them. "I'm still planning to see the boys Christmas day, if it's all right." She opened her car door.

"What's the hurry? It's only nine; let's go up to Louella's for a while. You drive; I'll follow you, but don't speed, Naomi." She wrinkled her nose at him flirtatiously.

Louella greeted them with what Naomi took to be an innuendo. "I'm glad to see you two still together." She glanced at Naomi. "Is he taking good care of you, honey?" Flustered, Naomi dropped her gaze. Apparently attuned to her, sensing her discomfort, Rufus put his arm around her in a protective gesture. Louella waddled off to get their drinks—ginger ale for Rufus and white wine for Naomi—and Rufus grinned wickedly and teased the woman encircled within his powerful arm.

"You're an open book, sweetheart. Lou wasn't saying what you were thinking, but believe me, by now you're both thinking the same thing. Baby, people cannot look at us and know what we've been doing."

"We aren't. I mean, there was just that one time, so you shouldn't put it that way." He was making her nervous. She did not want to be reminded of that night, what he had done to her, and how he had made her feel, but she *was* reminded of it, and when he slid his leg against hers beneath their table, she swooned. Rufus exposed his beautiful white teeth in a mesmerizing grin, forcing her to confess that he had achieved his goal.

Captivated, she tried to hide it with a frown. "All right! I know you're here, Rufus. Now, will you please get off of my case." He howled with laughter.

"Never, baby. Believe me, I mean never."

Louella brought their drinks and a cup of coffee for herself and took a seat opposite them.

"I enjoyed seeing your boys, Rufus. Bring them by again sometime soon, and I'll fill them full of ice-cream free of charge. How are they?" Naomi imagined that Louella could recall some interesting experiences with Preston and his passion for ice-cream.

"I think they're in mourning these days; apart from that, they're fine. Hellions, but fine."

"What or who are they mourning?" Louella inquired. Rufus showed his teeth in what passed for a grin, but his glacier-like eyes told the two women that the grin was plastic and the little metaphor about his sons' mourning shouldn't be taken lightly. Intuitively, Naomi knew Louella would discern that she was the source of the hurt that Rufus made no attempt to hide.

Louella sipped her coffee and leaned back. "Would you mind explaining yourself, hon? You writers have a way of making things clear by saying something other than what you mean."

Naomi didn't expect him to pull punches. Louella was more mother than friend to him, and he wouldn't mislead her or lie to her. "Naomi taught my boys how to express themselves with crayons and pencils," he told Louella, while his gaze scorched the woman beside him. "Now, they've got my house littered with drawings of her, and each one shows her either walking away or hiding from them. At least, they tell me that's what they've drawn. They've used up three pads of drawing paper in the last two days, and every sheet is taped to the wall along my staircase. Another one of Naomi's ideas. If that isn't enough, every other word is 'Noomie.' Noomie this and Noomie that. Sheldon doesn't even want me to read to him at night; he wants his Noomie. It's sending me up the wall."

Naomi shifted uncomfortably. She knew Rufus felt this more deeply than his words suggested; that it wasn't something she would be able to explain away.

"Tell them that I'll spend Christmas Day with them." It was weak balm for a searing pain, and she knew it, but what else could she do? She had to affect conciliation with Aaron, and no matter how much she loved Rufus and the twins, Aaron had to have priority. He deserved it. And until she understood him, what he wanted from her, and how he felt about Rosalie, she would be there for him no matter what. It would be unfair to encourage the boys to become more deeply attached to her. And Rufus. Well, she would face that when she had to.

She glanced at Rufus and shivered from the tremors that his hot, desire-filled gaze sent snaking down her spine. He might be annoyed with her because the boys needed her and she wasn't there for them, but he wanted her. Not that that meant much; she knew that Rufus put his boys before himself, and that he wouldn't let his libido interfere with their welfare.

Louella intervened in the long silence that followed Naomi's weak recompense. "Use the phone, honey. Kids love to get phone calls. 'Course, you could solve that another way, but I'm not one to meddle in other people's personal affairs." She drained her coffee cup, patted Naomi's shoulder, and went back to her customers.

"Have they really been asking about me? I just left there four days ago. I didn't think…"

"Four days are like four years to a child that age. Don't you know that?" He waved a hand in dismissal. "This is my problem; I created it, and I have to deal with it." He checked the time. "Naomi, I've got to relieve the sitter. Her husband will be there for her by ten." She considered letting him leave without her and decided not to test his patience or his temper. They would still have plenty of time for a leisurely talk, if he didn't intend to trail her home.

He parked in front of her building, and she drove into her garage. Raw nerves unsettled her as she walked into her building with the gentle guidance of his hand at her back. He was quiet and unreadable, and her nerves scattered wildly when they reached her door and he opened his hand for her key.

"Rufus?" He took a step closer.

"Give me your key, Naomi." His woodsy cologne and masculine scent tantalized hers, and his heat surrounded her, weakening her and seducing her, drawing perspiration from the pores of her thighs. Dazed, she handed it to him. He unlocked the door, walked in with her already in his arms, kicked the door closed, and bent to her.

"I need to nourish my soul. Open your mouth for me."

"Rufus…" She couldn't give in to him. She wouldn't. There was too much as stake: for her son, his children, Rufus himself. He was her world, but she had to push that aside. "Rufus, please. I don't want this."

"No, you don't. That's why you're holding me as if your life depends on it. Kiss me. Open your mouth and kiss me. Sweet woman, I need you." She whimpered and gave him kiss for kiss, twirling her tongue around his. Frantic to have all of him, she took his tongue into her mouth and held it captive there, feasting on it. She protested when he stepped away, separating them. But his heated, feral gaze warned her that he'd had as much as he could take. Then, in a gesture that contradicted his untamed look, he caressed her porcelain-smooth cheek with the backs of his fingers. Lovingly. Possessively. "Is that what you want from me right now? Do you want to make love with me?"

She nodded. "But I can't. I promised myself that I wouldn't go any further with you until I…until I got some things straightened out."

He wiped perspiration from his forehead with the back of his hand, braced his back against the door, and stoked the fire in her as he stroked her shoulders and then pulled her toward him.

"You've already gotten some things straightened out, I think," he told her bluntly. "When are you planning to tell me about it?" What had to be a startled look in her eyes must have told him he had guessed correctly, and she attempted to take a step backward, but his powerful arms gently but firmly imprisoned her.

"When?" he persisted. What did he know, and how had he

known it? she wondered. She was at a loss only briefly; the stakes were too high to allow herself to be sidetracked.

"When I have something to tell you, I will. You promised to wait patiently and I'm depending on you to keep that promise."

"I've been keeping it," he griped, "but we didn't discuss the duration of my patience, and believe me, it's petering out. Of course, you could say that's tough, but what about my boys? I know that you aren't their mother and that you aren't obligated to them in any way. This is what I wanted to avoid, but I didn't, and it's my fault, not yours, that they're hooked on you. No woman, not even their aunt Jewel, has ever given them the love that you have. They feel it, Naomi. And I feel it." She turned her face into his shoulder and groped for equilibrium.

"At tonight's board meeting, you did nothing to prevent boys' gaining access to OLC. I was present once when you defeated it single-handedly. Why did you change your position? And another thing. In the past, you've apparently refused all requests for interviews either from print journalists or video reporters. Now, all of a sudden, you don't mind. Maybe when I know the reason for these switches in concern, I'll know everything that I need to know. Right?" The word "right" was on the tip of her tongue, but her presence of mind saved her.

"I don't see anything so strange about it," she demurred. "If eleven members want boys in OLC, the one member opposed should accede. And as for that business about the interviews, I'm starting my New Year's resolution early."

Rufus pushed away from the door and put his hand on the knob, signaling his departure. "When you pass a mirror, try to avoid looking at it; you might get a shock."

"Whatever do you mean?" She knew precisely what he

had in mind, but she wanted the satisfaction of forcing him to say it.

Rufus chuckled humorlessly. "I like your nose, Naomi; I'd hate to see it start growing. What time are you coming to my place Christmas Day? Try to make it early. My boys will be unmanageable until you get there."

She looked at his hand turning the doorknob and then glanced up at his deliberately expressionless face. He couldn't leave her; in the four days since she'd seen him, her world had spun out of control. Without his presence and support, she'd had to face one of the most challenging ordeals that could confront a woman. And she'd needed him so badly that the pain of his absence had seemed physical. Need propelled her to him, and she reached up and pulled his mouth down to hers. She plowed into him, heedless of her vow to stay away, guaranteeing that it was he who was seduced. She chucked her inhibitions and made love to him as if she knew it would be the last time. Her soft hands held his face, and she kissed him until they were both breathless, until she was limp and he was strong and hard against her.

He didn't seek compliance; her traitorous body gave him his answer. He picked her up, carried her into her bedroom, and in a minute's time, had her clothes off and was stripping himself. She lifted her arms to him in invitation, impatient for him to join her, to unite them. But he coaxed, teased and tantalized her until she begged him for relief.

"Rufus, please..."

"Don't call me 'Rufus' when I'm with you like this; I want to hear something sweet and loving." Tremors shook her as he bent to her breast and toyed with her sensitive nipple until she lay helplessly open to his ministrations.

"Please, I..."

"Please, who?" he demanded, dropping his hand to the inside of her thigh and dragging his fingers slowly upward,

mercilessly, until she writhed beneath him in frantic anticipation.

"Please, love..." It erupted from her like lava from a volcano as his devilish fingers found their mark.

Later, when they lay sated, holding each other, her still-
ness told him she was already searching for words of denial.
She attempted to move out of his arm, but anticipating her
action, he pulled her back to him, nudged her neck, and bent
over her. He wanted a clear view of her expressive eyes.

"Don't tell me your sorry, Naomi, and that you didn't mean
for this to happen. I don't want to hear it. We needed this;
we needed each other. And it ought to tell you something.
There is nothing commonplace about what we feel for each
other, and it isn't going to go away." If he had been wearing his thinking cap and hadn't let his heart rule him, he'd
have taken her to bed four nights ago, when she'd packed her
things and left his house. But he loved her, and because he
couldn't bear to be the source of her discomfort, even indirectly, he had allowed her to call the shots.

"It isn't going away because you have decreed otherwise,"
she replied. "When we first met, you didn't want anything
to do with me; in fact...boy, this is funny. The merest suggestion of intimacy between us and both of us swore that we
didn't want it; we were practically insulting to each other. Me,
I was hoodwinked. What happened to you? Did you follow
my suggestion and get help?"

She had resorted to humor. Desperate humor, he decided.
And why? Minutes earlier, locked in his arms, she had been
as honest as a woman could be. Another one of her screens.
Irrefutable evidence that he had gotten too close. Well, he
wasn't going to make it easy for her.

"Naomi, I had begun to think that you'd given up that sly
trick of using wit and sarcasm to cover your true feelings.

Don't you dare trivialize what we just experienced. I suppose you figure that if you knock it down, it won't mean so much to you. Well, don't believe it." He pulled her body tightly up to his, letting her feel the need that surged in him. And he gloated with pure masculine pride when he felt the heat rise in her as he rotated his hips and she rocked beneath him, silently demanding his penetration.

"It means more to me than you could ever imagine, but it shouldn't have happened, Rufus. I told you when we were in New Orleans that I don't have anything to offer."

"And I told *you* that you *do* have something to offer me, and that I want it. I was prepared to leave here tonight. Why didn't you let me go? You knew what would happen if you so much as put your hand on me, and you went far beyond that. Why did you keep me here?" She squirmed beneath him, but he didn't ease up. He had too much riding on her acceptance of what for him was a forgone conclusion: she was his. He would do whatever he had to in order to make her acquiesce. He sensed her nervousness and knew it was because she didn't want to share her secrets with him, but he'd get those, too, he swore to himself. His pulse quickened as he gazed down at her.

"Why?" he persisted.

"I didn't think about it. I didn't weight the pros and cons. You needed me; you told me so, and I could feel it myself. It was powerful, like some kind of opiate." He sucked in his breath and let his gaze travel over her, seductively, possessively, until she sighed deeply and buried her face in his shoulder.

"I needed you, too, and something in me just reached out to you," she mumbled. "I had no control over it. I just couldn't bear to see you leave like that, and I needed you to stay. Am I making myself clear? It was both." It was clear to him, but he wondered if she understood it. It was time he let her know the man in whose arms she snuggled.

"Why, Naomi?" He held her close, feathering kisses over her face, neck, and shoulders. Maybe he wasn't giving her a fair chance, but he didn't really give a damn about fairness right then. He needed to know where he stood with her; his future and that of his children were bound up with her.

"Why, baby?" he persisted, in a voice that he intended to sound sultry and seductive, running his tongue around the rim of her ear and nibbling on her shoulder. "Come on. Tell me. Why can't you bear to see me hurt?" He put an arm around her shoulders and a hand under her buttocks, parted her legs with his knee, and let her feel the hard power of him poised at her portal of love, just out of reach.

"Rufus, I…"

"Didn't I ask you not to call me 'Rufus' when I'm with you like this? Didn't I? Now, tell me why you need me and why you couldn't deny me. Baby, open up to me." He hoped that by now, her senses were full of him. If not, I'll give her more, he vowed silently, as he felt her tremble with excitement and frustration from the feel of his warm, silken steel flesh so close, yet not a part of her. He teased and tantalized her until he felt her frantic movements signaling her desperation to feel the heat, passion, and protection of his male power. He was playing trump cards and didn't care if she knew it.

"Tell me why, baby."

"I…oh, honey, please. I can't bear it any more. I need you. Oh, God, Rufus, I love you so. I love you. *I love you!*" A shudder of relief escaped him as he entered her with a powerful surge of his body, cherishing her and loving her until their passion consumed them and left them spent.

A long while later, Rufus watched her steadily as he buttoned his shirt and secured his cufflinks. "Your mental wheels are busily turning again. Don't tell me you've found some more negative things to say about what's going on between us." His stance became aggressive, but he didn't allow his face to tell her anything.

"But, Rufus, nothing has changed."

He bent over her, grasped both her shoulders, and looked intently into her eyes. "Really, Ms. Logan? You told me that you love me, and, baby, you told very convincingly. I already knew it, but I had to make certain that you did. Now, as soon as you can trust me, *everything will change.*"

Half and hour later, having told the sitter good night and checked on his boys, he walked into his bedroom, fighting an uneasy feeling. "Everything will change," he'd told her, but she had denied it quickly and forcibly. Maybe he had misjudged her after all. She had secrets; he was certain of that. But did she erect barriers between them for some more compelling reason? Like her career? Was success driving her, as it had Etta Mae and his mother? He didn't want to believe he was so gullible, that his feelings for her had caused him to drop his guard completely, to accept her unconditionally, knowing what his bitter experience had taught him. His instincts cautioned him to be fair: after all, hadn't she deliberately risked and lost a lucrative account in order to take care of Preston while he worked? And what did that prove? That she felt guilty for having ignored the boys, even though she knew that they yearned to see her? Hell! How was he to know? He stretched out on his back, both hands beneath his head.

He had been in an emotional vortex, a sexual hurricane. Her passion had filled his nostrils with lush female scent, bruising his senses, robbing him of his very self. He could still taste her warm, sweet flesh and hear her moans of total surrender as they spun together into an otherworld, possessed by each other...it had been the sweetest torture he'd ever known. He loved her and wanted her, but he was definitely going to be more careful. Until he got some answers, he intended to pull back, but not so she'd know it.

"Everything will change!" Three days later, Naomi still pondered those words. What had she done? Her life was in total chaos. She couldn't even conceive of a solution, but she had let her resolve waver and had broken down and told him that she loved him. She couldn't even claim to have been in the grip of ecstasy. But telling him had felt so good, a powerful, cleansing release, a mental catharsis such as a guilty person must feel confessing a crime. How would she feel if she told him everything? Could a man change to the extent that he seemed to have done? She remembered that he hadn't mentioned love, though he'd forced her to confess. Maybe he believed in her; maybe not. She couldn't afford to risk it; she had set her course, and she would stay with it.

Shaking her head as if to deny existence of the dilemma, she walked up the steps of the red brick ranch house on Pershing Street in Silver Spring. The gaily decorated Christmas tree with its whimsical lights in the shapes of musical instruments greeted her through the picture window, giving the house a semblance of gaiety, a Christmas Eve welcome of its own. And it comforted her to know that Aaron lived in a home where the holidays were a time for caring.

Rosalie Hopkins opened the door and greeted her as she would a sister. She had a keen sense of disappointment that Aaron was at work that afternoon; she wanted to see him in his own environment, to know how he and his adoptive mother related to each other. There was so much she needed to learn, so much she had to know before she could begin to have peace about Aaron and herself. They entered the living room and she glanced at the wall unit that housed an elaborate music system.

"Who's the music buff? You or Aaron?"

"I am," Rosalie explained. "This is company for me when Aaron is occupied with his books, paints, guitar, and you-name-it downstairs in his private kingdom."

"He doesn't watch television?"

Rosalie seemed proud when she answered. "Rarely. He says it's a stupid waste of time. And I'm glad. It offers too much of what he shouldn't know and too little of what he should. Anyway, he's not a passive person. Have a seat. I'll be right back." She hadn't planned to visit, but Rosalie made tea and invited her to stay. Her gaze took in the warm, attractive room, it's well maintained appearance and the tasteful but simple furnishings. She saw nothing flashy; a child raised in this environment by such a woman as Rosalie would have garnered a worthwhile system of values. Rosalie returned with the tea and they talked for a few minutes, exchanging meaningless banalities. Then, abruptly, Rosalie rose, as if having arrived at a decision, and took her first to Aaron's room and then to his basement hideout.

Naomi touched his little league trophies and pennants and his first guitar and looked through his sketches and drawings, all neatly organized by subject matter and date. She gazed in wonder at his glee club photographs, dozens that chronicled his growth from about age six onward. Rosalie walked over to his desk and showed her a watercolor portrait under which was written, "Noomie." She struggled to hold back the tears, and when they came, Rosalie comforted her.

"I hope we can be close friends, Naomi," the older woman said hesitantly. "Aaron didn't tell me much, but he seems content, and that's about all I can ask, since you've been together only once. I do know that he hasn't been restless." Her smile was that of a mother having fond thoughts of a child, Naomi realized.

"He seemed more concerned about me and how I feel about his seeing you," Rosalie continued. "I'll be honest with you. I want his happiness, and I want him to grow to become a fine man, but no matter what, he'll always be my son. And I'll fight for that with my last breath."

She took the woman's hands into her own and reassured her as best she could. "You have nothing to fear from me, Rosalie; I'm only grateful that you are a compassionate person and that you seem to understand what I'm feeling. You've been more than gracious to me, and you've offered me your friendship; I won't abuse it. Another woman might have refused to let Aaron meet me, and I would never have known him."

Naomi looked with affection at the woman beside her whose name would never be included in Maude Frazier's social register, but who possessed more honorable traits than most of the socialites she knew. Her glance fell upon a tank of tropical fish nestled in a recessed cove in the hallway.

"What an odd assortment of tropical fish."

"My husband brought them to me from Honolulu. He always brought us something when he returned from his trips. Those Thai temple bells hanging from the ceiling along the hallway and down the stairs to the basement were his gifts to Aaron. My son likes to run his hand along them as he walks. He says he gets a different tune each time."

This home has been filled with love, she thought. Love between a man and wife and between them and Aaron. There was just one more thing.

"Rosalie, does Aaron ever go to church?"

Rosalie shrugged. "He always has, but since none of his friends go, he's become stubborn about it. I've decided not to make it an issue between us." Naomi laughed. She had behaved in the same way, but a lot of good it had done her. Just wait until Judd lowers the boom on him, she thought. She was happy…or she would have been.

Suddenly she wanted to tell this stranger about Rufus and her fear that he would find her contemptible if she told him about Aaron. She sensed that this woman had suffered and would understand and not scorn her. I can't dump on her, she thought; it would make sense. She handed her two packages; one containing a small bottle of perfume, and the other an artist's palette and brushes for Aaron, wished her and Aaron merry Christmas, and continued her rounds.

Her next stop was Marva's house, but she realized that though she loved Marva, she had no interest in visiting with her friend. She was sick of shielding her emotions from her closest friend, of living a double life. Judd and Aaron knew her secrets, and with them she was free. But she needed to be with Rufus, unfettered by fears of exposure. She needed to feel his arms around her. To bare her soul to him, confessing everything, and then to have him cherish her. But it wouldn't happen, and she had made up her mind to accept that. The more involved she became with Aaron, the more willing she was to sacrifice everything—Rufus included—for her son.

Naomi drove downtown to North Capital and P Street and parked in front of Linda's house. Walking slowly up the walk, she wondered whether she was doing the right thing, whether Linda would think her visit an invasion of privacy. The front door opened before she'd reached it, and Linda stood with it ajar, waiting. Naomi knew at once that the girl didn't want her to go inside. She handed Linda a beautifully wrapped package containing a book of reproductions of the paintings of Matisee and William H. Johnson. Linda eagerly tore open the package, stared at its contents, and gasped. She looked up at Naomi with glistening eyes and grasped her in a joyous, enthusiastic hug, her first gesture of affection toward her mentor. Startled, Naomi recovered quickly and pulled the girl to her in a motherly embrace.

"I'm going to keep this forever," Linda promised. Naomi wished her merry Christmas, swallowed the lump in her throat, turned, and left.

Chapter 15

Naomi opened the windows, turned up the radio, and let the crisp winter air flow in while the music swirled around her. She loved the English Christmas carols and hummed along as they filled her living room. How long had it been since she had welcomed Christmas morning? Years. This one wasn't perfect, not by a mile. She didn't have Rufus, and her son didn't belong to her, but Aaron was a part of her life and she knew that if she needed Rufus, he'd be there for her. Right now, she wasn't asking for more. She snipped the needle ends from the holly leaves and made a bouquet of holly and Santa Claus with his reindeers that she tied on her gifts to Preston and Sheldon. Then she wrapped her grandfather's gift—Klopshc's 1901 *Red Letter New Testament* that she'd found in a used bookstore, added Rufus's gift to the pile, and quickly dressed.

She looked in the mirror. Why hadn't she been born in a culture where men wore their hair long and women wore theirs short? She got her long, thick tresses into an attractive twist just as she heard a playful jingle of the doorbell. Who could that be? Her heart pounded furiously when she saw Aaron standing there, smiling shyly. She stepped aside, took his hand, and pulled him into the foyer. That seemed to amuse him; his sheepish grin tugged at her heart as he awkwardly handed her two attractively wrapped packages.

"We thought we'd give you these." He handed her the gifts. "My mom and me, I mean." She thanked him, risked putting an arm loosely around his shoulders, and walked with him into the living room.

"How come you only got this little tree? Couldn't you find a bigger one? It's nice, but…" His voice drifted off.

"There's only me, so I don't put myself out much when it comes to celebrations." He clearly didn't think much of it and didn't try to hide his disdain. He was blunt, too, she remembered, and figured he hadn't learned to misrepresent himself; she hoped he never would. He walked around the tree, pushed his hands into the pockets of his jeans, and shrugged.

"It's too little. Next year, I'll get you a big one. Well, maybe I oughta go. My mom's relatives are coming for dinner, and I have to help her. Uh…Noomie, my…er…your grandfather called me. He said I have to go out there and see him. Are you going to his house today?" She nodded, unable to believe her ears. He was planning on being a part of her life, and he wanted to meet Judd.

"If you're going this morning, can I bum a ride? I can't stay but a few minutes; my mom needs help with the dinner and stuff. But I promised him I'd go. What time you gonna leave?"

"I'll phone Grandpa, and we'll go right away." His quick glance and nonchalant shrug might have amused her, if she hadn't understood adolescent insecurity. He was nervous about meeting the old man. She drove past Bethesda's beautiful residential neighborhood, wishing that it was night and she could share with her son the elegant colorful Christmas decorations for which the area was so famous.

Aaron looked at Naomi, apparently surprised, when she parked in front of Judd's house, cradled her head in her arms, and leaned on the steering wheel.

"Uh, what's the matter, Noomie? You're not scared to go in with me, are you? I mean, you're not sorry you brought me, are you?" Her head snapped up sharply at his words, his misinterpretation of her action.

She patted his knee affectionately. "Aaron, I never dreamed I'd have the pleasure of bringing you to my grandpa. Do you know what it means to be so happy that you're a nervous wreck? I hardly realized I was driving, and that's dangerous. Sorry I brought you here? Honey, you're smarter than that—I'm sure of it."

His grin, brilliant and sincere, warmed her from head to the soles of her feet. "Just checking. Mom said I shouldn't do anything to upset you." Naomi looked at her child, a cocky, lovable boy, and understood the implication of his questions: he was insecure about her. He had really been asking her whether she was ashamed of him. She reached in the back seat for her handbag, squeezed his shoulder, placed her hand on the door, and paused.

"Aaron, I'm proud of you. You're a wonderful boy, and I know Grandpa will be proud of you, too." The astonishment and pleasure in his young face told her that her words had been precisely what he needed.

Judd opened the door before she rang the bell. "Well, well. Come in. Come in. Let me look at you. Come here. Come here." Judd feasted his eyes on the boy as he moved closer.

"I never thought I'd live to see my great-grandchild. Merry Christmas, son." Naomi stood with her back to the door, transfixed, as Judd put an arm around the boy, and the two went into Judd's study. Her grandpa hadn't said a word to her. Just then, he looked back at her.

"Merry Christmas, gal. Thanks for bringing him to me."

"Merry Christmas, Grandpa." She could barely get the words out.

The strange peace, the sense of right, of once more being a part of a family, was almost more than she could bear. If she had ever doubted that she had done the right thing, the tears that she saw in her grandfather's eyes erased that uncertainty. She wanted to remind Judd that they had no claim on the boy, that he shouldn't become too attached to him. But she said nothing. Christmas was a day of joy, and she hadn't the heart to cast a shadow over her grandfather's happiness. She didn't want to remember it herself, but experience had made her a realist.

Remembering how important it had been for her and Aaron to have privacy when they met, Naomi remained in the foyer and watched from there as the old man showed Aaron a picture of his maternal great-grandmother, his maternal grandparents, and his own mother as a child. The boy's questions indicated a keen interest in his roots, causing Naomi to wonder if anything other than identity had motivated him to locate her. A glance at her watch told her it was safe to assume that the twins had become uncontrollable and Rufus close to furious. Judd released them after getting Aaron's promise of another visit soon.

When Aaron got out of Naomi's car at his home in Silver Spring, she thought he looked at her as if there was something he wanted to say. So she smiled and waited, and when he only shrugged, thanked her for taking him to visit Judd, and ran into the house, she felt let down. What had she expected of him? She turned the Taurus toward the East West Highway, Chevy Chase, and Rufus. Rufus. She'd see him soon. Soon she'd be with him. Nothing would happen; he wouldn't even kiss her, but she'd see him. She'd be able to touch him. She eased off the accelerator; not point in getting a ticket. And no point in getting herself wound up over Rufus, because nothing had changed.

To leave her own child and spend Christmas day loving children who were not her own, even though she did love them, wasn't a thought that made her feel like dancing. And if she let her mind dwell on spending Christmas with the man she loved while not sharing it with him as lovers would, she might scream like a banshee. She laughed: that would be so far out of character that she'd voluntarily commit herself for mental observation. She slowed down as snowflakes dusted her windshield. Thank God for Judd. She could finally appreciate his favorite sermon: if you concentrated on your blessings, what you didn't have would seem less important. Well, old girl, she told herself, when you lay an egg, you challenge an ostrich, don't you.

Her heart soared as she glanced up at Rufus's sprawling house; in minutes she would see the man and his wonderful little boys. Common sense told her to calm herself, to walk carefully over the slick stones, but her feet seemed to take wing. The door opened before she reached it and the boys bounded out, almost knocking her down in their excitement and adulation. Tears of joy brimmed her eyes, but she refused to shed them. The children jumped into her arms, ignoring the beautifully wrapped packages, covering her face with kisses.

"Merry Christmas, Noomie," they cried in unison. "Merry, merry Christmas. We love you to pieces," they told her. She had told them that when she'd kept them while Rufus was in Nigeria. She put the packages on the floor just inside the door and hugged them feverishly, delighted that they remembered.

"I love you to pieces, too. Merry Christmas." She didn't

want to release them; their love and warmth filled a void, an aching emptiness. They laughed excitedly, but only she knew what their love meant to her.

When she could no longer postpone it, she straightened slowly, letting her gaze travel upward as she did so, past his powerful jean clad thighs and his flat belly and up to the tight curls visible from his open-collared T-shirt. The familiar pangs of desire gripped her, and she forced herself to shift her glance to a neutral object. But it landed instead on his hard, masculine biceps, and shivers rocked her as the vivid memory of them strong around her, holding her, seemed almost real.

Like a caged animal who'd just lost its battle for freedom, she looked unwillingly into his face, then quickly freed herself from his fierce, knowing look. But his strong, irresistible pull would not release her, and she admitted surrender and allowed her gaze to settle on his fiery eyes. She couldn't remember the torment of the past few days nor the pleasure of that morning with Judd and Aaron. Her five senses were focused on Rufus. The rumble of the passing car could have been the beat of his heart; the rising wind, his breath; even the odor of pine and bayberry that wafted toward her became his own scent. She took a deep, labored breath and rimmed her full lips with the tip of her tongue, mesmerized.

His eyes darkened to a glistening mahogany, his breathing quickened, and she didn't have to be told that under different circumstances, he'd have had her in his bed within minutes. The warmth of his hand when he touched her shoulder reached her through her clothing, and she leaned into him as he steadied her and quickly but tenderly pulled her into his arms. "Merry Christmas, sweetheart." She struggled to speak, but emotion muffled her words, and she could only cling to him.

In his strong arms, where she needed to be, peace and contentment flowed over her, chasing away the tension and the desire. The twins pranced around her like little magpies. Rufus squeezed her to him and released her—reluctantly, she realized—and she wrapped her arms around herself. She tingled from his warm smile, from the sweetness that she felt coming from him. She could almost dance for joy. The boys had become still and were silently gazing up at them. Then, as if on cue, they each took one of her hands and led her into the living room.

"Look at our tree, Noomie," Preston urged, as Rufus placed her gifts beneath it. She did look at it. Hundreds of little twinkling reindeer shaped lights danced on the nine-foot spruce; red and white candy canes, mistletoe, angels, and cherubs hung from its dark green branches; icicles, gilded pine cones, and red holly berries decorated its needles. "We did it with our daddy," Sheldon volunteered. Her gaze moved from the tree to the three of them, and beyond them to the crackling fire that warmed the great stone hearth. Carols filled the air. She had to struggle hard to contain her feelings. Opting for the safety of wit, she made herself smile and ask Rufus, "Is it all right if I bawl? Bawling is kind of like house-cleaning; you have to do it once in a while."

Rufus watched her fight the tears, and understood what she hadn't wanted him to see: as a youth, she hadn't had a family Christmas with all the frills. He draped an arm casually around her shoulders, wanting to share whatever she felt. She was made of stern stuff, he discovered, when she brightened up, swung around, and kissed him on the cheek. Before he could react, she gave the boys similar treatment.

"There," she announced cheerfully. "Thanks for letting me see your beautiful decorations. I love the tree. Now, I'd better get going; I don't want to interfere with your plans for the day."

"You can't go!" Sheldon screamed, and began to cry. Startled at his son's unusual outburst, Rufus snapped his head around. But Preston's quiet fury, with tears rolling silently down his little cheeks, was the real shocker. Rufus looked down at his son. He was going to have to cool down Preston's temper. He'd had enough personal experience with a quick temper to know how much trouble one could cause. He smiled inwardly. If he didn't have a quick temper, he'd never have met Naomi, and look what he'd have missed.

"She isn't leaving, boys. I'll make us a hot drink, and we can read some Christmas stories." His boys trusted him, but both looked at Naomi for confirmation. She smiled agreement, and he suspected that she didn't want to go, that she'd been polite when she'd said she had to leave. They sat by the fire and drank hot mulled cranberry juice while he read them classic Christmas stories.

"Now *you* read one," he suggested to Naomi.

"I'd rather tell one, if you don't mind." He nodded, and she told the story of three kings and the first Christmas. "And that's why we give gifts at Christmas," she told the boys. Rufus watched them nod to her as if in complete understanding. She began to fidget uncomfortably, and he figured he'd better make a move.

"Stay and have dinner with us, Naomi, unless you already have an invitation." Her deeply drawn breath warned him that she was about to decline.

"Don't worry," he told her, a genuine grin creasing his face. "I'm having it catered, so it'll be edible. Might even taste good." He winked. "Well, what do you say?" She looked longingly at the children, and he could see that she wanted to share their day, and the fleeting flicker of pain in her eyes told him that she might not want to leave him, either. If she loved him, as she'd said, surely she would want to spend Christmas with him.

"Cat got your tongue?" he asked her provocatively, deliberately reminding her of sweet moments they'd shared weeks earlier. He got the impression from her quickly raised brows that he'd surprised her. But he knew well that she could give as good as she got.

"You already know the answer to that one," she joshed.

"Well? We all want you to stay. Will you?" He wasn't going to beg her, and he wasn't going to ask her any more. He wanted to spend the holiday with her and his boys, but if it wasn't important to her, she could go whenever she wanted to. He shoved his hands in the pockets of his jeans and assumed an air of indifference.

"Rufus, I'd love to spend the whole day with you and the boys, but I promised my grandpa that we'd go out to dinner. I can't let him eat alone on Christmas day." He watched her lean against the back of the soft leather sofa, twisting her hands. Yes, she wanted to stay.

"Grandpa can eat with us, too," Preston explained excitedly.

"Can he, Noomie? Can he?" Sheldon pressed her. Rufus had already headed for the telephone. He laughed when Judd Logan answered on the fourth ring, because he knew that the telephone was right beside Judd's chair.

"Merry Christmas, Reverend Logan. This is Rufus Meade. Naomi is here with my boys and me, and we want her to stay for dinner. She says the two of you are going out. Now, why should you go to a restaurant when I'm having a big turkey over here that won't taste good unless Naomi eats some of it? Be over here in a couple of hours." Rufus had to dig into himself to contain his amusement. He knew that both Naomi and Judd were probably staring with their mouths open at his audacity.

"You're big on temerity, aren't you, boy?" he heard Judd say, after clearing his throat loudly. Rufus leaned around a broad column from which dangled the boys' collection of miniature crystal airplanes, got a look at the shock on Naomi's face and allowed himself a joyous belly laugh.

"Just taking a leaf from your book, sir. Well, what do you say? We'd love to have you, and you can meet my boys."

"Meet your boys, huh? I didn't know you had any. If my Naomi wants me to, I'll get over there. Where do you live?"

Rufus stood at the door with his boys, waiting to greet the Revered Judd Logan, as he got out of a big limousine that Rufus had ordered for him and walked unbowed up the winding stone walk. Rufus thought of his own father, how he'd have loved Preston and Sheldon, and gave silent thanks for Judd Logan. Kids needed grandparents, and for today, Judd would do just fine. Wondering about Naomi's decision to stay in the living room, he opened the door and extended his hand just as the boys ducked beneath his arms and gave the old man what was probably the best greeting.

"Hi, Grandpa," they said in unison. "Merry Christmas." Rufus shook his head in wonder. That ninety-four-year-old man didn't even see his proffered hand, but bent nimbly to the twins' level and exclaimed, "My heavens, you're twins. And good-looking ones, too." The boys dragged Judd into the house, and the old man hadn't so much as greeted him. Rufus stood at the door, his left hand absently rubbing the back of his neck. What was it about the Logans? They charmed his boys without even trying. He took Naomi to the kitchen with him, explaining that he wanted to fix Judd some mulled cranberry juice.

"He hasn't said a word to me, Naomi. What do you think he's up to?" He figured from her deep frown that she was as perplexed as he. After a moment she responded.

"My grandpa doesn't hold grudges, so he's not sore because you were smart with him. Anyway, he probably admired you for that. I think he's besotted with the boys. Right now they've got him down in their basement empire. I hope he's got sense enough to stay off their trampoline, but you don't rate with them unless you bounce around that thing."

"What about me? What do I have to bounce around on to rate with you?" He felt her tense slightly, but he didn't care; a man had to make hay while the sun was shining. He set the bottle of cranberry juice on the table without taking his eyes from hers and moved toward her. "What do I have to do, Naomi?" She backed away, and he moved slowly and surely to her until her back touched the wall. His heart skipped a beat at the suddenly accelerated pace of her breathing and the telltale quiver of her lower lip. Even as he reached for her, she came to meet him, her lips already parted in anticipation of what she knew he'd give her.

He used what strength he could muster and resisted kissing her. "I'm hungry for you, sweetheart, but I can't stand the punishment of a couple of kisses. I can't have what I need from you, so I'll just content myself with the fact that you're here with me and my boys. That's more than I'd hoped for, so I'll just wait." He'd always loved her smooth, delicate skin, dark like perfectly caramelized brown sugar. He let the backs of his fingers gently graze her cheeks. "Ah, Naomi, it isn't written anywhere that a person has to be perfect. You love me with all my shortcomings. Why can't you open up and…" He almost said, *Let me love you.* Maybe the problem was both of them, not just Naomi. He saw in her turbulent brown eyes a need as great as his own and eased away from her.

"You said you'd just wait, Rufus. Wait for what?" He grinned one of those grins that he'd come to realize unsettled her.

"You're kidding. Right?"

She shook her head. "I want to know." He rested his hip against the marble countertop and folded his arms. "We can take this up another time, if you'd like. In fact, I want us to do just that. But today's Christmas, and it feels good having you here. Judd, too, though he hasn't bothered to acknowledge my presence. Let's avoid deep talk, okay? Soul splitting conversation is bad for the digestion." He whirled her around and kissed her hard and quickly on her eager lips. Then he took a tray with the pitcher of cranberry juice and five mugs into the living room, let the caterers in, and called Judd and the boys upstairs. After teasing Judd about ignoring him, he served the drinks and announced that Judd would tell them some stories.

He liked the twinkle in the old man's eyes when he said, "Rufus—I expect I can call you that, since you got so familiar with *me* this morning—I see you like to play hardball. I practically ordered you to my house, and now you've commanded me to yours. We're even."

Rufus laughed. "I stand corrected, sir." He looked at his boys, each comfortably ensconced on one side of Judd, drinking in his every word. Rufus was happier than he ever remembered being, and pretty soon he was going to be even happier, he promised himself.

But for Naomi, while the day was far more than she'd expected, it was less than it could have been. She was sure Judd was happier than he'd been since he'd lost her grandmother. The years had seemed to fall away from him when he'd looked at Aaron. At least she'd given him that much. She'd hung back when Rufus and the boys had gone to the door to greet him, because to stand there with them would have been too much like a happy couple and their children greeting a guest. Too much like the scenarios of her dreams. And there was Aaron. She was thankful for the beginnings of a relationship with him, but she couldn't help wanting them to be together for Christmas dinner. She caught Judd watching her furtively and scolded herself for wanting it all. Four out of five wasn't bad; in fact, it was a pretty high percentage. But why couldn't she be with Rufus and the twins every day, all the time, forever? She closed her eyes tightly, calming herself. She wanted so badly to tell him, but she wouldn't be able to bear his contempt. Why should he judge her less harshly than he did his own mother?

Naomi realized that Judd was telling the boys a story about her one Christmas when she was a little girl. Embarrassed, she glanced quickly at Rufus and had to struggle to hide the excitement that surged through her as his heated gaze devoured her. She shook her head slowly, clearing her mind, trying to relieve the tension. Rufus grinned deliberately, and she laughed, grateful to him for undoing the damage he'd just caused. They both looked at Judd, whose knowing wink told them that their secret wasn't that anymore.

Rufus stood and extended a hand to Naomi. "Come on, everybody, let's open the gifts. I promised the boys we'd do it before dinner. They got some teasers this morning so they'd settle down. Sorry, we don't have presents for you, Judd."

"Your company is all the present I need. Being here is gift enough." Rufus grazed his jaw with his forefinger, deep in thought. Older people had no business living by themselves, not even when they were as independent as Judd Logan. No wonder the old man was so imperious; he needed companions.

"I hope you won't make this your last visit." He didn't doubt that his statement pleased Naomi's grandfather, who sat with an arm around each boy. They opened gifts and enjoyed the miracle of children at Christmas. Mr. Ernest, the caterer, announced that dinner was served, and Rufus reached for Naomi's hand.

"What kind of impression are you trying to give my grandpa?" she hissed, earning one of his wicked grins.

"He's grown, has been for years. It's been decades since anybody fooled Judd Logan, so I'm not depriving myself of the pleasure of holding your hand, thinking that he doesn't know what's going on with us. Come on. And I want you to sit opposite me at my table." They walked down the long hall toward the dining room ahead of Judd and the boys, holding hands.

"The two of you have so much in common that it's eerie," she told him, and he hoped her pout was pretense. "He's a Capricorn, born December thirty-first. What about you?"

Rufus laughed heartily and squeezed her hand. "Naomi, you won't believe this; my birthday is January second. I'm a Capricorn, but I'm not bossy, like Judd. No way." She looked skyward, as though invoking heavenly powers to deal with such blasphemy. Judd said grace, and Rufus told himself he had better start taking the boys to Sunday school.

Preston and Sheldon didn't want Judd to leave, but he soothed them by getting their promise to visit him. Rufus watched the limousine as it turned the corner carrying Judd Logan to Alexandria. If he ever got Naomi to marry him, could they make Judd a part of their family? If you've been head of your own house for seventy years, you're not likely to accept another man in that position. Well, he could build a guest cottage out near the little brook. He walked back into the living room; such thoughts were premature. He'd learned during his football playing days never to try running with a ball before he'd caught it. Still, when he told the old man his intentions about Naomi, Judd happily gave his blessings, along with a warning that getting her wouldn't be easy. Judd hadn't disagreed when he'd said that Naomi seemed weighted down with personal problems, and he hadn't seemed surprised that she refused to share them with him. "Get her to trust you deep down," Judd had said. "That's the key, son." He knew it was going to be tough, though he didn't understand why. And if she knew he'd spoken to Judd about them while she was out of the room, she'd be furious.

The boys didn't want to go to sleep. It wasn't just the day's excitement, he knew; they were afraid that when they woke up, Naomi wouldn't be there. She pulled a chair up between their beds, lowered the lamp, and sang softly to them, lulling them. Her soft, sultry voice soothed the boys, whose eyelids soon became heavy; but it didn't soothe him. His emotions splintered like ancient shards at the sights of her loving his children, nurturing them in a way that was new to them and that they seemed to love. As she kissed each of them good-night, he had to restrain a powerful urge to reach for her and hold her to him. But they no longer had chaperons, and he wasn't going to the brink with her tonight. If he touched her, she'd go up in flames, though nothing would have changed. And nothing would until she put her cards on the table. He was in this for the long haul, to win, and he was smart enough to realize that each time he gave her a chance to tell him no, saying no to him became easier for her. He rested a hand lightly on her shoulder.

"They're asleep. Let's go down and get something to drink." He took her hand and walked down the curved stairs with her, reflecting on her unusual quietness throughout the day.

"You haven't been very talkative, today, Naomi. Was it because of Judd's presence, or did something happen to make you so quiet and pensive?" He put the coffee on and set a tray, remembering to add pieces of the coconut cake that was Louella's present to him and his boys. They went into the living room and sat on the loveseat at a right angle to the fireplace.

Naomi smiled at Rufus's perceptiveness. "I've been awed, to tell the truth. I don't remember having spent such a wonderful Christmas with my grandpa. He seemed so much at home here. And he was happy. Are you really going to let the boys visit him?"

Rufus sipped his coffee and looked at her, rather sternly, she thought. "Naomi, if I told him I'd take the boys to visit him, that's what I'll do. I keep my word. And beside, you don't think Preston and Sheldon would let me forget that promise, do you? Why did you change the subject?" His voice lowered, and she sensed anxiety in him. "I really want to know whether you've been happy here today." She got the impression that he cared deeply about her answer.

She crossed her right leg and swung her foot, playing for time. For composure. She didn't want him to know how the day had affected her, what joining their families for the festive occasion had meant to her. With effort, she told him in a casual voice, "Rufus, I don't remember a day in my life that was happier than this one." Then, not wanting to sound overly sentimental, she joshed, "As a host, you're a class act, though the boys are already giving you a run for your money."

His smile was humorless. "Have you forgotten your promise not to cover your real feelings with clever repartee?" How could she forget it? By agreeing to that, she'd let him take away her props, leaving her vulnerable, without defense, against his powerful attraction for her. She was suddenly aware of the heat that emanated from him, of his strength and solid manliness. Quickly, she jumped up.

"I'd better go. It's seven-thirty, and I have to get up early tomorrow." She started toward the hallway, and he followed. She was glad he didn't attempt to persuade her to stay longer.

"And my grandpa will call me no later than six-thirty in the morning to give me his views on you and the boys," she went on. "I'm as sure of that as I am of my name." She reached for the doorknob, but his hard, masculine hand covered hers, halting her.

"When will I see you again, Naomi?" His heated gaze sent her pulse skidding rapidly, and she opened her mouth to give him a day, then thought of Aaron and turned away.

"We'd better leave things as they were, Rufus. I told you that if I ever get things together, I'll come to you, and we'll talk." The fire that she saw in his eyes suddenly became impersonal, and she knew he was about to lose a battle with his temper. She struggled not to panic when he suddenly closed the distance between them, towered over her, and pulled her into his arms.

"Have you ever seen a puppet as big as I am? One that you can dangle according to your whims, huh? Have you?" His words and tone sounded agreeable, but she knew by the fiery daggers in his eyes and the involuntary twitch of his jaw that he was spitting mad.

"Do I at least get a kiss for Christmas?" In his arms, under his spell, feeling his strength, she didn't have the energy or the desire to speak. He had only to lock his heady gaze on her to scramble her brain. He didn't wait for her reply, and she met his mouth with parted lips. She had expected his kiss to be an avalanche, a roaring fire. It wasn't, and she shuddered at its tender possessiveness and clung to him, saturated with need.

His eyes didn't betray his feelings, and she barely had control of hers. "What…what is it, Rufus? I thought you were furious with me, but you…you can't kiss me like this if you're angry—can you?"

"I hate to end Christmas Day like this, Naomi, especially since I don't remember being happier. But I'm tired of this. I'm almost thirty-five years old, and I didn't make out like this when I was nineteen. I'm serious about us, Naomi. I've told you that often enough, so I assume you know it and that when you're ready, you'll do something about it. When you *do* get around to it, I may still be serious, but there's a chance that I may not be. I hope you haven't mistaken passion for love, because there's an important difference." He walked her to her car. "Drive carefully, and don't play your cards too close to your chest. Oh, and call me so I'll know you're home safe."

Uneasiness stole over her when he walked away before she turned the key in the ignition. Was he preparing himself psychologically to stop feeling protective toward her? She pulled out of his driveway slowly, telling herself it was what she wanted, but she no longer believed that. She drove past the beautiful homes, festively decorated and welcoming, with shades up and blinds open. Many families were still at their dinner tables. She thought back on the day, and happiness surged through her. She'd had a real family Christmas, and she had shared the morning with Aaron.

Nobody's life was perfect; you changed what you could, and what you couldn't change, you accepted. Some people didn't, and that's why psychiatrists were rich. She laughed. They weren't getting a shot at her. She glanced at her small tree as she walked into her living room; it hadn't seemed so puny until Aaron had scoffed at it. The memory prompted a smile; he'd promised to get her a big one next year. She reached for the phone to call Rufus and stopped. What right did he have to judge her feelings for him when he hadn't once told her what he felt?

And how could he demand that she pour out her insides to him when he hadn't ever given her a solid reason for doing so? Maybe she wasn't the only one having a problem with trust. She kicked off her shoes and reached for the phone. Maybe he didn't reciprocate what she felt.

"Hi. I'm home. Thanks for a special Christmas. Kiss the boys for me. 'Bye." She hadn't given him a chance to do more than greet her. The phone rang, just as she'd expected.

"Good night, Naomi." Furious, was he? Her spirits soared

at the thought of Rufus battling his temper, knowing that he'd overreacted to her little mischief. "If I'm not careful, I'll go absolutely nuts over that guy, and then where will I be?"

Chapter 16

Naomi crawled out of bed, dragged herself into the kitchen and got a cup of instant coffee. Then she put on a pot of real coffee and waited for her grandfather's telephone call. Judd was as predictable as night and day, so she wouldn't have to wait long. She lifted the receiver on the first ring.

"Good morning, Grandpa. How are you this morning?"

"I'm surprised you're up so early after your late night, gal." She wanted to correct him about that, but he didn't pause. "I see you've finally got smart and found yourself a good man. You'd better latch on to him, gal; You don't find men like him often these days. And he's got two nice boys there. I want you to bring those boys out here, and I want my great-grandson to come over here and spend some time with me. That's a fine boy; you can see the Logan genes in him. Are you working today?" Naomi sighed. She should have known that having Judd with her at Rufus's home was going to cost her something.

"We'll see, Grandpa. It wouldn't hurt you to have a friendly talk with Rosalie Hopkins about Aaron. Don't forget, she's his mother." It hurt deep in her soul to say it, but she had to accept it. And Judd Logan had to do the same. "She and I are on good terms, Grandpa, so please don't upset her."

"What do you take me for, gal? Now, you bring those boys out here."

Naomi spread her bed linen across the chairs on her balcony to freshen up in the crisp, dry air. She raced back into the kitchen to the telephone and was disappointed to discover that it was Marva. Why had she hoped Rufus would call her?

They exchanged pleasantries and season's greetings before Marva asked her, "Are you going to the town meeting tomorrow night? The topic is teenage behavior, and Cat Meade's book is being discussed. I'd like to go, but Lije says he's sick of the subject."

"I'll call you later and let you know." Naomi sat on the kitchen stool long after their conversation was over. What was she to think? She'd spent eight hours with Rufus yesterday and he hadn't mentioned it. She'd show him. She'd go.

She and Marva arrived early and found seats in the front row of the small auditorium. Radio and television cameras, cords, lights, and other trappings of the trade alerted them to the significance of the occasion, as did the presence of some local leaders. How could she experience so many emotions simultaneously, she wondered, after the program began. Exhilarating pride in the man, in his dignity and bearing brought her shoulders upright. He was different, apart from other men. She knew a keen delight in the smooth, knowledgeable way in which he answered audience questions, but she was furious at some of the things he said. She couldn't wait to tell him off. To think that she'd almost been willing to believe him capable of understanding and accepting her. But no, he was standing by what he'd written in that book.

She rushed out at the end, before the applause died down, heedless of Marva's difficulty in keeping up with her.

"Naomi, for goodness' sake, what's the matter with you? Why are you so mad at him? I thought he was wonderful." Naomi slowed enough to let Marva catch up. She put an arm around her friend's shoulder, and they walked swiftly through the shadowy parking lot until she spotted Rufus's minivan. There was no sense in trying to explain the point to Marva. And besides, she wanted to hold on to her anger until Rufus got there.

As if sensing that the issue was a personal one between them, Marva gave Naomi an excuse when they saw Rufus coming toward them still some distance away, and went to find her car.

"Hello, Naomi. I was surprised to see you here tonight." She continued to lean against the driver's door, blocking his way.

"I'll bet you were. Probably as surprised as I was to learn about this from someone other than you."

She smiled, hoping to unsettle him. "Honest, Rufus, your views are outdated. If you backed into the twentieth century, just think how many people you could bring along with you. You've got a lot of fans." She grinned more broadly. "You going to give it a try?"

"That ploy won't work," he growled. "You're not ringing my bell tonight, sweetheart. I knew when I saw you in the audience that you'd be spoiling for a fight the first chance you got. I'm tired, and I didn't have time to get any dinner, so would you please let me get in my car?" She didn't move. A light shone almost directly above them, letting her see his face clearly. To her dismay, he wasn't angry, or even slightly annoyed, and she sighed deeply, feeling the fight go out of her. He must have detected it, because his face creased into a gentle smile.

"I know you're touchy about anything related to motherhood and the family, just as I am, so let's bury it for now, shall we? Come, let's get something to eat; I'll drive you back here later to get your car."

She stared at him, horror evidently showing on her face. "What is it, Naomi? Did you forget something?" Her laughter rang out in the quiet darkness, echoing back from the adjoining alleys. Marva and her matchmaking, she'd deal with her friend properly.

"I didn't forget anything, but Marva's forgot that she drove me here, and she's gone home." She moved from the door.

"My good fortune. Give Marva my thanks." A glance at his face told her that his joviality was real; he seemed to be glad that she was with him.

Truth. Maybe that would be her New Year's resolution. "I'd enjoy a light meal with you, Rufus." He opened the door and almost bodily put her into the van, then seated himself and looked down at her.

"Can you tell me why we stood out there nearly twenty minutes? This is the coldest night of the year." His broad, electric smile was all the warmth she needed, but she didn't plan to take the truth that far. His heat reached her through her coat when his arm grazed her leg as he shifted gears. She wouldn't move closer to him, but she knew she should make herself move away. She did neither and soon felt him do it again, deliberately this time, and with a little more pressure. Then her glance caught him observing her out of the corner of his eyes. She tried to think of a clever remark but could only sputter and finally double up with laughter.

"Go on. Press your luck, Meade."

He laughed with her. "Terrible, aren't I? Want to go to Maison Blanche?"

She shook her head. What kind of a mood was he in?

He shrugged elaborately. "Why not?"

"It's too rich for my taste this time of night. I couldn't eat a five-course meal. What do you say to Twenty-One Feral? Great lobster, and the potato-crusted salmon is to die for."

He turned onto L Street. "Sounds good to me." They were shown to a table not far from the pianist, who played a haunting blues. For a while, Naomi hummed along softly.

"Why did you stop? I enjoy your voice, even when you're only humming." He reached across the table and tucked a bit of hair behind an ear. Her heartbeat accelerated at the tender gesture, and she bowed her head. Warm sensations whispered within her at the touch of his index finger gently stroking her chin, a silent entreaty for her to look at him. Her glance swept upward almost of its own volition, as if she had no will of her own.

"Why?" he repeated, his warm, fawnlike eyes sending her intimate messages and daring her to give him back the same. She wanted to be angry with him for twirling her around as if she was a top, unraveling her just when she thought she had it all together.

"Why?" he persisted, even though they both knew her answer was of little importance.

"I'm not in the mood for the blues," she finally replied. "Blues can rip your insides out, just tear you up." His eyes widened in astonishment, but he let it pass.

"Are you in the mood for me?" Lightning-like thrills warmed her as the heat in his seductive gaze matched his words. Hadn't something similar happened the night before last, Christmas night?

"You aren't deliberately toying with me, are you, Rufus? Let's just resist that sort of thing tonight, okay?" But as the cool wine trickled down her throat and his seductive gaze commanded her submission, she ceased struggling against him. She didn't care if he was provocative; feeling his caress and being able to touch him was what mattered. Still, it might be best to get onto a different topic.

"My grandpa called and ordered me to bring Preston and Sheldon to see him. He also had a few nice things to say about you."

Rufus laughed. She liked his laugh, as opposed to some of his grins. When he laughed, he meant it. "Naomi, Judd called me before seven yesterday morning, and ordered *me* to bring the boys to see him. I told him I'd take them this weekend, and I intend to beat him at a few games of chess while I'm there."

Her eyebrows went up at his last statement. "Even though my grandpa is ninety-four, Rufus, he's a wizard at chess."

He must not have heard her. "I'm looking forward with pleasure to beating him." Their dinner arrived. A shrimp salad for her and grilled salmon steak with boiled potatoes and asparagus for Rufus. Naomi declined dessert, but Rufus helped himself to a heavy serving of chocolate cake with raspberry ice-cream. She wondered where he'd put it.

Between sips of espresso, Rufus prodded Naomi about her reaction to his talk earlier that evening. "Why did you get upset about my mentioning Rosie the Riveter? Everybody knows the American family hasn't been the same since the Second World War. I gave five factors that I thought were responsible for changes in the family, but you latched on to that one. Naomi, what is behind this? It's almost as if…why are you so passionate about it?" If only she wouldn't resort to wit, if she'd just talk to him, let him understand her. He needed to understand her, to know her, really *know* her. "Naomi, what is it?" He watched disappointed as she put a hand under her chin, propped her elbow on the table, and smiled wanly.

"I'd like to know what's behind *your* stubbornness about this, Rufus." Shaking his head in frustration, he signaled the waiter and ordered them additional cups of espresso. They had so much in common. And their attraction for each other was so powerful that he knew it might one day bring him to his knees. But not yet.

He watched the flickering candle flame in the hurricane lamp that lit their table. "You know, from time to time there's a barrier between us that I just can't figure out. We'll be on the same wavelength, singing the same tune, and suddenly you'll put up an impenetrable wall between us. I suspect it leads right back to what we're talking about now. To what my book is about."

He slid his left hand slowly down her soft right cheek, touching the silk he knew he'd find there, gently caressing the warmth that he suddenly needed. A shudder plowed through him, catching him unawares, when she sucked in her breath and lowered her eyes.

He took her hand, turned it over, and examined her long, tapered fingers, brushed the back with the tips of his own, and looked at her steadily. "I guess we can't discuss it. We're not talking about conditions in our community or anywhere else, for that matter; we're talking about ourselves, Naomi, and I don't think we'll ever agree. If we do, I suspect that'll be the day we both begin to live, really live. We need each other, but neither one of us is willing to settle for half a loaf. And neither of us should. Let's go."

Naomi raced anxiously to her front door the next morning, hoping that the caller was Rufus. She'd had a sleepless night with dreams and visions of her and Rufus at opposite ends of everything—buildings, streets, and poles, even a canoe. It was symbolic, she knew, but her flesh prickled at the memory of the eerie happenings in her dream. Shaking her head as if to clear her mind of all unpleasantness, she reached for the knob. Maybe their relationship wouldn't have stood a chance even if Aaron hadn't existed. Aaron...thoughts of him warmed her, and she smiled inwardly. Would she ever get used to having a thirteen-year-old child? Good heavens, he'd be fourteen tomorrow, she remembered. Shock riveted through her when she opened the door and saw Aaron standing there with a worried look, biting his bottom lip.

"Hi, I, uh…I hope I'm not disturbing anything." He looked at her, hopefully, she thought, and then kicked at the carpet. "My mom told me I could visit you anytime you don't mind. She said I ought to call or we oughta make an arrangement or something, but I figured if you were busy I'd just go on back home. I mean, it isn't like you were expecting all of a sudden to have me hanging around. My mom had to go to work, so…look, I'm sorry I bothered you."

She put an arm around his shoulder and pulled him through the door. Seeing his relief, she figured it wouldn't hurt to give him a hug. That seemed to relax him. Still holding his hand, she walked on back to the kitchen, where she had been testing designs for a sportswear logo.

"I'm glad you came, Aaron. Can I safely assume that you're hungry?"

He grinned broadly and settled more comfortably in the straight-backed chair. "Always. What you can't assume is that I'm not hungry. What are you going to cook?" She wondered what he'd do if she hugged him breathless.

"It's still breakfast time, so why don't I make us an old-fashioned country breakfast? You know—biscuits, sausage, grits, eggs, and fried apples. You can have hot chocolate." He wrinkled his nose in apparent disdain.

"What would you prefer, s—Aaron?" What would he do when she finally slipped up and called him "son?"

He crossed his left ankle over his right knee and smiled indulgently, knocking her breath away. "Coffee. Noomie, I'm too old to be drinking hot chocolate. That's kids' stuff." She laughed, and Aaron sat upright, staring at her.

"What's the matter?" What had she done to make him look so serious? Only a moment earlier he had been jocular, laughing at her.

"You've got a real pretty laugh. It reminds me of those temple bells my dad brought me from Asia. I never heard anybody laugh like that. Real nice." She hoped the smile that she'd tried to force on her face actually made it. He wouldn't understand tears of joy, she knew, as she fought to control her emotions.

When she could, she turned away from the stove and faced him. "My grandpa says that when he hears me laugh, it's like hearing my mother laugh. He says she loved to laugh. I don't remember her. What's in the bag, Aaron?"

"My skates. I didn't wear them 'cause I caught a ride with one of the neighbors. I also brought along the Christmas present you gave me. It's real cool. I was wondering if you'd give me a few lessons—you know, brushstrokes and mixing paints, stuff like that. I paint, but I haven't had any lessons." He moved slightly so that she could set his place at the table.

"Aaron." She sat across the table from him. It was time to put him straight about a few things. "I want you to visit me whenever you like, as long as it's all right with Rosalie. And I'll be happy to teach you anything I know, so don't be apologetic about asking. Rosalie showed me some of your watercolors, and I thought they were impressive." He drew his shoulders up and sat erect, evidently pleased by her compliment. "I'm glad you like to paint," she told him, patting his hand before turning to take the biscuits from the oven. "It's what I like to do best. If you have any problems with math or English, I can help you with that, too. I once taught both subjects to high school students. And if you need help with anything else, just ask me. If I can, okay; if not, we'll find someone who can."

She couldn't hide her amusement at the sight of his eyes

getting bigger when she placed the food on the table. He glanced at her from the corner of his eyes.

"I'm not triplets, Noomie. You of all people ought to know that." Laughter spilled from her lips. When she could calm herself, she noticed an expression on his face that proclaimed he'd witnessed the unusual. At her inquiring look, he explained.

"I'm not used to this laugh of yours yet. Too bad you can't sell it." He bit into a biscuit and gave her a thumbs-up sign.

She taught him the basics about mixing his paints and showed him some of the differences between brush techniques with oils and with watercolors. Laughter bubbled within her when he joked derisively at his mistakes and with his hand, patted himself on the back when he'd look at her, wink, and say, "I did good, right?" The third time he looked at his watch, she had the gloomy feeling that he was tiring of her company. Feeling stomach pangs, she looked at her watch.

"Are you hungry, Aaron?" His sheepish grin was answer enough, but he confirmed it.

"Well, I could use a hot dog or something. It's one-thirty already. Do you think we could drop in on my...your grandfather for a couple of minutes today or tomorrow? I'm not in school this week."

"He'll like that. I'll check and see which day is best for him. When we go, ask him what he wants you to call him." She pursed her lips. "I'm sure the two of you can work something out." They finished eating and she packed a bag of biscuits for Rosalie.

"What's wrong with your feet?" She saw him looking down at them with a worried expression.

"I'm a mess, and I promised my mom I'd try to be a little more tidy. She's a neat freak. I've got paint of every color on

my shoes. No wonder you're barefooted." She showed him
the laundry room where he could wash his sneakers and took
the opportunity to phone her grandfather.

"As far as I'm concerned, he can come over here and stay.
About today, I'm not so sure. Depends on how much Rufus
knows," he told her. Taken aback by his reference to Rufus,
she asked him what he meant and whether Rufus was there.

"No, but he will be shortly with those little boys of his."
She knew from the tone of his voice that he was withholding
his censure.

"I haven't told him anything, Grandpa, and I don't want
you to tell him." She could have added that he wasn't always
right. She hadn't yet made him eat crow for advising her not
to get in touch with Aaron; when she disobeyed him, look
how he acted. You'd think he'd spent his life looking for the
boy. He rapped out at her, getting her attention.

"Where are your ears, gal? I said, what do you take me
for? It's not my business, but you'd better hurry up and tell
him about it before this balloon pops right in your face. You
listen to me, gal. I've lived a long time. That's a good man;
you mind what you do." She told him she'd bring Aaron for
lunch the next day and hung up. This time she had to admit
Judd was right.

She leaned against the edge of the kitchen sink, waiting
for Aaron to return from the laundry room. Rosalie had done
a wonderful job raising the boy. He had good manners and
good habits. And there was much of herself in him. She'd
have to be careful not to go overboard, she reminded herself, because his mother was Rosalie Hopkins, a good, decent
woman. Would she have been as generous if their roles had
been reversed? She didn't think so; she doubted many women
would have been and she was going to do whatever she could
to make certain Rosalie never regretted what she'd done.

Aaron walked into the apartment in his stocking feet, holding his clean white sneakers high over his head. "I oughta get going, Noomie. I've got a few chores to do at home if we're going to Alexandria. Won't take me but half an hour." She explained that they'd be going the following day and noticed an involuntary twitch of his jaw. Was she about to learn something else about him?

"What's the matter? The old man doesn't want my company today, or you don't feel like taking me?" His humorless smile didn't fool her; he felt rejected. And his hard penetrating stare seemed out of character for the light-hearted boy with whom she'd spent the last four hours, but she sensed that it was part of him, that he could be harsh. He wasn't an easy one, and she'd better not forget it.

"Aaron," she told him in a soft voice, "Grandpa has company this afternoon. He said he'd rather you came tomorrow, when he can spend all his time with you. In fact, he said he wouldn't care if you went over there and stayed with him."

"He said that?" His face brightened immediately, and he didn't seem to need an answer, but treated her statement like a self-evident truth. He sat down and began pulling on his sneakers, and she sighed deeply. What a turnabout!

"Before I go, you want to tell me what you do for a living? I know you're an artist, but how do you make money doing this?" After explaining her work to him, she put on her coat and boots and informed him that she was driving him home. He didn't need to know that she was afraid for him to skate on the highways at the height of the rush hour.

"Phone your mom and tell her we're leaving. I don't want her to worry."

"She's still at work, but I'll phone her." He did, and when they got in the car, he looked at the bag in her hand.

"I sure hope you put some of those biscuits in there."

She patted his hand, aware that she no longer felt as if by

touching him she violated his privacy. "There's nothing here but biscuits, and you're going to tell Rosalie that I sent them to her." She put her arm across the back of the seat and looked at him.

"On your honor?" He grinned sheepishly, and she supposed that his little mannerisms would always pull at her heartstrings. She'd just have to get used to not hugging him at such times. He wouldn't have liked it at his age if he had been living with her all his life.

"I'm wai...ting." She sang the word.

"Okay, but you sure drive a nasty bargain. Why don't you just give me a couple of them now? That'll hold me."

She tossed him the bag. I'm a pushover, she thought, as she drove. Aaron tuned to a rock station, and her mind drifted to Rufus. What would he and Judd talk about? If only she could share with him her feelings about the morning she'd spent with Aaron. She couldn't judge whether she and her child had made any progress toward real friendship, because he had so quickly shown suspiciousness of her. She had never felt so helpless, but there was nothing she could do but wait; it was all up to Aaron. She glanced at him sitting there, seemingly without a care— his head resting on the back of the seat, his fingers tapping his knees to the sounds of rock—and looked quickly away. She had the urge to throw caution aside, tell Rufus everything, and pray that he'd take her in his arms and keep her there.

"Are you in a hurry all of a sudden, Noomie? Sixty is kinda fast in the city."

She took her foot off the accelerator. "Sorry. My mind wandered." She parked in front of the house, and her spirits soared when Aaron patted her shoulder and teased, "Thanks. You'd better get your pilot's license if you're planning to continue flying. See you tomorrow."

She stopped by a bakery and ordered a cake, bought some oils and other supplies, locked herself in her studio, and turned on the answering machine. Hours later, the burning in her stomach reminded her that she hadn't eaten dinner, and a glance toward the window informed her that it was dark and snowing. The telephone had rung several times, but the caller had hung up as soon as her message had begun. Satisfied with her logo design for a record company's new label, she prepared to leave. The telephone rang again, and moments later, she heard his hypnotic voice.

"Did you call me earlier?"

"Three times. I hate those infernal machines. You promised a magazine interview for OLC, and I'm thinking it would be more impressive if the story covered spokesperson for several of our foundations. I've spoken with an editor of *African Americans Today,* and she would like, say, five separate stories in the same issue. I'd write the overview, and you would be the lead. What do you say?"

He had the ability to burst her balloon without trying. Her heart had thumped wildly at the sound of his voice, at the chance that he'd missed her or just wanted to talk with her. But no—he'd called to talk business. She glanced over at her drawing board at the sketches of which she had been so proud, that had made her feel like skipping instead of walking to her car, and wondered how she'd let his impersonal manner suck away her good mood so easily.

"Could we talk about this some other time, Rufus? I've just realized it's snowing, and I'd better get home. I don't know what condition the streets are in." She thought she heard him sigh, but she wasn't sure.

"Wait there a few minutes while I step outside and check the weather. Stay there until I get back to you." He hung up before she could tell him she didn't want his on-again, off-again caring. She shouldn't have answered, she told herself, knowing that after she heard his voice, hardly anything could have prevented her from lifting the receiver.

She sat down at her drawing board to wait for his call and busied herself developing ideas for a cosmetics ad. At the knock on her door, she looked at her watch; almost twenty minutes had passed. She should have realized that he'd come. She opened the door to him and the blast of cold air that still swirled around him. She hadn't seen him in knickers before. The thick Scottish tweeds and knee-high leather boots suited him. With the heavy parka, they gave him the look of a rugged outdoorsman. He walked in without waiting for an invitation, and she gave full rein to the laughter that bubbled in her when she noticed the snowflakes sticking to the tiny black curls on one side of his head.

He lifted his brow quizzically. "I amuse you?" It was difficult at times to know whether he was serious.

"I didn't realize you'd come here. The weather must be terrible. Who's with Preston and Sheldon?"

He shrugged and unzipped his parka. "I left them with a sitter, a young boy who lives across the street. They had a great time with Judd this afternoon. I think they're ready to adopt your grandfather; they're crazy about him." He tilted his head to one side and narrowed his eyes slightly. Here it comes, she thought.

"I can't imagine why you were surprised to see me. You must have known I wouldn't let you drive in this blizzard if I could prevent it. I'll drive you home. Don't worry—I'll get your car to you tomorrow morning."

She frowned, nodding hesitantly. She was taking Aaron to visit Judd tomorrow and she wouldn't consider postponing their visit; it would be the first of her son's birthdays that she'd spend with him, and she'd already seen how quickly he could become suspicious of her.

"But I'll need the car by eleven."

"Then I'll have it here by eleven." She had to fight to hold down the panic; what if Rufus found Aaron at her apartment?

But she breathed a sigh of relief when it occurred to her that she could phone Aaron and tell him she'd pick him up. Letting the breath out of her lungs slowly, she mustered a little enthusiasm and agreed to his suggestion.

At her apartment door, he asked whether she planned to invite him in for coffee. "I haven't even had dinner yet, so you'd have a long wait for coffee," she hedged. She suspected that coffee wasn't his goal, but how could she deny him something so simple after his generous gesture, going out for her and driving her home?

"Ask me in anyway, and give me a chance to warm up before going back out there in that blizzard." She tried to ignore the coolness of his grin, the clear evidence that something displeased him. He walked in behind her, unzipping his parka as he did so.

"Don't be so melodramatic," she threw over her shoulder. "It's just a little snow." But she sensed before the words were out that he wasn't in a mood for humor.

"This place always looks so warm and inviting. Like you." He stood looking down at her, his eyes and facial expression unreadable.

She placed her hands on her hips, stood with arms slightly akimbo, and gazed up at him. Bravado seemed the best way to handle Rufus right then. "Rufus, I'm going to eat my dinner and you're going to drink a cup of instant coffee and then go home."

The message in his eyes carried the precision of words. "Want to bet?" they asked her, as he took a few steps closer, almost but not quite crowding her. She wouldn't let him see how he affected her and stifled the tremors that threatened to unbalance her.

"Don't start anything that we aren't going to finish. It's bad for my nerves." She laughed. "And we're as far apart tonight as we were last night. Nothing's change. You know that."

"Nothing's changed because you won't trust me; you won't share what's inside you, eating at you."

She looked past him to the refrigerator. "And *that's* because you've never shown me a good reason."

"Then you admit there's something." He moved closer but she backed up a step and looked at him steadily, neither confirming nor denying it.

He took his parka from the back of the chair, put it on and started toward the hallway. "I don't really like instant coffee. Your car will be here in front of your door at nine."

Another evening gone sour, she thought, as he reached out and dusted her cheek with the back of his hand. "Good night, Naomi." It seemed that lately their partings always left them further apart than when they'd gotten together. She warmed some leftovers in the microwave for dinner. Later, she called Aaron and told him she'd stop by for him at noon. Rosalie had enjoyed the biscuits. "You can send some more any time; they were delicious," Rosalie told her, and added, "Next time, stop in and visit for a while. You'll be welcome."

Rufus drove slowly. Considering his state of mind, he'd be smart to walk. Something about his driving her home had made her fearful, or at least sufficiently concerned to hesitate. It was understandable that she might not want him to go home with her, their libidos were almost certain to flare up if they were alone together. He knew he should wait until she straightened out whatever was bothering her, but he was increasingly doubtful that she ever would. Walking away no longer seemed an option for him; he loved her and needed her, and if she didn't come to him soon, he was going to force the issue. Failure wasn't something he was familiar with. He laughed at himself. He'd come full circle—from disliking her to letting her get into his blood. Then, he'd fallen in love with her, and if he knew anything at all, he knew this was for keeps. His mother would have loved her, too, he reflected.

Naomi and Aaron found Judd pacing the floor when they arrived shortly after noon, worried that the storm would interfere with their visit. After the most elaborate lunch she'd ever known Calvin to prepare, Naomi brought out Aaron's birthday cake. She wouldn't have thought that a person's smile could bring her so much pleasure. But there was more to come. Happiness flooded her when Aaron leaned over a chair that was between them, wiped the chocolate crumbs from his mouth with the back of his hand, and kissed her on the cheek. She had to try hard not to overreact. To her surprise, Aaron didn't want to leave, not even when she reminded him repeatedly of the slippery streets and encroaching darkness.

At the door, she heard her grandfather tell Aaron, "You can stop calling me sir and call me Grandpa. Won't hurt you one bit to do that." She watched Aaron closely for any sign of resentment, but didn't see any.

The boy looked at Judd in the eye and told him, "I know who you are, sir. If that's what you want me to call you, it's all right with me. Uh, s—I mean, Grandpa, my mom said she'd like to meet you. Maybe you could call her sometimes." He looked from one to the other. "Thanks for the birthday lunch and especially for the cake. Chocolate's my favorite." Naomi bit her lip. It had been on the tip of her tongue to say that Rufus also loved chocolate cake.

Aaron arrived the next afternoon, as agreed, for another painting lesson. His talent and swift mind impressed her. She realized as they worked that Aaron wouldn't hesitate to ask her any questions that came to his mind. She hoped it was become he felt comfortable with her. Maybe she could ask him about something that had been bothering her.

"Aaron, how did you feel about your adoptive father?"

"I loved him," he told her. "He was great, really great. We were real close, and I still miss him. But I always felt something wasn't right. I didn't look like anybody. I'm a lighter complexion than my mom and dad, and my hair's like yours, wild and woolly. Theirs was softer and, you know, tame. Most of my friends looked a lot like one or both of their parents. Now, you..." He put the scraper aside and looked directly at her. "I look like you. Just like you. It's eerie as...it's eerie. You must look like your dad, 'cause both of us look like Grandpa."

The telephone rang, and she reached for the extension on the kitchen wall.

"Hello."

"It's Sheldon, Noomie."

"Sheldon? Darling, where are you? Home?" She remembered that Rufus had said he was going to teach the boy how to dial her number. They talked for a few minutes.

"I have to go now, Noomie. I'm supposed to stay in my room because I've been bad. We miss you, Noomie, and we want you to come see us." She told the child that she missed him and Preston, too. He hung up and she suspected that he'd been caught outside his room. She went back to her drawing board, distracted. What had they been talking about before that call?

"What's the problem, Noomie? Who was that?"

She told him, adding cryptically, "The problem is that I can't have my cake and eat it, too."

"Yeah, wouldn't that be a blast?" he quipped. Then, as if sensing an undercurrent of emotion in her, he queried, "Is Sheldon the son of that man you told me you love? Remember the day we met? You told me that." He looked steadily at her, seeming to grow older by the second. "You said the guy had four-year-old twins." He touched his head with his forefinger. "I've got a memory like an elephant, Noomie; I never forget anything." She knew her silence whetted his appetite for more information, and because she didn't have any answers, he'd draw his own conclusion, indicting her.

"Why can't you go see the kid? Seems to me if he likes you so much he called you, you've been spending some quality time with him. Is it because of me you don't see them anymore?" She had promised him that she'd answer truthfully any questions he had about her.

She leaned back and rested her elbows on the drawing board. If she was going to keep his respect, she had to appear to be in control. "I don't see them as much as I did, because their father and I are not so close anymore." She watched his eyebrows shoot up and braced herself for more quizzing. He didn't disappoint her.

"Did he drop you?" She shook her head, an amused smile playing around her lips.

"I didn't think so. You didn't tell him about me, did you? You'd rather drop him. Look, if you're ashamed of me, just pretend I don't exist. I don't need to hang around here, and I can get to Alexandria by myself." Her mind raced as she searched frantically for words that would reassure him, prevent a break in their relationship. He reached for his jacket, and she grabbed his hand.

"Aaron, no man is worth losing you again." He stared at her long and hard, as if trying to see inside her, and she had to reach deep within for the strength to withstand his scrutiny without flinching. Suddenly, he shrugged nonchalantly, as if none of it mattered.

"Whatever. I'd better be going; my mom likes for me to be home before dark." He zipped up his jacket, slanted his head, and asked her, "Do you still love this guy?" She nodded. He looked at his feet, then directly into her eyes. "I'm not sure I like this. I'll see you in a couple of days." He gave her his thumbs-up sign and left, and she wondered if she was going to lose both of them.

Chapter 17

Rufus turned off his computer. He should punish Sheldon for having disobeyed him, but he sympathized with the child. Sheldon and Preston loved Naomi and missed her as much as he did. Preston translated his hurt into anger, but Sheldon's temperament was different, and he suffered more. He had tried to protect his boys from what they were experiencing with Naomi, but an hour after they'd met her, it was too late. They feel for her as instantaneously as he did. Naomi seemed to have a way with the Meade males.

He walked upstairs, opened the door to the boys' room, and found them huddled together on Preston's bed, whispering. He watched as Preston patted Sheldon on the back, seemingly comforting him. Rufus closed the door softly, went back to his office, and phoned Naomi. Sheldon didn't need punishment; it was Naomi who needed it. He greeted her, skipped the preliminaries, and told her he knew about Sheldon's call and what he had just witnessed.

"Give me a ring when you find a solution to this." He told her goodbye and hung up. By now she was hurting, and he was sorry, but he had to play the hand that had been dealt him. He loved her. He wanted her. But if he played by the rules, he'd never get her.

Naomi's hand rested on the phone long after she'd hung up. She'd thought when she'd established contact with Aaron that she'd begun to straighten out her life. But had she? Instead, she'd precipitated new relationships and situations that had taken on a life and momentum of their own, that were all tied up together, and that would someday have to be straightened out. "I'll cry tomorrow," she quoted, as she put on a jazz album to change her mood.

At nine the following evening, Naomi conceded defeat, locked the door of her little cubicle at OLC, and headed for her car. Her steps echoed thought the empty building, accentuating her aloneness. Tutoring was usually suspended during the holiday school recess, but Linda had agreed to meet her with a report on the retreat. She couldn't imagine why the girl hadn't come, had kept her waiting there on a blustery cold night in a barely heated building. She'd have thought Linda would be anxious to share with her what she'd learned about art and painting at the retreat.

She telephoned Linda the next day at the drugstore where the girl worked part-time and asked for an explanation. She didn't mind that Linda was unapologetic, but her indifference hurt. She explained carelessly that her mother had kept her at home and, as if she had become distrustful of Naomi, asked, "Why are you so interested, anyway?"

You couldn't beat teenagers for bluntness, Naomi thought, remembering her conversation with Aaron the day before, nor for cruelty. "Linda, I see in you myself as I was at your age, and I understand you. I know where you're headed and why, and I just want to be sure that you don't get there. I'm going to speak with your mother."

She called the woman immediately and was sorry she hadn't done it earlier. Linda's mother seemed to appreciate the call and promised to encourage and support her daughter. They agreed that Linda would help her mother after work, that Naomi would tutor the girl at her apartment on Saturday mornings, and that they would stay in touch. If only her other problems could be solved so easily.

She dressed and went to buy a present for Judd's ninety-fifth birthday and one for Rufus's thirty-fifth. Aaron hadn't called her, and she decided not to pressure him. Her eyes widened and she couldn't utter a sound when he opened Judd's door just as she reached for the knob.

"Well, what a surprise. I guess you weren't joking when you said you could find your way to Alexandria." She heard the hurt in her voice and didn't try to conceal it. Something akin to embarrassment flickered in his brown eyes, but he didn't give quarter.

"Today's Grandpa's birthday. I thought I'd come out and let him beat me at chess. You coming in, or are you planning to stay out there in the cold?" Before she could react to that series of questions, he released another at bullet speed. "You want to let me carry that for you, or do you want to just give me, er, the devil for getting smart at you when I left your place?" She succumbed to his charm, fully aware that he'd turned it on to ease things for himself.

"You said you'd see me in a couple of days. What happened?" she chided.

"I've been sorting things out," he told her casually. She supposed her uneasiness showed, because he explained, "I decided to talk to Grandpa and I feel a little better about it. Have you been to see Sheldon and his brother yet?" Looking up at him, she shook her head and could have sworn that he'd grown a few inches in the last three days.

His mouth curved almost cynically. "You have to get your act together, Noomie. Talk to the guy. You won't have any less than you've got now." As if to soften the blows of his words, he stroked her cheek with the backs of his fingers, and she had to fight back the tears. Rufus often did that, usually when he was leaving.

To complicate things, Rufus called to wish Judd a happy birthday, and the boys also talked with him, filling the old man's day with happiness and giving her a feeling of aloneness. She marveled at Aaron's silence as she drove him home. Like her, he didn't feel compelled to talk unless he had something to say. But as she swung off Georgia Avenue onto his street, he turned to her.

"You'd feel better if you talked to them. Happy New Year, Noomie." He bounced out of the car and up the steps, turned, and waved.

She usually spent New Year's Eve alone, so she didn't mind it. But she made some double fudge brownies in case she got into a blue funk. The sinfully delicious treats would cure most any ailment, or at least take your mind off it. She ate her dinner and had just settled down to watch the holiday festivities on television when the doorbell rang.

Her heart leaped in her chest when she opened the door and saw Rufus and his boys. She knelt and gathered the children into her arms, showering them with kisses, barely aware of the happy tears that streaked her cheeks. The boys hugged and kissed her, dancing excitedly, lavishing her with love. At last, she stood and looked into Rufus's eyes. If only he'd take her in his arms, if only he'd hold her and kiss her, as the boys had done. She dropped her gaze, unwilling to let him see what was in her heart.

Rufus looked down at Naomi, at the sweetness of her expression and the warmth in her smiling, tear sparkled eyes that nearly took his breath away. "We came to wish you a happy New Year."

When she glanced around, he figured she was looking for the boys. He knew they'd followed their noses and had gone looking for brownies, the fragrance of which enveloped the apartment.

"Come in. I always forget to ask you in." He stepped inside, noticing that she didn't step back to make it possible and guessed that she wanted him closer. He wasn't ready to accommodate her. Preston and Sheldon had wanted to see her and had tormented him until he'd brought them. He had wanted to see her, too, but unlike four-year-olds, he regulated his desires; they didn't regulate him. She looked up at him, seeming to beseech him, but he wasn't about to spend the rest of the night—and probably a lot longer—aching for her.

"I'm so glad you came and that you brought the boys. I don't think anything could make me happier."

His lips tightened with disdain. "Nothing? Why don't I believe you? Oh, I know you think you're telling the truth, but if nothing would make you happier, sweetheart, you'd find yourself with us more often. Maybe constantly." He grinned. "Right?"

She took his hand. "Come, let's see what the boys are into. I don't want them to open the oven." They found the boys on their knees, peering at the glass oven door. When she would have rushed toward them, he restrained her. "They won't get closer, and they wouldn't touch it even if it were cold." She put the brownies on the balcony to cool and made hot chocolate.

Rufus sat at the table, holding his empty coffee cup and looking over at Sheldon, who stood beside Naomi with an arm around her and his head resting in her lap. Then he looked down at Preston who, in an unusual gesture, had taken the same position with him. He had to do something. Couldn't she see that they all belonged together?

He stood abruptly. "They're getting sleepy, so we'd better be going." At the door, he gazed at her, letting her see everything he felt; love, loneliness, need. Her quick intake of breath told him that she'd seen what he'd wanted her to see. She lowered her head, and he swiftly pulled her to him, teased her lips apart, and thrust his tongue between them, taking from her what he needed and making sure that her night would be as lonely as his. He wanted to hold her to him forever, but she stepped away, clearly shaken, gasping. He winked at her, lifted the boys into his arms and left.

The new year is only two days old, Naomi thought, and my life is in a bigger mess than ever. How had she gotten herself into such a predicament? Linda was coming for her Saturday morning tutoring session, and Aaron had decided he wanted to visit. Moreover, he refused to accept her reasons for asking him to come in the afternoon and chose instead to take it as a rejection. When she explained that Linda was a fifteen-year-old teenager who needed her help, he had curtly informed her that if she'd rather help Linda, it was fine with him; and if she didn't want her friends to meet him, he didn't care to meet them. It hadn't occurred to her that he'd see it that way.

Her wait that afternoon for Aaron was fruitless, and she realized belatedly that he hadn't promised her he'd come. Dispirited, she called Marva in hopes that a good chat with her friend would lift her mood. They talked about everything but what bothered her, and she hung up feeling worse than before she'd called. She couldn't settle into her work, and when she found herself pacing the floor, she followed her heart and telephoned Rufus.

* * *

Rufus allowed their conversation to stall after an exchange of pleasantries. He wasn't going to engage in small talk with Naomi when there were so many important things they needed to discuss. Besides, he hated small talk. "Why did you call me, Naomi? You couldn't be interested in my views on the weather. I'm a journalist, not a meteorologist."

"I just wanted to talk, Rufus. Haven't you ever just needed to talk?"

"Give me some credit, Naomi, and level with me. I know you didn't call me at ten-thirty at night to talk about nothing. I thought that when we were in New Orleans, we progressed to the point where you could admit needing me. And later, we got to the point where you lay in my arms with me deep inside you and told me you love me." Softness colored his voice, and he had to clear his throat when it clogged with emotion. "What happened since then, Naomi? You promised me you would tell me what this is all about as soon as you knew. I have a feeling that you know, and that you've made up your mind that I'm expendable. But for one, your heart refuses to follow your mind, and you're in trouble." She offered no comment when he paused. "How am I doing so far?" he asked with pretended jocularity.

"*I—I* think I'd better hang up, Rufus. This isn't helping. Kiss the boys for me. Good night."

His hand automatically replaced the receiver, but he still heard the quiet tears in her voice when she'd asked him to kiss the boys for her.

As soon as she hung up, Naomi jumped up. How could she have forgotten that it was Rufus's thirty-fifth birthday? She hadn't even arranged to give his birthday present. She removed the receiver and punched in his telephone number. She'd given her relationship with Aaron the highest priority and had removed everything and everyone else from her central thoughts. But even the slightest problem, no matter how inconsequential, turned her mind to Rufus and her need of him. She got a busy signal, hung up, and dialed again. Maybe it was the feeling she had in his arms, after he made love to her, that bound her irrevocably to him. When he folded her to him and held her, she soared, secure in the knowledge that he'd keep her safe no matter what, even in the eye of a hurricane. She heard his magnificent voice and sighed. "Happy birthday, Rufus."

Naomi rubbed furiously at the finish on her Shaker rocking chair, one of the few things of her mother's that she'd kept. She sat on the floor in front of the chair, looking at it, but seeing her life. Shiny in places, paint bare in some, and coming apart in others. The doorbell rang, and she looked at her watch, wondering which of four or five people she'd find there at ten o'clock in the morning. Aaron.

Wide-eyed with amazement, she took the bird of paradise he handed her and opened her arms to him, trying without success to control the trembling of her body as he hugged her back. He was trying to make up for yesterday, she knew, though there'd been no need for that. But they'd just passed a milestone. Maybe it was a good omen.

"I was out of line, yesterday, Noomie. I don't know what got into me. I mean, just because this girl—uh, Linda—is a kid doesn't mean you like her better than me. Does it?" Her heart raced in her chest at his admission that he wanted to be important to her. She held his hand as they walked down the hallway to the kitchen.

"No. And in your heart, you know that. Thanks for the flower; when it dries, I'm going to press it in the back of the family Bible." She gave him a half dozen brownies and a mug of coffee.

A sheepish grin softened his face as he bit off a piece of brownie. "You are, huh? I'd better go. My mom's got me painting my bathroom. Say, this is terrific. I'll take the rest of this with me." He looked down at the rocking chair. "That thing needs a lot of work. Leave it till the next time I come over. I refinished a couple of things for my mom. She liked what I did. Look, I gotta split." She walked with him to the door, rested her hand on the knob, and waited. It was his move. His kiss on her cheek washed away a lot of the pain she'd felt the night before.

"Oh, Noomie. My school is having its annual parents' day program tomorrow night. The boys sit with their fathers and the girls with their mothers. They're having some big shot guest speak, but I didn't get his name. Grandpa agreed to sit with me. My mom said you could go along with her if you want to. She said be at our house by seven o'clock. You coming?" She nodded, too full to speak. She managed to grin at his familiar thumbs-up sign, closed the door, and went to finish her coffee.

Naomi leaned against the door, speechless. She knew that her grandfather was taken with Aaron, but she found it hard to believe that he'd go so far as to publicly acknowledge him. She went into the living room, picked up the portable phone, and dialed.

"Grandpa, did you tell Aaron that you're going to sit with him at his school's program tomorrow night? Won't that be the same as announcing that he's my son?" The old man cleared his throat. His reticence made her wary; she had never known him to be reluctant to express his views.

"Naomi, gal, we have to face this now. We've turned a corner, and there's no going back. Aaron wanted to go to church with me last Sunday, and I had to postpone it. I'm a minister of the gospel, gal, and I have to do what's right. I've thought about it, worried about it, and prayed about it, and I have to do this. I've been kept here for a purpose, to support my great-grandchild, maybe. I don't know. You took a stand and did what you felt you had to do. I admired your for it, even though I opposed it, and I'm glad you did it. Now, I have to do what I know is right. We'll face whatever comes together, Naomi gal. Just take my advice and do what I've been telling you. Talk to Rufus before it's too late." She'd barely hung up when the doorbell rang. She put the flower in a bud vase and placed it on the table in the foyer as she went to open the door.

Rufus felt a tightening in his stomach as the doorknob turned. He didn't know what he'd hoped to accomplish with this spur of the moment visit, but he couldn't stay away. He had to see her. She had been hurting when she'd called him last night, and it was a deep hurt. The startled look on her face when she'd opened the door and seen him standing there had quickly changed to welcoming warmth, and he knew she was glad to see him. She opened the door wider and stood back to let him in. He stopped before her. Close. Reading her eyes and the slight quiver of her lips. Oh, God, he needed this woman so badly.

"Ah, Naomi, come here to me, sweetheart." Miraculously, she stood wrapped in his arms, sobbing his name against his lips. A shudder ricocheted through him as her soft, warm body and roaming lips inflamed him. He picked her up and set her bodily away from him; he'd warned himself before leaving home that making love with her wouldn't solve their problems, would only exacerbate them. She tried to move back into his arms, but he restrained her gently.

"Hold on, sweetheart, we need to talk. How about some coffee?" They walked back to the kitchen, and she gave him a mug of coffee.

"Why did you call me last night, Naomi?" He waited until she sat down and deliberately faced her across the table. He had to see her eyes and the movements of her mouth: Naomi had spent so much time covering up her feelings that you needed a microscope to figure out what was going on with her.

"Are you going to tell me why you called me? Naomi, if I start making love to you, I can get you to tell me anything, but that's not what I want for us. Beside, it's a form of blackmail. You're so articulate, witty, and wicked when it suits you, why won't you talk to me? Are you willing to drop this? If you are, tell me. It won't kill me."

Naomi had been sipping her coffee, seeming to weigh his every word. She remembered Judd's advice of minutes earlier, but she couldn't banish her fear that if she told him everything, he would scorn her. "Rufus, why do you think I had a hidden motive for calling you?"

"I didn't come here for that, Naomi." How could she look so calm, knowing that she was skirting the truth?

She straightened up and looked directly into his eyes. Maybe she was going to level with him at last. She spoke softly, seeming to measure her words carefully.

"There's noting else I can tell you now, Rufus. I'm glad you came over here this morning, more than you could guess. And knowing that you'd have been there for me last night if I'd had a problem makes me happy."

He placed his cup on the table and stood. "That's it." Bitterness laced his voice. "That's all you've prepared to say to me?" She nodded. His hand touched his forehead in a mocking military salute.

"Stay there, honey. I can let myself out."

She got up slowly and put the few dishes in the dishwasher. She hadn't been able to deal with Rufus's questions; her mind had been on her narrow escape. If he had arrived five minutes earlier, he'd have found Aaron there. She tried to dismiss the feeling that she stood at a precipice, about to tumble into disaster.

* * *

Rufus stepped briskly up to the lectern. Next to writing, his greatest pleasure was in talking to young people, especially teenagers. As usual, before he began to speak, he let his gaze sweep his audience as he took its pulse. Why was Naomi there? If she wanted to see him, she knew where he lived. But this wasn't the time to think about Naomi, he told himself, and got down to the business at hand. He smiled appreciatively at the waves of applause that greeted him at the end of his twenty-minute talk. Reaching down for the small case that he'd brought with him, he stepped across the rostrum to the boys and girls who stood with their parents. He knew that the older boys weren't shaking hands with the speaker, but with Cat Meade, the former NFL wide receiver. Nonetheless, he hoped his message would have an impact on their lives. He handed each a key ring, a small gold-plated replica of a house, on the back of which was inscribed, *"Best wishes, Rufus Meade."*

He reached for the hand extended to him and looked into Judd Logan's face. "What are you…" His glance shifted to the right and the boy beside Judd. He managed to exchange greetings with them, finish his round, smile at everyone, and get off the stage. He had to find her.

As if she'd known he'd come, she remained seated, right where she'd been all evening, open and vulnerable. He walked up to her, knowing that if he said a word, he'd regret it. The people around them were just a faceless mass of human flesh; there was only Naomi, the woman he loved beyond all reason. The woman who thought so little of his capacity for caring and understanding that she couldn't tell him she had a teenaged son. If that boy wasn't hers, there was no such things as genes. He stared at her for minutes and said nothing. Talking would have been useful yesterday or that morning, but not now. He shook his head sadly, not caring that his disappointment showed, nodded to the startled woman beside her, and walked away.

Home at last, away from the fuss and adulation that he hated, away from the scene of his shocking discovery. At the door to his sons' bedroom, watching their peaceful sleep, he gave thanks for the one constant in his life: his love for his sons and theirs for him. Why couldn't she have trusted him? Why hadn't she realized that he'd have climbed mountains for her, and that he'd have made her problems his own, that all he asked in return was her trust, her faith in him? He walked to the window, drawn there by the howling winter wind, and looked out at the desolate, leafless trees, eerie shapes beneath the dark, cloudy skies. He'd never felt so disheartened, nor so alone.

He'd had clues, but they hadn't fit any pattern. At last he understood Naomi's protectiveness toward Linda and her sudden refusal to block the admittance of boys to OLC. Still, something didn't fit. If the boy was hers, where had he been? Naomi had said she was an only child, so that boy had to be her son. And the age fit the bits and pieces of information he'd gotten from her and Judd. *It's been over fourteen years since she let herself get as close to a man as she was to you last night. And I know that for a fact,* Judd had told him. That boy had to be about fourteen. He walked out of the room and closed the door. Something wasn't right, and he had to decide whether he cared enough to find out what was beneath it all. He wondered what she was thinking right then, whether she realized what she'd done.

Naomi looked up at the inquiring faces of Aaron and Rosalie and into the knowing eyes of her grandfather. "Come on, Naomi gal, we're the last ones here." His withered fingers grasped her shoulders, urging her to get up, and his old eyes softened with sympathy. She trailed them outside, hardly aware of her surroundings. At her car, Judd stopped her. "No point in crying over spilled milk, gal. You didn't tell him, and now he knows. Either find a way to patch it up, or forget him and get on with your life. Neither course is going to be easy. If I'd known this would happen, I'd still have sat with Aaron. It was past time for you to level with Rufus; you hadn't any right to let him care for you while you kept him in the dark about something like this. I kept your secret, but you know I didn't like doing it. I begged you just yesterday to talk to him. You're going to have to make the first move, and you'd better make it soon."

Naomi turned at the touch of Aaron's hand on hers. "I'll be over tomorrow morning, Noomie." She nodded. Ten minutes later, she walked into her apartment, too numb to do more than pull off her clothes and get into bed. She hadn't misinterpreted the cool disapproval in Rufus's eyes; he had condemned her without giving her a chance to explain. She had been right not to confide in him; he didn't care enough. And she'd have to straighten Judd out. She'd told Rufus many times that there couldn't be anything between them, so she couldn't be accused of leading him on.

She answered her door at eight-fifteen the next morning to find a very solemn Aaron standing there. He walked past her quickly, as if to avoid a greeting.

"If you didn't eat breakfast yet, I'll eat with you. All I did was get up, put my clothes on, and leave. My mom dropped me off." She wondered about his nervous chatter; it was unlike him. She put together a hearty breakfast and sat down with him.

"What's on your mind, Aaron?" She didn't plan to let him disturb her equilibrium, no matter what he said or did. Rufus had given her enough to deal with.

He chewed his bacon deliberately, swallowed it, and sipped some coffee. "What is Cat Meade to you, Naomi?" She hadn't expected his question to be so direct. Unfazed, she looked into her son's steely, accusing gaze. She no longer had a reason for evasiveness and secrecy; she could be herself.

"I love him, Aaron."

"I see. So he's the one. And you didn't tell him about me. He found out on his own last night, because I'm the spitting image of you and I was with Grandpa. Why didn't you tell him?"

"I didn't think I could handle it if he scorned me for having a child that was given up for adoption. He doesn't know that part yet, and he still judged me harshly, without hearing me out."

"Come on, Noomie. The guy got a shock. Do you think it would've been worse if you'd sat down and talked to him?" He sipped the last of his coffee, and she watched his young face sadden.

"I should have stayed out of your life. If I hadn't pushed my mom so hard to find you, you'd probably be married to the guy by now. But I'm not really sorry, Noomie, because now that I know you, I understand myself better. I guess I shouldn't have stuck so close to you and Grandpa, though. My mom says it's natural for me to like being around you, since you don't mind. But I'll disappear, if it'll make things better between you and Mr. Meade." He looked at her expectantly, and she hurt for him. He had chosen to take responsibility for the mess she'd made.

"Aaron, Rufus can't replace you in my life, any more than you can take his place. Try to understand that you aren't part of any solution to my problem with Rufus. And meeting you was my decision; a decision I have never regretted. Nor will I ever. You come here as often as you like and as long as Rosalie doesn't mind." He seemed more relaxed, and she hoped she'd put his mind at ease.

Later, he stood at her door, about to leave, more pensive than she remembered having seen him and without his usual swagger. "I hope you make up with him, Noomie. I like him a lot. Us guys in my class think he's a saint; he's practically our guardian angel. Sometime you can tell me how you met him." She laughed at the memory, and Aaron smiled broadly, as if glad to see the change in her. He left, but forgot his thumbs-up sign. If only he'd forget about her and Rufus; she knew she had to do just that. From Rufus's behavior last night, it was over between them.

Rufus sat in his office with Sheldon on his knee and Preston between his legs leaning against him and listened to Dick Jenkins drone on and on. He didn't usually discuss business with his boys hanging onto him, but Dick had dragged the appointment out for three hours. He had switched on the answering machine and didn't answer the phone, but when he heard, "I'm Aaron Hopkins. I met you last night," he picked up the receiver.

"Hello, Aaron. I can't speak with you right now. Give me your number, and I'll call you in five minutes." That should get rid of Jenkins.

"Aaron, this is Rufus Meade." The boy wanted to come and see him. He wasn't going to discuss Naomi with anyone, but he'd listen to Aaron, he decided. He opened the door an hour later to the handsome boy who looked so much like the woman he loved.

"Come in, Aaron." He noticed the boy's reticence and draped an arm loosely around his shoulder.

"Thanks for letting me come. Where are the twins?" He hadn't expected that Naomi would have told the boy about him and his children.

"They're about to have a nap." He poured two glasses of ginger ale and sat down, motioning to Aaron to do the same. "What can I do for you?" He watched Aaron take a deep breath, as if preparing himself for an ordeal.

"I'm fourteen, and I'm very reliable. So if you need a sitter sometime, or maybe someone to run errands or something, I'd be glad to do it without charge. Reverend Logan could give you a reference." He wondered what had given the boy such a guilt complex, but he wouldn't pry.

"Thanks, I appreciate the offer, and I may call on you, but I'll pay you the going rate. Never offer charity where none is needed, son. I hear my boys running around upstairs. Come, I'll introduce you." Sometime later, he dressed the boys for their trip to the library, listening to their chatter about their new friends, Grandpa and Aaron. What had prompted Aaron to seek him out? He remembered seeing him in the school gym, a bright, inquisitive kid, but the boy had never said a word to him. And he sensed Aaron's protectiveness toward Naomi. But why? Strange, that he'd never seen evidence of him in her apartment.

Rufus arrived at the *Journal* the next morning, a few minutes early for his appointment with Hector Shaw, its editor-in-chief. He'd left the boys with Jewel's husband, but he had been tempted to ask Aaron to stay with them. Hector rushed in at precisely nine o'clock.

"Sorry, Cat, but there was an accident, and I had to make a detour. Let's check the police headquarters and see if we can find out anything. There appeared to be several cars involved." He picked up the receiver, dialed and got down to business. It was routine, a part of the job.

"How old is he? Did you get his name? How do you spell that? Thanks."

He hung up and turned to Rufus. "A bad accident, but

no fatalities. Routine stuff. A kid on in-line skates. They took him to the hospital center. I'll put Joyce on it. She'll get the human interest aspect. Those skates are dangerous." He puffed on his stale pipe.

Rufus saw nothing routine about a kid getting hit. An odd sensation pricked the back of his neck. "How old is the boy?"

"Early teens. Why?"

Rufus knew that he only pulled at his chin when he was disturbed. He resisted doing it, but for some reason, he had an unaccountable edginess. "What is the boy's name?"

Hector checked his notepad. "Hopkins."

Rufus turned on his heel with the speed for which he was famous. "I'll speak with you later on. Right now I've got to get to that hospital," he called over his shoulder.

He found Naomi and Rosalie huddled together in the waiting room, frightened. "I'm Rufus Meade," he told Rosalie. Naomi's tear-streaked face and sad, reddened eyes clutched at his heart as she looked at him. "Rufus, this is my friend Rosalie Hopkins. We don't have any news yet. A car sideswiped him, and two other cars collided to avoid hitting him. He's in surgery. How did you know about this?"

"I was at the *Journal*." His mind raced, searching for a logical explanation of the relationship between the two women and Aaron. Hours later, a doctor informed them that Aaron had suffered internal injuries and a sprained knee, but would recover fully within a few weeks. He advised them to go home; the boy was in intensive care and wouldn't be allowed visitors for twenty-four hours. Naomi had said she was an only child and that she'd never married. Rosalie and Aaron had the same last name, but Aaron resembled Naomi, not Rosalie. Somewhere in there lay Naomi's reason for secrecy, he'd bet on that.

* * *

Naomi walked zombie-like into her bedroom and sat on the bed. Rufus had insisted on bringing her home, and she was grateful. The chill in her chest had nearly disappeared when she saw him coming toward her in the hospital, confident but concerned. "I think you should undress and try to sleep," he advised her. "I'll phone Judd. Then I'll run over to Jewel's to look after my boys, but I'll come back and see that you get dinner."

She tried to keep the weariness out of her voice so that he wouldn't think she was asking for his sympathy. "I don't expect that from you, Rufus, though I do thank you for being there today. It meant more to me than you could imagine. But I'll be all right."

His gaze seared her, and she shifted nervously under its impact. "I said I'll be back here. Give me your keys, and I'll let myself in." She gave them to him, wondering why he'd bother.

She awakened at his urging two hours later to a lobster dinner complete with white wine and chocolate mousse for dessert. He had set her kitchen table for two, adding candles and three calla lilies he'd brought her. He reached across the table, took her hand in his, and said grace, then proceeded to eat as though it was their daily routine. She loved lobster, but salty tears impaired its taste.

He spoke for the first time. Lovingly. Compassionately. "Don't worry, Naomi. The doctor said he'll be okay, and that there won't be any aftereffects."

She brushed away the tears and forced a smile. "If I'd known you could cook like this, I'd have asked you to marry me. With this kind of talent, I'd take a chance."

He looked steadily at her. "I'm glad you feel like joking, even if it's at my expense. And incidentally, if I can cook like this, why would I want a wife?"

She laughed; he could give as good as he got, though she figured he felt about as much like teasing as she did. She looked at him. *Oh, Lord. He wasn't joking.*

"I'm sorry." Poor recompense, she knew, but it was what she felt. They finished the meal, and he insisted on straightening up the kitchen. She took the flowers from the table and thanked him for them. He only nodded, and she realized too late that he wasn't a man to diminish his standard of behavior no matter what anyone else did. He would be gracious and considerate even if he wanted to throttle her. She walked out of the kitchen slowly, dispirited; from the way he acted, she could be a woman he'd just met.

She put the flowers beside her bed and crawled under the covers. "Life begins tomorrow," she told herself, "and if I can't have him, I'll just get along without him."

Her heartbeat accelerated wildly at the sound of his soft knock. "Yes?" Emotion clogged her throat, nearly strangling her. Was he asking to come in? He couldn't be!

"If you need me, Naomi, I'll be in your guestroom. I've just spoken with the doctor at the hospital. Aaron is comfortable and not in any danger. Good night."

"Goodnight, Rufus. And th-thank you."

Hours later, she turned on the light, unable to sleep. Was this how Rufus felt when she refused to tell him what kept them apart? When she got downstairs the next morning, Rufus had already left.

Each morning she joined Rosalie in Aaron's hospital room and sat there with her most of the day. And she watched the door impatiently every afternoon until Rufus arrived. She and Rosalie noticed that Aaron was brighter and more responsive during Rufus's visits. And Naomi became increasingly conscious of the bond that had begun to form between her and the woman who had nurtured her son. She gasped in astonishment at Rosalie's suggestion that Aaron recuperate at her apartment, explaining that she had lost two weeks' pay and couldn't afford to lose more.

Naomi remembered that Rosalie was a nurse and would have been the more logical choice as caregiver for Aaron. Her common sense told her that Rosalie's financial circumstances must be more modest than she had thought, and the knowledge saddened her. But she gloried in the chance to care for Aaron and to help him stay abreast of his schoolwork. She expected that Rosalie would be attentive to Aaron, visiting him daily. But she could not have imagined that Rufus would care for them and nurture them as he did, calling in advance for her shopping list, even cooking on occasion. She looked forward to his daily visits and especially to those times when he brought the boys with him. But the deep, aching need that spread through her each time she saw him remained unappeased when he left. How could he be so impersonal? Friendly. Caring. Considerate. And still so detached. She'd catch him looking at her and see the hot desire in his eyes immediately turn to cool disinterest. Chills coursed through her as she thought of him sitting beside her in Aaron's room or passing within inches of her, always with a smile that barely reached his lips and always avoiding touching her. He hadn't made a semblance of an overture toward her since that awful night, and she knew he wouldn't.

Judd visited Aaron nearly every day, and one afternoon, he followed Naomi into the living room. "He's giving you a hard time, isn't he, gal?"

"Oh, Grandpa, I made a terrible mistake. I just know it. He is completely unselfish and caring. I believe he might have understood if I'd given him a chance. He quietly takes care of us; if we need anything, we don't have to ask him, he just seems to sense it."

"You're being foolish not to tell him what's in your heart, gal."

"I can't, Grandpa. All those times he gave me the chance, I didn't take it. If he'd given me even a little sign, I'd go for it. But he keeps me at a distance."

Judd raised one eyebrow. "In my days, if a man cared for a girl, she could get him to do just about anything short of dishonoring himself. What's the matter with you young people?" Shaking his head, he left her standing there and went to the kitchen where Rufus was changing a recessed light bulb in the ceiling.

Rufus looked down from his perch on a ladder. He'd been expecting Judd to corner him for an inquisition. The old man looked up and squinted. "You're good about letting my Naomi depend on you, boy, but you're still giving her a hard time. I want to know exactly why you're here every day."

Rufus grinned. He cared a lot for Naomi's grandfather, but he wasn't going to let him treat him like a child. "You're meddling again. But I suppose it's too late to stop you; you've made a lifelong career of telling people what to do. Naomi is mine, Judd, and I am going to take care of her. And if you're smart, you'll refrain from tattling."

He watched Judd walk away with a pretended indifference, but he knew that his words had pleased the old man. Let Naomi figure out for herself the mistake she'd made with him. She was ready for a reconciliation, but he wasn't. He needed her. His body ached for her, and he missed her weird humor, and their warm camaraderie. But for the first time in his life, he appreciated the virtue of patience. He wasn't giving an inch until she came to him, opened her heart to him, and let him know that she trusted him completely and needed him.

Chapter 18

Naomi opened the door for Rufus, mumbled, "Hello," and left him to trail her as she walked back to her room. "Why didn't you let yourself in?" she threw at him over her shoulder, and blanched at his smooth retort.

"I was reminding myself that I don't really live here." She'd asked for that, but being with him constantly while he treated her like a discarded shoe was wearing on her. Nothing seemed to ruffle him.

She turned to him, tossing her head arrogantly. "Have no fear. *I* hadn't forgotten it." He grinned, and tremors shot through her as she stared at the dancing lights in his eyes and felt his blatant masculinity leap at her. But as quickly as he'd turned on the charm, he extinguished it, reminding her that they were still at odds.

"I'd like to take Aaron over to my place this afternoon, give him a change of scenery for a while. And he thinks he'd like to try using my on-line computer service, make friends with some fellows his age in Texas, California, or wherever."

He paused, and her hair crackled with electricity as he eyed her knowingly, like a man going in for the kill. "Whose permission do I get? Yours, or Rosalie's?" She turned away, uncertain as to her next move.

"I'm too tired to go right now, Mr. Meade," Aaron called from his room, letting them know he'd heard their conversation.

She fought against the tension that churned within her as Rufus's mouth curved in a mocking grin. "He's very protective of you. I wonder how he got so tired this early in the day while lying in bed. Preston could have thought up a better one than that."

Naomi sucked in a deep breath. How had it come to this? She tried to hide her vulnerability to him and lowered her eyes to prevent his seeing what she knew they mirrored. When she looked up at him, her heart pounded furiously at the pain in his eyes, the pain of a tortured person. Her hand went out to him of its own volition; taken unawares, he grasped it and clung to it for a moment. Then she watched unhappily as a curtain of indifference seemed to descend over him. Wordlessly, he turned and went into Aaron's room.

She went into her own room, closed the door, and telephoned Rosalie. "What shall I tell Rufus? If Aaron wants to go with him, do you mind?" She waited anxiously for Rosalie's answer, for this clue to their future relationship, for the first evidence she'd have of how far Rosalie would allow her tie with Aaron to go.

"Naomi, when Aaron is with you, he's responsible to you. If it's a question of policy, of course I must be consulted, but ordinarily, you decide. As time goes on and we get to know each other better, it'll be easier." Naomi wondered at her long pause before she continued in the same gentle voice. "I am definitely not suggesting that we share parenting; that wouldn't make sense. But I want Aaron to have a good, healthy relationship with you, and that means obeying and respecting you. So far, our relationship has been good for all of us. I'll be over after work."

Naomi paced the floor. She'd have to find out what Aaron wanted; then she'd speak with Rufus. He had deliberately put her on the spot, indirectly challenging her to explain the relationship between Rosalie, Aaron and herself, though she was certain he'd figured it out.

She found Aaron alone, pensive and anxious for her. He raised up and braced himself on his right elbow. "Noomie, I don't want you and Mr. Meade to be mad at each other because of me. I called my mom, and she said I can suit myself if you agree, so why don't you tell him I'll go to his place after lunch? I like him, Noomie, and I want to see those little rascals of his." He took her hand in his. "You have to make up with him. Promise."

Joy swelled within her. He cared for her, wanted her to be happy. She looked at her son, shook her head at the changes in him, and asked him a question that Rufus had once asked her. "I promise, but whatever happened to your gnawing wit? You've gotten so serious lately."

He placed his hand under his chin, knitted his eyebrows, and pretended to be an old sage. "We're dealing with serious stuff here, Noomie." Her musical laughter filled the room, and he laughed with her.

"I could use a good laugh." She glanced up as Rufus entered the room. Did his eyes always sparkle like diamonds, and did she feel seduced every time she saw him smile? Emotion muffled her words as he walked toward her, carelessly self-possessed. Her hand clutched her throat as she forced herself to speak calmly.

"Aaron wants to go with you, and there's no reason why he can't."

"None?" he asked sardonically.

Aaron heaved himself up in bed. "Mr. Meade, if Noomie says it's okay, it's okay." The both stared at Aaron; the testiness in his voice was unmistakable.

Rufus grimaced slightly. The boy could be touchy. "I'll be ready when you are, son."

Rufus observed that Aaron was unusually quiet. He had a right to be irritated; blood was thicker than water, he'd always been told. The boy knew he'd been putting pressure on Naomi, and he suspected Aaron knew why. He admired her strength, her old-fashioned grit. Strong men would have fallen under what she'd endured during the past month: his discovery of her secret; Aaron's near-fatal accident; her peculiar arrangement with Aaron and Rosalie; having a man she loved so close every day and so detached. He doubted that he'd have borne it all as gracefully. She was vulnerable and raw on the inside, and he was half mad with her for refusing to relent and talk to him. Lord, how he wanted to comfort her, hold her, love her. He sighed deeply. Stubborn woman!

Naomi used her afternoon of freedom to visit Marva. She needed to talk to someone who would give her the blunt truth. Judd had already voiced his thoughts, but he seemed to have taken out a life membership in the Rufus Meade for everything club and was biased. She knew immediately that she wouldn't be able to speak candidly with her friend. She found Marva knitting booties and unable or unwilling to consider any topic other than her marvelous pregnancy, as she called it. She left Marva, disappointed.

A letter in her mailbox gave Naomi cause for celebration. She telephoned Linda at home to tell her that if she maintained a B average until she finished high school, she'd have her choice of at least three universities with a full scholarship. Linda's screams and confessions of love must have attracted her mother's suspicion, because Linda's mother took the phone and inquired, with some hostility, as to the caller's identity. To Naomi's amusement, the woman's reaction to the news was identical to her daughter's. She couldn't hold back the tears that streaked her cheeks and colored her voice; Linda had a chance at a fruitful, happy life. It was up to her, and Naomi didn't doubt she'd seize the opportunity. Naomi had a sense of triumph, of having finished a difficult task, when Linda's mother invited her to have a meal with them. It had not been easy, but she'd made a friend.

She sat in a leather chair in her living room, sipped mint tea, and contemplated the changes in her life over the past half year. Her euphoria at Linda's good news disappeared. She hadn't known she'd felt so alone until Rosalie arrived.

"Why are you sitting here without lights, Naomi? Are you all right?" Maybe it was the concern with which she spoke, or even the quiet, compassionate way she had of talking. She seemed to invite confidence. A floodgate sprang open and within seconds, Naomi found herself pouring out her soul to this stranger who'd become her friend. She omitted nothing.

"What'll I do, Rosalie? I love him with every fiber of my being. He is my world, my life. I thought I could get him out of my mind and out of my heart, but now I know I can't. I love Aaron, and I need Rufus. I made a terrible mistake."

Rosalie walked over to the sofa, sat beside Naomi, and put her arms around the mother of her adopted son. "You carried a terrible load for a long time, Naomi, and because of unfounded fear, you kept it all inside. Just when the load got bigger, you found someone with whom you could share it, but you couldn't let go of the fear. You couldn't trust. Rufus hasn't been here for you night and day since Aaron got hurt just because he doesn't have anything else to do. Have you asked yourself why? My mother used to tell me that 'pride goes before destruction and a haughty stumble before a fall.'"

Her deep-set brown eyes misted, and for a moment, she seemed to be reliving a treasured experience. "I wouldn't let pride keep me out of the arms of a man like Rufus Meade." She went on. "Stuff your pride, Naomi. Let him know you have faith in him, that you trust him. It's all you need to do."

Naomi watched Rosalie's suddenly brilliant smile. "Now I know we're friends; you've never told that to anyone else. Well, I've always wanted a sister, and you'll do nicely."

"No, I haven't," Naomi, confirmed. "And now that I know what I've missed, never having had a sister, I'm definitely going to cherish the one I've got now. Let me get you some more coffee." They talked about their lives and familiarized themselves with each other until Rufus brought Aaron back.

"Will you stay for dinner? It's not much, but there's fried chicken." She wanted him to stay, and she couldn't keep the note of hope out of her voice. His leaving would have been easier to accept if he'd shown any reluctance, but he hadn't.

"I promised Preston and Sheldon I'd be right back. We'll have to do this again soon, Aaron; my boys and I enjoyed having you with us." He nodded to Rosalie and Naomi. "Good night. I can let myself out."

Rosalie had gone home, and Naomi sat by Aaron's bed, listening to his excited account of his afternoon with the Meade family. "He's a great guy, Noomie, Cat Meade practically walks on water."

He slanted his head in a sly grin. "Of course, you do, too—walk on water, I mean." Her eyes widened, and he patted her hand. "Don't get a big head now." She watched as his light olive toned face suddenly curled into a deep frown, his youthful expression becoming serious and strained. "What you told me about when I was born…you know…that stuff about the pressure those people put on you. I believe you. Now that I know you, I can't imagine that you'd willingly have given me up for adoption. I love my mom, Noomie; she's my mom. But I've got a real special place in here for you, too." He pointed to his heart. "I'm lucky my mom is the kind of person she is; otherwise I wouldn't know you."

He used the corner of the sheet to wipe away his mother's tears. "I'm going to try and be a son to you. I promise."

His words warmed her as would a brilliant light, and comforted her, completing the catharsis that had begun with her confession to Rosalie. "I didn't even pray for this, Aaron, because I didn't think it possible for you to love me; I was just hoping you'd like me enough to be with me sometime. You... you're my heart; you're precious to me, and I care deeply for Rosalie, too." She sniffled a few times and had to fight off her emotions. A woman's tears made a man uncomfortable, and sensing that, like most of them, Aaron had low tolerance for heavy emotional scenes, she rose. "I'll get us some ginger ale, or would you rather have a Coke with a couple of scoops of vanilla ice-cream?"

He rewarded the suggestion with a broad grin and his thumbs-up sign. "Noomie," he called after her. "You, my mom, and me are straight. Now all you have to do is get it together with Mr. Meade."

Rufus entered his house through the garage door and rubbed his arms vigorously. Washington wasn't usually so rough in winter, but the entire East Coast was in the clutches of a cold wave. He called a taxi for the sitter, sent her home, and ran upstairs to let his boys know he'd returned. He went back downstairs and made hot chocolate for the three of them, got a tray, and stopped. He could have stayed and had supper with Naomi. She had wanted it so badly, and her wordless entreaty had nearly made him lose his resolve. But if he allowed himself to weaken, all would be lost and she'd never open up to him. Unless she came to him, she wouldn't know that he didn't want to judge her, only to have her complete trust.

He rubbed the back of his neck. Being around her constantly, looking at her, and brushing against her for almost four long weeks had tested his self-control, tried him to the limits of his willpower. But he was damned if he'd give in. He swallowed the saliva that had suddenly accumulated in his mouth. Memories of her woman's scent in the heat of passion assaulted his olfactory senses, and he could feel again her long, silky legs rubbing against his, caressing him as she writhed uninhibitedly beneath him. His blood rushed through his body, telling him how long it had been since he'd loved her. Something had to happen; their standoff had to end, and soon. He picked up the tray and slowly climbed the stairs, deep in thought.

Naomi telephoned her grandfather early the next morning. He wasn't going to like what she had to say, but as he'd said, there was no going back.

"Naomi gal, you can't let well enough alone, can you? Why would you walk into that pit of snakes and present them with the ammunition they'll use to kill your chances? If you take Aaron with you to that school board meeting, you'll never be elected board president. You can find another way to let him know what he means to you."

She had expected him to react that way, but she had to make certain that Aaron would never again think her ashamed of him. She told Judd as much.

"All right, gal. I think you might regret it, but being president of that bunch of snipers is nothing compared to what Aaron means to us. If you'd listened to me, I would never have known my great-grandson. You go on and do what you have to do. You always did, and I'm proud of you."

"Thanks, Grandpa. Aaron loves us, and we've got to show him it's mutual. His last name is Hopkins, but he's family, and he accepts that. I'll let you know what happens at the board meeting."

She brought Aaron's breakfast to him and sat beside him with her own tray. "Noomie, I can eat at the table. You're spoiling me."

Her gaze swept lovingly over his handsome face. "I'm making up for lost time. Besides, I think you're wrong. Rufus told me the doctor said you shouldn't move around too much for another week yet."

As if he'd been waiting for that cue, he placed his tray beside him on the bed, put both hands behind his head, and leaned against the headboard. "You know, Noomie, I think Mr. Meade must be crazy about you. The radio said it was eight degrees and icy outside, and he drove all the way over here to bring you a bottle of milk and a carton of eggs that we could have done without. 'Course, I'm glad he threw in the ice-cream and Coke."

She knew he noticed the clatter of her cup and saucer as she placed them with trembling fingers on the table beside her. Her throat constricted in pain as she forced out her words.

"If he's crazy about me, you and he are the only ones who know it."

Aaron leaned toward her. "I'm a kid, Noomie, but somebody half my age would pick up on that. I've seen him looking at you, just as I've seen you looking at him. You mean he's never told you anything about how he feels?"

"Never, Aaron, and I don't want you to talk to me about it. There was a time when I might have been able to straighten it out, but it's too late now. At first, we didn't like what we saw in each other; then we got close, but I couldn't tell him about my life, so I kept a barrier between us. He figured it all out for himself that night, and I guess he couldn't accept it. Don't think badly of him, Aaron; this mess is my fault. I knew better than to get involved with him."

He seemed restless and his expression turned hard. "Does Mr. Meade know you love him? I mean, did you ever tell him?"

She looked down at her hands, remembering that night. He had pushed her over the edge, controlling her senses, igniting her, blackmailing her with her wanton hunger for his possession. Then his body had consumed hers with blazing tongues of fire as he'd driven her to mind-shattering ecstasy. Tremors colored her voice. "Once, I told him."

"And you still do." There was no question in his voice. "So how is this your fault? Why must you be the one to fix it? Let him sweat; only a fool would pass up a woman who looks like you, Noomie. And Mr. Meade is not a fool." He let out a long breath, as one who is disgusted. "Sometimes I wonder why adults think they know everything." Naomi took the remains of their breakfast to the kitchen, straightened up the room, and got dressed. She'd stopped wondering why Aaron's thinking so often belied his age; Rosalie had told Naomi that she and her husband hadn't shielded the boy, but had included him in all but the most private aspect of their lives. She tapped on his door, opened it, and leaned in. "I'm going to the supermarket; I should be back in about an hour." She grinned when he folded his fist and stuck his thumb up.

Cold fear knotted Naomi's stomach as she walked through the quiet house and up the stairs to Aaron's room. Intuition and the eerie silence told her that she was alone in the house. The door to Aaron's room stood ajar, the bed made, the room empty. She started to knock on the door of his bathroom, glimpsed the sheet of paper pinned to his pillow, and knew that he was gone. But why? He could barely walk without support. She picked up the paper and for the first time read his careless script.

Dear Noomie, I know it's not right to leave like this, but I think it's time I went back to my mom. I can look after myself now. Thanks for everything. And don't worry. I'm taking a taxi. I'll call you.
Love Aaron.

She had to fight the hysteria that welled up in her. What had caused him to leave so suddenly? He'd said he loved her and would be a son to her, and then he'd left, walked out on his word. She couldn't lose him; she *couldn't*. She couldn't find Rosalie's number at work. Wringing her hands in despair, she fought the urge to call her grandfather. She didn't know whether he could stand the jolt; Aaron had come to mean everything to him.

Oh, Rufus. I need you so! Her feet propelled her to the telephone beside Aaron's bed as if of their own volition. He answered on the first ring. "Rufus, it's me, Naomi. I went to the supermarket, and when I got back, Aaron had gone. His note said he was going home." She tried to control the trembling in her voice. "I can't lose him, Rufus. I can't lose him. I can't…"

He interrupted her gently. "Settle down, Naomi. It will be all right. Just wait until Rosalie gets home and we can get to the bottom of this. I'm surprised the boy didn't tell you he intended to go; he's always so straightforward."

She wiped her nose with her sleeve and took a deep breath. "That's why I'm worried. Something's wrong."

"Nothing's wrong, Naomi." His voice came to her strong

and confident. She knew he had no more information that she did, but his convincing assurance restored her hope. "I'll call you back in an hour or so," he told her. "Don't worry about it, now. Aaron is a good boy, and he's very responsible."

Rufus had registered his boys in a morning preschool program, and he'd already learned that there were benefits for him as well as for the boys. He could leave home suddenly without getting a sitter. He drew his parka on over his cashmere sweater, got into his Town Car, took the East West Highway, and within ten minutes was knocking on the door of the red brick house on Pershing Street.

The surprised look on the boy's face when he opened the door and saw him might have been comical if he hadn't noticed that Aaron was withdrawn, almost unfriendly. "May I come in, Aaron?"

"Sure, Mr. Meade. How did you know where I live?"

What an actor! This kid was mad as the devil about something, but he obviously didn't intend to show it. "I've driven Rosalie home several times. Aaron, Naomi is terribly upset about your leaving her like this." He walked into the living room and sat down. "She's nearly hysterical with worry."

"What's it to you? What do you care how upset she is?"

He could see that the boy would love to slug him. Whatever the problem, he was in the middle of it. "Aaron, this attitude is not one bit helpful. If you've got something to say to me, say it. I'd have thought our relationship merited honesty on both our parts." He watched the boy as the anger left him, and he dropped his head. Rufus waited. Aaron sat in the chair across from him, spread his legs, rested a hand on each knee, and observed him steadily, as if making up his mind. Suddenly, he leaned back.

"Mr. Meade, do you know what Noomie is to me?"

Rufus's eyebrows shot up. He hadn't expected this turn of conversation. "I'd have to be blind not to know. Why?"

Aaron slanted his head to the side in a gesture so reminiscent of Naomi that Rufus shifted uncomfortably at the vision he suddenly had of her. "If I hadn't pushed my mom so hard to find Noomie, you'd probably be married to her by now. She doesn't know how you feel about her, but I do."

Rufus sat forward, a frown furrowing his brow. "What are you talking about? Who is…Aaron, I don't need to hear this from you; I need to hear it from Naomi."

"If you needed to hear it from her, why didn't you ask her right out, Mr. Meade? Can't you see she's been miserable? I know I'm the reason you two can't get together. I hate to see her hurt; she's been hurt enough. If you loved her, you'd talk to her. She said you'd never told her whether you…how you felt about her, but she told *you*. You don't deserve her. I left this morning because if I'm not there, you won't go there every afternoon, and she won't have to be around you." He shrugged. "I just can't figure it out. You'd do anything on earth for her except tell her how you feel. I sure hope I don't grow up to be that stupid!"

Rufus laughed. "Stupid" wasn't one of the names he'd acquired, but maybe it was appropriate in this instance. Aaron's demeanor suggested that if there was anything comical about the matter, he hadn't registered it.

Rufus rose, walked over to Aaron, and extended his hand. "I'll put it right…if she'll let me. Thanks a lot. I'll let myself out." He smiled at the boy's knowing grin and thumbs-up sign. Had it been twenty-one years since he was that age? And had he been that self-assured? He looked at his watch. He didn't have enough time for a visit with Naomi before picking up his boys. He got in his car and dialed her on his cellular phone.

"Naomi, this if Rufus. I've just left Aaron. He's fine, and

you've nothing to worry about, believe me. I think he was just matchmaking," he told her cryptically, then added, "I'd like to come over tonight around eight-thirty, if it's okay with you." She agreed, and he hung up. If he was lucky, she'd be wearing that burnt orange dress.

He parked in front of the private day-care center and sat there, pensive. Aaron's words burned his mind, forcing him to see his own role in his volatile relationship with Naomi. He got the boys, drove home, and packed an overnight bag for them. He didn't like them to sleep away from home, but he had to straighten out the issues between him and Naomi, even if it took all night. He left his boys with Jewel and went home.

Naomi took a long, scented bath, tamed her hair into a French twist, and dressed carefully. It might be her last chance with Rufus, and she wanted to look her best. He'd said that dark women look good in pinks and reds, so she donned a lavender pink bra and bikini panties of silk lace that left her practically nude, looked over the pink corner of her closet, selected a wool crêpe dress of the same color, and slipped into it. She decided against pantyhose and wore garters instead. It was frankly a come-on, but she couldn't worry about that; this was war.

When her bell rang at exactly eight-thirty, she moved effortlessly and languidly toward the door, hot anticipation already beginning to steam within her. The frank appreciation in his sensuous gaze told her that the effort she'd made to please him had paid off. She took the beautiful crystal vase of red roses he handed her and stood back to let him enter. Then she placed the vase on the table, took his overcoat, and breathed a prayer of thanks that she'd had the foresight to dress well. He was the epitome of elegance.

He looked down at her as they entered the living room, but the warm anticipation she'd felt knowing she'd see him soon began to dissipate; his eyes were not smiling, but distant and wary. She sat on the sofa and nervous quivers knifed through her when he sat close beside her. He hated both pretense and small talk, so she knew he'd go straight to the point.

Rufus glanced at her as she sat patiently, hands folded in her lap, waiting for him to speak. "I'm a man on a high wire, Naomi; if I make one false step, I'll cripple myself for life. I went to see Aaron, to find out why he left you, but I learned far more than that. The boy is so perceptive and so blunt." He sensed her anxiety and suspected that she was nervous in anticipation of what Aaron might have told him.

"I had no right to ask of you what I couldn't give you in return, Naomi."

She gaped at him. "What do you mean?"

He ran his left hand over his tight, well groomed curls and took a deep breath. Attitudes he'd developed through his life had to be discarded; he'd thought he'd done it, but he realized now that he hadn't. "I asked you to trust me, to share with me what I now realize was the most personal of information. And I accused you of not trusting me, of being secretive and evasive. But you were justified; I've never given you a reason to trust me."

She squirmed beside him. "How can you say that? I've never met anyone more trustworthy than you. Rufus, please don't take responsibility for this…this situation. No one could have been a better friend than you've been these past few weeks." He smiled; she couldn't ever refer to their relationship as the mess that it was.

"I haven't given you the basis for the level of trust you needed and deserved. Oh, I know I came here and helped you and Aaron, did things for you for purely selfish reasons. I had to be with you, and I couldn't allow you to be without anything you wanted or needed." His glance swept over her profile. She was so beautiful, so elegant, and right now, she was so vulnerable. "And haven't you done the same for me," he asked her softly. "What I'm saying is that I self-righteously demanded that you bare your soul to me. I even pressured you into telling me that you loved me and reminded you of it on more than one occasion."

He turned sideways to look fully into her face and saw the tears that glistened unshed in her wide brown eyes. "Baby, don't cry. Don't. I can't stand it." Her lips quivered as her gaze shifted to his face. She lowered her eyes quickly, but he had seen the need in them, the simmering want, had seen her emotionally naked. There was so much that the wanted to say, had to say, but the fire-hot desire that suddenly blazed in his body muffled his words, extinguished every thought but that she wanted him. With a gut-wrenching sigh, he pulled her into his arms, and she reached for him, her lips parted and waiting for the thrust of his tongue.

Naomi opened up to him, a flower offering nectar and receiving life-giving pollination. She grasped the back of his head and held him to her. Hungry. Starving. She gave, and he took. She took, and he gave. He pulled away slightly, and she could see the fine sheen of moisture around his forehead that desire had wrung from him. If he walked away from her tonight, she couldn't bear it. It would be over, and she wouldn't allow it to end. She gazed drunkenly into his mesmerizing eyes, his beloved face. Why didn't he say something? Well, she thought recklessly, when the world didn't turn the way you were going, you walked the other way. Her hand reached out and cupped his chin, but his only reactions were the flicker of passion in his eyes and the slight quiver of his full bottom lip. She could hear the silence that surrounded them, silence so pregnant with the tension of desire that it spoke with a voice of its own. A groan escaped her soft lips, and she clung to him.

"Don't...don't leave me tonight." She wanted to beg him to

never leave her. His passion filled eyes drilled her as he seemed to look deeply within her, questioning her desire for him.

"I need you, Rufus. I'm not ashamed of it. I ache for you."

"Oh, God. Naomi, sweetheart, I need you, too. I'm hungry for you, out of my mind with it. All these weeks without you." Heated sensation streaked through her as his sweet mouth found her waiting, hungry lips. Jolts of fiery craving claimed her and she capitulated completely, her head lolling against his breast, her body limp with desire. He took her up in his arms and into her bedroom

He settled her on her feet beside the bed where he'd last loved her, faced her, and found her zipper with his fingers. She stepped away as the dress fell to her feet, and his breath was momentarily lost in anticipation of ecstasy as hot desire shot through him. She had dressed for him, had planned for them to make love. His gaze roamed slowly from her feet, moved up her long, shapely legs, and rested on the vee that cradled her sweet, moist tunnel, her citadel of love. Then it meandered slowly up to her full breasts, bare to his hot gaze except for the tiny scrap of nothing that caressed her nipples. She was beautiful. Intoxicating. How had he stayed away from her, denied himself the fulfillment that he needed so badly, that in his entire life he had found only within her arms? He shuddered violently with the fierceness of his arousal. Breath hissed through his teeth when her hand found his hard flesh and caressed him lovingly through his slacks. Shaking with desire, he picked her up, lay her gently on the bed, removed her intimate garments, and quickly stripped himself. His gaze drifted up and down the reclining body of his *naked maja,* a smile playing around his lips, unable to believe that she was his.

Desire gripped her and her body trembled in anticipation as she stared rhapsodically at the virile man who stood over her, powerful and beautiful in his nudity, his proud sex ready and eager for her. Her tongue slowly rimmed her slightly parted lips and her arms opened to him as her body took control of her mind. She gloried in her womanhood when he fell trembling into her waiting arms. His weight upon her heightened her need, fueled her impatience for his possession. She heard his softly murmured words of assurance, telling her of her beauty and that he adored her. He wrapped her to him and tension curled in the pit of her belly as his strong, hard legs brushed her and her nipples tingled against his chest. She felt the full measure of his hot, steely flesh against her belly and cried out in want.

Somewhere in the distance she heard a loud crash and twisted her body up to his. "It's all right, baby. Just the clock falling to the floor." Tremors swept her as his mouth covered hers tenderly, hotly, in a mind-drugging kiss, as if to rekindle her rushing passion. She strained against him in shameless supplication, but the continued his assault on her senses, curling his tongue around her nipple and pulling it slowly into his warm mouth, punishing her senses as he suckled her voraciously.

"Rufus, please…"

"Didn't I ask you not to call me Rufus when we're together like this? Tell me what you want. Tell me."

"Rufus, darling. I…oh God, honey, I'll die. Please, get in me." She felt his smile as he kissed her belly.

"We've got all night, sweetheart. Just give yourself to me."

Dizzying currents of heat danced through her body as his fingers strummed it, stroked it, played it skillfully like a priceless lyre, and she cried out, writhing and undulating beneath him. Desperate for consummation, her desire at fever pitch, she spread her legs and took his hard, silken flesh into her soft hands. He raised his head and looked down into her face with love-lit eyes. Then he pressed gently against her,

but she grasped his tight buttocks and thrust upward, sending a rush of air from him and a loud moan from her lips.

Her body quickly attuned itself to him, and she met his
powerful thrust as their bodies moved in perfect unison. Soon
the tide of ecstasy began to course through her and she tried
to hold it back, to stay with him.

"Let it go, baby. Let it happen. Give yourself to me. I'll be
with you all the way."

The waves of ecstasy began at her feet and spiraled
through her body, settling in her core and gripping the man
she held within her. She cried out from the sweet torture of
it as he buckled above and they flew together, their passion
undimmed, free.

Shaken beyond words, Rufus looked down at the woman
whose body encased him and kissed her tenderly and lovingly. Then, without releasing himself, he turned on his side,
bringing her with him.

"I love you, Naomi." He felt her body stiffen. "I have for
a long time. I realized it the night I got back home from Nigeria, and I should have told you then, before we made love,
because I knew." He held her closer when he felt the tremors
of her emotional reaction.

"I realize now that I didn't tell you because I didn't trust
you not to exploit it, and because I couldn't see you in the setting I envisaged for my boys and myself, even though I told
myself otherwise. Yet I asked you to trust me. I was wrong
in every way, and I know it. You're what I want and what I
need."

"Oh, Rufus, there's so much you don't know." He turned
to her and kissed her soft brown cheek.

"Not as much as you may think. And before you tell me
I want to say something, and it's important. Whatever happened to you in the past, Naomi, can't be undone, and it's not

what matters. What the past has made of you is what counts with me. I just want to know if you still love me."

"Oh, yes. I think I started loving you the minute I saw you. I'd watch you with Preston and Sheldon, how you loved them and how secure they were in your love. I knew you had a great capacity for love, and I wanted you to love me. I pushed you away because I thought because of your past experiences with your wife and mother, you'd reject me when you found out about Aaron."

She told him about her son, beginning with the day she'd learned of her pregnancy. "Once I knew he wanted to find me, I had to see him. And then I had to choose between the two of you. I couldn't let Aaron get away from me a second time."

Quietly, he thought over what she'd told him. She'd be a wonderful companion and lover, wife and mother. He had misjudged her badly, but she'd helped by misleading him. Judd was right; pain had to have been her constant companion. But not anymore; he'd see to that, if she'd let him. She began to squirm, to move away from him, and he tightened his hold.

"From now on, we trust each other. We could have spared ourselves a lot of sleepless nights and heartache if we'd believed in each other."

He rolled her over on her back and let her feel him growing within her. "If you'll marry me, I'll be a happy man, Preston and Sheldon will be delirious, Judd will be out of his mind, and Aaron will get off of my case. What about you?"

She sucked in her breath as his gaze consumed her and his intoxicating virility fired her womanhood. "I'll be ecstatic."

* * * * *